Praise for Elly Griffiths

'A memorable, breathless race against time . . . One of the most cinematic finales in recent British crime novels'

Daily Telegraph

'An admirably gutsy heroine'

The Times

'Griffiths weaves superstition and myth into her crime novels, skilfully treading a line between credulity and modern methods of detection'

Sunday Times

'A wonderfully rich mixture of ancient and contemporary . . . A welcome addition to a great series'

Guardian

'Griffiths' excellent series is well informed and original'

Literary Review

'The perfect ratio of anticipation, shock and surprise'

Independent

'A palpable sense of evil . . . Perfect for dark winter evenings'

Financial Times

'A sinister, life-threatening mystery that grips to its end'

Woman & Home

'The characters are constantly engaging – particularly the vulnerable Ruth – the writing is perceptive, as well as wryly humorous . . . This is recommended'

Spectator

Also by Elly Griffiths

The Crossing Places
The Janus Stone
The House at Sea's End
A Room Full of Bones
Dying Fall

ELLY GRIFFITHS

THE OUTCAST DEAD

First published in Great Britain in 2014 by Quercus Editions Ltd
This paperback edition published in 2014 by Quercus Editions Ltd

Quercus
55 Baker Street
7th Floor, South Block
London W1U 8EW

A CIP catalogue record for this book is available
from the British Library

PB ISBN 978 0 85738 893 3
EBOOK ISBN 978 0 85738 892 6

10 9 8 7 6 5 4 3 2

Printed and bound in Great Britain by Clays Ltd, St Ives plc

Typeset by Hewer Text UK Ltd, Edinburgh

For my children, Alex and Juliet

THE
OUTCAST
DEAD

CHAPTER 1

'And we ask your abundant blessing, Lord, on these, the outcast dead . . .'

There is a murmured response from the group gathered on the bank below the castle walls. But Ruth Galloway, standing at the back, says nothing. She is wearing the expression of polite neutrality she assumes whenever God is mentioned. This mask has stood her in good stead over the years and she sees no reason to drop it now. But she approves of the Prayers for the Outcast Dead. This brief ecumenical service is held every year for the unknown dead of Norwich: the bodies thrown into unmarked graves, the paupers, the plague victims, forgotten, unmourned, except by this motley collection of archaeologists, historians and sundry hangers-on.

'Lord, you told us that not a sparrow falls without our

Father in Heaven knowing. We know that these people were known to you and loved by you . . .'

The vicar has a reedy hesitant voice which gets lost before it reaches Ruth. Now she can only hear Ted, one of the field archaeologists, giving the responses in a booming baritone.

'We will remember them.'

She doesn't know if Ted has any religious beliefs. All she knows about him is that he was brought up in Bolton and may or may not be Irish. If he's Irish he's probably a Catholic, like DCI Harry Nelson who, however hard he denies it, has a residual belief in heaven, hell and all points in between. Thinking of Nelson makes Ruth uncomfortable. She moves away, further up the hill, and one of the people gathered around the vicar, a tall woman in a red jacket, turns and smiles at her. Ruth smiles back. Janet Meadows, local historian and expert on the unnamed dead. Ruth first encountered Janet over a year ago when examining the bones of a medieval bishop believed to have miraculous powers. It was Cathbad who put Ruth in touch with Janet and, even now, Ruth can't believe that her druid friend won't suddenly appear in the shadow of the castle, purple cloak fluttering, sixth sense on red alert. But Cathbad is miles away and magical powers have their limitations, as she knows only too well.

Words float towards Ruth, borne on the light summer breeze.

'Remember . . . lost . . . gone before . . . heavenly father . . . all-merciful . . . grace . . . forgiveness.'

So many words, thinks Ruth – as she has thought many times before – to say so little. The dead are dead and no words, however resonant, can bring them back. Ruth is a forensic archaeologist and she is well acquainted with the dead. She believes in remembering them, in treating their bones with respect, but she doesn't expect ever to see them again, carried heavenwards on clouds of glory. Unconsciously, she looks upwards at the pale blue evening sky. It's June, nearly the longest day.

A loud 'Amen' from Ted signals that the service is at an end and Ruth walks towards the knot of people sitting or standing on seats cut into the grassy bank. She approaches Ted but sees that he's talking to Trace Richards, another of the field archaeology team. Trace's aggressively alternative appearance – purple hair, piercings – belies the fact that she's from a very wealthy family and has, in fact, just got engaged to a prominent local businessman. Ruth has never really got on with Trace so she veers off at the last minute and finds herself next to Janet.

'I like this service,' says Janet. 'We *should* remember

them, the ordinary people. Not just the kings and the bishops and the people rich enough to build castles.'

'It's one of the reasons I became an archaeologist,' says Ruth. 'To find out about how ordinary people lived their lives.' She thinks of Erik, her ex-tutor and mentor, saying, 'We are their recorders. We set down their daily lives, their everyday deeds, their hopes and dreams, for all eternity.' But Erik is dead now and his hopes and dreams are forgotten, except by those people, like Ruth, whose lives he has marked forever.

'You've been digging at the castle haven't you?' says Janet.

'Yes,' says Ruth. 'Right near here, by the entrance to the cafe.'

'Find anything?'

'We think we've found the bodies of some prisoners who were executed.'

'How do you know they were prisoners?'

'Well, they don't seem to have been buried with much ceremony, no shrouds or coffins. Some have their hands still bound. And the bodies were lying prone, face down, north to south.'

'North to south?'

'Christian burials are usually west to east, head to the west, feet to the east.'

Janet nods thoughtfully. 'They really were outside Christian charity, weren't they? They might not even have committed very dreadful crimes either. In the early nineteenth century you could be hanged for being a pick-pocket.'

'I know,' says Ruth. She doesn't mention one particular skeleton, excavated yesterday, which she believes may be that of a woman who was guilty of a far more terrible crime.

'Can you date the bodies?' asks Janet.

'We can do Carbon 14 tests on the bones,' says Ruth. 'Look at any objects found in the grave, that sort of thing. And we know that convicted felons were mainly buried in the castle precincts in the mid to late nineteenth century. Before that they were sent to the surgeons for experimentation. It was actually a crime to bury them. And before that, of course, they were tarred and put in metal cages.'

'Gibbets.'

'Yes. Apparently, you could see human remains hanging in gibbets right up to Victorian times.'

'There's a Gibbet Street in the city,' says Janet. 'And Heigham Street used to be known as Hangman's Lane. Executions were big events in Norwich,' she continues, her voice dry. 'They were held here on Castle Hill. Some-

5

times there would be a fair or a market too, just to add to the merriment, then the bell of St Peter Mancroft Church would ring and the prisoner would be led out, following the chaplain and the prison governor.'

Janet, like all good historians, always makes Ruth think that she can actually see the past. She looks up at the castle, square and dark against the sky. She can almost hear the prayers of the chaplain, like the words of the vicar earlier, lost upon the air. Then the great bell tolling, the jeers of the crowd, the white face of the prisoner before the hood is pulled over his head.

'It must have been ghastly,' she says.

'Ghastly?' says a voice behind her. 'What's ghastly?' Ruth turns and sees her Head of Department, Phil Trent, apparently dressed for cricket in white trousers, open-necked shirt and a panama hat.

'Nothing,' says Ruth.

Phil doesn't pursue the matter. He rarely seems interested in what Ruth has to say although she is fairly popular with him at the moment because she has just got a publishing deal for her first book. The book, about an excavation in Lancashire, has nothing to do with Phil or the department but, nevertheless, he is taking a good percentage of the credit. Even so, he never usually shows any enthusiasm for her company but today he is positively brimming with bonhomie, seizing her arm and steering her away from Janet. Ruth looks back apologetically and Janet gives her a smile and an odd little wave.

'Fantastic news Ruth,' says Phil.

Ruth composes her face. The news could be promotion for Phil or new funding for the department. She doubts if it is anything to do with her. It could even be personal. Phil lives with Ruth's friend Shona and they have recently had a baby. Maybe they're getting married?

'You know our find earlier,' he says, lowering his voice.

'Our' is pushing it, Phil wasn't even on site when Ruth uncovered the woman's body, though he came quickly enough when he heard the news.

'Well, there's been some interest,' he says.

'From English Heritage?' asks Ruth, genuinely excited. If English Heritage fund a really big dig, who knows what they could find? Norwich Castle dates back to medieval times, there must be layers and layers of treasures beneath their feet.

'Better than that,' says Phil, his face holy with joy. '*Television.*'

Ruth drives home through apparently endless traffic. She has left the other archaeologists having a party in the castle grounds, with warm white wine and vegetarian snacks supplied by Janet. This is one of the worst things about being a working mother. Oh, the *work's* all right. You can make arrangements for the work. It's all the other stuff. The drinks after work, the leaving dos, the Friday nights when someone suggests a curry. All the times, in fact, when the important bonding gets done. Ruth has to miss all that, and she's lost count of the times when she's been the last to hear about a dig because 'we discussed it last night in the pub'. Phil is a great one for networking, he's always skulking off with a few cronies to plot over pasta but, then again, Phil is only a working father. Having children doesn't seem to impinge on his professional life at all.

But Ruth has no time to lie on the grass talking about the dead. As it is, it'll be past eight before she collects Kate from the childminder. Sandra is always very understanding but Ruth doesn't want to use up all her credit in one go. She never knows when she might need another favour. So she embarks on the tedious drive from Norwich to King's Lynn, all the way across the fattest part of the county. But as she switches lanes, gets stuck at red lights, and chooses countless short cuts which actually take more time but at least keep her moving, she isn't thinking about her colleagues or even about her beloved daughter. She is thinking about the body in the trench.

As soon as she saw it she knew. A skeleton, still clad in a few shreds of clothing, face down, arms tied behind its back. But what made Ruth catch her breath was what was on the end of one of the arms. An iron hook, almost rusted away at the point, crudely screwed into the carpal bone. When the body was excavated and she could see by the pelvic bones that it was female, she was even more convinced that she was looking at the skeleton of Jemima Green, otherwise known as Mother Hook. Even Ruth, who avoids 'real crime' stories like the plague (though she's actually quite interested in the plague), has heard of Mother Hook, probably the most notorious murderess in Norfolk's history. A so-called baby farmer, Jemima Green was convicted of murdering a child who had been fostered out to her in a nightmarish Victorian version of childminding. It was thought at the time that she may have killed as many as twenty more. She was one of the last women hanged at the castle, doubtless in front of a capacity crowd. Yet her name had lived on. Partly it was the grisly fascination of the hook. From Peter Pan onwards, metal limbs have added to the horror of panto-mime villains. And the fact that Jemima Green had a hook instead of a hand added to the idea of a woman lost to all natural instincts, a mother who killed instead of cherishing. The hand that rocks the cradle became an instrument of torture. Without realising it, Ruth starts to drive faster, almost missing the turning for the A47.

If they have found the remains of Mother Hook, the publicity implications are tremendous. There have been countless books written about Jemima Green, even a rather dubious musical comedy entitled *Hook, Line and Sinker*. No wonder a TV programme is interested. But every time Ruth thinks about the skeleton, still with a hood over its head, iron hook glinting in the light, she feels a chill to the bone. She almost feels like saying that she doesn't want to be involved in this dig any more but, remembering Phil's ecstatic expression, she knows that she has no chance of escaping.

Kate is asleep by the time she reaches Sandra's house, which only adds to Ruth's feeling of guilt. She carries her daughter out to the car but, as she manoeuvres her into the baby seat, Kate wakes up. 'Mum', she says accusingly.

'Hi Kate. We're going home.'

'Home,' says Kate, shutting her eyes.

Home. As Ruth drives through the summer evening, past the outskirts of King's Lynn, the tantalising glimpses of sea, the caravan parks filling up for the season, she thinks about their home, hers and Kate's. Ruth lives in an isolated cottage on the very edge of the Saltmarsh. For most of the year her only neighbours are the birds that fly above the coarse grass and sand dunes leading to the sea. Sometimes she has the company of her nomadic Indigenous Australian neighbour, Bob Woolunga, or the weekenders who have the cottage on the other side. But mostly it's just her and Kate. And mostly that's just how Ruth likes it. But recently, particularly this winter when they were snowed in for several days, she has begun to wonder if this is really the best place to bring up a child. Shouldn't she be nearer to civilisation, playgroups, Chinese takeaways, that sort of thing? The trouble is that Ruth doesn't always like civilisation very much.

It's still light when she reaches her house but the shadows are darkening. The security light (fitted by Nelson three years ago) comes on as she carries a still-sleeping Kate up to the front door. Ruth's ginger cat, Flint, greets them enthusiastically, weaving around Ruth's legs as she climbs the stairs with Kate in her arms. 'Don't wake up,' Ruth implores silently. She loves her daughter more than life itself, but the prospect of an evening watching TV with Flint and a glass of wine is more attractive than the thought of hours singing nursery rhymes and reading about Dora the Explorer. But though Kate snuffles and sighs when Ruth puts her in her bed, she doesn't wake up. Ruth tiptoes downstairs with Flint close on her heels. He wants to make sure that his supper is her highest priority.

Ruth feeds Flint, makes herself a sandwich and pours a glass of red. Then she pushes a pile of books off the sofa and sits down to flick through the channels. Cookery? No thanks, she has enough problems with her weight without indulging in cup-cake porn. Restoration Homes? No, her sympathy for people who buy million-pound mansions and then have trouble with dry rot in the orangery is limited. The News? Oh, all right then. She really should know something about the real world.

The screen shows a heavily built dark-haired man scowling at the camera.

'DCI Harry Nelson,' says the announcer, 'refused to comment today, but King's Lynn police confirmed that they are questioning thirty-seven-year-old Liz Donaldson in connection with the deaths of her three children.'

Now the picture is of a blonde woman, laughing as she holds her baby in her arms.

CHAPTER 2

By the time DCI Harry Nelson reaches home he feels as if he's been awake for several years. Seeing his wife's car on the drive he wishes, for almost the first time in their married life, that Michelle was out with the girls or visiting her mother, not waiting for him with a hot meal and wanting to know the details of his day. What can he say? I've been questioning a young mother, a woman not unlike you – attractive, independent, intelligent – asking her if she held a pillow over the mouths of her three children and choked the life out of them. I've been asking a woman who has just lost her third child whether her loss was not, in fact, tragedy but outright murder. I've been doing this in the face of open hostility from my team. Judy, who believes Liz Donaldson is suffering from post-traumatic stress disorder.

Clough, who says 'no mum could do a thing like that' though he knows that they can and do. Even Tim, who Nelson has brought down from Blackpool to be the calm voice of reason on the team, says he feels uncomfortable about the whole process. 'The coroner found natural causes in the cases of the first two children. It's possible that we're talking about a congenital health defect here.' Possible but not, in Nelson's view, probable. He's been involved in cases like this before and he knows that it goes against all human feelings to believe a mother capable of killing her children. As a devoted father he finds it rather insulting to realise that people are all too happy to pin the blame on Daddy. But Mummy . . . Mummy's different.

Michelle comes out of the kitchen when she hears his key in the lock. As usual she looks beautiful, still wearing her work outfit of tight grey dress and high heels. Her blonde hair is tied back in a complicated French plait and her careful make-up is only slightly smudged around the eyes. The house is filled with the savoury aroma of shepherd's pie. It is true, as Nelson's mother is always telling him, that he really does have the perfect wife. What would it be like to come home to Ruth? She'd probably be slouched on the sofa with her cat, drinking wine and watching intellectual crap on the telly. Nelson shakes his head, annoyed with himself. Why the hell is he thinking about Ruth?

'Hi love,' says Michelle, inclining her scented head for a kiss. 'Good day?'

'Bloody awful.'

'Your mum rang to say she'd seen you on TV.'

Nelson groans, opening the fridge and searching for a beer. As if things weren't bad enough, now his mother's on the warpath.

'It's that case,' he says. 'The woman with her kids. All the press are on to it. We've even had calls from the States. Whitcliffe's in seventh heaven.'

Gerry Whitcliffe, Nelson's boss, adores publicity. One of the many ways in which he and Nelson are diametrically opposed.

'Do you really think she did it?' asks Michelle, getting the plates out of the oven. 'Killed all three of her children?'

Nelson sits at the kitchen table and holds the sweating beer can against his forehead. 'I don't know,' he says wearily. 'But I have to consider the possibility. That's my job.'

The problem is he does think she did it. As soon as he saw Liz Donaldson, he suspected her. He hadn't been the first on the scene when the hospital had reported a sudden infant death. That had been DS Judy Johnson with her training in child protection and family liaison, not to mention bereavement support, grief counselling and all the rest of it. Judy had visited the Donaldsons' home with the family doctor, following police procedure. She had asked sensitive questions and had seen the site of death (a cot in an upstairs bedroom). Judy had reported that the mother displayed the calm, almost disconnected, manner of a person deeply in shock. That had set Nelson's alarm bells ringing for a start. Calm? Disconnected? If anything happened to one of his daughters he'd be climbing the walls. He remembered the occasion last summer when Kate was in danger and Ruth's wild eyes as she'd clung to him, begging him to save their daughter. Calm certainly didn't describe either of them. But Judy said that it was a perfectly natural reaction. 'She'll be feeling unreal, almost as though she's sleepwalking. Remember, she's already lost two babies. She won't be able to believe that it's happening again.'

But, of course, it was this tragic history that had sent Nelson to Liz Donaldson's door. One infant death and you get a caring family officer, three and you get a DCI with a notebook and a nasty suspicious mind. Judy had accompanied him, checking all the time that he was being sympathetic enough. And he had felt sympathetic, of course he had. The woman had just lost a child, for God's sake. And Liz Donaldson was, at first glance, very likeable. She was tall and slim with short, blonde hair and a low, attractive voice. She had greeted them that day without animosity, seeming to accept the continuing police intrusion as just another burden that she had to bear. She had been on her own, which surprised him. Judy said there was a husband but they were separated.

'That was quick. The kid was only a few months old.'

'*David* was eight months old,' said Judy, emphasising the name. 'And the marriage hadn't been going well for some time. The deaths of Samuel and Isaac put a tremendous strain on the parents.'

'All boys,' Nelson had commented.

'Yes. Which makes it more likely that we're looking at some genetic disability.'

Biblical names, thought Nelson. But he kept this thought to himself.

Liz had invited them in. The terraced house was painfully tidy, the smell of lilies almost overpowering. Lilies for death, Nelson's mother always said. The front room was full of cards and flowers. Nelson wondered if Liz had been thinking about David's birth, less than a year ago, and whether the house had been full of flowers then. But now, of course, the tone was muted. Mauves and purples, footsteps on sand, angels and sad teddy bears. Deepest sympathy, in our prayers, safe in the arms of Jesus. Sitting on the edge of Liz Donaldson's sofa, Nelson had surprised himself with a powerful animal instinct to run, to put as many miles between him and this tragedy-filled room as possible. But Judy was leaning forward, asking Liz how she was doing, whether she was getting enough sleep, enough support . . .

'Mum's just left,' said Liz. 'Bob was here yesterday but he was in pieces, poor thing. Sometimes I think it's harder for men.'

Bob must be the ex-husband, Nelson noted. He thought he detected something almost smug in Liz's tone. Bob was going to pieces but Liz sat, pale yet still undoubtedly whole, answering their questions with sad dignity.

'I'm so sorry, Liz,' said Judy. 'But we'll have to ask some questions about Samuel and Isaac. Is that OK?'

'It's OK.'

'Samuel was six months old when he died and Isaac just over a year?'

'That's right.'

'Did you ever find out anything about the cause of death?'

Liz looked away, gazing unseeingly at a card showing

a lurid night sky etched with the words 'Safe in heaven'. 'Sudden Unexplained Death in Infancy. That was what it said on the certificates.'

Nelson and Judy already knew this, having seen the paperwork. SUDI is coroner code for an unexplained death which doesn't need further investigation. Nelson wondered who carried out the autopsies.

'Must have been hard,' said Judy, 'not having any answers.'

'It was almost the hardest thing,' said Liz. 'We just didn't know why. Neither Bob or I smoke, we're not asthmatic, neither of us have any heart problems. When Sammy died it was just possible to think that it was just one of those terrible things. But when Isaac was taken . . .'

Taken, thought Nelson. Odd choice of word. But Judy had been sympathising and empathising, all the time skilfully extracting the pattern of events. They had found Samuel dead in his cot one morning, with Isaac he had seemed listless and floppy, they had rushed him to hospital but he had died in A and E. David, like his older brother, had been found cold and blue after an afternoon nap.

'I knew he was dead,' said Liz, 'but I kept trying to revive him. I kept on, even after the paramedics told me it was no good.'

Nelson made a mental note to check this story.

'You're a nurse, aren't you?' Judy was saying.

'I was. Before I had . . . before the boys were born.'

The boys. It made them sound like a family, a happy band of siblings. But Liz Donaldson only ever had one child at a time, each boy dying before his brother was born. Nelson tried, and failed, to think how this must feel. He remembers now that Liz had suddenly leant forward and grasped Judy's arm.

'Do you have children?'

Judy had looked for a moment as if she might not answer but, in the end, she said, very quietly, 'Yes.'

'How many?'

'A boy. Just over a year old.'

'Keep him safe,' Liz Donaldson had said. 'Keep him safe.'

CHAPTER 3

Phil is already at the site by the time Ruth arrives in the morning. The dig was originally a low-key affair, organised because the council wanted to build new public toilets. Usually in these situations the archaeologists' role is simple: they come in before the builders, survey the area for any unusual features and dig a few trenches. There is an unspoken agreement that unless they unearth the lost ark of the covenant, building work will continue regardless. All the archaeologists can do is mark the find and take samples for posterity. Ruth often thinks that there must be multi-storey car parks and office blocks all over the country built on top of Roman farmsteads and dead kings. But, as with everything, money talks and building contractors tend to have more money than archaeologists. Toilets are more important than old bones.

But the possible discovery of Mother Hook has changed everything. As she walks down the slope, Ruth sees not only her head of department but the county archaeologist and a man in red spectacles taking photos with a digital camera. Ted is also there, drinking coffee from a flask and looking sardonic.

'Here she is,' says Phil with massive bonhomie, almost managing to convey the impression that Ruth is late though she is, in fact, five minutes early.

She walks over to the trench, which is fenced off from the main picnic area. Behind them the cafe rises up out of the grass like a giant glass bubble, and opposite, across the bridge, the castle squats, square and secretive. They excavated the woman's body yesterday. Now samples have been sent for Carbon 14 and DNA testing. Ruth's job today is to examine the context, the grave cut, looking for clues in the infill, searching for any objects – glass, pottery, coins – that might help her to date the burial. She would like to be able to get on with this in peace but Phil is still hovering excitedly. Ruth notes that he is dressed in his best Indiana Jones casuals – safari shorts and a short-sleeved shirt – though she can't remember the last time that she saw him do any actual digging.

'Mark, let me introduce you to Ruth. Mark, this is Dr

Ruth Galloway, Head of Forensic Archaeology. Ruth, this is Mark Gates.' Voice lowered reverently. 'A TV researcher.'

Blimey, thinks Ruth, that was quick. Phil must have been on the phone as soon as he saw the bones. She shakes hands with Mark Gates who looks at her appraisingly, as if considering how she'll look on TV. Probably wondering where he can get a wide angle lens.

'So you're the lady who discovered the bones,' Mark is saying.

Ruth doesn't like to be called a lady, but it's too soon to get into that sort of conversation and she doesn't want Phil to start rolling his eyes in a humorous 'man surrounded by feminists' way so she just smiles and says yes, she excavated the skeleton but there are still lots of tests to be done.

'But you're almost certain that it's Jemima Green, Mother Hook?'

'Well, the dates seem about right . . .' begins Ruth but Phil cuts in, 'Oh, absolutely certain. A woman with a hook for a hand. Who else could it be?'

'Captain Hook in drag?' suggests Ted from the trench. Phil ignores him.

'Because if it is her,' says Mark, addressing himself to Ruth, 'my programme would be very interested. Very interested indeed. It would tie in with one of our specials.'

What is his programme, wonders Ruth. He doesn't look as if he's from *Time Team*. Probably some academic archaeology series. On the History Channel perhaps.

'What programme's that?' asks Ted.

'*Women Who Kill*,' says Mark, allowing a certain ghoulish relish to enter his voice.

Nelson is also discussing women who kill. Unfortunately for him the discussion is with Madge Hudson, criminal profiler, privately described by Nelson as Queen of the Bleeding Obvious. Also present are DS Judy Johnson, DS Dave Clough, DS Tim Heathfield. Tim joined the team at the start of the year, transferring from Blackpool where he had been the protégé of Nelson's old friend Sandy MacLeod. He has proved a good addition to the squad, calm and professional, always respectful to his colleagues, deferring to their local knowledge. But there's no doubt that Judy and Clough are both wary of him. Clough distrusts new people on principle, if they are men and graduates, fitter and better-looking than him, his suspicion hardens into open hostility. Judy, who Nelson thought might get on with Tim, seems even more dubious. Their shared resentment has made Judy and Clough draw closer, a miracle in itself, Nelson thinks. He doesn't know how Tim feels about his new teammates.

Apart from one slightly cynical comment about being 'the only black policeman in Norfolk' Tim has shown no sign of not fitting into his new environment. His smooth, polite manner makes it oddly difficult to ask personal questions but Nelson supposes that he ought to try.

Now Madge beams round the table, blissfully unaware of the cross-currents of antipathy.

'We're looking at a woman here,' she begins, reaching, in Nelson's opinion, new heights of Bleeding Obvious. 'A woman suspected of killing three of her children. Now a woman who kills her children is often suffering from depression.'

You don't say, thinks Nelson. There was him thinking that infanticide was a sign that everything was going well.

'But often they can present a very good facade. Looking perfect can be very important to them.'

Despite himself, Nelson thinks of Liz Donaldson's spotless house. She had been wearing slippers, he remembers, so as not to spoil the carpets.

'Are we talking about Münchausen's?' asks Tim.

Clough gives him a dark look, which Nelson notices. Clough always becomes irritated when Tim uses words that are more than two syllables long.

'Münchausen's Syndrome by Proxy,' corrects Madge.

25

'I think it's possible. Münchausen's,' she turns to Clough, 'is a psychiatric disorder where the subject feigns illness in order to gain attention. In the case of Münchausen's by Proxy they feign illness in other people, often children, sometimes actually causing the illness themselves.'

'I know what it is,' snaps Clough. 'There was that case of a nurse, wasn't there?'

'Liz Donaldson's a nurse,' says Nelson before he can stop himself.

'Beverley Allitt,' nods Madge, 'convicted of murdering four children in her care and attempting to kill three others. One theory was that she was suffering from Münchausen's by Proxy.'

'Still got life though, didn't she,' says Clough.

'Yes, she was detained at Rampton Secure Hospital. The Judge recommended a minimum of forty years. Actually DCI Nelson makes a good point.'

Nelson looks as surprised as anyone to hear this.

'Individuals with Münchausen's often have some medical knowledge. Liz Donaldson was a nurse. She'd know about symptoms and treatment. She'd know exactly what the doctors and nurses were looking for.'

'That was a long time ago,' says Judy. 'She hasn't worked since her first child was born.'

'That could be significant in itself,' says Madge. 'She may have missed the kudos of being a nurse. She may have wanted to prove that she was as clever, or cleverer, than the medical staff attending her children.'

'By killing them?' Nelson can't stop the incredulity creeping into his voice. He suspects Liz Donaldson but the idea that she murdered her children in order to look intelligent seems to him dangerously simplistic. He can just imagine the Defence's reaction if the CPS tried that one in court.

Madge remains calm. She once told Nelson that his hostility to her was actually a sign of admiration, even attraction. Since then, Nelson has tried to avoid her as much as possible. The trouble is that Madge is almost always called in on the big cases. Nelson's boss, Superintendent Whitcliffe, thinks she's brilliant.

'Women kill for the strangest of reasons,' she says now, smiling seraphically.

'So do men,' says Judy. 'I mean Münchausen's doesn't just affect women. What about the husband?'

'Münchausen's by Proxy primarily affects women,' says Madge. 'And I understand the husband wasn't present when any of the deaths occurred. Which, incidentally, might be a factor. Liz may have been trying to reclaim her husband's attention. She might also have resented the fact that Bob's career was going well while hers seemed to have stalled.'

Madge seems to be on first-name terms with both of the Donaldsons, though they have never met. Once again, career envy seems a very flimsy motive to Nelson. Michelle gave up her job as a hairdresser when their children were born. She'd gone back to it when the girls were at secondary school. As far as Nelson can remember, there hadn't been any angst about it. It was just what you did.

'It's all conjecture though, isn't it?' says Clough. 'I mean, there's no evidence.'

And that's the problem. There is no real evidence. They are still waiting for the autopsy on David. The deaths of the first two children were recorded as 'unexplained' but Nelson has wheeled in an army of experts who say that the reports could point to asphyxiation. It was this that led Nelson to bring Liz Donaldson in for further questioning. Somehow, though, the press got wind of it and, with no further evidence forthcoming, he has had to release her without charge. He is aware that he walks a knife edge. The press coverage is teetering between evil child killer and wronged mother. One false move and Nelson himself will be the big baddie in all this. Then Whitcliffe will sack him and he'll still be no nearer to finding out who killed Samuel, Isaac and David.

Thinking of those names, he says now, 'Could there be a religious link? All three boys had biblical names.'

'Liz Donaldson isn't religious,' says Judy. 'She had the boys baptised in the Church of England but there's no record of churchgoing. It's not as if she was Born Again or,' a swift glance at Nelson, 'Catholic.' Judy, like Nelson, was brought up a Catholic.

'Why pick religious names then?' says Nelson.

'They're fashionable aren't they?' says Clough, whose first name is David. 'Lots of kids these days called Noah and Joshua and the like. Doesn't mean anything.'

'Isaac was almost sacrificed by his father,' says Tim. 'Samuel was called by God. David was the chosen one. They're also all Old Testament prophets.'

'You seem to know a lot about it,' says Clough.

'I was brought up in a highly religious household,' says Tim mildly. 'I'm agnostic myself.'

That figures, thinks Nelson. He has already noticed that Tim likes to keep his options open.

'That's an interesting line of thought,' says Madge, giving Tim a warm smile. 'The child as sacrifice.'

Nelson thinks of something Ruth once told him about children being buried under doorways, sacrifices to Janus, the Roman God of beginnings and endings. Aloud he says, 'This isn't getting us very far. We're awaiting the autopsy results on David. If there's any evidence of suspicious circumstances, we'll get Liz Donaldson in again. She's bound to crack soon.'

'I wouldn't be too sure,' says Madge. 'Remember she might almost enjoy pitting her intelligence against yours.'

Judy snorts, as if implying that Nelson is bound to come off worse in any battle of wits.

When Nelson gets back to his office, his PA, Leah, tells him that his warlock friend has called.

'Cathbad?' says Nelson.

Judy, who is hovering in the doorway, gives an involuntary exclamation.

Nelson turns. 'Did you want me, Judy?'

'No.' Judy backs away.

Left alone, Nelson calls his friend who is, strictly speaking, a druid and not a warlock. He misses Cathbad, who recently moved to Lancashire. Raving mad though he undoubtedly is, you can always rely on Cathbad for some interesting conversation.

Cathbad comes straight to the point. 'Liz Donaldson is innocent.'

'What do you know about it?'

'I just know,' says Cathbad, maddeningly elliptical as ever.

'Oh, OK then. I'll call off the enquiry. Nice of you to call.'

'Sarcasm is a defence mechanism, Nelson.'

'I need all the defences I can get.'

'I know Liz Donaldson,' says Cathbad, softening slightly. 'She's a lovely person. It's unthinkable that she should do something like this.'

But the unthinkable does happen, thinks Nelson. I think about it all the time. Aloud he says, 'I can't discuss the case with you, Cathbad.'

Cathbad sighs. All the way from the north, Nelson's country. 'Be careful, Nelson,' he says.

'Careful of what?'

'If you convict an innocent woman, you'll be cursed.'

This, Nelson knows, is not a joke.

CHAPTER 4

Ruth begins the long drive home in a less than placid frame of mind. She had been looking forward to a peaceful day's digging but Phil has ruined it by hanging around with his TV pal, asking stupid questions.

'Find anything interesting?' Mark peered into the trench, scuffing the perfect edges with his trendy red converse.

'Some glass,' replied Ruth, pointing to the neat row of objects on the tarpaulin. 'Looks Victorian.'

'Why would there be glass buried here?'

Ruth sighed. 'All sorts of reasons. It's in the topsoil which is just a jumble of accumulated objects, rubbish, builder's debris, that sort of thing. There may be no association with the body at all.'

'What if you found something really exciting? Her diary, for instance?'

Ruth didn't ask why Jemima Green's diary would have been buried with her. It's possible that the woman couldn't even read and highly unlikely that she kept notes of her crimes. *Feb 8th 1866 Busy day. Went to market, scrubbed floor, killed a child.* Instead she said, dryly, 'That really would be a significant find. Excuse me. I must get on.'

When Mark saw her brushing dirt from a piece of bone, his excitement knew no bounds.

'Is that human? Looks like a child's.'

'Animal,' said Ruth. 'Probably a sheep.'

'I'd love to have some shots of Ruth cleaning bones,' said Mark to Phil. 'Do you have any spare bones we could use?'

'Oh we've got lots of bones,' said Phil heartily. 'Bones all over the shop in our department. Isn't that right, Ruth?'

Ruth ignored him.

As a matter of fact, Ruth did find something rather interesting in the trench. Luckily she made the discovery when Phil and Mark were at lunch (she'd declined the invitation to join them though Ted had acquiesced on hearing the word 'pub'). She was just thinking about sitting down for a solitary sandwich when she saw something glinting amongst the chalky soil. Brushing away the dirt she saw that it was a medallion, silver alloy perhaps, tarnished and green with age. Ruth peered at it, trying to make out the image. It seemed to show two heads. Madonna and child? St Christopher? Didn't he carry the infant Jesus somewhere (to a soft-play centre perhaps)? She thought of Janus, the two-faced god and of Hecate, the goddess of witchcraft, sometimes depicted with three heads. Or could the image be something more unusual and more sinister? She sat back on her haunches, thinking. There was no guarantee that this medal belonged to Jemima Green but it was found at about the right depth. In any case, it was a curiosity. She imagined Mark's frenzied excitement: 'Was Mother Hook a devil worshipper?' On a sudden impulse she slipped the medal into her pocket.

Now, driving home, she wonders why she concealed the find. It goes against all her training as an archaeologist. All finds must be logged, recorded, photographed, written up in the report. I'll do it tomorrow, she tells herself. When that Mark isn't around. And the medal probably isn't anything. Some builder's St Christopher that slipped off when they were shifting the earth to make the car park. But, deep down, she knows this isn't true. The layers above Jemima Green's body were all in place. This soil hasn't been moved for over a hundred years.

Ruth thinks of Erik, her tutor at university and once the man she admired most in the world. It was Erik who discovered the Bronze Age henge on the beach near the Saltmarsh. The henge dig, which took place thirteen years ago, is still a golden memory for Ruth. The wide clear sands in the early morning light, the tide rushing in across the marshes, the first sight of the wooden henge, the sacred circle still complete after some four thousand years. Some local people – Cathbad included – wanted the henge to stay where it was, exposed to the wind and the tides. Erik had sympathised. 'Sometimes the best thing we can do is to leave something where it was meant to be.' But higher authorities had prevailed and the timbers were removed to a museum. Would Erik approve of Ruth removing Jemima Green's medal? He would probably think that it should remain with the dead woman, her one pathetic example of grave goods. But, on the other hand, he certainly wouldn't have approved of *Women Who Kill* and would definitely have considered Ruth a more fitting guardian than Mark Gates or Phil.

Thinking of Erik makes Ruth feel restless. When she gets home, rather than going into the house, she decides to walk with Kate across the sand dunes to the sea. It's a beautiful evening, limpid pools of blue and gold, the seagulls flying low over the waves. The walk across the marsh can be dangerous but Ruth takes a path discovered long ago, two thousand years ago in fact. It's an Iron Age causeway, constructed many years after the henge but, in Erik's opinion, connected to it. 'This is sacred land, Ruthie. A crossing place. A bridge between land and sea, between life and death. People have known that for thousands of years.' All that is left of the causeway is a series of wooden posts sunk into the earth. Ruth follows these now, Kate skipping along at her side, thinking of the time when she first found the path, lost on the marshes at night. And Cathbad, of course, had known all along. She is so deep in the past – recent and ancient – that the sound of her phone is a shock. But when she looks to see who's calling, it's not a surprise at all. Cathbad.

'Hi Cathbad. I'm walking across the Saltmarsh with Kate.'

She thought he would respond to this – the Saltmarsh is one of his favourite places and Kate is one of his favourite people – but Cathbad's voice is tough, businesslike.

'Ruth. Have you heard about Liz Donaldson?'

'Who?'

'Liz Donaldson. The woman accused of killing her three children.'

For a moment Ruth is no wiser and then she sees a woman's face, a laughing blonde-haired woman holding a baby.

'She was on the news the other night,' she says.

'Yes. There's been a lot of coverage. It's Nelson's case you know.'

'I know.' She thinks of something. 'I didn't think she'd actually been accused. The report I saw just said she was being questioned. Nelson refused to comment.'

Cathbad laughs, rather bitterly. 'Yes, he's doing that a lot at the moment. They took her in for questioning. There was no evidence so they had to let her go again. But it's obvious what they think. The police think she did it.'

'And you don't?'

'No. I know she didn't do it. I know Liz. She's a friend of Delilah's, she used to babysit for the kids. She's a lovely woman. She would never harm anyone.'

Ruth is silent. Delilah is Cathbad's ex-girlfriend and they have a child together, though she must be almost grown-up now. But that's not what is making Ruth's heart beat so fast. Delilah was the mother of Scarlet Henderson, the little girl whose disappearance first led to her collaboration with DCI Harry Nelson. It was Scarlet's death that plunged her into this terrible world where children can be killed and horror is never far from the surface. Sometimes Ruth feels that she would give anything to go back to her pre-Scarlet life but she knows that this is impossible. Kate's second name is Scarlet.

'I didn't know you were still in touch with Delilah,' she says. After Scarlet died, Delilah and her family moved away from Norfolk.

'We speak on the phone now and again,' says Cathbad. 'Maddie's at university now. Leeds.'

'Have you talked to Nelson?' asks Ruth. 'About Liz Donaldson?'

'Oh, I've talked to him,' says Cathbad. 'I've told him that if he doesn't stop hassling Liz he'll be in for some serious karmic backlash.'

'What did he say to that?'

'He said he'd take his chances.'

Ruth can just imagine the exchange. She has reached a narrow gravel spit with water on each side. Kate tugs at her hand, wanting to jump in the puddles. 'No, Kate. You haven't got your wellies on.'

'Is that Hecate?' Cathbad's voice softens. 'Give her my love.'

'Her name's Kate,' says Ruth. But her voice too is soft.

'Ruthie,' says Cathbad. 'I want you to talk to Nelson.'

'Me?'

'Yes. You've got a special bond with him. I want you to convince him that Liz is innocent.'

Ruth is silent, walking along the path through the beautiful and dangerous marshland. Has she got a special bond with Nelson? He's Kate's father but she knows that he will never leave his wife. She has come to terms with that and, if it still hurts, she keeps the pain to herself. As a forensic archaeologist she has helped the police on several occasions and, whilst Nelson has always respected her professional opinion, she can just imagine his reaction if she tries to interfere on a case that has nothing to do with her.

'He won't listen to me,' she says. 'He'll say it's none of my business. And he'd be right.'

'Ruthie . . .'

'Don't call me Ruthie.' Only Erik was allowed to use that name.

'Think about it,' says Cathbad. 'This woman has lost three babies. She's been through the worst nightmare that you can imagine, the darkest places of the human heart. And now the police want to say that she killed her own children.'

Maybe she did, thinks Ruth. But she knows there is no

point saying this to Cathbad. He is on one of his crusades. She can hear it in his voice.

'I'll try,' she says at last.

'Thanks Ruthie.'

CHAPTER 5

'Let me get this straight. Cathbad thinks she didn't do it so I have to back off? Case closed?'

It isn't going well. It's Sunday afternoon and Ruth, Nelson and Michelle have taken Kate to a horse rescue centre near Yarmouth. Ruth had thought that it would be hard to imagine a more innocent place for her to raise the subject of Liz Donaldson. Nelson and Ruth are watching Kate ride a donkey and the fields are full of adorable ponies saved from fates worse than death. But, whilst the setting may be idyllic, the situation isn't entirely free from tension. Under an uneasy agreement brokered two years ago, Nelson sees his daughter maybe once every two weeks. Michelle knows about Kate's parentage and often accompanies Nelson on these visits. It would be too much to say that she has forgiven Ruth but she is always scrupulously polite to her and is genuinely fond of Kate. The future, though, remains uncertain. Nelson's role in Kate's life has not been made public and even his own daughters do not know that they have a half sister. Ruth sees storm clouds ahead. Nelson has already shown signs of wanting to be involved in the choice of Kate's school, for example. What happens when he wants to come to parents' evenings? And when Kate is old enough to question the exact nature of her relationship with the man who takes her on day trips and buys her inappropriate gifts? She calls him 'Dada' but she calls all men Dada, even the postman. Ruth doesn't like to think what this means.

But today the sky is clear. It's another beautiful June day and Kate is shouting with delight as she is led around the paddock. Last summer's trip to Blackpool may have dark memories for Ruth, but for Kate its abiding legacy is a love of donkeys. And a fear of roller coasters. Michelle has gone to get coffee (she often leaves them alone for tactful, but rationed, spaces of time) and Ruth has seized her moment. Nelson, though, is glowering.

'Did Cathbad put you up to this?'

Of course he did, Ruth wants to shout. Bloody Cathbad. How can he still be pulling the strings from two hundred miles away? But all she says is, 'He says he knows Liz Donaldson very well.'

'I'm sure he does. I'm sure he knows all sorts of nut-cases.'

'Is that what she is, a nutcase?'

Ruth looked up the case last night. There are any number of internet experts prepared to bet on the odds of three children from the same family dying from cot death. Articles range from 'The horror of mums who kill' to 'A mother's worst nightmare'. Other cases are trawled out: mothers jailed for killing their children, only to be released when new medical evidence comes to light, mothers who poison their babies and then act the heart-broken parent for the cameras. She can see them all, the mothers and their babies, in endlessly repeating patterns, like wallpaper. She sees Mother Hook too, in the one surviving photograph of Norfolk's worst murderess. A square, heavy-browed face, scowling out of the gentle sepia. There was a gruesome lullaby written at the time: *Don't cry little darling. Don't cry little dear. Don't cry little darling. Or Mother Hook will hear.*

Kate waves. Ruth and Nelson wave back.

'Look Ruth,' says Nelson, in the voice that he uses when he's trying to be reasonable. 'I'm sympathetic to any parent who loses a child, but three children are dead and I've got to keep an open mind. That's all I'm doing. Keeping an open mind.'

'She's a friend of Delilah's,' says Ruth.

Nelson doesn't respond to the name. He stares straight ahead but Ruth knows that he's not seeing Kate wobble past on her donkey. He's seeing the Saltmarsh at first light, the seagulls calling overhead, the sudden silence as the sand revealed its secrets. Nelson's hand is clenched on the gatepost. Ruth has a crazy desire to touch it.

'Delilah was an irresponsible hippie,' says Nelson, his voice harsh. 'It's no recommendation being a friend of hers.'

'Liz used to babysit for the children,' says Ruth. She doesn't say 'she may have known Scarlet'. She doesn't have to. She knows that Nelson is thinking about Scarlet, about the family. There were three other children too.

'If she's innocent she's got nothing to worry about.'

'Do you think she's innocent?'

'Like I say, I've got an open mind.'

'What do Judy and Clough think?'

'Judy thinks she's the bloody Virgin Mary. Clough believes everything he reads in the *Sun*.'

'What about Tim?' Ruth, too, is a little wary of Tim. They met in rather inauspicious circumstances and Ruth feels that Tim – like his old boss Sandy – slightly disapproves of her.

'Tim's just doing his job. He's a good copper.'

He looks as if he's about to say more, but at that moment Kate's ride comes to an end. Excited children rush to the fence to claim the next go. 'Dada!' shouts Kate as she is lifted out of the saddle. 'Look at me, Dada.' Michelle arrives just in time to see Nelson's fleeting expression of pure delight.

Nelson and Michelle leave soon afterwards. Ruth thinks that Michelle may have had enough for one day, especially after a carthorse slobbered on her pink cardigan. But before Ruth can go, Kate demands that they visit Ranger. In a weak moment last year Ruth agreed to sponsor Ranger, a bad-tempered Shetland, and many pictures of his cross, hairy face now adorn their fridge. Ranger sends nice letters to Kate, enthusing about eating carrots and frolicking in the fields with his mates, but when they meet face to face he usually seems distinctly underwhelmed. Today is no exception. Visitors aren't allowed to feed the horses, so when Ranger realises that they aren't about to be forthcoming with the carrots he turns his back on them.

'Oh, look at his tail,' says Ruth in desperation, 'Isn't it swishy?'

She is aware that another couple are doing their best to interest their child in the ponies.

'Look,' the father is saying, 'Lovely gee-gees. Look Michael.'

Michael. Ruth turns. A ginger-haired father is holding a baby on the gate. The mother stands nearby with an empty pushchair. She looks rather bored.

'Judy?'

'Ruth! Fancy meeting you here.'

'Oh, Kate and I love the horses,' says Ruth airily. What would have happened if Judy had seen her with Nelson earlier? What if she'd heard Kate say 'Dada' . . .

'Ranger's naughty,' says Kate.

'He looks naughty,' agrees Judy. 'I'm a policeman so I can tell.'

Kate looks at her dubiously. The policeman in her 'Going to Work' book doesn't look anything like Judy.

'You know Darren don't you?' Judy is saying.

'We met at your wedding,' says Ruth.

'Well, I was there all right,' laughs Darren, holding the baby in front of him like a trophy. 'Have you met our little superstar?'

'He's grown so much,' says Ruth. 'I hardly recognised him.'

'It was his first birthday last week.'

Michael looks at her out of big brown eyes. He's very dark, far darker than the pink-skinned Darren or pale, freckled Judy.

'The boss was here,' says Judy. 'Did you see him?'

'Nelson? Oh yes. He was with Michelle.'

'Wouldn't have thought horses were their thing,' says Darren.

'The boss likes horses,' says Judy. 'It's Cloughie who's scared of them.'

'Kate,' says Ruth, wanting to change the subject. 'Come and say hallo to the lovely baby.'

'Hallo baby,' says Kate, without enthusiasm.

'Can you say "Kate",' says Darren to Michael. 'Can you say "Hallo Kate"?'

Michael looks intently at Kate but declines to comment.

'Kate's growing too,' says Judy. 'How old is she?'

'She'll be three in November.'

'Do you remember that time I babysat? In the snow-storm?'

'Yes,' says Ruth. She doesn't think she'll ever forget that night.

'Heard anything from Cathbad?' asks Judy.

'Yes. I spoke to him on Friday.'

'I never thought he'd stay up there,' says Judy. 'Living on his own in the middle of a forest.'

'It's not exactly a forest,' says Ruth. 'I think he likes it. He's got his dog and he works part-time at the university.'

'I never thought he'd stay,' says Judy again. She turns and fiddles with the straps on the pushchair.

'Is that the druid chap?' says Darren. 'Maybe he's joined a coven. He lives in Pendle doesn't he? Pendle witches and all that.'

'A druid isn't the same as a witch,' says Judy. 'Come on Darren, we'd better get Michael home. He's a nightmare if he doesn't have his nap. 'Bye Ruth. 'Bye Kate.'

Ruth watches them go. Darren turns to wave but Judy has her head down, pushing the pushchair fast over the uneven grass. Ruth feels anxious, though she couldn't have said exactly why. She leans over to give Kate a cuddle and Ranger comes up behind and butts her, hard.

CHAPTER 6

That night Ruth dreams of Scarlet. She is walking over the Saltmarsh with Nelson, the wind is in her face and the skies are howling. She is in the henge circle with Erik, he is whirling round in a purple cloak until he is a hundred feet tall and his face is made of stone. She is searching in the dark, digging with her bare hands, knowing that if she gets there in time, Scarlet will be saved. She is watching as the police carry Scarlet's body over the sands, knowing that she has failed. She is looking at Scarlet asleep in her bed but then Scarlet has turned into Kate and Ruth wakes up, mouth open in a silent scream.

She looks at her alarm clock. Six o'clock. Thank God, she doesn't have to go back to sleep. She lies in bed, listening to the seagulls and thinking about her dream.

Does she still feel guilty about Scarlet in some way? Or is it just the Liz Henderson case and the disturbing link to Delilah, that Liz babysat for the family? Or maybe it's the body in the trench and the look of unholy glee on Mark's face when he talked about 'Women Who Kill'. *Don't cry little darling. Don't cry little dear.*

Ruth shifts in her bed. Her backside feels a bit sore after the headbutt. Bloody Ranger. She'll cancel that standing order today. She knows she won't though. Kate counts on getting a birthday card from her pony. 'Why the big horse? Big horse it's your birthday . . .'

Ruth switches on the radio. The *Today* programme fills the room, those lovely soothing morning voices. Weather updates, racing tips, Thought for the Day, the Dow Jones, John Humphrys interrupting. Ruth feels herself relaxing. Surely nothing can be wrong with the world if the *Today* programme is on? Isn't that meant to be one of the signs of a nuclear bomb attack, if the *Today* programme goes off air? Well, humanity seems safe today. She'll get up when Thought for the Day comes on. There's only so much metaphysical musing she can take in the morning.

By the radio, next to the baby monitor and Ruth's battered wrist watch, is the medallion. Ruth picks it up and turns it over in her hand. Did it belong to Mother Hook? The silvery metal glints in the light. She traces the outline of the two heads. Does it show the Madonna and Child or some other image? She doesn't know if Jemima Green had any religious affiliation. She sighs. She has a feeling that she will soon know more about Mother Hook than she has ever wanted to know. Phil reports that Mark is 'really keen' on including them in his programme. 'He wants to feature you, Ruth,' said Phil, sounding surprised. 'He says you're a natural.'

Didn't natural once mean simple, thinks Ruth, getting out of bed and feeling for her slippers. She can just imagine herself looking simple on television, her great moon face peering into the camera (isn't TV meant to put on a stone?), stumbling over her words and her feet, her uninspiring appearance picked over by a million twittering experts. 'Make-over needed for TV's Ruth.' 'How to avoid Ruth Galloway's Wardrobe Disasters.' Surely Phil with his slick charm would be a better choice? Or even Ted who, she is sure, would quickly acquire a cult following. What if she's a complete failure or, worse still, a success? Her friends would think it highly amusing and her mother would be horrified to see her daughter involved with such an ungodly programme. Ruth allows herself a quick grin. It's not all bad then.

Ruth pads across the landing. Kate is still asleep. She might even be able to have a bath (luxury) rather than just a quick shower, but as soon as she starts to run the water an imperious voice from the other room calls 'Mum'.

'Coming Kate.' Ruth may be the face of *Women Who Kill* but Kate will always be the star turn in this house.

'Are you sure?'

'I'd bet my bollocks on it.'

Nelson sighs. He is speaking to Chris Stephenson, the police pathologist, and, whenever you talk to Chris, his bollocks are sure to come into it somehow.

'I'm on my way to the station,' he says, pulling out into traffic with the minimum of care. 'I'll meet you there.'

'OK, Chief.'

As he weaves through the morning traffic, Nelson wonders why it irritates him when Chris Stephenson calls him 'Chief' but he doesn't mind his team calling him 'Boss' or 'Guv' . . . Maybe it's because he knows that the pathologist doesn't see him as his superior, or even his equal. For Stephenson the police are a lower form of life, an opinion he inexpertly conceals under a veneer of hearty laddish-ness with the men and unsubtle sexism with the women. Speaking of women, Judy should have been present at the autopsy. Why hasn't he heard from her yet?

She calls as he is taking the turn by the Campbell's Soup tower.

'Stephenson found fibres in David Donaldson's nose and mouth.'

'I know. He called me.'

Judy makes an exasperated noise. 'Why? He knew I'd make a report. Probably thinks women can't understand words like asphyxiation.'

'Is that what he thought it was? Asphyxiation?'

'He said it was the most likely cause. No bruising round the mouth but the eyes were bloodshot and there were clear traces of fibre.'

'Fibres from what?'

'A pillow, he thought.'

Nelson parks in the slot marked 'Reserved for DCI Nelson.' Some wag has replaced 'DCI' with 'Admiral'. He takes his phone off hands-free and waits for Judy to make the next move.

'Shall I bring her in, Boss?'

'I think it would be better,' says Nelson.

Ruth gets Cathbad's message just as she is leaving the lecture theatre. She always turns her phone off during lectures, and, in the old days often used to leave it off all day. But now she turns it on again as soon as she can. There is always the chance that there might be *the* message. The one telling her to come quickly because Kate is hurt, is ill, has been abducted by a serial killer in a clown mask. These days her imagination resembles a late-night horror film. It's what being a mother does to you.

But today's message says simply 'Call me'. Cathbad's name flashes up impatiently but Ruth waits until she is back in her office with a cup of coffee before calling back. She has a feeling that she might need caffeine.

'What took you so long?' says Cathbad.

'I was giving a lecture.'

'I thought term was over.'

'It's the summer school.'

Ruth enjoys teaching summer school. The students are always keen, often they are older people who have always dreamt of being archaeologists, merchant bankers inspired by *Time Team*, old ladies with a surprisingly detailed knowledge of Bronze Age burial customs. There are usually lots of foreigners too, because the university needs the money: Americans with complicated dietary needs, earnest Chinese students, casually elegant Italians. Next week they'll go on a dig. Who knows, this year they might even find something.

'They've arrested Liz,' says Cathbad.

'I thought they'd let her go.'

'They did but they've taken her in again. This morning. Judy . . .' He pauses. 'Judy and another one.'

Ruth thinks that this is how Cathbad sees the world these days. Judy and everyone else. But Cathbad stayed in Lancashire precisely to give Judy a chance to get on with her life, to forget their affair and concentrate on her marriage. He can't really complain if she's doing just that.

'How do you know?'

'Delilah told me. She rang me because she thinks Nelson's my friend.'

'He is your friend.'

'Nelson's a policeman through and through. He doesn't have friends.'

'That's not fair.'

'Maybe not.' There's a silence. Ruth wonders where Cathbad is. At work? Walking on the Pendle Hills with his dog, called Thing, at his side? Sitting alone in the little cottage that once belonged to a witch?

'I did try to talk to Nelson,' she says. 'But he just said that he was keeping an open mind.'

'Since when have the police been open-minded?' Cathbad's anti-police feelings go back a long way, to the death of a friend in the Poll Tax riots of the 1980s. But usually he exempts Nelson from these strictures.

'Nelson wouldn't arrest her without a reason,' says Ruth, wondering why she's defending him.

Cathbad obviously wonders the same thing. 'What would Erik say if he could hear you now? Norfolk police's PR department.'

'Don't take it out on me,' says Ruth. 'None of this is my fault.'

'Oh no,' says Cathbad nastily. 'It's nobody's *fault*.' He rings off.

Ruth drinks her cold cappuccino and wonders how Cathbad always manages to make her feel so guilty. It's not her fault that his friend's been arrested. For all she knows, Liz Donaldson *could* have killed her children. It certainly seems too much of a coincidence for three babies in one family to die of unexplained causes. But haven't there been cases like this before, where the mother was accused but turned out to be innocent? Ruth doesn't know and, quite honestly, she doesn't want to know. Her dreams are already full of abducted and murdered children; she doesn't want to add Liz Donaldson to her list of nightmares.

A perfunctory knock at the door and Phil's beaming face appears.

'Yes?' says Ruth unhelpfully.

'Having a coffee break, Ruth? I just came to tell you the good news.'

'What is it?' She has a feeling that she might not share Phil's definition of good news.

Sure enough.

'The TV people definitely want to include us in their programme on Mother Hook. We've got permission for a dig at the castle and a crew is going to film it all. We're going to do some of it at night. With *arc lights*.' Phil looks as if he is about to explode with excitement.

'Is this *Women Who Kill*?' She tries to put sarcastic quote marks around the title.

'That's right.' Phil misses the irony. 'An hour-long special. They're going to interview me.' Phil swells still further. No wonder he's so happy. He's always longed to be a TV expert. 'And they're going to feature you digging. They're very keen on digging.'

That suits Ruth. The longer she is hidden in a trench the better.

'And they're bringing in a well-known historian. Frank Barker. Have you heard of him?'

'No.'

'He's an American,' says Phil, as if this is an occupation.

'What does an American knows about a nineteenth-century Englishwoman?'

'He's an expert on the Victorians,' says Phil. 'He's done a lot of television.'

Christ, he's even starting to sound like a media buff. *He's done a lot of television.* God help us.

'There's a meeting tomorrow,' says Phil. 'I said you'd be there.'

'I can't wait,' says Ruth.

CHAPTER 7

Tim is pleased when Nelson asks him to go with Judy to bring Liz Donaldson in. Judy and Clough usually pair up, leaving Tim with the keen but distinctly junior Tanya. This would be a chance to bond with Judy, whom he admires as an officer but finds rather enigmatic as a person. He often hears Judy laughing with Clough or Nelson but with him she's always utterly serious, polite and pleasant enough but strictly unsmiling. Well, she's not going to be smiling today. Cases with children are always tough and this one seems to have hit Judy hard, probably because she's got a young child herself. In fact, the one time Judy almost unbent with him was when he showed her pictures of his twin nieces. 'I don't know how people cope with twins,' she'd said, 'I find it hard enough with one.' 'Have you got a picture of your son?' he had asked. 'No,' she said, closing down immediately, though he knew for a fact that Baby Michael was her screen-saver. Well, perhaps this job – harrowing though it may be – would give them a chance to get to know each other better.

They drive to the Donaldsons' house as soon as they get the nod from Nelson. They don't speak much on the way. Tim is driving and he hasn't quite got the geography of King's Lynn straight in his head. Judy promps him in a brisk monotone. She's a local girl, Tim knows.

Liz Donaldson answers the door. She's in a pink track-suit and Tim wonders if she was on the way to the gym. He's a gym addict himself and would understand the impulse to lose yourself in exercise. Judy, though, gives the outfit a rather surprised look.

'Liz,' said Judy, 'we have to ask you to come to the station with us. We need you to answer some questions for us.'

'Can't I answer them here?'

'We need you to come to the station?'

Liz looks from one face to another. 'Am I under arrest?'

By Tim's reckoning she has asked this question far too soon but Judy replies calmly, 'No, but we'd like to ask you some questions under caution.'

'In line with the Police and Criminal Evidence Act 1984,' adds Tim, thinking he might as well come across as the unsympathetic cop who sticks by the rules.

'Attendance is voluntary,' says Judy, shooting a rather unfriendly look at Tim.

'I'll come,' says Liz. 'Can you give me a few minutes to get ready?'

Tim assumes that she's going to change out of her tracksuit, but when she emerges a few minutes later she's still a vision in pink. It's only when they are half way to the station that he realises what she has done. She's put on her make-up.

There are a still a few reporters camped at the front of the station so Judy tells Tim to drive around the back. As they hustle Liz in through the door, Tim can hear Tom Henty, the grizzled desk sergeant, bellowing at the press pack. 'You'll get nothing from us until such time as DCI Nelson makes a statement.'

'Have you got new evidence?'

'Has she confessed.?'

'Has this brought back memories of the Scarlet Henderson case?'

'Why . . .'

'How . . .'

'Vermin.' Henty slams the door.

Nelson is waiting in the lobby, trying to keep out of the sight lines. Tim hears him ask the sergeant, 'Who asked that question about Scarlet Henderson?'

'Some woman reporter, I think. Young. That's her in the green jacket.'

Tim thinks for a second that Nelson looks rattled; far too rattled, surely, for some fairly innocuous questions from a fairly innocuous group of hacks? But then he turns to Tim and Judy and he is his normal self, brusque but in control.

'Take Mrs Donaldson into Interview Room 2, Johnson, and then we'll have a quick team meeting.'

Nelson begins the briefing at a gallop. 'We can only keep the suspect in for twenty-four hours without charge so let's get our interviewing strategy right. How did she seem?'

'Calm,' says Judy. 'Self-composed.'

'She asked us to wait while she put her make-up on,' puts in Tim.

Judy shoots him another black look. 'I don't see that that's relevant. Most women put make-up on before they leave the house.'

'Do you?' mutters Clough. Judy pretends not to hear him. Tim gives Judy a sideways glance. Her face looks shiny and make-up free. She has nice freckles, he notices.

'I think it could be significant,' says Nelson slowly. 'It could mean that she's putting on a different face for us.'

Tim thinks this is a rather perceptive comment. Nelson has grown-up daughters, he remembers. Judy, though, snorts contemptuously. Nelson carries on, 'Has she called a lawyer?'

'Yes,' says Tim. Liz made two phone calls before they left the house. One to her ex-husband and one to her lawyer.

'Who's her solicitor?'

Judy answers. 'Nirupa Khan.'

Nelson groans. Tim gathers that Ms Khan is not a personal friend. 'Well, we'd better get going double quick. Nirupa will have her stopwatch going. Johnson.'

'Yes Boss.' The briefing room is small but Tim notes that Judy has moved as far away from him as possible. 'I want you to take the lead on this. Be sympathetic. You're a young mum, you know what it's like to have a crying baby, all that kind of thing.'

'I'm not bringing Michael into this.' Judy looks mutinous.

'Shall I do it?' Tanya chimes in. 'It might be too distressing for Judy, having a young baby and everything.'

Tim suppresses a smile. He has already noticed that Tanya always volunteers for everything, whether it's meeting the chief constable or going on the afternoon chocolate run.

Judy shoots a distinctly unfriendly look at her colleague. 'I'm all right, Tanya. It's my job.'

'Yes, I need Judy's expertise here,' says Nelson. 'Tim, you back her up.'

'OK, Boss.'

'In the meantime, Cloughie and I will talk to the husband. We should speak to the grandparents too. Anyone else?'

'Liz mentioned a babysitter,' says Judy. 'Justine something.'

'Good. We need anyone who can help us build up a picture of Liz Donaldson as a mother. Tanya, you check her record of hospital attendance with all three children.'

'We've already done that.'

'We may have missed something. Do it again. Then you can go out with Rocky and talk to the neighbours.'

Tim notes that Tanya looks less than delighted. He has already come across PC 'Rocky' Taylor, the slowest man in British policing. As a pairing, it's not exactly Cagney and Lacey.

Tom Henty appears in the doorway. 'Miss Khan is here, Boss. She says she hasn't got all day.'

'Charming,' says Nelson. 'OK. Let's get to work.'

Tim has to admire Judy's style. She starts off low key, leaning confidentially across the desk.

'Are you OK, Liz? Have you got everything you need?'

'I'm OK.' Liz Donaldson is sitting patiently, hands clasped in her lap. The pink tracksuit looks almost shockingly bright in the basement interview room. The hastily applied make-up looks garish, lips too red and eyes too dark. She appears calm but Tim thinks that there is something defeated in her posture, as if she has already been convicted and is waiting for sentencing.

'You kept her waiting nearly half an hour,' says Nirupa Khan.

Nirupa Khan is small and neat, with black hair drawn back into a tight ponytail. Tim thinks that she is trying to appear older and tougher than she actually is. The black suit adds a few years, as does the hair style. Her manner is brusque and aggressively charmless. Tim can see why she and Nelson draw sparks from each other.

Judy doesn't rise to the comment or mention that the lawyer only arrived ten minutes ago. She continues to address Liz in the same calm voice.

'You know why you're here, Liz? The autopsy on David has raised a few questions.'

'What sort of questions?'

'The pathologist found traces of fibres in David's nose and mouth.'

Tim knows what Judy is doing. Keep saying the name, that's what the books say. The more you can make the suspect concentrate on the dead child, rather than the manner of their death, the better. He sees Liz flinch away from the words and thinks that Judy too looks rather sick. Must be hard doing this when you've got a child yourself.

'What does that mean?' asks Liz, her voice steady but her hands tense on her lap.

'It suggests that David was suffocated,' says Tim.

'Suffocated?'

'Liz,' says Judy. 'Why don't you take us through the events of last Tuesday again.'

Liz looks at Nirupa who nods slightly.

'It was afternoon,' she says. 'I'd taken David to the mother and toddler group and he'd fallen asleep in his pushchair on the way back. When we got home I carried him upstairs, put him down to sleep in his cot and went back downstairs. I did some housework then I made myself a cup of coffee. I sat on the sofa and I went to sleep. I was . . . I was very tired. David wasn't sleeping much and nor was I. When I woke up it was almost five. I couldn't hear a sound from the baby monitor. I thought that David had been asleep a long time. It's usually only an hour or two in the afternoons. I went upstairs and he was lying face down in his cot.'

'Did you put him to sleep face down?'

'No, I knew it was dangerous to do that. I put him on his side.'

'Was there a pillow in the cot?'

'No. They shouldn't have pillows until they're a year old.'

'Was he still in his outdoor clothes?'

'No. I'd taken off his jumper and trousers. He was just in his vest and nappy.'

She knows all the answers, thinks Tim. He's read up on it and knows that children can die because they're too hot or because they've suffocated on a pillow. Judy must know this too, that's why she's asking these questions again. Christ, why does anyone become a parent? The worry would kill you.

'When did you realise something was wrong?' asks Judy.

'I think I knew as soon as I went into the room,' says Liz, twisting her hands together. 'I turned him over and his face was blue and his skin was cold . . .' Her voice dies away.

'What's the point of this line of questioning?' says Nirupa, leaning forward to pat her client on the shoulder. 'I assume you've been through all this before.'

'New evidence has emerged,' says Judy. She, too, leans forward.

'Was anyone else in the house, Liz? When David died?'

'No. I was on my own.'

'When did you call the ambulance?'

'Immediately. I had my phone with me.'

'That's efficient,' says Judy. 'I always leave mine downstairs.'

Nice touch, thinks Tim. But Liz is ready for it. She looks coolly at Judy. 'I always have mine with me.'

Tim, says, 'It must be tough having a baby who doesn't sleep.'

'I didn't mind,' says Liz quickly. 'He was teething.'

'How long since you'd had a proper night's sleep?'

'I don't know. A week or so.'

'Bet you didn't know whether you were awake or asleep half the time.'

Suddenly Liz stands up. In her pink tracksuit she towers over Judy and is on eye level with Tim.

'I know what you're doing and I didn't kill David

because I was tired or because he was crying or because I didn't know what I was doing. I didn't kill him. I loved him. And, you know what? I've got all the time in the world to sleep now. I've got no husband, no babies, and you're probably going to put me in prison for life. I just hope I go to sleep and never wake up.'

She collapses back into her chair, sobbing, tears making streaks down her cheeks.

'Interview suspended,' says Judy into the tape machine.

Nelson is about to drive over to interview Bob Donaldson when Tom Henty informs him that Mr Donaldson is in the waiting room.

'He wanted to see his wife . . . ex-wife . . . but I told him that it wasn't possible.'

'OK. I'll have a word with him.'

'He's a bit upset,' warns Tom.

'I'll be gentle with him.'

Nelson takes Bob up to his office so it seems less like an interrogation. He's slightly disappointed not to be able to see Bob Donaldson at home as he likes to observe people in their own environment. You'd be surprised, he'd told his team, how many clues you can get from a person's record collection. 'No-one has records anymore,' objected Clough, but he'd got the point.

Now Clough stands back to let Bob precede him into the room. It's a shame that Clough looks so much like a nightclub bouncer, thinks Nelson, it hardly creates a cosy impression. But at least he's stopped eating crisps.

Nelson asks Bob if he'd like a cup of coffee. Ruth always tells him that the station coffee is vile but people seem to like him to make the offer. Sure enough, distressed as he undoubtedly is, Bob requests a white coffee ('not too milky') and two sugars. Nelson dispenses a glowering Clough to get the drinks.

'Thank you for talking to us,' he says.

'What have you done with Liz? What's happening?'

'Mrs Donaldson is being questioned by two of my officers.'

'She didn't do it, you know. Liz would never have harmed David.'

Bob Donaldson is a nervous-looking man, slight and pre-maturely balding. Nevertheless Nelson knows that he has a glamorous new girlfriend and lives in Pott Row, a much sought after village on the outskirts of Lynn. There must be more to him than meets the eye. Nelson casts his mind back for Bob's profession. Something to do with computers . . .

'Programmer,' says Bob impatiently. 'I'm a computer programmer. I want to know what'll happen to Liz. You can't keep her here without charging her.'

'Everything's being done by the book, Mr Donaldson,' says Nelson. 'Mrs Donaldson has her lawyer with her.'

'Nirupa?' Bob relaxes slightly. 'Good. I rang her as soon as I heard from Liz.'

'Very sensible,' says Nelson, wishing that Bob had been slightly less sensible. And was there something suspicious about running so quickly for a lawyer? Probably not. 'Innocent men don't need lawyers' had been a favourite adage of his former boss, but Nelson knows that they often do.

Nelson tries to get the discussion back on track and even attempts a smile. 'I'm DCI Harry Nelson and this . . .' as the door opens on Clough, who seems to have brought half the chocolate vending machine as well as the coffees, '. . . is DS David Clough. We'd just like to ask you a few questions.'

Judy had interviewed Bob Donaldson as part of her preliminary investigations. She described him as 'pleasant but a little colourless'. He and Liz were married for seven years, during which time they had three children and lost three children. Nelson can see the dates as if they are written on Bob's worried face. Samuel: born 2008, died 2008. Isaac: born 2009, died 2010. David: born 2010, died 2011. A list to make a stone weep.

'You and Mrs Donaldson are separated,' he says now. 'Is that right?'

'Yes, we separated at the beginning of the year. It was all very amicable. Liz is a lovely woman. There's no way she could have done a thing like this.'

'A thing like what?'

Bob stares at him. 'Are you playing games with me? I know you think she killed David. You probably think she killed Samuel and Isaac too. All our beautiful boys.' His pale blue eyes fill with tears.

'We're not making any assumptions,' says Nelson. 'Nevertheless there are circumstances around David's death that concern us and we have to investigate them. We wouldn't be doing our job otherwise.'

'What sort of circumstances?'

Nelson isn't about to tell him yet. 'I believe you have a new partner, Mr Donaldson.'

'What's that got to do with anything?'

'Just trying to build up a picture.'

There's a silence while Bob wonders whether to answer then says, in a voice made up of equal amounts of pride and resentment, 'Yes. Aliona. We've only been together a few months.'

'What does she do, Aliona?'

'She's a student.'

Nelson says nothing. After a moment, Bob says, 'I met

her when I did some teaching at the university. She's a good bit younger than me but she's very mature.'

I bet she is, thinks Nelson. Aloud he says, 'What did Liz think about you going out with someone new?'

'She was fine about it,' says Bob. Too quickly.

'Must have been hard for her, left alone with a young baby. Especially when you consider the history.'

'Of course it was hard,' says Bob. 'But things had got to the stage when it was worse to stay together.' His voice drops. 'It was torture.'

'Torture?'

'I didn't mean that,' Bob backtracks quickly. Nevertheless it is there, hovering in the air. Torture. Surely an odd, melodramatic choice of word.

'It's just . . .' Bob turns to look at Clough, as if begging someone else to understand. 'The marriage was over really, but when Liz got pregnant again we decided to give it another go. But sometimes you can't go back. I wanted to leave as soon as David was born but Liz was so depressed . . .' He stops.

Nelson and Clough exchange a look. There was no mention of post-natal depression on Liz Donaldson's medical notes.

'She was depressed?' prompts Nelson.

'No.' Bob backtracks again. 'It wasn't full-blown depression. She was just tired. David wasn't sleeping, I was working all hours . . .' He stops again, as if he's aware that he's making things worse.

'When did you leave?' asks Nelson, his voice hard. Nothing excuses abandoning your child, he thinks. But then a voice inside his head says: isn't that what you did?

'In February.'

'Depression all over then? Liz feeling full of beans?'

Bob can hardly miss the antagonism but he says, with an attempt at dignity, 'There was never going to be an ideal time to leave.'

'I should imagine not. David must have been, what, three months old?'

'Four.'

'And you met Aliona when?'

Bob hesitates. 'Well, I already knew her.'

'I see.'

Nelson can see Clough looking at him and knows that he sounds too disapproving. With an effort, he says in a more neutral voice, 'Did you keep in touch with Liz and David?'

'Of course,' says Bob. 'I saw David every week.'

'When did you last see him before he died?'

'The day before,' says Bob. Tears begin to roll down his

cheeks but he makes no attempt to check them. 'I saw him just the day before. He looked so well and happy. He was just starting to crawl.'

'And Liz? How did she seem?'

'I didn't see Liz. The babysitter was with David when I picked him up.'

So, far from the break-up being amicable, Liz Donaldson couldn't bear even to see her husband on his access visits. That must be the explanation, surely?

'The babysitter?'

'Justine Thomas. A lovely girl.'

She's next on the list, thinks Nelson.

'How long had Justine looked after David?' he asks.

'Since he was born. She looked after Samuel and Isaac too.'

'Great names, your boys,' says Clough.

Bob looked surprised. 'Oh, thank you.'

'From the Bible, aren't they?'

'I think so, yes. To be honest they were Liz's choices. I prefer simple names for boys.'

'Was Liz religious?'

'No. She'd turned her back on all that stuff.'

'What stuff?'

'She was brought up a Seventh Day Adventist,' says Bob.

Nelson doesn't know anything about Seventh Day Adventists but the name stirs memories of another case involving a baby. In Australia, wasn't it? Something about Ayers Rock and a dingo. He'll look it up after the interview.

'So she had no strong religious beliefs?'

'No.' Bob sits up and rubs his hand over his eyes. 'Look, what are you getting at? Liz wasn't a religious maniac, she wasn't depressed, she wasn't mad. She didn't kill David. You've got no evidence that says she did.'

Nelson pauses to straighten the papers on his desk before replying. 'The autopsy suggests he may have been suffocated,' he says.

CHAPTER 8

Justine Thomas agrees to see them but says that she is working.

'But you can come here. My boss won't mind.'

'What does she do?' asks Clough as they head out of town, Nelson at the wheel, Clough eating a bacon sandwich.

'She's a nanny. Works full time for a family in Chapel Road.'

Clough whistles. Not easy with a mouthful of bacon. 'They must have a bob or two.'

Chapel Road is known locally as Millionaire's Row and it's not hard to see why. It's a leafy area next door to the Sandringham Estate and some of the houses look fit, if not for a queen, at least for a member of minor royalty. The Rectory, inhabited by the family who employ Justine

Thomas, is a sturdy Victorian house set back from the road and surrounded by trees. Nelson thinks that it could be the setting for one of those God-awful costume dramas the girls like to watch. Even Clough chews more respectfully.

Justine, who meets them at the door, is a small woman (both Nelson and Clough think of her as a girl) with short hair and a sensible manner. She is carrying a baby and another child clings to her legs.

There are three children she explains, as she leads them into what she refers to as 'the playroom', but the eldest is at school. As far as Nelson can see the playroom is bigger than his entire house, a huge sunny space with French windows leading out onto the garden. Justine puts the baby into a playpen and gets the older child playing with some bricks.

'Hope you don't mind,' she says, 'but it's easier in here because they can entertain themselves.'

As the room contains more toys than Hamleys, Nelson can believe this. But after a few minutes the little boy abandons the bricks and starts trying to climb on Justine's lap.

'He's a bit clingy,' she says. 'He'll settle down in a bit.'

Strange to cling to the nanny rather than your mother, thinks Nelson. Clough is probably thinking the same thing because he says, 'They're pretty young to be left with a nanny, aren't they?'

'Poppy's just over a year,' she says, indicating the baby. 'Scooter here is nearly three. Bailey, he's the one at school, is five. I've looked after them since Bailey was a baby.'

Clough leans over to shake a rattle at Poppy. Nelson still can't get over the names. *Scooter*. What were the parents thinking? They give their poor kids outlandish names and then push off and leave them to be brought up by a girl that looks younger than his daughters.

'I'm twenty-two,' says Justine, in answer to his question. 'I became a nanny straight from school. I love it.'

'And you looked after all Liz Donaldson's children?'

'I wasn't their nanny but I babysat sometimes.' Her face clouds as she gently disentangles Scooter and puts him back on the floor. 'I can't believe that you've arrested Liz.'

'New evidence has come to light,' says Nelson. 'I can't say more at present.'

'You can't believe that she killed those babies. It's impossible.'

'We're trying to build up a picture of Liz,' says Nelson. 'What can you tell us about her?'

'She's lovely,' says Justine. 'She's been through so

much.' Samuel and Isaac dying, Bob leaving her. I don't know how anyone could stand it.'

Maybe she didn't stand it, thinks Nelson. Maybe she cracked and, for whatever reason, killed her last surviving child. Or did she kill all three of them, this lovely woman admired by all.

'When was the last time that you saw David?' he asks.

'The day before he died.' Justine's eyes, like Bob's earlier, fill with tears. 'Bob was coming round and Liz didn't want to see him so I went and waited with David. It was my day off.'

'Was Liz still upset about her old man leaving?' asks Clough.

Justine's eyes flash and, for a second, she looks like a completely different person. 'What do you think? He left her for a girl who was barely out of school. Aliona.' She says the name with a mock Russian accent. 'She's younger than me. Did you know that? He left Liz alone with a young baby and he knew what she'd suffered. I'll never forgive him for that.'

'Had Liz forgiven him?' asks Nelson.

'She never criticised him, not even to me, but I think she was still pretty sore about it. She said it hurt too much to see him with David. That's why she went out that day.'

'How did David seem?' asks Clough. 'Was he under the weather at all?'

'No,' says Justine. 'He was his usual smiley self.' She brushes away tears with the back of her hand. 'He was such a lovely baby.'

Nelson thinks that the one person who is hardly ever discussed is David Donaldson. Yet he was eight months old. He knows from his own children that by eight months they have powerful personalities. He has seen pictures of David – a blond blue-eyed moppet straight out of central casting – but he has never really thought about his character. Was he cheerful? Serious? Did he like cars or teddies? Did he have a passion for Thomas the Tank Engine? He asks now.

'Oh, he was a sweetie,' says Justine. 'Not a grizzler like Scooter here. But then he had his mummy at home with him. He had nothing to grizzle about.'

'Was he healthy?' asks Nelson. 'A good eater?'

'Liz sometimes used to worry that he wasn't gaining weight,' says Justine. 'But he was pretty healthy. He had a few colds and sniffles, nothing serious.'

Nelson knows that David had visited the doctor several times, always for minor ailments. But he had never been admitted to hospital. Surely, if Liz Donaldson was suffering from Münchausen's by Proxy, she would have taken him to A&E a few times?

'And how was Liz with him? Loving? Patient?'

'Yes.' Justine looks at him defiantly over the head of Scooter, who has climbed back onto her lap. 'She was a perfect mother. And I'll say that in court.'

On the way out, Clough asks what Justine's employers do. 'Must have plenty of cash by the look of this place.' Justine says that they run a toy company.

'So, what do you think, Boss?' asks Clough as they make their way back through the leafy streets. 'Did Liz Donaldson do it?'

'I don't know,' says Nelson, speaking slowly and driving quickly. Too quickly. A speed bump jerks them both out of their seats.

'Jesus, Boss,' says Clough. 'Are you trying to kill us?' It's usually the junior officer who drives and Clough wishes he had insisted on this protocol.

Nelson puts on the brakes. They take the next bump at thirty and almost miss the mini-roundabout altogether.

'Have you got enough to charge her?' asks Clough, holding on to the safety handle.

'I don't know,' says Nelson again. 'Chris Stephenson thought the autopsy definitely pointed to asphyxiation. But David could have suffocated by rolling on to his front.

Remember, Bob said that he was just starting to crawl? He would have been mobile enough. There were fibres in his mouth but no bruises on his face. It's all too ambiguous. And Liz Donaldson doesn't have any record of mental instability.'

'There was the depression,' Clough reminds him.

'We've only got the husband's word for that. And wouldn't it be enough to make you depressed, your husband going off with some foreign bimbo?'

'She could be a religious nutter. What was that about the Seventh Day Whathaveyous?'

'Seventh Day Adventists.' Nelson had looked them up after the interview with Bob. 'They believe in observing the Sabbath and preparing for the second coming.'

'They all do that. Even your lot.'

Nelson ignores this reference to the Roman Catholic Church. 'There was that case in Australia,' he says, 'where a baby disappeared in the outback. The mother claimed that the baby was taken by a dingo but she was charged with murder. They were Seventh Day Adventists and there was a lot of guff in the press about the church believing in infant sacrifice. The baby was called Azaria and there was some talk that it meant "sacrifice in the wilderness". All rubbish as far as I can make out. The woman was acquitted later.'

'Shame,' says Clough. 'We could do with something that links Liz Donaldson to a bunch of child sacrificers.'

'Instead she seems to be a perfectly normal woman. No-one's got a bad word to say about her.'

'I thought you had her down for it,' says Clough.

Nelson doesn't answer for a few minutes. He doesn't like to think that Clough can read him so well. 'I do suspect her,' he says again. 'There are just too many co-incidences. All three children dying when alone in the house with her. And there's something about her. She's altogether too perfect for my liking. Her house is perfect, she was the perfect mother, she looks perfect. It's just too . . . manufactured.'

'Maybe she *is* perfect.'

Nelson laughs. 'Nobody's that perfect. You'll find out when you have kids.'

There's a brief silence and then Nelson says, 'I just don't know if we've got enough for the CPS. There's the forensic evidence but that could be challenged. We can paint a picture of this depressed, psychotic woman but she'll be sitting in the witness box looking like Mary Poppins.'

'I always thought Mary Poppins was psychotic,' says Clough.

*

They park the car behind the station and walk round to the front. As they approach they see a young woman coming down the steps. She has long blonde hair and is wearing a green jacket.

Nelson puts a hand out to stop Clough. 'That girl,' he says, 'she was one of the reporters this morning.'

Clough squints at the retreating figure. 'She's a looker all right.'

'How can you tell from the back?'

Clough leers. 'I can tell.'

Nelson sighs. Since splitting up with Trace last year Clough has reverted to full Benny Hill mode. He has had a stream of girlfriends but none has lasted more than a few weeks. Nelson thinks that Clough was deeply hurt by the news of Trace's engagement, although of course he'd never admit it and Nelson would never ask.

He asks Tom what the reporter wanted.

'She wanted to talk to you,' says Tom. 'I told her you were out on a case.'

'What did she want to talk to me about?' asks Nelson.

'Scarlet Henderson.'

CHAPTER 9

Ruth is making breakfast when she hears the news that Liz Donaldson, 37, has been charged with the murder of her son David, eight months old. She stops, toast in hand, wondering whether Cathbad knows this latest. It's only on the local news (she has switched from Radio 4 to get a traffic update) so it's possible that he hasn't heard. She wonders whether to tell him but decides against it. Bad news travels fast and, besides, Cathbad has his sixth sense to rely on.

'Toast,' says Kate, waving an imperious hand.

'Please,' says Ruth. She has been trying, without much success, to get Kate to say 'please' and 'thank you'. Strange, when you think how easy it was to teach her the words to *Incy Wincy Spider* or even *Thunder Road*.

She gives Kate the toast and pours herself another cup

of tea. She'd better get a move on. She needs to drop Kate at the childminder's at eight and then get into the university for the meeting with the dreaded TV people. She imagines them incredibly cool and trendy, wearing designer outfits and those little glasses that make everyone look clever. She peers at herself in the kettle. She's wearing her normal work-day uniform of black trousers and loose white shirt. Her only concession to summer is leaving off her black jacket. Does she have any cool, trendy clothes? The newest item in her wardrobe is an all-weather cagoule for digging. She doubts if this counts.

'More toast,' says Kate, wiping her hands on Ruth's sleeve.

Eventually she makes do with a red scarf wound round her neck. People like Shona are born knowing what to do with a scarf but Ruth is always left with too many loops.

'Red, red, red,' sings Kate softly. It's her favourite colour. Ruth wonders what this says about her character. Ruth's own preference is for cool green.

As they set out along the Saltmarsh road, Ruth slots in a nursery rhymes tape. Kate objects immediately. 'Thunder Road,' she demands.

'Please,' says Ruth automatically, but she is only too

pleased to swap the wheels on the bus for Bruce and his car waiting by the screen doors, ready to scorch off across the black heart of America. She sings along as she drives. It's a beautiful morning, the mist just rising from the sea, the sky high and clear.

Kate sings too. 'Woo thunder road, woo-oo thunder road.' They pass the roundabout and the caravan site and the boarded-up pub then take a turning inland. Ruth looks at the clock on the dashboard. Seven-fifty but that's five minutes slow so it's . . . She drives between overhanging trees and takes the turn onto the Lynn Road.

What happens next seems almost dreamlike. One moment Ruth is driving along the familiar road, the next a car is heading straight for her. She can see the driver's shocked face and hears Bruce singing about promises being broken. Even as Ruth brakes and swerves she thinks of Kate, sitting happily in the back seat. Oh God, don't let Kate be harmed. If Ruth dies surely Nelson will look after Kate, and even if he insists on a Catholic school at least she'll be safe with him and Michelle. All this passes through Ruth's mind in the split second between pulling out onto the road and finding herself in the hedge.

'Are you OK Kate?' she asks.

'Yes,' says Kate in a very small voice. Ruth looks round

88

and her daughter smiles at her, almost as if she is reassuring her. Clarence Clemons is beginning a saxophone solo. After a few seconds Ruth becomes aware that someone is banging on her window. She tries to wind down the window, can't find the handle and opens the door instead. She gets out, dimly aware that her legs are shaking.

A man is standing on the grass verge. His car, a black Lexus, is on the opposite side of the road. Ruth notices a dead rabbit in the gutter and hopes that it wasn't an innocent victim of the crash.

'Jesus Christ,' the man is saying. 'Are you OK?'

'Yes,' says Ruth and her voice sounds strange and dreamy. 'Look at that rabbit.'

'You need to sit down,' says the man, 'you must be shocked. Look, it was all my fault. I was on the wrong side of the road.'

An indignant squawk from the back of the car rouses Ruth.

'Kate,' she says. 'Coming darling.'

'Oh God,' says the man, 'you've got a baby in there. Is she OK?'

Ruth opens the back door and lifts Kate out. She stands there, holding her daughter.

'Is the baby OK?' says the man again.

'I'm not a baby,' says Kate scornfully.

'Sorry, honey,' says the man. 'I can see you're not. Are you all right, sweetheart?'

'I'm nearly three,' says Kate. 'Not a baby.' In fact, she's just over two and a half but Ruth doesn't correct her.

Ruth thinks she should put a stop to this conversation. 'Shouldn't we be exchanging numbers or something?' she says.

'Sure,' says the man, getting a notebook from his pocket. 'But, like I say, it's all my fault. I thought I'd got used to driving on the left but I guess I lost concentration.'

Ruth notices for the first time that he has an American accent. He's a tall man, powerfully built with thick grey hair. There's something rather powerful about him too, even though he is apologising and promising to pay for the damage. Ruth thinks of a sheriff or an old-style New York cop. Maybe it's just the way he drawls his rs.

'Is your car damaged?' says the man, handing Ruth a page from the notebook.

'I don't think so,' says Ruth, scribbling. Her ancient Renault looks pretty battered but then it always looks like that. Nelson often mutters about her needing a new car. 'Something safer for Katie.' She won't tell him about today's adventure.

'I think I swerved just in time,' she says. 'I must have

driven right over to the other side of the road.' As she says this, she realises that she doesn't remember anything after swerving to avoid the Lexus.

'But you might have whiplash,' says the man. 'I think you should see a doctor.'

Whiplash always sounds dodgy to Ruth. 'I'm OK,' she says.

They exchange addresses and Ruth puts Kate back into the car.

'Look,' says the man. 'I'm not sure you should drive. You've had one hell of a shock.'

'I'm OK,' says Ruth again. 'And I've got to go. Got to drop my daughter off and I'm late for work.' She gives him a bland, social smile. 'Goodbye.' She has to stop herself from adding 'nice to meet you'.

She starts up the car and bumps over the verge, back onto the road. In the mirror she can see the American standing by the hedge, gazing after her.

She doesn't tell Sandra about the crash as she doesn't want to get into the whole 'are you all right, have a cup of tea, are you sure you haven't got whiplash' thing. Kate seems unconcerned and that's all that matters. Besides, now Ruth really is late. The TV people are coming at nine and she'd wanted to have half an hour to prepare herself but it's now eight forty-five. So she gives Kate a quick kiss, says goodbye to Sandra and dives back into her car.

She feels fine until she gets to the university. Then, as she's parking outside the Natural Sciences block, she sees her hands shaking on the wheel. She turns off the ignition and notices, with a kind of detached interest, that now her whole body is shivering. For God's sake Ruth, she says to her reflection in the driving mirror, pull yourself together. You've got to impress Phil's TV mates. She attempts a professional-looking smile but realises that she's grinning like a loon. And now she can't stop smiling. It's as if she's had four cups of espresso, a totally spaced-out feeling, not unpleasant in a way, but not terribly helpful today of all days.

She manages to stop smiling and shaking as she climbs the stairs. Calm, she tells herself, calm and professional. Oh God, where's her scarf, her cool TV scarf? She feels at her neck. She must have left it in the car or even at the side of the road where she had the accident. Never mind, you don't need a scarf to look like a good archaeologist. She pushes open the door to Phil's office.

The room seems to be full of people. Dimly, as if looking through water, Ruth sees Phil, a woman in jeans and a tall, grey-haired man.

Phil is doing the introductions. 'And this is Frank

Barker, the celebrated historian,' he is saying. 'Poor Frank's a bit shaken up. He had a shunt on the way here. Some woman driver.'

And Ruth realises that Frank is holding her red scarf, like the favour of some fallen knight.

CHAPTER 10

Ruth stands frozen to the spot. 'You,' she says at last.

The man, Frank Barker, is looking equally stunned. He glances down at the scarf and then back to Ruth as if wondering how the two came to be in the same room.

'My God,' he says. 'It was you . . .'

Phil, who has been looking rather put-out (he doesn't approve of tension unless he is the cause of it), says suddenly, 'Oh I see! Ruth – you were the woman driver. That's priceless.'

'It was entirely my fault,' says Frank.

'Sue him, Ruth,' says the woman, who has remained seated, her face impassive. 'Sue him for every penny he's got.'

'It's no big deal,' says Ruth, sitting down at the conference table. 'I'm sorry I'm late.'

'You had to drop your daughter off,' says Frank. 'How is she?'

'Fine,' says Ruth shortly. She doesn't like the way that Phil is still chuckling and the woman (what was her name? Danielle something) is still staring at her.

'Here,' Frank pulls out a chair. 'Sit down. I'll get you some coffee.' Ruth sees a cafetiere and real china cups laid out on a tray. Phil must have brought them from home. The university only runs to plastic cups from a vending machine. There are biscuits too.

'Are you sure you haven't got whiplash?' says Phil. 'You can make a mint out of whiplash claims.'

'Just another way for lawyers to get rich,' says the woman, leaning forward to fill up her cup.

'I haven't got whiplash,' says Ruth, through gritted teeth. 'I'm fine. It's no big deal. Shall we get on with the meeting?'

'Good idea,' says Phil. 'Now that the two experts have bumped into each other, ha ha.'

Ruth is pleased to see that no-one else laughs. The woman, who turns out to be the producer, hands out glossy information packs showing a shadowy figure of a woman brandishing a knife.

'This is the franchise,' she says briskly. Her voice is an odd mixture of transatlantic drawl and upper-class English. '*Women Who Kill* is a series about notorious woman murderers. It tends to be a bit sensationalist. Corinna Lewis presents it and she's not exactly one for subtlety, but I've been called in to do this one and I want it to be a bit different, more accurate historically. That's why I want to involve Frank here.'

'So not too many close-ups of the famous hook,' laughs Phil. 'No screams in the night.'

'No,' says the woman, deadpan. 'None of that. The thing is, we've got a different angle.'

'What Dani is saying,' Frank leans forward, 'is that we've got some pretty compelling evidence that Jemima Green may have been innocent.'

'Mother Hook innocent?' exclaims Phil. 'You're kidding! What about all that *Don't cry little darling* stuff?'

'A myth has grown up around her,' says Frank, 'but that's all it is. There was never really any evidence against her.'

'I thought she killed all those children and gave their bodies to the grave robbers?'

'She obviously knew the Resurrection Men,' says Frank, and Ruth thinks that he's choosing his words carefully, 'but there's no evidence of any murders. Some of her charges did die but then infant mortality was high.'

'She was convicted of one murder,' says Dani. 'Joshua

Barnet, the child of a single mother, died in Jemima's care. The mother, Anna Barnet, accused Jemima of murder and the court believed her.'

'She couldn't produce the body,' said Frank. 'That counted against her.'

I bet it did, thinks Ruth. Aloud she says, 'So this programme is going to be an exoneration of Jemima Green?'

Dani and Frank exchange glances. 'It's not quite that simple,' says Dani at last. Ruth finds the producer rather intimidating. She's a small woman with close-cropped black hair and precise bird-like movements, who gives the impression of knowing exactly what she's doing. Phil is completely mesmerised.

'Frank has his theories,' Dani is saying, 'but we've no evidence one way or another. The trouble is that the producers are wanting to make a very different sort of programme – this hook-handed monster, this evil woman. You know the sort of thing.'

Phil, who has been saying this sort of thing ever since they found the bones, says, in a shocked voice, 'God, I hate all that sensationalism.'

'Me too, Phil,' says Dani. Phil looks smug. 'But we'll have to put a bit in because that's what this series is all about. What I hope is that Frank – and Ruth here – can balance it with some hard-headed fact.'

'If there's anything about the bones themselves,' says Frank, looking at Ruth, 'that gives us a more rounded view of Jemima, that would be a real boost.'

Ruth notices that Frank, like so many other academics before him, is now on first-name terms with his subject. She also sees that Phil is dying to be included amongst the hard-headed experts.

'Bones can tell us a certain amount,' she says cautiously. 'Age, health, diet, that sort of thing. Generally speaking, bones can't always tell you how someone died but they can tell you how someone lived.'

Phil looks rather irritated. 'Bones can tell us a bit more than that, Ruth. Tell them about the case up in Lancashire.'

'No,' Dani interrupts him. 'That's just the sort of thing that we'd like to hear Ruth say on camera. There's too much guesswork in documentaries these days.'

'We could get a facial reconstruction,' says Phil. 'They're always good. Pricey though, but if the TV company's paying . . .'

Dani grimaces slightly. 'We haven't got a massive budget, I'm afraid. Anyway, that's the sort of thing I want to avoid. I'd rather hear a few sober facts from Ruth.'

Ruth tries to look suitably sober. She can sense Phil's frustration from across the table. He had been so sure that his particular brand of charm would be perfect for TV but it turns out that they're looking for dull professionalism instead.

'I'd love to have a look at the place where you found the bones,' says Frank. 'Is that possible?'

'Yes,' says Ruth. 'I'll take you, if you like. It's about an hour's drive away.'

'We can go in my car if it's easier,' says Frank.

'No thanks,' says Ruth. 'I'd rather get there in one piece.'

'Jesus, when you came into the room I thought you'd come to arrest me.'

'I thought I was seeing things. And when you held up my scarf . . .'

Ruth is cutting her way through the mid-morning traffic. Frank sits beside her, completely relaxed, long legs folded into the tiny car. It's funny, thinks Ruth, it's as if they've skipped several stages in the getting-to-know-you process (a process which, for Ruth, can take several years). Now she finds herself laughing with Frank about their first meeting, even teasing him gently when she asks how an American has ended up as an expert on Victorian murderesses.

'I'm not an expert exactly but the Victorians fascinate

me. They weren't nearly as buttoned up as people think. I mean it was the age of Freud and Marx as well as the age of Dickens. There was Strauss telling them that the Bible wasn't true, Darwin saying they were descended from apes, there's a new middle class taking over, and the Queen goes into mourning and never comes out again. It's no wonder they were all a bit mad.'

'What about Jemima Green? Was she mad?'

'I don't think so,' says Frank seriously. 'She wrote a diary almost up to the moment of her execution and it's very lucid, not the work of a madwoman at all.'

'She kept a diary?' Ruth thinks of her scorn when Mark mentioned a diary. Clearly the TV man had better instincts than her.

'Yes, it's very interesting. I've done quite a bit of research on Jemima Green. Shall I tell you about it?'

'OK,' says Ruth. 'It'll take my mind off crashing.' Despite her earlier protestations she is finding driving slightly stressful.

'Well, Jemima was born in Saxlingham Thorpe, not far from Norwich. She was the youngest of nine children so I suppose money was tight, but she did go to school and could read and write. Her diary's very well written and there are poems too. She trained as a nurse and worked in a mental hospital for a while. Then she lost her hand in a farming accident. Her father was a farmer and she was probably helping him with the harvest. There was a lot of new farming machinery at the time and accidents were common. Anyway, Jemima must have been desperate. She was twenty-nine, unmarried, she had to find some way to make a living.'

'So she became a baby farmer.'

'Yes, she took in unwanted babies. A sort of childminder.'

Ruth thinks of Sandra and shivers. But Sandra is a highly trained professional, a mother of three, not some nightmare Victorian hag. Nevertheless she has to stop herself looking round at Kate's baby seat. Only a few hours before she can see her again.

'The 1834 Poor Law Amendment meant that fathers didn't have to provide for their illegitimate children,' Frank continues, 'so there would have been no shortage of desperate women knocking on Jemima's door. Jemima took in the babies and then arranged for them to be adopted.'

'Except she didn't, did she? She killed them instead.'

'We know she arranged for some to be adopted. She kept quite meticulous records. There were a few cases at the time of baby farmers deliberately letting their charges die from neglect but there doesn't seem to have been any record of this with Jemima. All the witnesses testified that the children in her care were clean and well-fed. Like I said, there were some deaths but then infant mortality was high. When she came to trial there were stories of her killing hundreds of babies, but there's no evidence for any of this.'

'What about the baby she was accused of killing?'

'Joshua Barnet. He was the child of a governess, a respectable woman by all accounts. She handed him over to Jemima when he was just a few weeks old. The mother, Anna Barnet, seems to have kept in regular contact. Maybe she hoped to be able to reclaim him. Anyway, Joshua was never given up for adoption. When he was about a year old, Anna Barnet arrived to visit her son. She was told that he had died but Jemima Green wasn't able to produce his body. Anna was frantic, as you can imagine. She persuaded the police to search Jemima's house, which took some doing as the police weren't particularly interested in foundling children. In fact, the police force as we know it had only just been formed. Anyway, the police found opium and blood-stained baby clothes and, most suspicious of all, something called 'The Book of Dead Babies'.'

'The Book of Dead Babies?' Ruth skins crawls. She wonders if Dani, with her preference for hard-headed facts, knows about this.

'Jemima Green said it was a list of children who had died of natural causes while in her care. She wrote their names in a book and beside each name was a poem. Strange little poems. But there was no record of any of the children being buried. One of the rumours was that she'd given the bodies to the Resurrection Men.'

They are getting close to the castle, its square walls rising up above the city. Ruth edges through the traffic, looking for the turning for the car park.

'You mentioned them earlier. Do you mean the grave robbers?' asks Ruth.

'Yes. They had a lot of other names too: the sack men, the body-snatchers, the burkers – after Burke and Hare. There was a lot of hysteria about this in the mid-1800s. The medical schools needed bodies for dissection and the Resurrection Men supplied them. The 1832 Anatomy Act was meant to stop the trade because it gave doctors the right to use unclaimed bodies from workhouses and poor hospitals. The unclaimed poor, they called them.'

The unclaimed poor. It reminds Ruth of the service for the Outcast Dead. *We will remember them.*

'How did the Resurrection Men get the bodies?' she asks.

'They'd look for freshly dug graves,' says Frank, 'then sneak in at night and dig up the corpses. People started to bury their loved ones in iron coffins for protection. There was the famous case of the Italian boy. Three resurrectionists called Bishop, Williams and May were touting the body of a young boy around the medical schools. The authorities grew suspicious and it emerged that it was the body of a fourteen-year-old street boy called Carlo Ferrari. Carlo had been murdered – drugged and drowned in a well – so that they could sell his body for dissection. John Bishop wrote a full confession admitting that rather than just digging up dead bodies he actually killed people to order. He had a list of the corpses he had provided and it included lots of children. Children's bodies were always in demand.'

'And is that what they thought about Jemima Green? That she had killed the children to provide bodies for the resurrectionists?'

'That's what they said. There were cartoons of her putting children in her sack like some kind of evil Santa.'

They have reached the entrance to the underground car park, a great round O like a giant hobbit hole. They take the steps up to the castle grounds, passing the outdoor theatre where the service for the Outcast Dead was held. Today it's full of schoolchildren with clipboards and felt-tip pens. The castle looms above them, its sides smooth and featureless like one of the pictures about to

ELLY GRIFFITHS

be coloured in by the children. The grass bank is studded with daisies. Ruth and Frank stand looking up at the fortress.

'It was Norman originally wasn't it?' says Frank.

'Yes,' says Ruth. 'You can still see the remains of the Norman keep inside the castle.'

'So the Victorians built a nice tidy case to enclose it all,' says Frank. 'Typical.'

Ruth gives him a sidelong glance. His tone is light but she can tell an authentic historian when she sees one. She knows that he is seeing the castle, not as a twenty-first-century tourist attraction, but as an eleventh-century garrison. Or maybe he's seeing the nineteenth-century prison, the gibbet only yards from where they are standing.

'Do you really think Jemima Green may have been innocent?' she asks.

Frank turns to look at her. He has very blue eyes, Ruth notices. 'There was no real evidence against her,' he says. 'Even the opium wasn't really that unusual at the time. There was a popular children's medicine called Godfrey's Cordial, also known as the Mother's Friend, that basically contained syrup and opium. No, what really condemned Jemima was her appearance. You've seen the photograph. That face, the hook. And she was a big woman, like a giantess some of the reports said. Add that to The Book of Dead Babies and she was as good as hanged.'

Ruth, who has also been called a big woman, thinks of the body in the trench. Was she also guilty of condemning Mother Hook on her reputation alone? She thinks of Mark Gates peering into the grave. *Women Who Kill*.

'And then there were the accusations of witchcraft,' says Frank. 'Anna Barnet testified that Jemima Green always wore a silver medal round her neck depicting the devil and his daughter.'

They are crossing the bridge that leads to the castle entrance. Ruth stands stock still as the schoolchildren swarm past her. The devil and his daughter.

CHAPTER 11

Nelson stares unenthusiastically at the faces ranged before him. Next to him his boss, Superintendent Gerald Whitcliffe, is positively vibrating with excitement.

'Remember what you learnt in the media management course, Harry,' he keeps saying, 'press conferences are vital for improving police PR.'

Nelson, who only lasted half a day on the media management course, doesn't see why addressing a group of bored and hostile reporters, most of whom think the police spend their time taking bribes or beating up prisoners, should help anyone.

'We've got to show them the modern face of policing,' says Whitcliffe. 'Prove that we're not all Neanderthals.'

'Europeans have up to four per cent Neanderthal DNA,' says Nelson. He learnt this from Ruth.

Whitcliffe ignores him, he is too busy beaming in a modern and caring way at the correspondent from the *Guardian*. Goodness, even the *nationals* are here.

'OK,' says Nelson, 'let's get started. Who's first?'

Someone asks about evidence, giving the impression that Nelson routinely arrests people just for the fun of it. Nelson glowers in a distinctly prehistoric way. Whitcliffe chips in seamlessly, talking about the rights of suspects but also (with a caring smile) the rights of 'the real victims here, the children.'

Pass me the sick bag, thinks Nelson. He tells the reporter from the *Telegraph* that yes, he has consulted the CPS and, in his opinion, there is enough evidence to bring Liz Donaldson to trial.

'Will you be relying on expert witnesses?' says the man from the *Mail*, with a slight sneer.

'We may bring expert witnesses, yes,' says Nelson. 'I can't say more at this present time.'

'*Sub judice*,' explains Whitcliffe with a smile. 'I'm sure no-one wants to jeopardise this investigation.'

'DCI Nelson, are you haunted by mistakes made on the Scarlet Henderson case?'

A low murmur in the room, the hacks turn to investigate this new voice, sounding so much younger and angrier than anyone else. Whitcliffe looks questioningly at Nelson who seems to have been turned to stone.

The voice belongs to the blonde girl, the one in the green jacket. Nelson stares at her, trying to remember where he has seen her before.

'You missed vital clues in the Scarlet Henderson case. Do you think you've done the same here?'

'We're not able to discuss previous cases,' says Whitcliffe. 'But you might remember that we brought the murderer of little Scarlet to justice.'

'By accident,' says the girl. 'After you suspected her totally innocent parents.'

As Nelson still seems incapable of speech, Whitcliffe says, 'Well, if that's all for today, thank you for your time.'

He turns to Nelson, planning to have a supportive word about dealing with hostile questioning but his Chief Inspector has already disappeared into the crowd of journalists.

'Wait a minute!'

The girl turns, flicking her long hair back from her face. She's very pretty, with pale skin and wide-apart green eyes. She looks far too young to be a journalist.

'Who are you?' asks Nelson.

'I'm Maddie,' says the girl. 'Maddie Henderson.'

Henderson. Nelson thinks back to Scarlet's family. Delilah and Alan. The bohemian mother with her bare feet and ravaged prettiness, the thin-faced father whose nervous behaviour had certainly aroused suspicion at the start of the case, the younger brothers who had been quite excited by the presence of the policemen – and the eldest daughter, slightly apart from the rest of the family. He looks at the girl again.

'You're Scarlet's sister.'

'Yes.'

'How old are you?'

'I'm nineteen.'

As the father of daughters Nelson knows that teenage girls can look completely grown-up or they can look like children. Maddie Henderson, disconcertingly, flits between the two. Her face is young – no make-up, pale eyelashes, slightly chapped lips – but her manner is that of an adult, an angry adult at that.

'Are you a journalist?' he asks.

For the first time, she hesitates. 'I'm studying journalism. At Leeds Met.'

'Why did you want to speak to me?'

'I saw that you'd arrested Liz Donaldson for the murder of her children. I remembered when Scarlet first went missing, how you'd behaved around Mum and Dad. I know you suspected them. Hippies, dropouts, letting their kids run wild. I remember you digging up our garden. You thought we'd killed her.'

'You're wrong,' says Nelson. 'We had to follow every line of enquiry but your parents were never suspects. I give you my word.'

Maddie is still glaring at him. The other journalists have all left but Nelson knows, from the burning sensation in his back, that Whitcliffe is still in the room.

'Look, why don't we discuss this somewhere else?' he says. 'I'll buy you a coffee.'

'I don't drink caffeine,' says Maddie.

'A milkshake then,' says Nelson, rather wildly, trying to think of drinks his daughters used to enjoy.

'I don't believe in taking milk from baby cows,' says Maddie but she accompanies him to the door. Something in her expression, half challenge, half acquiescence, reminds him of someone. Then he remembers. Alan Henderson isn't Maddie's father.

Cathbad is.

Ruth and Frank make their way towards the excavations. Ruth is thinking about the revelation that Mother Hook's medallion could be a black magic talisman. She feels a sudden atavistic fear about having the thing in her house. She must get rid of it. She'll take it into the university tomorrow. But then she thinks: is it likely? Do they make medals showing Lucifer and Little Miss Lucifer? Did the devil even have a daughter? Aside from the one in old Christopher Lee films, that is. Frank seems to be suggesting that the case against Jemima Green consisted mainly of superstition and hearsay. The story of the satanic medal could be just another example. Anna Barnet must have had an interest in making Jemima seem as evil as possible. Ruth walks on, deep in thought, and doesn't notice when Frank offers his hand to help her over the ditch at the bottom.

The trench is covered with a tarpaulin. Ruth pulls this aside and displays the neat oblong of earth. A measuring pole lies beside it.

'Hasn't there been a lot of building work here?' asks Frank.

'Not in this area. It's a little apart from the other prisoner burials. That's why we were surprised to find anything here.'

'Do you think that was deliberate? Because she was so reviled?'

'I don't know,' says Ruth, 'but it was certainly a deviant burial. Skeleton was prone, for a start.'

Frank nods. 'Being buried face down indicates disapproval in lots of cultures.'

'And there was no shroud or coffin,' says Ruth, 'we're hoping that there's not too much contamination but . . . it may be difficult getting DNA samples.'

'But you're in no real doubt that it's her?'

'Well, evidence does point that way,' says Ruth cautiously. 'We'll get a date from the Carbon 14 tests though, as you know, that'll only give us a margin to play with. And we'll do stable isotope tests. That'll tell us if she was from the Norfolk area.'

'By analysing the minerals in the bones?'

'Yes. Bones renew themselves, so they're a good snapshot of where a person spent their last years. To find out about their early years, you need to look at the teeth.'

'It's fascinating,' says Frank. 'I wish I knew more about forensics.'

I wish I knew less, Ruth thinks. She says, 'But you know a lot about the times she lived in. That's fascinating too.'

'Yes.' Frank looks across at the castle. Another group of children in bright red blazers are going in through the gates, laughing and chattering. But in spite of this, the building still looks grim and unwelcoming, a smooth square fortress squatting on a hill. 'Jemima would have been a prisoner at a time when they were experimenting with the separate system. Have you heard about that?'

'I think so,' says Ruth. 'I've seen the chapel at Lincoln castle. It's the spookiest place I've ever been.'

'The separate system was a way of keeping prisoners completely isolated. It was first used in the Eastern State Penitentiary in Philadelphia. Penitentiary, of course, meaning to do penance. The prisoners literally had no contact with anyone. They had to wear masks at all times, and when they were exercising they held a rope knotted at intervals to keep them apart. Even in chapel the prisoners were kept in separate little boxes, unable to see anyone except the minister. You can see that at Lincoln. The idea was to stop criminals consorting with other criminals, crush the so-called criminal sub-culture. But, of course, there was a major drawback.'

'What was that?' Ruth can think of several.

'They went mad,' says Frank shortly. 'Human beings who have no contact with other human beings go mad. At some places they had to build special mental hospitals next to the prisons. Eventually there was a real outcry against the system. Elizabeth Fry was one of the first people to condemn it.'

Ruth has always felt rather an affinity with the great prison reformer who is a local heroine. There is even a statue of her in the grounds of the university. When in doubt she often asks herself 'What would Elizabeth Fry do?'

'When did they stop using the separate system?' she asks.

'By the end of the nineteenth century but there are still some prisons in use today – like Pentonville – that were built for the separate system.'

Pentonville reminds Ruth of a Monopoly board. She was always the dog and her brother the top hat. She really must give Simon a ring. Thinking of home reminds her that she's hungry. She could suggest that they stop off at the museum cafe for a sandwich. Or would that be too forward? What would Elizabeth Fry do?

But before she can ascertain this, Frank says, 'Do you fancy some lunch? I know there are some great pubs in town.'

They go to a pub near the centre of Norwich. It's an irregular slice of a building, tucked away down an alleyway near Maddermarket. There doesn't seem to be a straight line in the entire place; the floor tilts, the beams bow outwards and the doors and windows fit together like a complicated jigsaw puzzle.

'It's like being on board ship,' says Frank, putting the

drinks onto the table and watching them slide slowly southwards.

'It's supposedly built on top of a mine,' says Ruth. 'There were chalk mines in Norwich once. The whole place is riddled with tunnels.'

'I like it,' says Frank. 'I love Norwich. All those churches, all these pubs, Tomblands, the cathedral, the castle. Layers and layers of history.'

'Yes,' says Ruth. 'I sometimes think that we're walking over bones all the time. All those bodies beneath our feet.'

'That's what I love about Britain,' says Frank. 'In the States we get excited if something's a hundred years old. Here, that's modern. I mean, you've got New College in Oxford that was built in thirteen hundred and something.'

'Whereabouts in the States are you from?'

'Seattle. I did my first degree there but then I came to Cambridge as a post-graduate. Man, I just love the fens,' he says, leaning back in his chair and grinning with perfect American teeth. 'It's flat and grey and scary as hell but I love it.'

This almost sums up Ruth's own feelings about the Saltmarsh but she doesn't say so. Instead she asks how a Cambridge academic ended up talking about murder on TV.

'I went back to the States and taught at Stanford U for a while. Some local TV company was making a programme about the Industrial Revolution and they asked me to appear. I was only on screen for five minutes, talking about nineteenth-century looms, but for some reason they asked me back to do another programme. One thing led to another. I'm still not sure how it happened myself.'

He smiles self-deprecatingly but Ruth can see why Frank is in so much demand as a TV expert. He has unquestionable authority but the laid-back accent and the lazy charm stop him from seeming too threatening. She keeps having to remind herself that she's only known him for a day.

'I've never been to Seattle.' says Ruth. She has, in fact, only been to America once, on a weekend trip to New York with Shona, but she's not about to admit this.

'It's a fine place. A hundred and fifty days of rain a year. That's why they call it the emerald city.'

'Sounds like England.'

'I just love England. I'm becoming more of an anglophile as I get older.'

Ruth wants to ask how old he is. He has grey hair but his face is tanned and unlined. He could be any age.

'Do you live in England now?' she asks.

'I've got a flat in Cambridge and a family house in Seattle,' he says. A family house, thinks Ruth. Does he have a family? A wife? She noticed earlier that he was wearing a wedding ring. She is about to ask another question but their food arrives and there's the usual hassle of finding knives and forks, salt, pepper, napkins. Ruth is having a ploughman's (which always sounds more slimming than a hot meal unless of course you count all the bread and butter) but Frank has gone for the full pie and mash option.

As Ruth tries to cut her cheese into very small slices, Frank says, 'The kids are grown up now but I still like to keep a place where we can all be together.'

'How many children have you got?'

'Three. Fred's twenty-five, Jane's twenty-two and Sean's twenty. Jane and Sean are at university, Fred's working in Africa.'

Ruth is just thinking that they have very normal names for Americans when Frank says, as if he has been holding these words back, 'I'm a widower.'

Ruth doesn't know what to say. She doesn't think she's ever met a widower in real life. 'I'm sorry,' she says at last.

'Ali died five years ago.' says Frank. 'I'm getting better at saying it. It's a terrible word, isn't it?'

'Yes,' says Ruth, 'like something from Dickens.'

Frank laughs. 'Dickens would have given me a golden-haired moppet to console me instead of three stroppy teenagers.'

'I bet they did console you though.'

'Yes,' agrees Frank, 'they did.' He takes a drink of beer, then he says, 'Ali and I got married young. We'd planned to have a lot of time together when the kids left home but it didn't work out like that.'

'How did she . . .?'

'Breast cancer. They didn't spot it in time. She was forty-six when she died.'

Ruth tries and fails to think of something to say. What can you say to a man who has lost his wife? At least if she was religious she could say something about heaven. She thinks of the prayers for the outcast dead. *Not a sparrow falls without our Father in heaven knowing.* Did He know about Ali Barker? Did He care?

Frank breaks the silence.

'Are you married, Ruth?'

'No.'

'I know you've got a daughter. How old is she?'

Was it only this morning that Frank made Kate's acquaintance? It seems years ago. Ruth is seized by a sudden tiredness. She'd like to put her head on the uneven wooden table and sleep for a week.

'Her name's Kate. She'll be three in November. I'm not with her father. I never have been.'

As she says this, she wonders if it's true. She's never been in a proper relationship with Nelson but, over the last three years, there have been times when she's felt closer to him than to anyone in the world.

'Tell me more about Phil,' says Frank. 'Is he a bit of an asshole?'

Ruth laughs, grateful that she doesn't have to talk about herself anymore and always glad of an excuse to slag off the head of department.

Nelson's meeting is not going so well. Maddie accepts a peppermint tea but shudders at the thought of eating anything. She's too thin, thinks Nelson. His own daughters are slim, but when she takes off her jacket, Maddie's arms are wand-like, the bones too near the surface. She's nervous too, picking at the skin around her nails and jumping when anyone enters the cafe. But there's also a confidence there, the self-assurance that allowed her to gatecrash a press conference and demand a hearing. Perhaps it's not so much confidence as belief, a complete and utter conviction that she is in the right. Maddie might be shaking in her thin T-shirt but she glares at Nelson like a martyr about to go to the stake. She reminds him a lot of Cathbad.

'Why was it so important for you to see me?' he asks. 'I saw you at the station the other day.'

Maddie pushes back the hair from her face. Her eyes are extraordinary, bright green with flecks of gold. Nelson tries to remember what Cathbad's eyes are like, just your average set he thinks, nothing like this.

'I wanted to stop you,' says Maddie. 'I know Liz is innocent. She used to babysit for the little ones sometimes. She wouldn't hurt a fly.'

'She's a friend of your mum's isn't she?'

'Yes. Liz was training to be a nurse but she did some babysitting to make extra money. She used to look after the boys, and Scarlet when she came along. She became a family friend. Mum wasn't very well after Scarlet and Liz was really kind. Used to take us all out to give Mum a break. I was twelve when Scarlet was born and I thought I was grown up but I wasn't really. Liz understood that. She used to talk to me. I could tell her things I couldn't tell Mum and Dad. Stuff about school, friendships, things like that. '

Nelson remembers Maddie in the days after Scarlet's disappearance. They had questioned her, he remembers, but she was out on the day that her little sister vanished. Scarlet had been playing in the garden with her seven-year-old twin brothers. One minute there and the next minute gone. Lost forever. For almost the first time, he wonders what that was like for Maddie. She was older, she may have felt responsible, she was certainly aware of her parents' suffering. It's interesting too that Delilah hadn't been well after Scarlet's birth. Liz would have witnessed this. She'd been kind, Maddie said. Was she also storing up symptoms for later? How long after Scarlet's death were Liz's children born? He'll have to check.

'I'm sure Liz was kind,' he says, choosing his words carefully. 'If she did this thing, it was probably because she was ill.'

'Is that what you're saying?' says Maddie quickly. 'It's all down to post-natal depression?'

'I can't discuss the case with you,' says Nelson. 'You know that.'

'Mum cried for years,' says Maddie, glaring at Nelson as if it was his fault. 'Literally for years. Can you imagine what that was like?'

'No,' says Nelson. 'I can't.'

'She blamed herself because she wasn't watching Scarlet. I heard you asking her "How long was it before you realised that Scarlet was missing? You mean you left her alone all that time? Why weren't you checking on her?" Jesus, it was like she was in court. Guilty of having five children and a shabby house. Guilty of having wind chimes and talking about Brother Sun and Sister Moon. I saw it all in your face.'

Is that fair, wonders Nelson. He had certainly thought Delilah casual to the point of neglectful. He'd disapproved of her bare feet and the aromatic smell of Alan's cigarettes. Had it shown in his face? But he had never underestimated her loss and grief. He had almost killed himself trying to find Scarlet.

'How's your mum now?' he asks. 'I heard she'd moved away.'

'She's better,' says Maddie. 'She has to function for Ocean's sake. She's only four.'

Of course, there was a baby. Ocean. Jesus wept.

'Where's she living?'

'Blackburn.'

Nelson is jolted by this. Blackburn is near his territory. Nelson was born and brought up in Blackpool and, whilst he now accepts that he will probably never live there again, he still thinks of it as home. The thought of Delilah being so close is curiously disconcerting. As if his past is tracking him.

'Do you see much of . . . your dad? You know he lives up north now?'

Maddie smiles. 'Cathbad? I can't think of him as Dad.

Yes, I've been seeing quite a lot of him. Alan will always be my dad but Cathbad's a pretty special person.'

Nelson can't deny this. 'He's a one-off, is Cathbad.'

'It was his idea that I should talk to you,' says Maddie, turning her mermaid's eyes in his direction. 'He said you'd be sure to help me.'

'Did he now?'

'Yes. He says that you share a psychic bond.'

And the worst thing is, Nelson thinks this might be true.

CHAPTER 12

'We've come to the beautiful city of Norwich to discover the truth about one of Victorian England's most notorious murderesses. A woman whose name still strikes terror into the hearts of mothers and children everywhere. Mother Hook. The so-called baby farmer who killed her charges for profit. The hook-handed killer who slaughtered innocent children and wrote their names into a ledger chillingly entitled The Book of Dead Babies.'

Corinna Lewis stops and pauses impressively, staring into the camera. Ruth, who is dutifully standing in the trench for an action shot, reflects that there is little sign of Dani's even-handed approach in the presenter's script. What had Dani said? That Corinna wasn't one for subtlety. Ruth amuses herself by cataloguing Corinna's favourite words: 'terror', 'slaughter' and 'chilling' are definitely three. She also likes 'shadowy', 'horrific' and 'innocent'. So far all these words, except the last, have been used to describe Mother Hook.

'Archaeologists digging in the grounds of this ancient castle,' continues Corinna, 'made a chilling discovery. The bones of a woman with a hook for a hand. I'm at the dig now with Dr Phil Trent, Head of Archaeology at the University of North Norfolk. Phil, tell me about your find.'

It was my find, thinks Ruth, as she digs and scrapes, conscious that the cameras may be on her. She can hear Phil talking in his new TV voice. One of the researchers told him to smile just before he spoke, 'it makes your voice sound really warm'. By the sounds of it, Phil has been grinning away for hours.

'It was really exciting, Corinna,' he says ('Use Corinna's name' urged the researchers). 'I knew at once that it was something really significant. It was the right age, for one thing, and it was a woman. Then I saw the hook and . . . well . . . wow.'

Well wow, thinks Ruth. Is that the sum of your intellectual input? A PhD in archaeology, years of experience and research. *Well, wow.* And it's impossible to tell the age of bones just by looking at them. Carbon 14 tests can give a clearer picture but they can be out by as much as a hundred years. The only real clues are in the context, the objects found in the earth beside the body. Phil won't mention this, it's far too boring. Besides, the most significant find is still on Ruth's bedside table.

'Do you get frightened, Phil, looking at the skeleton of such a monstrous figure?'

Phil laughs modestly. 'Well, I'm an old hand at digs but I have to confess there was a slight frisson, here.' He pats his chest.

'Cut!' Dani's voice rings out from behind the camera. 'Don't bang your chest, Phil. It makes the microphone boom. Let's take a quick break folks.'

I've been trying to tell Phil not to bang his chest for years, thinks Ruth, straightening up. She thinks that Phil looks rather chastened. Dani is talking to him and she can see him nodding vigorously. Probably agreeing to do a full-frontal striptease for the cameras. She can tell just by Phil's body language that he's in awe of Dani. He's standing just that little bit too close and laughing just a little bit too loudly. Shona said that she'd be along later to watch the filming. Ruth will be interested to see her reaction. Ruth's friend Shona, once a glamorous free spirit, has been in a relationship with Phil for almost three years and they have a baby son, Louis. Ruth is fond of Shona but she doesn't always trust her. She wonders how much Shona trusts Phil.

Ruth hopes that there'll be more interruptions and that they won't get round to her interview today. Dani had said that filming would take four to six weeks but they've been here all day and, as far as Ruth can see, they've only shot about ten minutes of film and most of that was Corinna telling the horrific/terrifying/chilling story of Mother Hook.

'Good game, isn't it?' Frank is leaning into the trench. He is wearing jeans and a check shirt and looks rather like an intellectual Indiana Jones. Ruth is sure that this is deliberate. Frank is also due to be filmed today.

'Does it always take this long?' Ruth climbs carefully out of the trench. The runners usually provide tea and coffee in the breaks and she doesn't want to miss out. It's surprisingly tiring, standing still for hours.

'We're doing well,' says Frank. 'Dani's good at moving things along.'

'What do you think she's saying to Phil?'

'Probably telling him to cut down on the theatrics and put in some history. She's going to be spitting mad at Corinna's script.'

'Can't she tell her to change it? She's the director after all.'

'It's not that simple. Corinna's quite a big star and the Women Who Kill programmes are always heavy on blood and gore. That's one reason why I've never done one before.'

'Why did you do this one then?'

'Because Dani asked me. I've done a few history programmes with her. She really knows her stuff.'

'What about Corinna? Have you worked with her before?'

'No, but I know of her. She used to be quite a well-known actress but then had a career break to bring up her children. Now she's becoming famous all over again.'

'She's certainly making it all sound very dramatic.'

'Yes,' says Frank. 'It's a bit over the top for me, I must admit. But you'd be surprised how the most serious people become drama queens when they're on camera. Look at Phil.'

'He's always like that.'

Frank laughs and takes two polystyrene cups from a passing runner. 'You wait till it's your turn.'

'I'm dreading it.'

'You'll be great. Just be yourself.'

'People always say that,' says Ruth. 'It's surprisingly unhelpful.'

'Frank!' Suddenly Dani is beside them, a tiny figure in jeans and combat boots. 'Can I have a word?'

'Sure,' says Frank, not moving away from Ruth.

Dani glances at Ruth and obviously decides that she is harmless. 'What do you think of Phil?'

'He's not telling us much,' says Frank.

'No. I think he's a bit of a tosser. We need someone with a bit more weight.' She turns (rather unfortunately, as far as Ruth is concerned) to Ruth. 'What about you? Aslan said you were good.'

Aslan is a gloriously-named researcher. Ruth blushes. 'Did he? Well . . .'

'The thing is,' says Dani. 'We need someone to give us some archaeology, otherwise it's all going to be Corinna flitting around talking about ghoulies and ghosties. Frank here will give us some proper history, won't you?'

'I'll certainly try.'

'So we need some proper archaeology to go with it. OK, Ruth? We'll do a longer interview with you.'

'OK,' says Ruth. Phil is looking over. She waves back cheerily.

'Carbon 14 is present in the earth's atmosphere in the form of gas carbon dioxide. Plants take in the gas through their leaves, animals eat the plants, carnivores eat the animals. So we all absorb the Carbon 14 and, when we die, we immediately stop taking it in and the Carbon 14 in our bones – or in the wood of trees, for example –

starts breaking down. So by measuring the amount of Carbon 14 left in a bone, or a piece of charcoal or cloth, it's possible to estimate its age.'

Ruth stares fixedly at the red light in front of her. The cameraman gives her a discreet thumbs up. The sound engineer brings the furry microphone closer to her mouth.

'So,' says Corinna, glancing down at the notes in her hand, 'how accurate are these tests?'

'Well, they're very useful when we're dealing with ancient finds where we just want to know the date within a certain historical period. But with modern finds it's more problematical. Radiocarbon dating can be skewed by sudden surges in the radiation, for example sunspots or solar flares. So we would only be ever able to give a date within a range of, say, a hundred years.'

Corinna seems to find this answer exasperating. 'So are you telling me that Carbon 14 tests won't give us a definite date for the skeleton of Mother Hook?'

'Yes,' says Ruth.

'Cut!'

Corinna turns round. 'Dani! Can I have a word?' She stalks away, stepping carefully over cables. Ruth is left alone with the cameraman. She finds him rather a soothing presence, much less frightening than Dani or the researchers. 'Was that OK?' she asks.

'Great,' says the cameraman. 'I love all that stuff. Never miss *Time Team*. Corinna won't like it though. She wants you to tell her exactly what Mother Whatsit had for tea.'

'You need stable isotope analysis for that,' says Ruth. She feels surprisingly exhilarated. After the first nerves, it hadn't been so terrible after all. She'd had nightmares about being struck completely dumb in front of the cameras but, in the event, she had just imagined that she was talking to a room full of students and the words had come quite easily. She wonders what she looks like though. Dani had told her to dress casually so she's wearing linen trousers and a loose blue shirt. Corinna, on the other hand, is in a tight red dress and high heels.

A runner brings Ruth coffee and she drinks it gratefully. She feels quite important for a moment. She can see Phil watching her and a flash of red hair which shows that Shona has joined her partner. But who's that next to Shona? Ruth looks again. There's no disguising the breadth of those shoulders, the thick greying hair, the scowl. Christ, it's Nelson.

'Are you ready to go again, Ruth?' Dani appears beside her.

'Did you ask the police to come?' asks Ruth. She gestures towards Nelson who ignores her. 'It's just I know that man over there.'

'Oh, we had some trouble clearing the traffic,' says Dani airily. 'But it's all sorted now. I've got a letter of authorisation.' She pats her pocket.

Ruth isn't convinced. She knows that Nelson would never lower himself to be involved with traffic calming. But, if not, why is he here?

'OK,' says Dani, darting behind the monitor. 'Can you tell us about Carbon 14 again? Straight to camera this time, Corinna's taking a break.'

Ruth goes again. She talks about Carbon 14, stable isotope values and the importance of calibration. She ignores Dani and addresses herself directly to the sympathetic cameraman. She tries not to think about Phil or Nelson or whether her stomach is sticking out. When it's over, Dani says 'I think we can use this,' which Ruth takes to be a compliment. The cameraman gives her another thumbs up and Ruth finds herself free to go. She walks slowly back towards the knot of people standing behind the catering van. Shona waves but Ruth is looking at Nelson. He's accompanied by two young women; one looks like she might be his daughter, the other, a slim figure with long blonde hair, also looks vaguely familiar.

'Hallo Nelson.'

'Quite the TV star.'

'Hardly.' Ruth laughs, rather wildly. The girls are looking giggly and awestruck. Ruth looks round to see the source of this excitement but nothing much is happening on the set and the film people are all in a huddle round the monitor. Then it occurs to her that they are in awe of *her*. Because she's on TV. Wonders will never cease.

'You know my daughter Rebecca.' Ruth doesn't know Rebecca though she's certainly interested in her, partly because she's Kate's half-sister. Rebecca Nelson is a good-looking girl with Michelle's grace and Nelson's dark hair. She shakes hands with Ruth and says how cool it must be to be on television. 'I'd like to get into TV,' she says. 'I'm doing media studies at uni.'

Ruth distrusts any discipline with 'studies' in the title but she smiles at Rebecca and wishes her good luck with her ambition.

'The girls heard that there was some filming at the castle,' Nelson is saying, 'so I thought we'd pop over to see what was happening. This is Maddie. Maddie Henderson.'

Ruth looks at the blonde girl. Maddie. Cathbad's daughter. Scarlet's sister. She remembers her dimly from four years ago. Then she was a watchful adolescent, now she seems to have grown into a beautiful young woman with something of her father's other-worldly manner. She wonders how on earth Maddie has ended up in Nelson's company, best buddies with his daughter.

Nelson seems to know what she's thinking. 'Maddie came to see me. She had some questions about a case. She's studying journalism. She was staying in a squat so I invited her back to our place.'

This seems to leave a hell of a lot unanswered. What case? And why is Maddie, who she knows is at university up north somewhere, in Norfolk? Didn't Cathbad say that the family had moved away? But Nelson is frowning in a way that doesn't invite further questioning. Rebecca asks what they are filming.

'It's a programme called *Women Who Kill*,' says Ruth. 'About Jemima Green. Mother Hook.'

'Oooh.' Rebecca and Maddie look at each other in delicious horror. 'Mother Hook. *Don't cry little darling*. I used to have nightmares about her when I was younger.'

Nelson looks outraged. 'Who told you about her?'

'Oh Dad! Everyone knows about Mother Hook. She killed all those babies and cut them up with her hook.'

'There's no evidence for that,' says a voice behind them. Frank is smiling at the girls, clearly more used to admiration than Ruth.

'You're the history man, aren't you?' says Rebecca. 'I saw you on that programme about Jack the Ripper.'

Frank looks at Ruth. 'I get all the classy gigs.'

'Nelson,' says Ruth, nervous though she couldn't have said why. 'This is Frank Barker, a historian on the programme. Frank, this is DCI Harry Nelson, of the King's Lynn police.'

Frank looks politely interested, Nelson glowers. Ruth feels that she needs to explain why a senior policeman would be visiting her on the set. Should she mention the traffic?

She is saved by Shona, who floats over to kiss Ruth on both cheeks and tell her that there's a button missing on her shirt.

CHAPTER 13

Nelson drives back through the rush-hour traffic, listening to Rebecca and Maddie chatting and feeling as if he's gone back in time. Though he'd complained then, he misses the days when he provided an unpaid taxi service for his daughters, lurking outside parties ('Don't get out of the car, Dad!') and freezing on the touchline at netball matches. When he'd invited Maddie back to his house he'd been motivated by a vague desire to save her from a squat described (admiringly) as 'a proper commune, like in the Sixties'. If he could save Maddie from three nights of free love and marijuana, perhaps Cathbad might forgive him for arresting Liz Donaldson. Michelle had been happy to invite Maddie to stay – she likes Cathbad, and perhaps she too missed the time when the house resembled a non-stop pyjama party. Only Rebecca had been inclined to grumble. She had just arrived home from university and had counted on having the house to herself. Her older sister, Laura, who took her finals last month, was on holiday in Ibiza. 'I've got *essays* to write, Dad,' Rebecca had said from a recumbent position on the sofa. 'You and Mum never seem to appreciate how hard I have to work.' But, in the end, she and Maddie had hit it off immediately. Before the evening was over, they were huddled under a duvet watching *CSI Miami*. Nelson, watching them, reflected that he had never really understood women.

But he had been happy to see the two girls enjoying themselves. When he first met her, Maddie had struck him as dangerously intense and nervous. Within minutes of meeting Rebecca, she was just another incomprehensible female, giggling at videos on YouTube and rolling her eyes whenever he told a joke. So when Rebecca had expressed an interest in the filming, he had volunteered to drive into Norwich. Was it because he had hoped that he would see Ruth Galloway? He doesn't like to think that he could be so obvious, though, by the look that Michelle gave him, she obviously suspected his motives. It's just that I feel like a change of scene, he told himself, an afternoon off after a week investigating the most horrible crime imaginable. He'd expected the programme being filmed at the castle to be one of those earnest productions where they dig for five days, find half a pot and then pretend to be happy about it. But when he got there he found Ruth making a programme about a notorious child killer. It's irrational, he knows (given their history), but he expects Ruth to be somehow above such sordid matters. And then his daughter had come out with all that stuff about Mother Hook. He'd been quite shocked. He likes to think that he has shielded his daughters from most of the horrors in life. He'd forgotten how much teenage girls like horror.

He'd been amazed at how relaxed Ruth had seemed on the set. She is confident, he knows, when she's in her professional world, but he'd thought that TV might bring out some of her better-hidden insecurities. But she seemed to treat the camera like an old friend, chatting animatedly about Carbon 14 and all those processes that she has so many times tried, and failed, to explain to him. For one ridiculous minute he had almost felt jealous. But he's not jealous, he tells himself; he has no right to be. And if Ruth wants to consort with silver-haired American TV stars, that's her choice. He stops with a jolt at a red light.

'Dad!' says Rebecca from the back seat. 'I was putting on my make-up.'

'Why do you need make-up when you're in the car?'

'Maddie and I thought we might stop off at Lynn. Meet up with some people from school.'

Nelson is about to answer when his mobile rings. He has forgotten to put it on hands-free. 'Can you get that, love?' he asks Rebecca.

But it's Maddie who picks up the phone from the foot-well.

'It's a text from someone called Clough.'

He shouldn't let Maddie see the message but he's too impatient to wait. 'What does it say?'

'*Justine T wants 2 talk 2 u. Says she has imp info.* Is that Justine Thomas?' asks Maddie. 'She's a good friend of mine.'

Nelson drops the girls off in the centre of King's Lynn and drives straight to Chapel Road. Justine had said that she might be collecting Bailey from school. Sure enough, the sweeping drive is empty, and when Nelson rings the doorbell the sound echoes through the house. He looks at his watch. Three-thirty. She should be back soon. He decides to take a quick stroll around the garden. It's the usual middle-class paradise of decking, terracotta urns and children's play equipment. There's a Wendy House that looks like a miniature Tyrolean cottage and a vast climbing frame that probably needed planning permission and a light on the top to warn off low-flying planes. Suddenly a picture flashes into Nelson's mind, a high-definition memory, so clear as to be almost painful: Scarlet's brothers playing on a half-finished climbing frame in their wilderness of a garden. That had been a very different creation – reclaimed timber and old tyres – but the intention had doubtless been the same, to provide a safe place for children to play. He thinks of Scarlet's twin brothers; Maddie said that they were eleven now. They had been playing with Scarlet when she disappeared. Do they still think about her? Do they still run and laugh and climb? Murder has deep roots, he thinks, and casts long shadows. Scarlet's brothers were only seven when she died but he wonders if they ever played so innocently again.

Justine's car, a shiny Golf, crunches over the gravel. Nelson goes to meet her. He admires her calm, unflustered movements as she lifts Scooter from his car-seat and unfolds Poppy's pushchair. Bailey, a tiny figure in a purple blazer, glares at Nelson from under his pudding-basin fringe.

'Who's this, Justine?'

Nelson hears the authentic, born-to-command tones under the babyish lisp, an attitude probably fostered by the purple school blazer. Michelle had insisted on send-ing the girls to private school, a decision he still regrets. He hadn't wanted his daughters to grow away from him, to rhyme 'bath' with 'hearth' and to sneer at people who put brown sauce on their chips. But Michelle had wanted to give them the best, 'a real chance in life'. Is that what his parents want for Bailey? Full-time nanny, pre-prep, Suzuki violin lessons? Ruth will be just as adamant, he knows, though in her case she will be demanding a state school in the most ethnically mixed, socially deprived area she can find in North Norfolk. His opinion won't count much with her either but, then again, what does he know? He hated school himself.

'He's a visitor,' says Justine, brightly but with a faint suggestion of steel. 'Say hallo, Bailey.'

'Hallo,' says the tiny plutocrat.

'Hallo,' says Nelson. He considers ruffling the boy's hair and then decides against it.

'This way,' says Justine. Poppy is in her pushchair and Scooter refuses to be put down so Justine balances him on one hip.

'Shall I hold him?' offers Nelson.

'I'm afraid he won't go to you. I'm OK. I can manage.'

She does, admirably, and within a few minutes they are all seated in the sunny playroom, the children drinking juice and eating raisins. 'Their parents don't like them to have cakes.'

'Do they tell you what to feed them?'

'Yes,' says Justine. 'I've got a list and I have to plan my menus for the week. I don't mind. I like to be organised.'

'You said you had something to tell me.'

'Yes.' To Nelson's surprise, Justine gets out her mobile, the latest iPhone. New car, state-of-the-art phone, she must be earning a good wage from the toy company owners.

'I'm still Facebook friends with him,' she is saying. 'I kept meaning to unfriend him but I never got round to it.'

Nelson is lost. He knows about Facebook, of course. At one time his daughters were never off it and even Michelle has an account. He can't see the point of it himself – in his view friends are people you can have a pint with, not names on a screen – but he doesn't think of it as evil either.

'What are we talking about?' he asks.

Justine looks surprised. 'Bob. Bob Donaldson. I was checking my Facebook page – I don't go on it that much these days – and I saw this.'

She puts the phone in his hands. He squints at it. Is text getting smaller or does he need glasses? Justine takes a swipe at the screen and the words get bigger. There's a picture too, a tiny square of a man holding a baby. 'Bob Donaldson,' he reads: 'June 14th. 2 Massey Avenue, King's Lynn.'

'That's his house.' says Justine. 'The house he shared with Liz, I mean. He must have enabled location finder on Facebook. You can add a specific location and the phone knows when you're there.'

'June 14th,' says Nelson. 'That was the day David died.'

'Yes,' says Justine. 'He said he wasn't in the house that day but he must have been lying.'

'What does the message say?' Nelson holds the phone up to the light.

Bob Donaldson's status report is brief. '*We'll never be parted again.*'

CHAPTER 14

'Why didn't you tell us that Bob was in the house?'

Liz Donaldson looks at him wearily. Nelson thinks that her two days in custody have changed her beyond measure. As a prisoner on remand she is wearing her own clothes but she seems institutionalised just the same, grey-faced and dead-eyed. She stares at Nelson and Judy as if she can hardly be bothered to speak to them.

'I didn't know,' she says.

'Look, Liz,' Judy leans forward. 'We know he was there. Why are you trying to protect him?'

Liz shuts her eyes. 'I didn't know. I woke up half way through the afternoon, not really awake, you know, like I was dreaming, and I thought I heard his voice on the baby monitor.'

'What was he saying?' asks Judy.

'He was singing a lullaby to David.'

Judy and Nelson look at each other. 'Why didn't you tell us this earlier?' asks Nelson.

Liz opens her eyes and they are full of tears. 'Because I thought I was dreaming. I wanted him to come home so much, to be with me and David, to sing lullabies to his son, I thought I was imagining things. Then, when I woke up, David was dead and everything was over. Everything.' She starts to cry in earnest, letting the tears fall onto her lap.

'Liz,' says Judy. 'What happened when you last saw Bob. Did you argue? Did you tell him that you wanted him back?'

Liz's voice is suddenly hard. 'You might say we argued. I told him that if he divorced me he'd never see David again.'

Back at the station, Nelson opens his office door to be met by the welcoming party from hell – Superintendent Whitcliffe and Madge Hudson.

'What's this I hear about you arresting the husband?'

Nelson tries to edge past his boss. 'I'm bringing him in for questioning. I've received information that places him at the scene.'

'What information?'

Nelson sits at his desk, trying to take control. Madge smiles as if she sees through this obvious bit of body language. Addressing himself to Whitcliffe, Nelson explains about the Facebook message. He's sure the superintendent has an account, complete with pictures of himself relaxing under palm trees or whatever he does in his spare time.

'Who's bringing him in?' asks Whitcliffe.

'DS Clough and DS Heathfield.'

'They should be able to handle things.'

'I think so. He's hardly an intimidating type, physically at least.'

'I always thought the husband was a possible suspect,' says Madge.

'In that case,' says Nelson, 'it's a pity you didn't mention it before.'

'That's not how it works,' says Madge. 'You know that.'

No? thinks Nelson. How does it work then? But Whitcliffe is regarding Madge with the trusting gaze of a volunteer about to be sawn in half by a stage magician.

'Family annihilators often act out of a perverted desire to protect,' she is saying. 'They convince themselves that their children would rather be dead than face a future without them. Typically, these actions are triggered by divorce or some other family trauma.'

'Don't family annihilators usually wipe out the whole family?' asks Nelson.

'Who knows if Bob has struck before? You said yourself that the deaths of Samuel and Isaac could be suspicious.'

'Why would he kill the older boys? He wasn't in danger of losing them.'

'How do you know? Maybe this isn't the first time that Liz has threatened him with losing custody.'

She has a point, though Nelson isn't about to admit it.

'Did the wife confirm that he was in the house?' asks Whitcliffe.

'She says she heard his voice on the baby monitor but she thought she was dreaming.'

'That's very plausible,' says Madge. 'She would have been almost in a fugue state, disassociated, wandering between waking and sleeping.'

Nelson thinks of something Ruth once told him about marshland. Because it's neither land nor sea, but something in between, prehistoric man had thought that it was a sacred place, a liminal zone, half way between life and death. This is why bodies and treasure are often found buried in marshes, to mark that boundary. Was Liz stuck in her own liminal zone, dazed from sadness and lack of sleep, unable to distinguish between dreams and reality? He thinks too of Judy's first diagnosis, that Liz was suffering from some sort of post-traumatic stress syndrome. Sometimes Judy can be very astute.

'What were the exact words of the Facebook message?' asks Whitcliffe.

'We'll never be parted again.'

'That fits,' says Madge. 'Bob will have convinced himself that David would only be truly his if he was dead.'

'If that's what he was thinking, why didn't he kill himself too?' asks Nelson. 'That would be more logical.'

Madge smiles pityingly. 'We're not talking about logic here DCI Nelson, we're talking about psychosis.'

But Nelson knows that there's usually logic, even if it's of a warped nature, in every crime. That bothers him. But the fact remains that Bob lied about his whereabouts. That's never a good sign. His phone rings.

'Nelson.'

'Boss, it's Clough. Bob's done a runner. Scarpered just before we got here. His girlfriend's having hysterics.'

Running away. That's not a good sign either.

Ruth drives home, tired but still on a high. She has delivered several pieces direct to camera and Dani said that she had 'a certain presence' which, according to Aslan the researcher, was the highest possible praise. Corinna, baulked of horrific chilling drama, stormed off in a huff, and Frank said on camera that he thought Mother Hook may have been innocent. It had all been very exciting. Phil was inclined to be sulky at first about Ruth's sudden rise to prominence but he had cheered up when he was filmed talking about the latest DNA technology. Even Shona had managed to get in on the act, standing in the trench in a very unacademic-looking leather mini skirt.

But now she's exhausted. She picks Kate up from Sandra's and starts the last weary leg of the journey. She goes cross-country, past picturesque villages too remote to be on the tourist trail. The sun is low over the flat fields, and as she gets nearer the coast she sees the seagulls circling, their feathers turning pink as they head towards the sea. She is fed up with driving, though, and is it her imagination or has the car developed a new and sinister rattle? She hopes that it wasn't the result of the collision. Frank has said that he will pay for any repairs but she dreads having to go to the garage and face the whole 'what's the problem darling? do you know where the engine is?' farce. She doesn't know anything about cars but she doesn't think that's because she's a woman. Max, for example, once spent two months putting unleaded in a diesel car.

She thinks about Max now as she takes the turning for New Road. He loved the Saltmarsh, and archaeology –

and her, as it turned out. He had even wanted them to have a baby together, a sibling for Kate. But Ruth had ended the relationship last year. When it came down to it, it just wasn't *enough*, sharing interests, enjoying the same things. Her mother had been horrified. This was the second time that Ruth had ended a relationship with a personable man for the most frivolous of reasons. 'I just wasn't in love with him, Mum,' Ruth said apologetically. 'Love!' her mum had responded. 'What's love got to do with it? He'd have been a lovely stepfather for little Katie. You're so selfish sometimes, Ruth.'

Is she selfish, she wonders. She certainly has her life the way she wants it – a job she loves, a daughter she adores, a companion animal to share her home – and she knows that she would find it hard to compromise this existence for any man. Even in her fantasies of Nelson leaving Michelle (which do occur, despite herself), they never progress beyond the first ecstatic love-making. She never thinks about Nelson actually living in the tiny cottage, hogging the bathroom, leaving his giant policeman's boots on the stairs, wanting to watch the football instead of *Prehistoric Autopsy*. They would kill each other in a week.

The marshlands lie all around her now, the sacred no-man's land that leads to the sea. Looking at the display on the dashboard, Ruth realises that it's June twenty-second. The summer solstice was yesterday. At this time of year it's not unusual to see the flickering lights of bonfires at night, or the hand-held torches of another group of alternative thinkers as they trek over the sands in search of the henge circle. Ruth always thinks of will-o'-the-wisps, the spirits of dead children some say, eyes in the darkness. But last night there was nothing. Maybe it's because Cathbad is no longer here to lead the ritual, scattering libations and wielding the burning brand. Cathbad is far away, perhaps celebrating the solstice with fellow Lancashire druids on top of Pendle Hill. Ruth feels sad. She is also uncomfortably aware that in two days time there will be a significant anniversary of her own. She will be forty-three.

The little house is close now and, as ever, Ruth's spirits lift at the sight of her blue gate, the trees beyond it bent flat by the winds. She releases Kate from her baby seat and her daughter, in tearing spirits after a refreshing nap, runs into the house in search of Flint.

'Flinty! Flinty!'

He'll be hiding under my bed by now, thinks Ruth. She dumps her bag on the sofa and wonders if she can be bothered to cook any supper. Does cheese on toast count as bad mothering? Kate is banging on the back door. She thinks that Flint might be in the garden. Ruth unlocks the door and lets Kate wander out. It's a safe space, the house is one of a terrace so the only way out is back through the house. Besides the whole garden is just twelve feet long and contains only uncut grass and a gnarled apple tree. Ruth puts three slices of toast under the grill, one for Kate and two for her. After a second's thought, she adds another piece. She can hear the seagulls calling from the Saltmarsh and the faint hum of the electric grill. Nothing else. She goes to the back door. A breeze is blowing through the long grass and a single magpie sits in the apple tree. There is no sign of Kate.

Ruth's heart turns to ice. How can Kate have disappeared? She has only been in the garden two minutes. She must have come back into the house when Ruth's back was turned. But as Ruth runs upstairs she hears, like an answer-phone message from the past, Delilah's voice: 'I only left her for a few minutes. She was playing in the garden.' Oh, dear God and all the pagan spirits, don't let anything happen to Kate. She isn't upstairs. Ruth thunders back through the house in search of her phone. She'll call the police. Nelson. He'll come immediately. He loves Kate as much as she does. He'll find her. Hasn't he promised that he'll always look after her?

It's a few moments before she realises that there's a

man in her kitchen. He's holding Kate in his arms and the room is full of smoke.

'Hallo,' he says. 'I'm Bob Donaldson. I'm afraid the toast's burnt.'

CHAPTER 15

At first Ruth doesn't register the name. Bob? Bob Donaldson? But even as her mind struggles, her body acts quickly. She grabs Kate from the stranger and holds her tightly. Kate wriggles. 'Down,' she says, 'down.' The man watches with an indulgent smile.

'Liz Donaldson's husband,' he says helpfully.

Liz Donaldson. The woman accused of murdering her son. Delilah's friend. Cathbad's cause of the day. Why on earth is her husband in Ruth's house? She puts Kate down but keeps hold of her hand.

'How did you get in?' she asks.

'I hid in your shed,' says Bob, as if this is totally reasonable. 'I climbed through from the neighbour's garden. The house seemed to be empty.' Ruth's neighbours only use their house for occasional weekends. Not for the first time, Ruth curses them for their careless townie ways. But why is this man, who is smiling at her so pleasantly, climbing through gardens and hiding in sheds? Suddenly Ruth feels very alone in the little house on the edge of the marshes. She wants to ring Nelson. She wants it so badly that she's surprised that her phone doesn't start dialling spontaneously. But her phone is in her bag on the sofa. She starts to back away.

'The thing is,' Bob is following her. 'The police are after me.'

'Really?' croaks Ruth.

'They think I killed David. Maddie rang me and warned me that they were after me. Lovely girl, Maddie. They've got some stupid Facebook message that apparently proves that I was at the house that day.'

'Were you at the house that day?' Ruth echoes rather wildly. She has reached the sofa now and tries, unobtrusively, to reach for her organiser bag. This means letting go of Kate's hand. Set free, the child bounces away happily.

'Stay here Kate,' calls Ruth. She doesn't want her daughter out of her sight.

'What a lovely little girl,' says Bob. 'I always wanted a daughter but I had three sons. They're all dead now.'

'I'm sorry,' says Ruth. Her hand is frantically sweeping the sofa. Where is the damn bag?

'How could they think I killed David?' Bob's voice is rising. 'I loved him. You'll tell him, won't you Ruth?'

'Tell who?' She is openly searching now. Keys, purse, a tampon, they all come flying out of the various pockets, but her phone is nowhere to be seen.

'DCI Nelson. Maddie says that you're very close to him. I want you to tell him that I'm innocent.'

Why does everyone think I've got influence with Nelson, thinks Ruth. And Maddie seems to have inherited her father Cathbad's talent for interfering. Why can't they all leave her alone?

Bob comes closer. He puts his hand on Ruth's arm. She can see the sweat on his face, his eyes are glittering behind his glasses. Should she scream? Who would hear?

But they both jump when Kate speaks loudly and clearly. 'Dada?' She has found Ruth's phone and is clearly having an important conversation.

'She's so clever,' says Nelson for what feels like the hundredth time. 'She actually rang me herself.'

'It was pure luck,' says Ruth. 'She just pressed random buttons.' She doesn't like to admit that Nelson's number, as one of her 'favourites', automatically appears on screen when the phone is activated. Nelson, hearing his daughter's voice and a strange man in the background, had jumped in his car and driven straight round to New Road. He had been rewarded by the sight of his prime suspect sitting on the sofa telling Ruth his life story. Kate had still been playing with the phone (she was having a long conversation with Flint).

Bob hadn't seemed surprised, or even unduly distressed, at the sight of Nelson.

'DCI Nelson, we were just talking about you.'

'Bob Donaldson,' said Nelson, 'you're under arrest for the murder of David Donaldson. Do you understand the nature of the charge?'

'I didn't do it,' said Bob. 'Ask Ruth. She knows.'

'I don't,' retorted Ruth, grabbing hold of Kate and retrieving her phone.

'You do not have to say anything,' intoned Nelson. 'However, it may harm your defence if you do not mention when questioned something which you later rely on in court. Anything you do say may be given in evidence.'

'I didn't do it,' said Bob. 'Tell him, Ruth.'

After a police car has taken Bob away, Ruth makes more toast for a ravenous Kate and she and Nelson sit with their daughter in the kitchen, an uncomfortable parody of a happy family.

'She's so clever,' says Nelson again. 'I couldn't believe

it when I heard her voice on the phone, clear as a bell.'

'She is clever,' says Ruth. 'She gets it from me.'

Nelson doesn't rise. He takes a piece of Kate's toast and asks Ruth how Bob managed to track her down.

'I think you've got Maddie to thank for that,' says Ruth.

'Bloody hell,' says Nelson, when Ruth has explained. 'Why would she do a thing like that?'

'I don't know. She knew Liz, presumably she knew Bob too.'

'And she's a friend of Justine's – the babysitter – that's how she must have heard that I was on Bob's tail. She knew that Justine had rung me.'

Ruth doesn't like to criticise Maddie. She knows that Nelson has endless tolerance where the young are concerned (far less for his fellow adults). Nevertheless, she does feel that Cathbad's daughter has some explaining to do.

'Why is she in Norfolk at all?'

'She wanted to talk to me about the case, the death of David Donaldson. It brought back memories of . . . of Scarlet.'

Ruth can imagine how this will have affected Nelson, but even so it doesn't quite ring true for her. Why would Maddie come all the way down from Leeds to harangue

Nelson about a case that didn't concern her at all? OK, it might have reminded her of her sister's disappearance, but why did she feel that she had to confront Nelson in particular?

'What's Maddie like?' she asks.

Nelson smiles. 'She's a bit like her dad. Very intense and other-worldly, talking about energies and negativity and whathaveyou. But in another way she seems very adult. She's the same age as Rebecca but she seems a lot older. I think she's had to grow up fast.'

Ruth guesses that Nelson still feels guilty about the events that caused Maddie to grow up too quickly. It's this guilt which has made him take the girl under his wing. But Ruth must be a nastier person than Nelson because she still feels suspicious. Maddie seems to have infiltrated the Nelson family. Why?

'How long's she staying?' she asks.

'Just a couple of days,' says Nelson. 'She gets on really well with Rebecca.'

'What does Michelle think?'

Nelson shoots Ruth a look. It's rare for her to refer to his wife by name. 'She likes her,' he says rather defensively. 'It's nice to have the house full again.'

Ruth says nothing. She knows that Nelson misses his daughters when they are away. She feels that she would be only too glad to see the back of two moody adolescents but Nelson is different. He is far more motherly than her.

'Do you really think that Bob Donaldson killed his baby?' she asks.

Nelson hesitates before answering. 'We've got information that places him at the scene, he lied about his whereabouts. It doesn't look good.'

Ruth thinks how like a policeman he sounds, 'places him at the scene . . . whereabouts.' It's a kind of pompous shorthand. They all do it.

'He did seem a bit weird,' she says.

'Yes, but you'd be surprised how often the weird ones are innocent. It's the normal-looking ones you've got to watch out for.'

Ruth looks at him. 'Do you still think Liz might be guilty?'

'No,' says Nelson. 'Looks as if she's in the clear. Especially if he confesses.'

'Why would he do that?'

'You'd be surprised,' says Nelson again. 'Sometimes it's a real relief to tell someone the truth.'

But sometimes people confess to crimes they didn't commit, thinks Ruth. She doesn't say this to Nelson. He's a Catholic, he knows all about the fatal glamour of the confessional. For a few minutes they sit in silence. Nelson entertains Kate by cutting her toast into shapes, hearts, diamonds and stars. Suddenly he says, not looking at Ruth, 'Who was the bloke on the film set?'

'Which bloke?' says Ruth, though she thinks she knows.

'Grey-haired. American. Pleased with himself.'

'Frank Barker,' says Ruth. 'He's a historian. I told you.'

'Do you know him well?'

Ruth can't resist saying, 'I only met him yesterday. I crashed into him.'

Nelson is predictably outraged. 'I'll have him for dangerous driving. Katie could have been killed.'

'I said I wouldn't press charges,' said Ruth. 'No-one was hurt.'.'

'You need a new car. That thing's a death trap.'

'My car's fine. Don't fuss, Nelson.'

'Fuss!' Nelson looks shocked. 'I never fuss.' Ruth forbears to remind him that when she chose Sandra as a childminder Nelson ran no less than three police checks on her. She knows that this excessive concern is his way of compensating for not being able to be a full-time father to Kate. Doesn't stop it being irritating though.

'If I make some money from my book I might buy a new car,' says Ruth.

'Or if you become a TV star.'

Ruth laughs. 'Hardly. I'll probably never hear from them again.'

CHAPTER 16

But Ruth hears from Dani the very next day. They have the Carbon 14 and isotope results and she wants to film Ruth discussing them with Phil and Frank.

'Just very casual,' she says. 'Three professionals together.'

In Ruth's experience, if you get three archaeology professionals in a room together, violent disagreement usually follows. But she doesn't say this. She is also furious that Phil has obviously told Dani about the results before sharing them with her.

'I thought we'd film at the university,' says Dani. 'Dreaming spires and all that.'

Has she seen the University of North Norfolk, thinks Ruth. Brideshead, it isn't. But she says nothing because, deep down, she wants to be filmed dispensing wisdom to Phil and Frank. She wonders if they'll give her a clip-board to carry.

When she gets to the university, she finds that the lights and cameras have been set up in one of the science labs.

'It was too poky in the archaeology department,' explains Aslan. 'We liked the light in here and all those Bunsen burners and jars with "Biohazard" written on them. It's what the viewers expect a lab to look like. It's a pity we haven't got one of those glass boards to write on, like in *Prehistoric Autopsy*.'

Ruth agrees that a glass board would have been awe-some. Privately she wonders how they got the notoriously prickly Head of Science to agree to the filming at all. Perhaps she too isn't immune to the magic of TV. The science department always reminds her of Cathbad, who was, until recently, a technician here.

Phil bustles over, wearing a pristine white coat. It makes his face look very brown. Or is he wearing tinted moisturiser?

'Looking forward to talking about the reports, Ruth?'

'I haven't read them yet,' says Ruth.

Phil looks momentarily discomfited and hands over a paper folder. 'I meant to give it to you earlier. It's very much what we expected anyway.'

Ruth flicks through the report. The bones are of an adult female and they are estimated as being about a hundred and fifty years old. Phil's right. There's nothing new here. The bones show the woman to have been fairly healthy, though the teeth have faint brown ridges which might point to periods of childhood malnourishment. This would tie in with Frank's story of Jemima Green's early years. The stable isotope results also point to the subject being from the local area. Mineral analysis shows a low marine diet, fairly typical for someone living about twenty miles inland.

Dani prances over. She's wearing a frayed denim mini skirt and, from the back, looks about ten.

'Right, we'll start off with you walking down the corridor. Phil, you ask Ruth what's in the report. Ruth, you explain. Emphasise the fact that the bones are the right age. Then we'll have you in the lab looking at the bones themselves. Is there anything else of interest?'

Ruth mentions the teeth.

'Brilliant. Frank!' Dani calls.

Frank wanders over with a Styrofoam cup in his hand.

'Frank, Ruth is going to say that the teeth show that Mother Hook had a deprived childhood. Can you say a bit about that?'

'Sure.'

'Then we'll just have a long shot of the three of you with the bones and Corinna can do a voice over.'

Ruth can just imagine how this will sound. 'So these are definitely the bones of the horrific monster known as . . .' No room for doubt or ambiguity or a hundred years either way.

A make-up girl appears and starts dabbing at Ruth with a sponge. 'Do you think they should be wearing coveralls, Dani?' she asks.

Please say no, begs Ruth silently. She looks like a Teletubby in paper coveralls.

'No, lab coats will do,' says Dani. 'Ruth, maybe you should have your hair up. It would make you look more academic.'

'Er . . . Dani?' Phil is smiling engagingly.

'Yes?'

'Perhaps I could do the explaining and Ruth could ask the questions. After all I am the Head of Department . . .'

'Nah. She's our bones lady. Five minutes, people!'

By lunchtime Ruth feels as if she has walked down the corridor a thousand times. Again and again she has smilingly explained to Phil and Frank that the bones found in the trench are the right age to be those of Jemima Green. Time after time she has examined the bones, holding them up to the light and trying not to notice when strands of hair escaped from her bun and fell into her eyes. She is utterly fed up with the sound of her own voice saying that brown ridges in the teeth could indicate a period of arrested development such as illness or malnutrition. She never before realised how a simple action can become almost impossible if you perform it enough times. By the end of the morning she has almost forgotten how to walk. Her mouth aches from smiling and her hair has finally given up the fight against the pins and hangs limply round her face.

'One more time,' says Dani. 'Let's go from the bit about the teeth. Dex, come in for a close-up of the tooth on Ruth's hand.'

Ruth holds out the tooth, wishing that her hands didn't look so rough and unfeminine. She hasn't even got an expensive watch or bracelet to liven things up. Still, at least this way you can't see her nails. She explains again about the ridges.

'That ties in well with what we know about Jemima Green,' says Frank. Ruth admires his ease on camera. Every time he says these words it's as if he's saying them for the first time. 'We know she had a very poor childhood, she was the youngest of nine children and her father was a farmer in Saxlingham Thorpe, just around the corner from here. These were very tough times for small farmers. New machinery was coming in and making it almost impossible for smallholders to make a living. And, of course, it was probably an accident with one of these new-fangled farm machines that cost Jemima her hand.'

This is only conjecture, as far as Ruth can make out, but Frank knows his audience. Ruth can imagine that Dani will illustrate Frank's last remark with a close-up of the infamous hook. It's clever too that he keeps calling her 'Jemima'. But Ruth thinks that it'll take more than using a cosy first name to get the audience on Mother Hook's side, especially when Corinna is painting her as Dracula's more bloodthirsty sister. Also, by no stretch of the imagination is Saxlingham Thorpe near King's Lynn.

'OK,' says Dani. 'Let's call it a wrap. Thanks Phil and Ruth. That was great.'

Ruth stands up, relieved that she will never have to suck in her stomach for the camera again. But Phil, on the other hand, seems rather disappointed.

'Is that it?' he asks.

Dani is looking into the monitor. She glances up. 'Yes. Except for the night dig, but you won't have to speak then.'

Won't have to speak. Ruth can see the horror of this reverberating in Phil's mind. He looks around the laboratory, at the cameras and make-up girls and researchers ready to record his latest words of wisdom. She can just imagine Phil contrasting this with a typical day at UNN – lectures, seminars, funding meetings, the continual battle to get people interested in any discipline that doesn't involve field trips to New York.

The Head of Department seems to be coming to a decision. He beams round at the room. 'In that case,' he says, 'I'd like invite you all to a meal at Iagos tomorrow. We're celebrating Ruth's forty-third birthday.'

Ruth walks across the landscaped lawns that lead to the car park. She is still absolutely seething. How dare Phil use her birthday as an excuse to suck up to his new TV friends. She is sure that without Shona he would have had no idea that her birthday was coming up. *And* he told everybody how old she will be. The worst thing was that everybody, including Corinna, Aslan and Dex the cameraman, said they'd be there. So now Ruth is stuck with celebrating her birthday at an over-priced restaurant in the company of people she hardly knows and who, she is sure, she will never see again. Even Frank, asks a sly voice in her head. Does she care if she never sees Frank again? Shut up, she tells the voice. Frank is a TV star, the George Clooney of armchair historians. He would never look twice at her.

Despite her rage, Ruth feels slightly soothed as she walks beside the ornamental lake. The campus is looking its best in the soft summer sun. Although the students have all gone home, the summer school residents are draped picturesquely on the grass, some are playing football and one is even flying a kite, brilliant red against the blue sky. A radio is playing and she can hear the sound of laughter and faint shouts from the tennis court behind the humanities block. It's like a blueprint for an ideal community – all ages and nations coming together in the pursuit of knowledge. Ruth knows that this Utopian vision won't stand close examination. In reality, all the holiday students are middle class and most are middle aged. But if she doesn't look too closely it feels like the new Jerusalem, Norfolk style.

In the car park, though, there's a sight which jars with the idyll. A police car and, beside it, DS Judy Johnson talking on her phone. Ruth waves but doesn't approach. After a few minutes, Judy puts away her phone and strolls over.

'Hallo Ruth.'

'Hi Judy. What are you doing here?'

Judy grimaces. 'Missing child alert. We had a tip-off that he was seen near the university.'

'Oh God,' says Ruth. 'Have you found him?'

'False alarm,' says Judy. 'That was the station just now. He's been found safe and sound at home. The mother just panicked when she couldn't see him in the garden.'

'Thank goodness.' Ruth thinks of Kate and pushes the thought away. She doesn't like to think of what must lie behind Judy's false alarm – the panic, the growing sense of dread, the frantic searching, the call to the police. Then the sighting in the garden, the child perhaps concealed by a tree or a playhouse. The passionate embrace, the tears, the slightly shame-faced second phone call. Even so, it seems to her that there is now a slight cloud over the perfect summer day.

'Nelson says you're making a TV programme,' says Judy. 'I saw the trucks.'

'We're a very small part of the programme,' says Ruth, feeling slightly proud all the same. 'They finished filming us today.' Suddenly she has an idea. Why shouldn't she invite some of her own friends to the dreaded birthday dinner?

To her surprise, Judy is enthusiastic. 'Great! I've always wanted to go to Iagos and it'll be a real treat to go out on my own.'

'Bring Darren too if you like.'

'No,' says Judy. 'He can babysit.'

Ruth will have to sort out babysitting too. She can ask Clara, her regular, or maybe Sandra will help. This is another time when she misses Cathbad, who was always happy to look after Kate. But, then again, if Cathbad were here, he would definitely be going to Iagos. He loves socialising, even if he does call it 'absorbing positive energies.'

'See you tomorrow then,' she says to Judy.

'Yeah. Thanks, Ruth.'

Judy gets into the police car and is driven away by its uniformed occupant. Ruth is just opening her car door when she hears someone calling her name. She looks round. It's Frank, carrying two leather-bound books.

'Ruth! Glad I've caught you.'

'Do you want a lift somewhere?'

'No. You're OK. I've got my car and I've just about mastered driving on the left now.' He grins and Ruth finds herself smiling back.

'No, I wanted to give you this.' He proffers one of the books. 'It's Jemima Green's diary. You said you'd like to have a look.'

'Oh, yes.' Even so, Ruth feels a curious reluctance to touch the thing. It's the same feeling she had when she first saw the bones in the trench. Don't get involved with Mother Hook. Don't let her get involved with you.

'I was looking through it last night,' says Frank, as if the writings of a murderess are ideal bedtime reading, 'and something struck me when she was writing about Joshua Barnet. I've made a note. I'd be interested to see what you think.'

'OK. I'll let you know.'

'There's The Book of Dead Babies too,' says Frank, holding out the other volume.

'Thanks,' says Ruth. 'Thanks a lot.'

'See you tomorrow then,' says Frank. 'I'm looking forward to it.'

'Me too,' says Ruth, putting the books in her car. 'Me too.'

CHAPTER 17

The police car drops Judy at the station. She doesn't want to go in and hear the latest on the Donaldson case – how everyone always knew it was the father all along. She has always believed in Liz's innocence, but now that she has been released she can't escape a slight uneasiness. Why didn't Liz mention earlier that she thought she might have heard her husband's voice on the intercom? It's all very well for Madge to say that Liz was in a fugue state, but she always seemed perfectly rational when interviewed. And she has always said that she was alone when David died. Bob is still denying that he was ever in the house that day. Will he be the first killer to be convicted by Facebook? Superintendent Whitcliffe says that it's a test case. He seems to find this very exciting.

It's three o'clock. If she leaves now she can collect

Michael from the childminder and have three hours alone with him before Darren gets home. She has plenty of overtime owing after all. Making her mind up Judy walks quickly to the car park. She doesn't want to run into Clough and have to listen to a barrage of thinly veiled criticism. 'Half day is it?' 'Your turn to pick up from nursery?' It's so unfair. She hasn't taken a single day off since she had Michael. Darren says that she is working harder than ever.

She relaxes when she's on the road. Judy loves driving, and before she was married cars were her greatest extravagance. She still regrets giving up her high-powered jeep for a sensible Fiat but at least it has plenty of poke. She whizzes through the gears and is first away at the lights, allowing herself a little smile of satisfaction in the rear-view mirror. Tosser. Serve him right for putting go-faster stripes on a Ford Focus.

She has phoned Debbie the childminder to say that she will be early, but when she arrives at the neat little house in Castle Rising there's no one at home. Fuming, Judy calls Debbie to be told that she and 'the kids' are still at the park.

'I'll meet you there,' says Judy, cutting off further explanation.

There's no reason why Debbie shouldn't have taken

the children to the park – it's a lovely day after all – but Judy is irritated all the same. She doesn't like Debbie saying 'the kids', it reminds her that as well as Michael Debbie looks after two other children, jolly three-year-old twins called Archie and Tom. This is perfectly legal – Judy has checked – childminders are allowed to care for up to six children, though only one of these can be under one. In theory, Judy likes the fact that Michael has the company of Archie and Tom, in practice she resents anyone who takes attention away from her precious baby. Of course, in a big family children have to fight for adult attention, it's perfectly normal. But that's another thing. Judy doesn't like Debbie saying 'the kids' because it sounds as if the children are hers.

The playground, in the shadow of the castle, is a pleasant grassy space. Approaching through the trees, Judy has plenty of time to observe, and she has to admit that Debbie is doing a good job of supervising Michael in the sandpit while still keeping an eye on the boys on the swings.

'Careful, Mikey,' she is saying, 'not in your mouth.'

Judy suppresses a perfectly irrational urge to say that Michael can eat sand if he wants to. Also to scream, 'Don't call him Mikey.' She never shortens her son's name, though Darren often refers to him as 'Mike'.

'Hi, Debbie.'

'Hi, Judy. You took me by surprise. Look Mikey, it's Mummy.'

Michael looks at her solemnly. He's a silent child, not like Ruth's Kate, who was practically talking in sentences at a year old. Michael has a few favourite words, but mostly he prefers to observe. Like his dad, Judy can't help thinking. Now he raises his arms to Judy and she lifts him up, burying her face in his dark hair. He smells gorgeous – sand and grass and crayons.

'I'll take him home now,' she says. 'Have you got his stuff?'

Like most children in day care, Michael travels with more equipment than a travelling circus: nappies, spare clothes, comfort blanket, toys. Debbie hands Judy his bag and says cheerfully that she'll see her tomorrow.

'Bye Judy. Bye Mikey.'

'Goodbye,' says Judy. As she turns away she can hear Debbie singing as she pushes the boys on the swings. Does she like them more than Michael?

Judy's love for her son has taken her by surprise. When he was born, a lovely midwife called Linda told her, 'You'll never know love like it.' And she was right. Judy has always distrusted strong emotion. When she studied *Wuthering Heights* at school she found it cringe-making. 'I cannot live without my life! I cannot live without my soul!' It was all so embarrassing and unnecessary. She has never felt like that about Darren. She loves him, of course she does, but it's a calm and adult affair. They have been together since they were sixteen, they know each other inside out, so much so that often they find themselves with nothing to talk about, unless they fall back on discussing the wonders of Michael.

Cathbad was different. Judy has never felt that she knew him at all, but when she thinks back to that first night they spent together – stranded in a snow-bound cottage – her whole body feels as if it is on fire. He was Heathcliff, if you like. The outsider, the figure from the darkness. And you don't plan a future with Heathcliff. Not if you've got any sense, you don't.

Judy and Darren live in a small modern house on the outskirts of the village. Darren has worked hard on the garden and this summer his hanging baskets are a joy to behold. But Judy, taking Michael out of his car seat, thinks that they too are somehow embarrassing. All that red and pink and cascading foliage. These days she prefers grey and blue, cool colours, the accents of winter. She remembers Cathbad appearing out of the snow, cloaked and mysterious. There's no point dwelling on the past, she tells herself, opening the newly painted front door; this is the present, this is reality. And, as happens so often these days, she realises that she is crying.

Ruth has also collected her child from the childminder and she, too, is home. But unlike Judy, Ruth feels pure satisfaction at being in her own space, alone apart from Kate and Flint who don't count. Feeling slightly guilty (it's a lovely afternoon, they should be on the beach), Ruth puts on children's TV and settles down by the window to read Jemima Green's diaries.

February 5th 1859

Cold day but I have a fire in the parlour which keeps my little birds warm. Worried about R's chest but have wrapped him in paper which seems to do some good. Visit from Mr G. He is always so good to us. Left five shillings.

Ruth glances across at Kate, wide-eyed in front of *Dora the Explorer*. What would it be like to have one warm room in the house, no television, none of the unnecessary but necessary adjuncts of modern life? Jemima Green's diary seems almost to have been written in code. Ruth assumes that the little birds were the children, unless Jemima has a particularly tame flock of sparrows.

But wrapping up a child in paper? What's that all about? Ruth reads on.

February 10

R's chest worse. I can ill afford a doctor but fear one must be consulted. There is a brightness in his cheeks which one does not like to see, it reminds me too grievously of dear sainted A. I will take him to Doctor H tomorrow.

But, if Doctor H was consulted, it was in vain.

February 21

My beloved R is dead. He breathed his last in my arms. Martha and I laid him out and all the children kissed him goodbye. Dear R! A sweeter child never lived. Mr G says that this is why God has taken him but I cannot hold to that view. But Mr G gave me two guineas so I must be grateful. I have written R's name in The Book.

'The Book' must be The Book of Dead Babies, currently lying on the sofa between Flint and Kate. Ruth doesn't feel strong enough for The Book right now. Instead, she turns to the page marked by Frank. It is two years after the death of R and now J preoccupies Jemima's thoughts. Ruth assumes that J is Joshua Barnet.

October 10

I do think that my little J is an angel. No wonder his mama does not want to give him up. He is the goodest baby but occasionally there is an absence which disturbs me. J will stare into the distance, eyelashes fluttering, as if he has seen a vision. Mr G says some children are not long for this world – they see the angels and long to be with them. I pray this is not true. When he is in one of his absent moments, J will smack his lips as if he is tasting heavenly nectar. Maybe it is his mother's milk which he misses though I give him milk sweetened with sugar. Mr G kindly gave me a shilling to buy more Godfrey's Cordial.

Ruth is starting to dislike Mr G with his handouts and religious truisms. Is he just a philanthropist (she imagines him in the Victorian tradition with tall hat and pained expression) or something more sinister?

November 1

J's mother is a cold woman. Today J would not go to her but cried for me. The mother became angry and said that she would take my angel away from me. I begged her to leave him here where he is happy. She said that she was seeking new lodgings and when she had found somewhere suitable would call for 'her boy'. Poor J clung to me when she had gone and his eyelids fluttered more than ever. Has he seen the angels?

Ruth reads this with mixed feelings. The first of November is Kate's birthday, which makes it worse. Jemima does seem to love the child but Ruth finds herself identifying strongly with Joshua's mother. There have been a few occasions – not many, but seared upon Ruth's heart – when Kate has not wanted to leave Sandra. Ruth remembers how, seeing Kate clinging to the childminder, a corrosive anger rose within her. She's stealing my child's affections, she had thought, ignoring the obvious fact that it was good that Kate liked Sandra and wanted to spend time with her. But she should like Ruth *more*. Jemima Green called Joshua her angel, but he's not her angel, he's his mother's angel.

On November 18 is the following entry:

Today my angel left this life. He had seemed perfectly contented in the morning. His nose had bled a little but this is not unusual. I staunched it with a wet cloth. Then, just after luncheon, his eyes began fluttering. I thought he was having one of his absent moments and I went to hold him, as this often helps. But oh so suddenly his little body went rigid in my arms. I called for Martha but by the time she arrived he was gone, his face so angelic in its stillness. I was heart-broken, it was some hours before Martha could wrest the child from me. But as we laid him out I came to a decision. Mr G shall not have him. She shall not have him. I shall lay him with Emily and Susannah, where Rowan will stand guard. Then I will always know where he is. Saint Michael will protect my angel child.

'Hola!' calls Dora from the screen. 'Hola!' shouts Kate. Even Flint looks as if he might conceivably say something in Spanish. Ruth looks back at the diary, at the faded copperplate hand. It occurs to her that Jemima Green wrote very well for someone who had little formal schooling. What did Frank say about her early years? She'll have to ask him again. She turns to Frank's note.

'Think J may have been suffering from epilepsy,' he has written, 'Symptoms of petit mal include gazing vacantly into space, fluttering eyes and involuntary movements of the lips. Interestingly these fits are sometimes called absence seizures and Jemima calls them 'absent moments'. It sounds as if J may have had a more serious fit and died, perhaps as a result of choking. The way she describes his body going rigid is typical of grand mal.'

So Joshua may have died of natural causes but Ruth can't help feeling that there are still a great number of unanswered questions. Who is Mr G? Why does Jemima say 'Mr G shall not have him'? It sounds as if Jemima kept Joshua's body from his mother (Ruth has her own feelings about this) but where did she bury him? Who are Emily and Susannah? Where is the rowan tree that will stand guard? She looks out of the window, across the miles of grey-green grass. She could ring Frank and discuss the diaries (she still has his number from the accident) but something stops her. Frank obviously wants to recruit her to Jemima Green's cause but Ruth still feels reluctant to excavate this particular site. Mother Hook may be innocent but the truth is that Ruth is still afraid of her. She doesn't like the talk of little birds and angel children. Her skin crawls at the thought of 'laying out' children, combing their ringletted hair and preparing them for death. She knows that Victorians often commissioned portraits of their dead children and this knowledge makes her heartily glad that she was born in 1968. And as for The Book of Dead

Babies . . . Ruth wants to throw the dreadful thing into
the North Sea.

'Clap Mum!' shouts Kate. 'Clap to find Dora's hat.'

Ruth claps loudly, hoping to drown out the past.

CHAPTER 18

The evening is sticky from the first. Ruth finds herself sitting between Corinna, resplendent in sequinned black, and Dani, wearing her usual jeans and T-shirt. Judy is opposite and Frank, much to Ruth's irritation, is at the far end of the table. Phil manages to make it clear both that he is the host and that he's not paying. Ruth knows from previous experience that when the bill comes he'll take out a calculator and work out exactly how much each person's meal cost. He does buy a bottle of Prosecco, though, and presents Ruth with the first glass.

'Happy birthday Ruth!'

To Ruth's embarrassment, some people have even brought presents. Dani gives her a scarf and Corinna a signed photo of herself. Frank gives her a book, 'open it later'. Shona and Judy both give her perfume and Phil says, 'We don't do presents, do we Ruth?' You don't, thinks Ruth, but she's all too happy not to have a gift from her Head of Department. That really would be embarrassing.

Things perk up when the first courses come. The food is lovely and Ruth's starter, scallops in chilli sauce, is so good that she has to stop herself wolfing it in one mouthful. A low marine diet, she thinks. Typical for this part of Norfolk. Corinna picks at her tricolore salad. 'You have to be so careful on television,' she says. 'If you put on a pound people start sending you abusive tweets.'

'I can't be bothered with Twitter,' says Dani, who, despite her tiny size, is demolishing a plate of antipasti. 'All those idiots telling each other what they had for supper. It's death by a hundred and forty characters.'

'I've got over a thousand followers,' says Corinna frostily. 'I owe them something.'

'Lady Gaga has thirty million followers,' says Dani.

'Do you prefer acting or presenting?' Ruth asks Corinna. 'Are they very different?'

She meant to flatter Corinna by alluding to her previous experience but it seems that she has said the wrong thing.

'I'm a serious actress,' she says. 'I've played Hedda and Lady Macbeth. This is just a sideline.'

'What have you been in lately?' says Aslan from across the table. Ruth looks at him quickly but his handsome face shows only innocent enquiry. Corinna's eyes flash.

'It may interest you to know,' she says, 'that I took a career break to have children. I didn't want to farm them out to a nanny or a childminder, I wanted them to have a proper old-fashioned childhood. I wanted to have the full experience of motherhood.'

As opposed to the rest of us, thinks Ruth, who are just playing at being parents. She catches Judy's eye across the table.

'I've got a childminder,' Ruth says. 'She's very good. Kate loves her.'

'But does the childminder love her back?' asks Corinna. 'It's just a job to her, remember.'

Ruth thinks of Jemima Green, who certainly seems to have loved her charges. Does Sandra love Kate? Does Ruth even want her to love Kate? On the whole she thinks it's more important that Sandra keeps her safe. Love can be a dangerous business.

'Lots of childminders really care for the kids they look after,' says Dani. 'I've got a lot of sympathy with them. I remember babysitting as a teenager.'

'Michael seems to like Debbie, his childminder,' says

Judy. 'She looks after two other children so it's good experience in socialising.'

'My children socialise brilliantly,' says Corinna. 'Everyone loves them.'

'How old are they?' asks Ruth.

'Mungo's fourteen and Alicia's twelve. They're both very talented. Mungo plays three instruments and Alicia's already been in several commercials.'

Ruth notes that Corinna's old-fashioned mothering does not preclude her from getting her children in front of a camera.

'I was a nanny once,' cuts in Dex the cameraman. 'A manny.' He laughs. 'The thing that got me was the weird names posh people give their children.'

'Yes,' says Judy. 'My boss told me about this family who've got three children with really bizarre names, Bailey, Scooter and Poppy, I think. They've got a nanny. Apparently the parents hardly see their children.'

Judy must be a bit drunk, thinks Ruth, or she would never be talking about work. She wonders who this family are and why Nelson was discussing them.

'I adore unusual names,' says Corinna. 'But then I'm a very original person.'

*

Ruth is grateful for Phil's suggestion that they move around between courses. She had been hoping for a chance to speak to Frank but finds herself between Shona and Aslan. Shona is being chatted up by Dex, 'Seriously, you're way too good-looking to be a lecturer. You should be on TV.' Shona is laughing and flicking her hair around. Ruth knows that she too thinks that she's wasted on the University of North Norfolk. How long before she's making a cutting-edge series on Shakespeare, striding around Stratford-on-Avon in a lace top and leather trousers?

Ruth is left with Aslan. She learns that he's twenty-four and studied English at Oxford. He's always wanted to work in TV and is very grateful to Dani for giving him the chance. He's a militant socialist who wants to destroy the status quo from within. 'How did you get the job on *Women Who Kill*?' asks Ruth. 'Was there lots of competition?' No, Aslan admits, fiddling with his fringe, his dad was at Westminster with one of the producers and just, basically, had a word. Aslan tries hard to show an interest in Ruth's life but she's aware that teaching archaeology in a little-known university can hardly compete with white-water rafting in New Zealand (something Aslan did on his gap year). She's just embarking on a description of a dig that's boring even herself when a voice says, 'Hey Aslan, shift up and let me talk to the birthday girl.' Aslan shifts with alacrity and Ruth finds herself next to Frank.

'Having a good time?'

'Wild.'

'Not your kind of thing huh?'

'Oh no,' says Ruth hastily. 'I'm really enjoying it. It's lovely of everyone to come. It's just I don't much like being the centre of attention.'

'I know what you mean. My kids organised a surprise party for my fiftieth. It was one of the worst nights of my life.'

So he's over fifty, Ruth can't help thinking. Aloud she says, 'But you must like being the centre of attention. You're a TV star.'

Frank laughs. 'I'm not a TV star. I'm just a historian who pops up on the cable channel now and again.'

Ruth, remembering Rebecca's reaction on meeting Frank, thinks that he protests a little too much. Even amongst the TV people, he has a certain star quality. It's not that he's the glossiest or best-dressed – in fact she is sure he was wearing that corduroy jacket earlier – it's more that he's the only person not looking around to see the effect he's having on the others. He seems entirely at ease with himself, a rare quality on television or off it.

And there's no doubting that he is rather good-looking. She can see Shona glancing in their direction, clearly wondering what Ruth can have to say to such an alpha male.

'Did you read the diaries?' Frank is asking.

'Yes. I won't be able to sleep for a week.'

'I'm sorry.'

'It's OK. It certainly seems that Mother H may have been innocent. There's even an explanation for the blood-stained clothes – Joshua had a nosebleed on the day he died. Did they read the diaries in court?'

'Yes, but they weren't given much weight. Likewise the maid, Martha, gave evidence that Jemima had really cared for the children but she was disregarded because she'd been an unmarried mother herself.'

'Martha?'

'Yes. Jemima had taken in the mother and child together. The boy grew up to be a successful lawyer and philanthropist. He always believed in Jemima's innocence.'

'Who was Mr G? He seems a bit sinister.'

'Ah,' Frank looks mysterious. 'I've got my theories about Mr G. Look, why don't I take you to Saxlingham Thorpe one day? The farmhouse isn't there anymore but there's a ruined church and lovely views. It's a really pretty place. We can have lunch in a pub and I can tell you about Mr G and the rest of the background.'

'OK,' says Ruth. 'I'd like that.'

'Sometime next week?'

Ruth is about to answer but Shona, unable to bear it much longer, has appeared at Frank's shoulder. 'Hallo. You must be Frank. Ruth's told me so much about you.'

At the end of the evening, after Phil has divided up the bill, there is a general move towards taxis and cars. Frank offers Ruth a lift but she says that she is going with Judy, who insisted on driving so that Ruth could have a drink. She wonders if Judy's had a drink herself but she seems perfectly sober as they walk to the car park.

'It was a great night, Ruth. Thanks for inviting me.'

'Thanks for coming. I needed a friend to protect me from all the TV types.'

'They were OK. I liked Dani and Dex was a real laugh.'

'What about Corinna?'

'Oh, she was a nightmare.' Judy clicks her key to open the car. '*I wanted to have the full experience of motherhood.* Silly cow.'

It's quite cosy bowling home through the dark lanes. Judy drives fast but well, hands at perfect ten-to-two position. She puts in a CD and for a while they just listen to

Elvis Costello singing about Alison and how the world is killing her. Ruth rests her cheek against the window and thinks about Kate and Nelson and Frank and Jemima Green. *I shall lay him with Emily and Susannah, where Rowan will stand guard.*

Taking the turning for the Saltmarsh is like driving into nothingness. There are no street lights, no houses, no landmarks, just inky blackness that seems to press in on all sides. They could be driving through the sky for all they know. There's no moon, not even the ghost lights on the marshes to guide them on their way. Judy's headlights seem only to illuminate a few yards ahead, as if the dark is somehow solid.

The car bumps over the uneven road. Elvis sings a melancholy song about shipbuilding. Judy says, 'I keep thinking of the time that I drove over here in the snow. This is where I saw Cathbad. Jesus, he just appeared out of the night like some wraith.'

'He does have a habit of appearing out of nowhere.'

'That's why I can't believe that he's gone.'

Judy talks about Cathbad as if he's dead but he's alive and well, living in Lancashire. Ruth knows that he's staying away because he wants to give Judy a chance to make it work with Darren. She wonders if she should say this now. Judy must know that Ruth knows about her relationship with Cathbad but they've never discussed it. They are friends but their friendship has strict limits. They have never talked about Ruth's relationship with Nelson either.

'Bloody Cathbad,' says Judy, and it sounds as if she's crying. 'How could he do this to me?'

'He loves you,' says Ruth.

'Does he?'

'I know he does.'

They drive in silence for the next few minutes. Ruth sees Clara's car parked outside her house, just as it was that night in the snow.

'Do you want to come in for a cup of tea?'

'No thanks. I'd better get back.'

'Thanks for the lift.'

Judy raises her hand in acknowledgement. As Ruth watches, she performs a complicated three-point turn and then the car is lost in the darkness.

The Book of Dead Babies

For A

> *You never spoke yet we miss your silence*
> *You never walked but we miss your step.*
> *Dearest Child, sweet Babe*
> *Now you are singing and dancing with the angels.*

Your cheek was cool and soft as snow
Precious Girl, we loved you so.

For R

The rocking horse is riderless now
The soldiers sad without their friend.
Oh we miss your laugh and your ready chatter
Your sleepy smile at the day's end.
Sleep well, my Babe, my little Angel Boy
The time was short and yet so full of joy.

For J

Mothers have no favourites, that is known
But the heart has secrets that can ne'er be shown.
I loved you my Child with a Mother's heart
Though another bore you, you were mine by rights
Of love and kindness.
Oh the painful nights
Without you, my most Precious Son
But you, at least, I see in my most secret eye
Because, my Child, I know just where you lie
And when the good Lord calls me from this life of pain
I will lie beside you and hold you in my arms again.

CHAPTER 19

Saturdays are the worst, thinks Cathbad. Weekdays aren't too bad. He works as a lab assistant at the university four mornings a week. Then he comes home and takes Thing for a long walk. In the evenings he reads or watches TV. He has started writing the story of his life though it's harder than you'd think. The things he wants to say – about his mother and grandmother and the importance of the old ways – seem stubbornly out of reach. Sometimes he abandons autobiography altogether and writes letters to Michael. These he tears up before he is tempted to send them.

He has made some friends. There is a local druid community and they are welcoming enough, though tediously devoted to pub quizzes. He has been out with the other technicians a few times, there is even an attractive redhead in the Modern Languages Department who has made overtures of more than friendship. But Cathbad's heart is frozen. He doesn't think he will ever be able to love a woman again.

Saturdays are bad because he imagines Judy and Darren in their little house, having breakfast, reading the papers, deciding what to do with their precious free hours. Worst of all, he imagines Michael in his high chair, smiling at Darren and calling him Daddy. He sees the family in slow motion, like the end of a romantic film, laughing as they run along beaches and eat ice creams and cuddle furry animals. Lou Reed's *Perfect Day* plays in the background. He tells himself that Judy will probably have to work at weekends, that she hates ice cream and isn't sentimental about animals. It doesn't help much because it reminds him what Judy is really like. She's his polar opposite: she's measured and rational, not given to flights of fancy or messages from the spirit world. She likes fast cars, he drives an ancient Morris Minor. She understands the Tote, he bets on horses with unusual names. He believes in the Pagan Gods, the Virgin Mary and anyone else who might be helpful in a crisis. Judy trusts only in her wits and the police procedure handbook. Why, then, does he miss her so much? Why do other women – not only the redhead but the female druids with their homespun skirts and books on homeopathy – seem so pallid in comparison?

But this Saturday Cathbad determines to invest in positive energies. He takes Thing for his early-morning run, breathing in the heady air on top of Pendle Hill and asking the spirits of earth and sky to watch over them. Then he returns home full of good intentions. Cathbad's cottage was once owned by a witch and this, to him, makes it a highly desirable residence. He speaks to Dame Alice now as he feeds Thing, makes coffee and listens to the news on the radio. The rumbling Radio 4 voices remind him of Ruth. 'Dame Alice, Wise Woman, help me to get through today without thinking of Judy.' There is no sign from Dame Alice but Thing looks at him hopefully, wagging his tail. Cathbad pats the dog and wonders how to fill the next few hours. He could go into Clitheroe for the market, he could do some work in the garden, he could write the next chapter of his memoirs. He could burn some herbs and try to meditate, or he could walk to Fence and have lunch in a pub. He's so lucky, the world is wide open to him. He sighs and goes to look up Judy's house on Google Earth.

Judy is not running along the beach to the strains of Lou Reed. She is with Darren and Michael in the car, on their way to see Darren's parents. It's another sunny day, though there are clouds gathering in the sky that promise rain before nightfall. Darren is singing along to Radio 2 and even Michael is beating time with his cuddly giraffe. They are going to the seaside (Darren's parents have moved from King's Lynn to Southwold). What could be better?

'Bet Mum and Dad will think that Michael's grown,' says Darren.

'They only saw him two weeks ago.'

'He's growing all the time.'

Michael is actually rather small for his age. It annoys Judy that Darren talks about him as if he's a prizefighter or a rugby forward. 'He's a champ. Look at those arm muscles. He'll be a devil in the scrum one day.' Michael has long eyelashes and sensitive fingers. Judy thinks that he may grow up to be a concert pianist.

'Wonder if we'll get in the sea today,' says Darren.

Judy shivers. 'It'll be freezing.'

'Not for our champ,' says Darren. 'He's tough.'

Judy says nothing. She leans forward and switches over to Radio 4.

Ruth is also at the seaside. She and Shona are walking along the seafront at Cromer. Ruth is holding Kate by the hand and Shona is wheeling Louis in his pushchair.

'Out!' shouts Louis. 'Out! Out!'

'When we get to the beach,' says Shona. She's wearing a short flowery dress and looks like something from a retro catalogue. Louis, on the other hand, looks very contemporary indeed. He's a few months older than Michael but twice as big, a ginger-haired heavyweight with a penchant for camouflage and loud noises.

'Out! Sea! Now!'

Kate puts her fingers in her ears.

They walk past the helter-skelter and the pier. The tide is going out and people are already setting up deckchairs and windbreaks on the sand. The sun is warm but, looking towards Overstrand, Ruth can see grey clouds gathering. 'Tears before bedtime,' her mother used to say. She really must ring her parents tomorrow.

'Catch a crab,' sings Kate. 'Catch a crab, a crab, a crab.' Nelson once caught a crab fishing from Cromer pier and Kate has never forgotten it.

'Maybe later,' says Ruth. She knows that she and Shona will never be able to catch a crab. It's a man thing, like skimming stones (Nelson can do that too).

They release Louis from his chair and walk down the steps to the beach. Ruth spreads out a blanket and Shona finds the buckets and spades. Ruth is wearing a skirt for once and she stretches out her legs in the sunshine.

Shona is kneeling beside Kate, filling a castle-shaped bucket with sand. Ruth is filled with an unexpected wave of happiness. It suddenly seems a very wonderful thing, to be sitting on the beach with her friend and their children. Kate's face is stern with concentration as she turns the castle upside down. Louis beats his spade on a thermos flask. The sun sparkles on the sea and from the pier comes the tragic tinny tune of the merry-go-round. She closes her eyes.

'Ruth?'

Shona is looking at her, shielding her eyes from the sun.

'Mmm.'

'What's going on with you and the American guy? The one that looks like George Clooney.'

'He doesn't look like George Clooney.'

'He looks more like George Clooney than anyone else in Norfolk.'

Ruth has to acknowledge the truth of this. 'Nothing's going on,' she says. 'He's working on the programme, that's all.'

Last night Ruth had opened Frank's present. It was a book of poems, leather-bound and old-looking. *Poems* by Alfred Lord Tennyson. Ruth had sat looking at it for some time. She hasn't read poetry since A-Level English, many years ago. What was Frank trying to tell her with this gift? That she was a fellow intellectual? That they share an interest in the much-maligned Victorians? Or maybe it was just an old book that he had lying around.

'Nothing's going on,' she says again.

'You seemed to be having a very cosy chat last night.'

'We were talking about Jemima Green.'

Shona pulls a face. 'I don't know how you can bear to think about that monster. Killing all those poor children. She must have been pure evil.'

'Actually,' says Ruth, 'there was a good chance that she was innocent. She was only convicted of one murder and there was just circumstantial evidence against her.'

Shona stops Louis from upending the thermos. 'You're joking! What about that "Don't cry little darling" stuff? What about the body snatchers and the devil worshipping?'

'A myth grew up around her. She was a scary-looking woman with a hook for a hand. Who was going to believe that she was innocent?'

Ruth thinks of Mr G and of the The Book of Dead Babies. She read a few of the poems this morning (she couldn't face it at night) and, while on the one hand they are rather touching expressions of quasi-maternal love, on the other hand they scare the hell out of her.

'Well, it'll make a good TV programme,' says Shona. 'Mother Hook was innocent, shock horror.'

'I don't know how the finished film will end up,' says Ruth. 'Dani says she wants to tell the truth about Jemima Green but Corinna keeps putting in all this stuff about evil and monstrous mother figures.'

'Corinna was lovely,' says Shona. 'I had a long chat with her last night. She quite understood when I told her that all I really wanted to do was to stay home with Louis. I really hate leaving him at the nursery.'

Ruth knows that Shona hadn't wanted to return to work after her maternity leave but Phil had insisted, saying that they needed the money. She can just imagine Corinna sympathising with this viewpoint, though calling her lovely seems to be stretching it a bit.

'And she's so gorgeous,' Shona is saying. 'I hope I look just as good at her age.'

Actually, by Ruth's calculations Corinna isn't much older than Shona, but Ruth has noticed before that her friend has a tendency to round figures downwards. Shona always describes herself as 'mid-thirties' but she is, in fact, almost exactly the same age as Ruth.

'Corinna wears a wig,' she says now. She learnt this interesting fact from Dex the cameraman.

Shona ignores this. 'She was telling me how she took

a career break to bring her children up. I wish I could do that.'

'You'd miss work,' says Ruth. When she went back to work after having Kate she had cried at the sight of her office with its sign on the door, 'Dr Ruth Galloway, Head of Forensic Archaeology'.

'Children are the most important things in the world,' says Shona passionately. 'They're so innocent and pure.'

As she says this, there is a loud cry from Kate. Louis has jumped on her sandcastle and is in the process of attacking her with his spade.

Google Earth is a wonderful thing, reflects Cathbad. He has never been to Judy's house but now he knows it in detail. The square of garden, the red front door, the dwarf conifers separating it from its semi-detached neighbour. Judy's jeep is parked outside. According to Ruth she has a new car now. Usually Ruth doesn't mention Judy and he doesn't ask, but this piece of information slipped out and was grasped greedily. The image was obviously taken in winter – the trees behind the house are bare – now the garden will probably be full of flowers. In the photo there's a skip outside. Maybe Darren was doing some home decorating. He looks the type who's handy with a socket set. Is Judy really happy with him? The last time they spoke, when Cathbad told her that he was staying in Lancashire, Judy had said, 'Don't worry about me. I'll cope.' Is that what she's doing? *Coping?* He hopes not, he wants so much more for her than that. He wants her to be wildly, ecstatically happy. He knows that despite her reserve Judy is capable of such heights. Only a really passionate person could be so restrained. He stares at the house as if by the intensity of his longing he could conjure Judy and his son, standing in the front garden and waving at him. But the little house is still, a tiny dot in the vast Google universe.

Tim is at the gym. He goes to the gym every day before work, but on Saturdays he has a proper session, ending with a sauna and a swim. He takes his time, pausing to stretch between machines, setting himself targets and limits. It's not as if he has anything else to do, after all. Tim doesn't regret the move to Norfolk, his career was stagnating in Blackpool and he wanted to be nearer his family, but he does miss his friends. In Lancashire he still used to see the old university crowd and there was always something to do on a Saturday night: cinema, pub, dinner dates. Increasingly, though, he found himself attending house-warming parties and even christenings as yet more friends succumbed to marriage and domesticity. At nearly thirty, Tim still thinks of himself as a young man, far too young to be thinking about duvet sets and the Ikea catalogue. He's had affairs – short, intense periods of love and lust – but he's never met anyone with whom he'd want to visit a DIY store. 'Maybe, in Norfolk . . .' his mother had said hopefully, but Tim thinks it's unlikely, given that he's hardly spoken to a woman outside of work.

In fact he doesn't really do anything except work and go to the gym. Weekends stretch ahead of him: workout, then solitary lunch in the pub, then maybe a run before settling down to an evening of crap TV. Sundays are the worst; he even finds himself feeling nostalgic for the days when his mum used to force him to go to church. One Saturday Clough did invite him to play five-a-side football. Tim enjoyed it immensely, the tough (frequently filthy) game, the drinks afterwards, the camaraderie and the banter. But Clough never asked him again. Now Tim wonders if he blew it by scoring a hat-trick. He knows that Clough regards him as a threat, but Tim is the new boy with everything to prove. Clough and Judy are formidable officers, he saw that immediately, and there's a tight bond between them. Tanya did make overtures of friendship but Tim distrusts her. She's too obviously on the make and, besides, he saw her in the gym once. Any woman who can do that many sit-ups is borderline unhinged. Nelson is a good boss – compared to Sandy MacLeod he's the Angel Gabriel – but he's never shown any tendency to favour Tim over his existing officers. Tim doesn't want favours, all he wants is the chance to prove himself. He's as ambitious as Tanya, it's just that he's learnt to hide it better. His childhood in Essex was fairly tough. His brothers were always getting into trouble but Tim kept his head down. He was a bright student, determined to go to university and escape the fate of most of his schoolfriends (dead-end job, dead-end relationship, living all your life in the suburb where you were born). But that doesn't mean that he's a wimp, as Sandy used to imply. Privately he thinks that he could take any of his new colleagues in a fight, except, perhaps, Tanya. In the gym, though, he can let his aggression show. He does so now, straining every muscle on the rowing machine in an effort to beat his previous best time, bringing his chest forward to his knees, shaking the sweat from his eyes.

When he gets up, he thinks he might have overdone it, he is out of breath and his legs are buckling. Time to stop. He heads for the changing room, has a freezing shower and changes into swimming trunks. Fifty lengths and then he deserves a half-pint with his lunch. As he pushes open the doors to the pool area, he is hit by the smell of chlorine and the sound of screaming. That's the worst thing about Saturdays, the pool is full of children, jumping in, having races or just bobbing up and down in arm-bands. The mothers, hair undisturbed by the breaststroke, chat and gossip at the side of the pool, completely ignoring their offspring. His mother would never let him run wild like that but Tim can't ever remember seeing his mother at a swimming pool. She would certainly never have been able to afford the prices at a place like this.

Tim makes his way to the fast lane, a segregated haven for real swimmers. As he does so, he sees a woman getting out at the other end. She's got a great figure, he notices immediately, though he doesn't think she's young. The woman takes off her bathing cap and shakes out long blonde hair. She's walking towards Tim and he delays his entry into the water so that he can get a proper look. She's seriously good-looking, tall and statuesque like a young Jerry Hall. She's wearing a simple black costume that leaves nothing to the imagination and, as she walks, she smoothes the material across her buttocks. Bloody hell. Good at guessing ages, Tim thinks that she's in her late thirties but she walks like a goddess. As she passes Tim she smiles. He dives into the deep end, puzzled yet pleased. Does he know the woman or is it possible that she was giving him a modest come-on?

Then, as he reaches the other end, the awful realisation dawns. He knows where he has seen the goddess before. When he first joined the King's Lynn force, Nelson invited him to his house for Sunday lunch. A proper roast with all the trimmings. Cooked, he now realises, by the blonde bombshell in the black swimming costume.

The rain starts just when Ruth is putting Kate in the car. She doesn't mind too much. They've had a good day but Louis has punched Kate just one too many times and now they've both had enough. The lowering clouds give Ruth the excuse she needs to set off soon after lunch. Left to Shona they would have had to have a cream tea and then a fish and chip supper in Cromer. Ruth remembers this trait in Shona from their child-free days. She was always the last to leave a party, the one who suggested making a night of it, having breakfast on the beach, staying over until Monday. Now she's the last to leave theme parks, and if she's invited out to supper she'll take Louis with her, feeding him pasta and letting him fall asleep on the seat beside her. But Ruth knows that she herself has become boring. She likes Kate to be in bed by seven, and she sitting on the sofa with Flint by eight. Even after a day in the sun, she's longing to be home with a cup of tea. That's what being forty-three does to you.

'What a shame,' says Shona, putting up a spotted umbrella. 'We could have made a real day of it.'

'We had fun though,' says Ruth, feeling guilty. 'We must do it again soon. Are you going home too?'

'Oh I thought we might just walk in the rain for a while,' says Shona. 'What do you think, Lou Lou?' Louis glares at her balefully from under his rain cover.

'Home,' chants Kate. 'Home, home, home.'

Ruth raises her hand in farewell and they are free. She watches Shona shrinking in her mirror, a tiny flowery figure. If Ruth were a better friend, would she have stayed and walked in the rain too? But there's only so much of Louis that Kate can take and, if she's honest, only so much of Shona that Ruth can take. Take Shona's admiration for Corinna, for example. Ruth can see that Corinna is glamorous and successful but how could Shona actually seem to enjoy her company? Maybe beautiful people are drawn to each other. Certainly Corinna has never shown the least interest in Ruth, even when they are filming together she wrinkles her nose at Ruth's untidy hair and her laborious scientific explanations. Ruth knows that Corinna would be happier appearing with someone like Shona, they could discuss the evil of Mother Hook while the camera rested lovingly on their glossy hair and razor-sharp cheekbones. Well, bad luck.

It's Ruth who is the expert and Corinna is stuck with her – cagoule and all.

And Ruth had resented Corinna's comments about working mothers. It's all right for her, with unlimited funds and probably a supportive husband (Ruth is sure there's a husband in the background somewhere). She can afford to take a career break and spend quality time with her supremely gifted offspring. Ruth doesn't have a husband and she has to work. Of course, she also wants to work, which complicates things. She's ashamed to find herself thinking that Kate is probably brighter than Corinna's children anyway.

It's raining heavily by the time they reach home. An afternoon for cuddling down on the sofa and watching TV. And that's just what they do. Ruth puts on a DVD of *The Lion, the Witch and the Wardrobe* and soon they are lost in snowy Narnia. Mr Tumnus reminds Ruth strongly of Cathbad. She should give him a ring. She knows that he's missing Judy. He never asks about her but there's a longing in his voice when he mentions Norfolk or the police or anything from his old life. And Ruth misses Cathbad. It's unfair, she knows, but she secretly blames Judy for Cathbad's self-imposed exile. Why did she have to have an affair with him anyway? Why does everything have to be so complicated?

The phone rings and Ruth is convinced that it will be Mr Tumnus himself. Instead it is someone far more surprising.

'Hi Ruth. It's Simon.'

'Simon!'

Simon. Her brother. The top hat from the Monopoly games. Why on earth is he ringing her?

She tries to keep this question out of her voice. 'Good to hear from you.'

'Yeah, well . . .' She can hear Simon shuffling, as he always does when he's embarrassed. 'It's been a long time. Did you get my birthday card?'

'Yes, thank you.' Simon always remembers Ruth's birthday although she often forgets his.

'Did you have a good day?' he asks now.

'Yes. I went out for a meal with some friends.'

'Good,' says Simon heartily. Then, after a slight pause, 'I was wondering, were you planning to come down to see Mum and Dad this summer?'

'I suppose so,' says Ruth, her heart sinking. Her parents spend part of every summer at a Christian camp but they're sure to have plenty of time free to nag Ruth about her sinful (i.e. unmarried) lifestyle. 'I haven't fixed a date yet though.'

'The thing is, Ruth . . .' Shuffle, shuffle. 'I wondered if I could come and see you.'

'Come and see me?'

'You know, for a bit of a holiday. Me and the boys.'

Simon's children – Jack and George – must be about ten and twelve. Ruth sees them at Christmas and the family gatherings that she can't avoid and, by and large, she gets on well with them. Better than she does with her sister-in-law at any rate.

'Is Cathy coming too?' she asks.

'No, just me and the boys. We could bring a tent, camp out in the garden. It'll be fun.'

'Fun,' echoes Ruth rather doubtfully. She can't really remember ever having fun with Simon. Two years older, Simon seemed to exist on a different planet. He liked football and other sports and, unlike Ruth, he was also willing to attend church youth club and summer camps. They did go on a family caravanning holiday every year and that's where Ruth remembers playing Monopoly and sometimes card games, sitting at the pull-out table while the rain thundered against the roof. Apart from that Ruth seems to have spent most of her childhood reading, devouring H. Rider Haggard while Simon played outside in the street with his friends. She doesn't dislike her brother but she can't recall having a single serious conversation with him. Simon left school to work in a building society and married Cathy when he was twenty-three. Ruth, lost in the world of university and archaeology, barely gave him a second thought. When she had Kate, Simon was supportive in a passive way. He didn't argue her case with their parents, but he did at least seem to acknowledge that childbirth was generally considered a positive life event. Ruth remembers being touched when he sent a present before Kate was born – it seemed to imply that he, unlike their parents, was actually looking forward to the new arrival. For that alone, she supposes that she owes him something.

'Of course,' she says. 'I've got a spare room as well. I'm sure there'll be space.'

'And it'll be nice for the boys to see something of Katie.'

'Yes,' says Ruth, thinking that Kate will love having the boys in the house. She adores older children. It makes Ruth sad sometimes.

'Great. Can I come on Tuesday?'

Now Ruth really is taken aback. She had assumed that Simon was talking about some vague date later in the summer. But today is Saturday, he's proposing to arrive in three days' time. It makes her wonder how long Simon has been thinking about this holiday. But, then again, she's got nothing special planned.

'Yes,' she says. 'Tuesday's fine.'

'See you then, Ruth.'

'Bye Simon.'

Judy drives home through the rain. She's at the wheel because Darren had a drink in the pub with his dad. She doesn't mind. She prefers to drive; it gives her an excuse for not talking. There is something soothing too about the rain, the windscreen wipers moving to and fro, Michael asleep in the back seat. After a while, Darren's head drops and Judy feels as if she really is alone in the world, the captain at the helm of the *Titanic*, steering ahead through the ice floes. Back and forth go the wipers, the water washing against the windows, car headlights glowing in the half-dark. Judy wishes that she could drive on forever, that her husband and son would remain in an enchanted sleep, that she could keep going until the landscape grew wilder and the Pendle hills surrounded them and she was outside Cathbad's cottage, the sinister witch's dwelling that she has never seen.

But, all too soon, she sees the signs for King's Lynn and Castle Rising. By the time they get home it's ten o'clock and the rain is heavier than ever. Judy carries Michael straight up to bed while Darren gets the bags out of the car. How can they have so much stuff just for a day out? Darren's mother has given her some clothes for Michael and Darren's dad insisted on presenting them with six bottles of his home-made wine. Judy likes Darren's parents – she has known them since she was a teenager – but sometimes their anxious solicitude is just too much. Why does her mother-in-law always have to say that she's looking tired? Why does her father-in-law always have to make the same jokes about the police force? 'She's got you bang to rights, son.'

'Cup of tea, love?' asks Darren as she comes downstairs.

'Thanks.'

Her phone rings just as she's sitting down in front of the television. The boss. Work.

'Leave it,' says Darren.

'I can't. It might be important.'

'Johnson.' Nelson's voice has an edge that she has only heard on one other occasion. 'Come quickly. We've got a child abduction.'

'Where?'

'Here. At Lynn. It's Poppy Granger. The family where Justine Thomas is a nanny.'

CHAPTER 20

By the time Judy arrives at The Rectory there are already three police cars in the drive. She sees sniffer dogs disappearing into the shrubbery, and the SOCO team is hard at work erecting an awning over the front door so that there is only one way in and one way out. These preparations confirm what Judy already knows: the odds are that Poppy is somewhere in the house. When a child disappears two things are always in the minds of the investigating officers – the child is usually still nearby and the perpetrators are probably members of the family.

The rain batters against the temporary plastic sheeting. The uniformed policeman at the door greets Judy with a nod. 'The boss is through there.' Nelson is in the sitting room with two people who must be Poppy's parents. Tim is also there, a fact that fills Judy with fleeting, though quite violent, resentment. She left the house the moment she got Nelson's call. She knows that she lives nearer to Chapel Road than Tim does. His presence can only mean one thing. Nelson called him first.

'Johnson,' says Nelson with obvious relief. 'This is Donna and Patrick, Poppy's parents. Donna, do you feel up to telling Judy what happened?'

Judy notes the use of her first name. Nelson is trying to be sensitive with the family, no easy matter when the house is swarming with policemen who obviously believe that your child is secreted somewhere on the premises. Donna, a tall thin woman in an incongruously short night dress, is clutching a child of about three. Another, older, child sits solemnly on the sofa between his parents. Of course, the uproar must have woken the whole family. The father, Patrick, is fully dressed, holding his iphone as if it's a security blanket.

'I went to check on Poppy before I went to bed,' says Donna. 'Her cot was empty. I thought at first that Patrick must have got her up, but when I went down to the study he was still at the computer, working. I ran back upstairs and then I saw that the window was open. It was raining and the wind was blowing the curtains in.'

'What time was this?' asks Judy.

'About nine. I was having an early night.'

Judy looks at her watch. Ten forty-five. Poppy has been missing for less than two hours. There's still hope.

'Did you search the house?'

'Yes. I went into the boys' room, just to see if they'd taken Poppy for some reason, but they were both asleep. Patrick searched downstairs. When we couldn't find her, we called the police.'

'Were the doors locked?' asks Judy.

Donna and Patrick look at each other. 'No,' says Patrick. 'But that's not unusual. I was still up. I always lock all the doors when I go to bed.'

'Back door and French windows were open,' says Tim. 'SOCO are looking at them now.'

Judy looks at the little family on the sofa. She'd like to talk to them separately but knows that's not possible yet. She takes a seat next to Donna and leans forward, wanting to establish some sort of connection.

'Donna, can you talk us through this evening? What happened when you gave the children their tea, put them to bed. Try to tell us everything, however trivial.'

Donna looks away. For a moment she appears almost embarrassed.

'Well, Justine was here. The nanny, you know. I don't normally have her on a Saturday but it was a bit hectic and Patrick was working and . . .' Her voice trails away.

'It's OK,' says Judy. 'So Justine was here?' (In the background, she can hear Nelson saying to Tim, 'Justine Thomas. Get hold of her.' Tim leaves the room.)

'Yes, Justine made tea for the kids and she played with the little ones. I helped Bailey with his homework.' Judy looks at the older boy. Surely he isn't old enough to have homework? 'Then Justine bathed Poppy and put her to bed. I watched TV with the boys. *Total Wipeout*.'

Judy smiles. 'My son loves that.' This is patently untrue – Michael is far too young for *Total Wipeout* – she's just desperate to create a bond with Donna.

It works because Donna smiles wanly. 'Then the boys had their bath and I put them to bed. Poppy was already asleep when we got upstairs.'

'When did Justine leave?'

'About half past seven.'

'Then what did you do?'

'I said goodnight to the boys, then I had a bath and got into my night things. I was so tired. I went downstairs to watch some TV.'

'What did you watch?'

'*The Wire*. We get it in box sets.'

Of course they do. Families like the Grangers don't watch TV with everyone else, they have box sets.

'But I was falling asleep in front of the TV so I decided

to go to bed. I looked in on the boys and Bailey was still awake, so I told him to go to sleep and then I looked in on Poppy and . . .' Without warning her face crumples and she starts sobbing violently. The child on her lap – Scooter, Judy supposes – slides off and goes to play with some bricks on the floor. Patrick reaches over and starts patting his wife's shoulder. Ineffectual, thinks Judy. She notes that Patrick Granger took no part in the bedtime routine.

'It's OK,' says Judy. 'It's OK. We'll find her.'

There's a timid knock on the door and a young policeman appears. Judy knows him by sight, she thinks he might be from the Norwich station. Where is Clough, she wonders. She suspects that he's hard to track down on a Saturday night.

'We've found something, Boss.'

The constable tries to keep his voice down but his words electrify everyone in the room. Patrick jumps to his feet, Donna lets out a cry that's almost a groan.

The policeman is handing Nelson a piece of paper in a plastic folder.

'We found it pinned to the Wendy House.'

Wordlessly, Nelson shows the paper to Judy and the Grangers.

She's safe with me. The Childminder.

Donna slumps forward as if she's about to be sick, Bailey and Scooter both start to cry. Judy and Nelson stare at each other as the door opens again to admit Clough, panting and tucking in his shirt.

'*The Childminder*. Bloody hell, what's all that about?'

'Your guess is as good as mine, Cloughie.'

The boss sounds tired, thinks Judy. It's two o'clock in the morning and they're back at the station. The streets around The Rectory are closed off and sniffer dogs are due to search the house and grounds again at dawn. 'Try to get some sleep,' Judy said to Donna and Patrick, knowing that this would be impossible. When she left the Grangers, Scooter and Bailey were both asleep on the floor but the parents looked as if they would never sleep again. 'What did you think of the parents?' asks Nelson now.

'I think they're in shock,' says Judy. 'I can't believe that they're involved in any way.'

Nelson looks as if he's about to remind her of the statistics but thinks better of it.

'What about the actual childminder,' asks Clough, 'Justine Thomas. Anything on her?'

A voice from the door says, 'She's got an alibi.' They look up to see Tim with a tray of coffees from the machine. He's brought chocolate too.

'Have you spoken to her?' asks Nelson.

'Tracked her down at a nightclub in Lynn. She's got an alibi for the whole evening.' He looks at Nelson and then away again. 'She was with Maddie Henderson.'

'Maddie?' Nelson sounds shocked.

'She still staying with you, Boss?' asks Clough, unwrapping a Mars bar.

'No. She said she was going to friends.'

'Well, apparently she's been staying with Justine,' says Tim. 'She says she was with her from the moment that she got back from the Grangers.'

'Do you really suspect Justine?' asks Judy. 'I thought she was meant to be the perfect nanny.'

'I don't know,' says Nelson wearily. He rubs his hand over his eyes. 'It's just . . . when we spoke to her, Cloughie, do you remember what she said about David, Liz Donaldson's baby? "*He was a sweetie, not a grizzler like Scooter here. But then he had his mummy at home with him. He had nothing to grizzle about.*" There was real bitterness in her voice, as if she hated her employers for not staying at home with their children. I wondered if she could have taken Poppy to teach them a lesson.'

'But then where is Poppy now?' asks Tim.

'I don't know,' says Nelson. 'But I think we should get a search warrant for Justine's flat.'

'Do you really think that she'd leave the baby there and go out clubbing?' asks Clough.

Nobody says anything but they're all thinking the same thing – if Poppy's dead she can be left alone with impunity. And, if she's not dead, where is she?

'It's a classic locked house situation,' says Tim, taking a swig of coffee.

'What the bloody hell does that mean?' asks Clough.

'I was thinking of that famous Victorian case,' says Tim. He never seems to get wound up, which irritates Clough even more. 'The Road Hill House murder. Little boy taken from his bed in the middle of the night. Everyone in the house, all the family and servants, were under suspicion.'

Judy knows the case he means. She read a book about it, *The Suspicions of Mr Whicher*. Thinking of how the book ended, she voices something that has been in the back of her mind ever since she saw Donna, Patrick and their sons sitting on the sofa.

'The baby in the Road Hill House case was murdered,' she says. 'They found his body in an outhouse. And his sister did it.'

They all look at her. Clough blankly, Tim sceptically, Nelson with slowly dawning comprehension.

'The Grangers' other children are tiny,' he says. 'Are you saying one of them did it?'

'No,' says Judy. 'But Donna said that the boys were asleep when she went into their rooms looking for Poppy, and a minute earlier she'd said that Bailey was still awake.'

'Bailey's five,' says Nelson, thinking of the little figure in the purple blazer. 'Do you really think that he abducted his sister, hid her, maybe even killed her, and then kept quiet about it?'

'He could have resented her,' says Judy stubbornly. 'Youngest child and all that.'

'I'm the youngest child,' says Nelson. 'My sisters were jealous of me but I don't remember either of them trying to do away with me.'

'Stranger things do happen,' says Tim mildly. 'Maybe we ought to talk to Bailey.'

'We won't be able to talk to him without his parents present,' says Clough.

'Then we'll talk to all three of them.'

Judy is grateful for Tim's support but she finds his calm, rational tone irritating.

'What about the note?' she says. 'Anything on the hand-writing? We can compare it with Justine's for a start.'

'We'll get it analysed first thing,' says Nelson. 'I think it was significant though that it was stuck onto the

Wendy House. Makes you think that it might be someone who knows the house and garden.'

'Mind you,' says Clough. 'That Wendy House is visible from the road. It's bigger than my flat.'

'Whoever wrote it was well prepared,' says Judy. 'The note was in a plastic folder. They must have known that it was going to rain.'

'You don't think the toddler wrote the note then, Judy?' asks Clough. 'Precocious little fellow is he?'

'He's not a toddler,' says Judy between gritted teeth. 'He's five and at school. And I never said that he abducted Poppy, just that he might know something about it.'

'OK,' says Nelson. 'That's enough for now. Go home all of you and get a few hours' sleep. We'll meet here at seven. The press'll be onto it by then so we'll have to issue a statement. I've already spoken to the Super.'

Whitcliffe is on holiday in Tuscany but Nelson wouldn't put it past him to be on the first plane back. As his team leaves, Nelson starts to draft a press release but his mind keeps going back to another case, something that happened nearly fifteen years ago.

Poppy's disappearance doesn't remind him of a classic Victorian closed house murder, it reminds him of the abduction of Lucy Downey, the case that nearly killed him.

CHAPTER 21

Nelson had been in Norfolk just three years when Lucy Downey disappeared. According to Michelle the move down south represented promotion, more money, the chance of a better life (unspecified) for their daughters, two and four at the time. All the same, Nelson had to be persuaded. He liked Blackpool CID, his mates, football on a Saturday. The south seemed alien and somehow untrustworthy. London would have been all right but when he first looked at King's Lynn on a map he had felt a twinge of real foreboding. Norfolk looked worryingly remote out there to the east. It was nearer to Scandinavia than to France. And was it his imagination or was there really no motorway? No, looking closer, he saw that there were only two A roads and they seemed to meet in King's Lynn. The rest of the county was veined with winding single carriageways that meandered their way to the coast. No-one would ever visit Norfolk on the way to anywhere else. It's a one-way street, he had thought, trying to drown out Michelle's talk of private schools and swimming lessons, a road to nowhere.

And, at first, the job too had seemed a dead end. Sure it was promotion, but most of the work seemed to involve low-level drugs and crime. King's Lynn was yet to acquire its immigrant population and the town seemed inbred to the point of claustrophobia. Then, in 1997, a little girl called Lucy Downey was snatched from her bed in the middle of the night. Nelson can still see the curtains (pink with Disney princesses) blowing through the open window. He remembers Donna Granger's words: *It was raining and the wind was blowing the curtains in.* Is history really going to repeat itself? It had taken him ten years to solve the Lucy Downey case, if 'solve' isn't too glib a word to choose. He knows that this failure still hangs over his reputation as a detective. And now he has another missing little girl, another grieving family, another potential child killer on the loose.

It's still raining. If Poppy is in the open somewhere, what sort of condition will she be in? He tries to remember the child in the playpen. She'd looked healthy enough but she's still a baby, completely dependent on adults. Ruth says that this dependency, peculiar to humans, is why our species developed its superior brain-power, but his own brain does not seem particularly powerful just at the moment. It's the low point of the night, three a.m., the time when the sick are most likely to die. For Nelson, it's the waiting that's unbearable. He can't get a search warrant until the morning. The search teams will start again when the sun comes up, which will be in about an hour's time. If he was sensible he would catch a couple of hours sleep but he can't sleep, not with a child missing out there in the dark and the rain.

He makes another coffee and tries to collect his wits. He mustn't let memories of the Lucy Downey case cloud his judgement on this one. It's not the same. There's the note, for one thing. Somebody called 'The Childminder' claims to have taken Poppy. Does this mean that they will, in fact, mind her? This is what he had said to Donna. 'Whoever's taken Poppy wants to look after her. That's positive. It also means that they've left a trail and we're more likely to catch them.' But is this true? Notes aren't always helpful. The police in the Yorkshire Ripper case had been badly distracted by letters claiming to be from 'Jack'. Nelson too has had his share of sinister notes and cryptic clues. The truth, as he knows to his cost, is rarely cryptic.

He had been surprised at how much he liked Donna Granger. He had expected her to be a typical middle-class 'having it all' mother. Instead, she's a thin, ungainly woman with more than a trace of an estuary accent. She must have worked hard to achieve the perfect house and the perfect family. Nelson, like Judy, is not sure just how much the husband contributes to the process. Donna may be an absentee mother who needs a nanny to cope with a rare evening alone with her kids, but she loves her children. Nelson is sure of that.

And what about Justine Thomas? She may have an alibi but Nelson still can't forget the look on the nanny's face when she'd described Scooter as a 'grizzler'. He remembers the little boy clinging to the young childminder. 'He won't go to you, I'm afraid.' The children certainly adore Justine. Is this normal? Is this healthy? He remembers the elderly lady, 'Auntie Amy', who occasionally used to make tea for his daughters when Michelle went back to work. They had liked Auntie Amy (Michelle makes sure that they still remember her birthday) but there had been no danger of them confusing the elderly figure at the kitchen stove with their real mother. But Justine is young enough to be the Granger children's mother or, at the very least, an older sister. Does she feel that close to them? Does she want to be more than a mere employee?

And why does the link with Maddie disturb him so much? He had wanted to take care of Cathbad's daughter, to protect her from the by-products of Delilah's hippyish upbringing (dubious squats, for example) and from her own crusading nature. He's not quite sure why he felt this way. Maybe because Cathbad had once risked his life to save Katie. Maybe because he still feels bad about Scarlet. Maybe just because Maddie's about the same age as his older daughters. And now he feels irrationally let down by her. There's no reason why she shouldn't have been with Justine last night. She told him openly that they were friends. But it bothers him that Maddie knows both Liz Donaldson and Justine Thomas, two women who have recently been connected with the death of a child. Maybe three children, if you count Samuel and Isaac. And now another child with close links to Justine has gone missing. It could be a coincidence, but Nelson has learnt not to trust coincidence.

The phone rings. It's the search team. No sign of Poppy in any of the surrounding streets but there was one curious sighting. A man returning from the pub saw a short-haired woman pushing a pram in the vicinity of Chapel Road. It may be nothing but why would someone be taking a baby for a walk at ten o'clock at night in the rain? 'We'll appeal to the public in the morning,' says

Nelson. 'Someone else must have seen her.' He'll organise door-to-door in the morning too. Get all units on the case.

Justine Thomas has short hair, he remembers.

By the time the team come in at seven, Nelson has already been back to Chapel Road. Donna and Patrick were still awake, sitting like grey ghosts in their state-of-the-art kitchen. The search team was in the garden again, raking through flower beds, dredging the lily pond, taking up the decking. The climbing frame loomed out of the early morning mist looking sinister, like a scaffold.

'Why are they still searching here?' asked Patrick. 'She's probably miles away by now.'

'We need to be sure that we've checked thoroughly,' said Nelson. 'It's just possible that she may have wandered into the garden. The back doors were open.'

'She could never reach the handle,' said Donna. Her eyes filled with tears again. 'She was just wearing her little nightie,' she says. 'The one with the Dalmatians on it. She'll be frozen.'

'It's summer,' said Patrick. But the day was cold after the night's rain. Let's hope she's still able to feel the cold, thought Nelson. But he didn't share this depressing thought. He left, assuring the parents that one of his team would be back in a few hours.

'Can you send the policewoman from last night?' asked Donna. 'I liked her.'

Giving thanks for Judy's empathetic qualities, Nelson promised that DS Johnson would be with them as soon as possible.

Nelson also visited the man who saw the woman pushing a pram. Woken at six, bleary-eyed (either from the early start or the night in the pub) the man was a poor witness. Yes, he was pretty sure it was a woman. She had short hair and was wearing trousers but you can just tell, can't you? Did she seem in a hurry? She was walking fast but it was pissing down . . . raining hard. He was walking quickly himself. He hadn't taken the car (virtuously) because he knew he was going to have a few drinks. How many drinks? A couple of pints. Maybe three. Perhaps four. What about the pram? Was it one of those old-fashioned ones with a hood? No, more like a push-chair. A buggy then? Yes, a buggy with big wheels. Colour? He couldn't remember. It was dark, after all. Nelson had checked with the Grangers, remembering seeing Poppy in her pushchair, that day with Justine. Poppy's pushchair (a state-of-the-art affair, a Range Rover for toddlers) was still in its usual place, in the utility room. Nothing else was missing.

He holds a briefing at seven. The team are alert, despite

their lack of sleep. Everyone is keen to get on with the job. Nelson dispatches Judy and Tanya back to Chapel Road. Tim is given the job of dealing with the media. He will appear on local radio and TV, asking for the public's help in finding Poppy (or Baby Poppy as she will inevitably be known). He will also mention the sighting of the woman with the pushchair. Clough looks slightly mutinous but Nelson knows that he's made the right choice. Tim is articulate and handsome, people respond well to him. Whitcliffe will also be pleased to see Tim representing the force because, in his words, 'he represents our ethnic inclusivity'.

'Come on Cloughie,' says Nelson. 'You're with me.' Nelson notices that Clough brightens at this news. Probably thinks that being with the boss means the chance of action.

Armed with his search warrant, Nelson drives to Justine's flat. He too is feeling better at the prospect of action. The rain has stopped and he allows himself the hope that Poppy might be alive somewhere. Perhaps even now she's gurgling happily in Justine's arms. But Justine was out at a nightclub last night says another, more pessimistic, voice. Would she have left Poppy alone in her flat? And if Justine doesn't have Poppy, where the hell is she?

Justine lives in a flat over a shop in the Vancouver

Centre. The shops aren't open yet, which means that Nelson and Clough are able to make a fairly discreet entrance, parking at the back amongst the bins and old cardboard boxes. Nelson bangs on the door. 'Police! Open up!'

There's a scuffling noise and the door opens an inch. 'What do you want?' Nelson recognises Justine's voice. She sounds scared.

'I've got a warrant to search these premises. Don't make me force an entry.'

The door opens. Justine stands there wearing a t-shirt and knickers. Her hair is standing on end and she looks bleary-eyed.

'I don't understand. Is this about Poppy? Have you found her yet?'

Nelson notices Maddie standing in the background. She too is wearing a t-shirt and infinitesimal shorts. Nelson glances at Clough and is pleased to see that his expression is strictly professional.

'I've got a warrant to search your flat,' Nelson repeats.

'Oh my God.' Justine stares at him. 'You think I've taken her.' And she starts to laugh hysterically. Maddie puts an arm round her shoulders, glaring at Nelson.

'Excuse me,' Nelson pushes past them into the main room.

The search doesn't take long. The flat is tiny, a bed-sitting room, thin slice of kitchen and a shower room. The girls sit on the bed, arms round each other, staring at them. In the corner of the room, behind a laundry basket, Clough holds up a plastic bag.

'Baby clothes.'

Nelson goes to look. The bag contains an outfit of clothes suitable, according to the label, for a child of between twelve and eighteen months. A pink and white striped dress and pink tights.

'It's a present for Poppy.'

'When's her birthday?'

'March. But it's not a birthday present, I just thought she'd look sweet in them.'

'You're a very devoted nanny,' says Nelson.

'Yes.' Justine's chin tilts up. 'I love them.'

The search yields nothing, not even a dodgy cigarette end or a tab of E. Nelson turns to face the two girls, one blonde, one dark, huddled together like a picture of per-secuted innocence.

'Justine, can you take me through what happened yesterday evening? From the time that you arrived at The Rectory to the time you left.'

'You don't have to answer,' says Maddie, her father's daughter.

'It's OK, Mads.' Justine sits up straighter. 'Donna rang at about four. She asked if I could help with bedtime, make tea, that sort of thing.'

'Was this something that had happened before? You getting called in on your day off?'

'Yes,' says Justine. 'Donna finds it hard to cope with the three of them. She hasn't got any routines, you see. She's not used to it.' Her voice is neutral.

'What about Patrick?'

'Patrick?' Now something like a sneer does cross Justine's face. 'He was shut away in his office, working apparently, but when I went in to offer him some coffee he was on level fifteen of Angry Birds.'

'Angry Birds?'

'It's a computer game, Boss.'

'So you helped Donna with the bedtime routine?'

'Yes. I made the kids some tea and played with the little ones for a bit. That let Donna spend some time with Bailey. He gets a bit jealous sometimes. She did his homework with him – ridiculous, a kid that age having homework – but at least he had her full attention. Then Donna and the boys watched some TV. I gave Poppy her bath and put her to bed. Then I went home.'

'When you put Poppy to bed, did you notice anything different?'

'No. I put her in her cot and put on the nightlight – it wasn't dark, but it plays a tune and it helps her sleep, Then I kissed her goodnight and went downstairs.'

Nelson makes a note to ask about the nightlight. Was it still on when Donna went to check on her daughter?

'What about the window?' he asks. 'Was it shut? Locked?'

Justine stares at him. 'It was certainly shut because I pulled the curtains. It was still light outside. I don't know if it was locked.'

'Had Poppy ever tried to get out of the window?'

'No. She wasn't an inquisitive child, not like Bailey. That boy is into everything. She hadn't been walking that long.'

Nelson looks at Clough. 'OK, Justine. That's it for now.'

Justine stays sitting on the bed but Maddie gets up, as if to make sure that they're really going. 'Just one thing,' says Nelson at the door. 'Do you know anyone who might call themselves The Childminder?'

Justine blinks at him. 'What?'

'Someone left a note saying they had Poppy. It was signed 'The Childminder'.'

Justine's face is as white as a sheet. Whiter, in fact, than the rather dubious linen exposed on her bed.

'How horrible,' she whispers.

'Does it mean anything to you?'

'No.'

On the way downstairs, Nelson wonders whether to share his fears with Clough. But, not for the first time, his sergeant surprises him. As they get into the car, he says, 'She talked about her in the past tense.'

CHAPTER 22

Ruth wakes knowing immediately that it's Sunday. It's not that she can hear bells (Norwich's famous fifty-two churches are well out of earshot) or that she hurries to dress in her Sunday best for church (though, in South London, her parents will be doing just that). It's more that the day has its own atmosphere – less exciting than Saturday, less depressing than Monday. Sunday mornings, in particular, have a mood of their own, easy as the song says. After lunch Ruth will still experience that old Sunday afternoon dread – a heady mix of undone homework and uniform drying by the fire, cosy and sad at the same time. She'll get the Dread even though she doesn't have to go to work tomorrow. Summer School is over and the holidays have officially started. But as soon as the Sunday evening programmes come on the television –

costume dramas, antiques and the countryside – the
Dread will descend.

But now, as she makes coffee and settles Kate with her
toys in a patch of sunshine, it is purely easy. Ruth sits
with her coffee at the table by the window and reads
yesterday's paper. The rain has stopped and the marshes
are steaming gently. Flint jumps onto the table and
arranges himself, with geometrical precision, on the
exact article that Ruth is reading. She pushes him off.
She'll get dressed in a minute, catch 'The Archers'
omnibus and maybe take Kate for a walk. Nelson is
coming to take her out in the afternoon. Then she needs
to start getting the house ready for Simon and the boys.
Oh God, this probably means going to the supermarket
and buying pizzas and things like that. What do almost-
teenage boys eat? Ruth recalls that Cathy is extremely
fussy about food, dissecting meals for traces of forbidden
substances like mushrooms and peanuts, much to her
mother-in-law's irritation. 'Whoever heard of a child
being allergic to mushrooms,' Ruth's mother was heard
to mutter. Well, Ruth won't buy mushrooms. In fact,
better to avoid vegetables altogether. Maybe they'll have
a barbecue, eat burnt sausages by the light of a camp fire.
It's possible, she supposes, but she can't quite see it happening. She wishes Cathbad were here. He'd light the fire

in a trice and probably organise wild games on the beach into the bargain. Cathbad is one of those strange creatures universally acknowledged to be 'good with children'.

Well, Ruth might not be a natural entertainer but she'll try her best to be a good aunt for a few days. Maybe she should buy a kite or something. She wonders what happened to the old Monopoly board . . .

'Your cousins are coming to stay,' she says to Kate. 'That'll be fun, won't it.'

Kate carries on stacking bricks, obviously underwhelmed. From his vantage point on the table, Flint blinks at her. He certainly won't enjoy the addition of two large tail-pulling children. Hang on, isn't one of them asthmatic? Ruth is sure that everything in her house is coated with a fine layer of cat's fur. Just as well they're camping in the garden. Should she mow the lawn? Bob usually does it for her but he's still away in Australia. Oh well, they can have fun playing in the long grass.

Ruth sips her coffee and tries to get herself in a positive frame of mind. She's looking forward to seeing her nephews, of course she is. It's just that she had been planning to get a bit of work done. She needs to check the proofs of her book. She still can't quite believe that she's become a person who has *proofs*, almost as if she's

ELLY GRIFFITHS

a real author. The book, *The Tomb of the Raven King*, was surprisingly easy to write. She finished it just before Christmas, pouring out the story of the buried king and also all the fevered emotions surrounding the discovery. It had been therapy, if you like. She hadn't had much hope of getting it published and had been amazed when the first publisher she contacted expressed interest verging on enthusiasm. She had travelled to London to meet her editor (her editor!), an extremely keen young man called Javier. Before long she had a contract, a book jacket (a moody shot of ruins in the mist) and a marked increase in respect from Phil. She still won't be able to believe it until she sees the finished book. It's due out in the autumn.

Still, the proofs can wait for now. Family is more important. She'll go upstairs in a minute and start sorting out bed-linen. After she's listened to 'The Archers' of course.

But, at ten o'clock, just as the jolly strains of 'The Archers' fill the air, the phone rings. It's Michelle.

'Hallo,' says Ruth warily.

'Hallo, Ruth. Just to say that Harry won't be able to make it this afternoon. He's been called away on an urgent case. You've probably seen it on the news.'

Ruth hasn't seen or heard the news but she says that

she quite understands. She knows that it's very good of Michelle to ring her at all. Michelle sounds resigned, as if she's had to cancel such arrangements many times before. In her position, Ruth knows that she'd soon come to resent the urgent cases that take priority over everything else. But then Ruth never will be in Michelle's position.

After Michelle rings off ('Love to Katie'), Ruth turns on the TV, still with the Archers quarrelling bucolically in the background. A familiar face fills the screen. 'Detective Sergeant Tim Heathfield of the King's Lynn Serious Crimes Unit,' reads the caption, in solemn capitals.

'. . . anything at all,' Tim is saying, 'that might help us trace Baby Poppy. She's a little girl, not much more than a baby, away from her mum and dad. She must be very scared right now. Please, if you have any information at all, call us on this number . . .'

Ruth stares at Tim's earnest face, feeling as if he's addressing her directly. And, as always, when confronted with an appeal like this, she immediately feels guilty. *Does* she know anything about this disappearance? Poppy, the name sounds strangely familiar. Poor little girl, and poor Nelson too. She knows that all policemen hate cases involving missing children, but for Nelson the reminders of Scarlet and Lucy must make it almost unbearable. She finds another news channel and learns that Poppy was taken from her bed in the middle of the night. Police are anxious to trace a woman seen pushing a pram in the vicinity of the house, if only to eliminate her from their enquiries.

'Dora,' says Kate in a commanding voice.

'In a minute,' says Ruth. 'I'm just watching my own programme.'

'Dora,' repeats Kate, clearly not thinking much of Ruth's taste in early morning TV. Ruth sighs and gives in. She usually tries not to switch on the television in the morning but today seems to be going downhill. She finds a children's programme and goes back to the radio. She doesn't know why she feels so jolted by the news about Poppy. Perhaps because there's just too much bad news about children at the moment. She thinks of Liz Donaldson, whom she has never met, and of Bob Donaldson, standing in her kitchen and begging her to intercede with Nelson. She thinks of Mother Hook and The Book of Dead Babies. She remembers seeing Judy in the university car park on Friday, the missing child alert that had turned out to be a false alarm. And now a child is missing for real.

The buzzing of her phone makes her jump. At least it's her mobile, which means it's more likely to be good news.

'Hi, Ruth. It's Frank. Frank Barker.'

'Oh. Hi, Frank.'

'You remember we were talking about visiting Sax-lingham Thorpe? Well I wondered if you fancied going one day next week.'

'I'd love to,' says Ruth, 'but my brother's coming to stay on Tuesday.' As she says this, she thinks how normal it sounds. As if she and Simon were sane, well-adjusted adult siblings, continually having shared holidays with their mingled happy families. She doesn't mention the missing child.

There's a slight pause and then Frank says, 'Well, what about Monday? Apparently it's going to be a good day. There are going to be "sunny spells". I love the British weather forecast.'

Ruth hesitates. For some reason, it feels wrong to be planning a day out when Nelson is on the trail of a lost child. But, then, what on earth can she do to help?

'I'll have Kate with me,' she says.

'Great. I'd love to meet her again. I'll be sure not to call her a baby this time.'

'OK,' says Ruth at last. 'That would be fun.'

As she puts the phone down, she remembers why the name Poppy sounded familiar. Bailey, Scooter and Poppy. The children with outlandish names. Can it be the same child? She sends up a prayer to whoever's listening. Please look after Baby Poppy.

Judy squats on the floor next to Bailey and Scooter. They're building a police station out of Lego. Nelson has taken Donna and Patrick to the TV studios in Norwich where they're going to film an appeal for Poppy. Judy had encouraged Donna to do this. 'It can really help. If the . . . the perpetrator sees the parents it makes them think about the child as a human being. It could make them put themselves in your shoes.' Privately she wonders if Donna will be able to go through with it. During the morning, as each hour went by and Poppy wasn't found, Donna seemed to disintegrate before their eyes. By lunch-time, she was sobbing hysterically on the sofa. Patrick wasn't much help but then he was clearly in shock him-self. It was only Judy's urging that had got her up and dressed and ready for the broadcast. Judy wishes that she could have gone with Donna to the studio but someone needs to look after the children. Tanya, standing by the window and fiddling with her phone, is no help at all.

'The policeman has a big gun,' says Bailey, clicking several pieces of Lego together.

'That is big,' says Judy. 'It's bigger than the police sta-tion.'

Bailey points the gun at his brother. 'Bang bang. You're dead.'

Scooter starts to cry. He, too, has spent most of the morning in tears.

'Come on, Scooter,' Judy cajoles. 'Let's put this tower on the top.' There is Harry Potter Lego mixed in with the ordinary stuff so the police station is starting to take on a distinctly exotic appearance. It has stained glass windows and an astronomy tower (complete with owl). Judy feels that it's a look that could catch on.

'Shall I put the TV on?' asks Tanya. 'See if we can see the appeal.'

Without waiting for an answer she switches on the set.

'Look, there's Mummy,' says Bailey.

Donna is crying, her face contorted in a way that's painful to watch, but she is still managing to speak. Patrick sits beside her as if turned to stone.

'She's our little baby. We miss her so much. Please, if anyone knows anything at all, please let the police know. She's my baby, my little girl . . .'

Judy looks at Tanya. They both have tears in their eyes. Bailey is watching solemnly, sucking a Lego man.

'Poppy's hiding,' he says suddenly.

Judy turns to look at him. 'What?'

'Poppy's hiding. We play hide and seek with Justine

sometimes. She's waiting until Justine tells her to come out.'

Judy leans towards the little boy. 'Bailey,' she says. 'Does Justine knows where Poppy is?'

Bailey's eyes are blank. 'Justine?'

'Yes. Does Justine know where Poppy is? Has Justine hidden her?'

Bailey shrugs. 'I don't know. Poppy's gone missing. Mummy said.' And he puts the Lego man back in his mouth.

Ruth and Kate are walking along the shingle path to the beach. Ruth has been shopping and has bought a range of food high in E-numbers and low on mushrooms. She and Kate ate chips at the supermarket cafe (who knew supermarkets had cafes, it's a whole new world) and now Ruth has acquiesced to Kate's demands for the sea. It's a beautiful day and, as they reach the sand dunes, the beach is spread out before them like a present. It's almost deserted. The Saltmarsh beach, accessible only after miles of trekking across the marsh, is not on the usual tourist trail. There are always a few hardy souls who think the journey is worth it for the view and the sand but Ruth doesn't begrudge them their place in the sun. As long as they don't try to talk to her, that is.

They pause at the base of the dunes. Ruth thinks of that other journey, four years ago, to find Scarlet's body. Please God, don't let the search for Poppy end the same way. She remembers Cathbad lighting a bonfire on the sands – 'Saint Bridget accept our offering' – and she includes Saint Bridget, whoever she is, in the prayer. This is sacred land, Cathbad would say, otherwise why would those unknown Bronze Age Britons have bothered to build a henge, way out here between the earth and the sky? Why would later people have built the causeway, that snaking path that leads across the treacherous marshland to the sea?

Kate is pointing back towards the grassland.

'Poppy!'

Ruth jumps. 'Where?'

But then she sees that her daughter is pointing at the flowers blooming amongst the wind-blown shrubs, blood red against the green. She wonders who taught Kate to identify a poppy.

'Come on Kate,' she reaches out her hand. 'Nearly there.'

Five o'clock and Donna and Patrick are still not back. Nelson must have taken them into the station for some reason. Or maybe Donna has collapsed and needs hospital treatment. The children are getting restive and Judy reckons it's probably time for their tea. She's sure Justine has some fairly rigid routines in place but she's not exactly available to help. Justine has been taken in for questioning. Tim's with her now.

'Do you want to make them some tea?' Judy asks Tanya, just to see what response she'll get.

Tanya looks horrified. 'Me? I don't know what children eat.'

Judy doubts whether Scooter and Bailey would enjoy afternoon tea cooked by Auntie Tanya. As far as she can make out, Tanya exists on energy drinks and cereal bars. So Judy makes scrambled egg on toast and they eat it in front of the TV, something apparently strictly forbidden by Justine. 'Though Mummy lets us sometimes.'

Afterwards Judy leaves Tanya with the washing-up and takes the children into the garden. They run in delighted circles, glad to be free of the house and its stultifying atmosphere. Bailey scales the climbing frame and Judy helps Scooter onto a swing. All this equipment, she thinks. Their back garden is only big enough for a tiny sandpit. Still, Michael loves playing in the sand, spending hours sifting and sorting. Maybe he'll grow up to be an archaeologist. Like his dad.

'Look at me!' shouts Bailey from the top.

'Be careful,' says Judy. The last thing she wants is for one of the children to be injured in her care. *Tiny tot in horror fall. Policewoman to blame.*

'Why don't we play a game?' she says.

'Hide and seek,' says Bailey, swinging on the rope.

Judy looks at him. She still thinks that Bailey has something that he wants to tell her. Maybe the game will unleash that memory or observation, whatever it is. She had better be careful though. She doesn't want another of the Granger children going missing.

'All right,' she says. 'But just in this part of the garden. OK? Just where the play stuff is.'

'Count to three hundred!' shouts Bailey, jumping up and down.

'I'll count to fifty,' says Judy. And she'll make damn sure to keep her eyes open too.

Scooter seems a bit uncertain. Through her fingers Judy can see him circling her slowly before crouching down behind the seesaw. Bailey has disappeared in the direction of the Wendy House.

'Coming!' she calls. 'Ready or not.'

After a show of searching that has Scooter in giggles, she 'finds' him and hoists him onto her hip. He clings to her like a monkey.

'Where's Bailey?' she asks. 'Where's your brother?'

Scooter giggles again and buries his face in her hair. She thinks that she can see Bailey's red t-shirt behind the Wendy House.

'Is he over here?' She doesn't want to find him too soon. He's older, after all, and deserves a proper game.

'Is he in here?' She tries the playhouse door. She won't go inside. She knows the search teams have practically taken the place apart. She'll just pretend to look.

'Bailey! Are you in here?'

She pushes open the door. The search teams have done their work well. The child-sized furniture – mini kitchen with table and chairs – is all back in place. But there's something else too. Something pink in the corner. Something that moves.

'It's Poppy,' says Bailey, appearing at her side.

CHAPTER 23

'And she was in the playhouse all the time?' says Ruth.

'She certainly wasn't there all the time,' says Nelson. 'We searched the Wendy House thoroughly on Saturday night and again this morning. Even took the floorboards up. But this afternoon, when I was with the parents at the TV station, Johnson was looking after the other kids. They were playing some game in the garden. Johnson looked in the playhouse and there was Poppy.'

'Was she OK?'

'Right as rain. A bit cold and hungry but otherwise fine. And she was dressed warmly. That's the biggest clue we have really. When she went missing she was just wearing her nightdress. When Johnson found her she was wearing a pink all-in-one thing, fleecy with feet attached.'

'God. I can't imagine what Judy would have felt. What did she do?'

'She picked up the little girl and ran like hell for the house. She wasn't sure if she was hurt or not at the time. Fuller called me immediately – I was driving the parents home – and we were there in minutes.'

Ruth can just imagine the way Nelson must have driven to cover those last few miles.

'What did the mum do?' she asks, though she feels as if she can see the scene for herself.

'It was one of the best moments of my career,' says Nelson. 'She just grabbed the baby from Johnson and collapsed on the floor, sobbing and laughing. The husband sort of fell on top of her and soon the whole family were in this little heap on the kitchen floor. Johnson and Fuller were crying like a couple of babies.'

'What about you and Clough?'

'Oh we're tough.' Nelson grins, 'Well, I think Cloughie had something in his eye. I was just so relieved. You know, I really thought she was dead.'

Ruth and Nelson are in her tiny garden, drinking tea and watching Kate play with her Native American tepee (a present from Cathbad). It's nearly nine o'clock but warm and still light. When Nelson had rung to say that Poppy had been found and that he'd be round to see Kate when he'd cleared up at the station, Ruth had said, 'Don't worry about us, you must be exhausted. Go home.' 'No, I want to see her,' Nelson had replied and Ruth can understand why. She has only been peripherally involved in Poppy's disappearance and yet the experience has made her want to treasure every moment with Kate. Even now, she's reluctant to take the little girl to bed. She just wants to watch her playing in the shadowy garden, shuttling to and fro between the tent and the apple tree, intent on some complicated business of her own. She understands why Nelson wanted to see his youngest daughter, to check with his own eyes that she was safe and happy.

'It's a hell of a relief,' Nelson says again, his eyes on Kate. 'When you find a missing child alive, it's the best feeling in the world. But the case isn't over. The perpetrator's still at large and we haven't got much to go on really. The note – assuming it's the same person – the change of clothes, that one sighting.'

'Do you think that was her? The woman with the pram?'

'I don't know, but no-one's come forward, which seems suspicious in itself. And why would anyone be wheeling a baby in a pushchair at ten o'clock at night in the pouring rain?'

'Maybe the baby wouldn't sleep. I used to take Kate out

for drives. Up and down New Road at twenty miles an hour. Anything to get her to close her eyes.'

Nelson smiles. He looks shattered, Ruth thinks. There are dark circles under his eyes and when he puts his empty cup down on the grass his hand is shaking.

'How long since you slept?' she asks.

He runs a hand through his hair. 'I don't know. I didn't go to bed last night. It'll have to be another early start in the morning too. Can't afford to let the trail go cold.'

'You can't afford to crack up either.'

He laughs. 'Don't worry about me, Ruth. Like I say, I'm tough. I'd like to give Johnson a day off though. She's really taken this case to heart.'

Judy lies on the sofa, eyes closed. The exhilaration of finding Poppy has given way to an exhaustion so complete that, as soon as she sat down, she felt as if she had sprouted tendrils that would root her to the spot forever. But the exhilaration has not disappeared. She can still feel the glorious weight of the little girl against her shoulder as she ran towards the house, stumbling over the flower beds, the two boys chasing after her. She remembers Tanya's shocked face as she stood at the door, not knowing whether the pink bundle in Judy's arms was moving or not.

'She's alive,' Judy had panted. 'Call the boss. Now!'

While they waited for Nelson, Judy had propped Poppy up on the kitchen table, not daring to let go completely. So far the little girl had not uttered a sound but she was awake, her blue eyes round as she stared impassively at the two policewomen.

'She's not that cold,' said Judy. 'She can't have been in there long.'

'Christ,' said Tanya. 'She must have been put there while we were in the house.'

'The clothes are different,' said Judy. 'Remember, Donna said she was in a nightdress.' She patted the pink babygro. 'Feels as if she's got a clean nappy too.' Tanya shuddered slightly.

'Hallo, Poppy,' said Judy. 'Hallo darling.'

Scooter was crying quietly in the corner but Bailey suddenly appeared carrying a squashy toy zebra. 'Look Pops! It's Stripes!'

Poppy had burst into noisy sobs. Judy gathered her into her arms as the door opened and Donna exploded into the room . . .

'Judy?' Darren is leaning over her. 'You ought to be in bed, love.'

Judy opens her eyes. 'How's Michael?'

'Fast asleep.'

Judy thinks of Poppy sandwiched between her parents as they lay on the kitchen floor, a sobbing, shuddering human pyramid. Incredibly, when Donna had finally got to her feet, Poppy had fallen asleep, mouth open, cheeks flushed.

'Is she OK?' Donna had asked Judy. 'She's not drugged or anything?'

'I don't think so,' Judy said. 'She seemed perfectly alert when I found her. But you'll need to get her checked out at the hospital.'

'There's an ambulance outside,' said Clough. They were the first words he had spoken though Judy had seen him surreptitiously wiping his eyes.

'Thank you,' Donna said to Judy. 'How can I ever thank you?'

'I didn't do anything really.'

Now she remembers something else. 'She smelt of perfume,' Judy says to Darren. 'Poppy smelt of the play house – you know, that typical shed smell – but she smelt of perfume too. Something expensive.'

Darren pulls her to her feet. 'You can tell Nelson in the morning.'

Judy leans against her husband as they walk towards the stairs. He smells of home.

CHAPTER 24

'It's what's called a shifted village,' says Frank. 'In medieval times the centre would have been here, just north
of the church. Now it's a mile away along the A140.'

Ruth looks around her. It's almost too perfect, a landscape painter's dream of a ruin. The walk, through dense
woodland choked with nettles and cow parsley, had been
hard going, especially for Kate (Frank had to carry her
for the last half mile), but the abandoned church was
worth it in the end. The trees, thick with summer foliage,
hid the ruins until the very last moment. Then, suddenly,
they were standing in an open space, the walls, still with
their high arched windows, rising up into the sky and
the branches reaching out to form their own vaulted
ceiling. Apart from a skylark singing somewhere up
above, there was perfect silence all around them. Now

Kate runs from wall to wall, laughing as she touches the mossy stones. For Ruth, though, the place has a curiously solemn feel – not unhappy, just sombre, as if the space between the walls is charged with something beyond the stillness and the isolation. Erik would have said that it was sacred land but Ruth doesn't believe in any of that, does she?

'When was it ruined?' she asks, sitting on a low wall to get her breath back. 'Would Jemima have come to this church?'

Frank shakes his head. 'The church was abandoned in the seventeenth century. I suppose her family would have gone to the church in Nethergate.'

'She would have known this place though,' says Ruth, looking up at the sky, bright blue between the leaves.

'She would,' agrees Frank. He takes Kate's hand as she skips from stone to stone. He's good with her; not pushy, in the way that adults sometimes are with children, but quiet and respectful. Kate has already honoured him with a full-length rendition of 'Wind the Bobbin Up', including gestures.

Ruth walks through a doorway which is still eerily intact, a gateway to nowhere. She's in another church-shaped space, probably a side chapel. The south wall still stands and includes two alcoves with statues on plinths, their faces worn smooth by wind and rain.

'I wonder who these were,' she says.

Frank and Kate are following. 'The Church was dedicated to Saint Mary,' says Frank. 'So maybe one of them was her.'

Ruth looks at the stone shapes, it's impossible to tell if they were meant to represent male or female figures. There's a suggestion of a flowing robe, but that doesn't prove anything. She remembers the time that she visited Norwich Cathedral with Janet Meadows, looking for the statue of Bishop Augustine. The cathedral was vast and magnificent but this little country church has something of the same feel about it. A sense of peace, of withdrawal from the rest of the world. Ruth thinks of the words of Mother Julian, Julian of Norwich, another woman commemorated in the cathedral. *All shall be well and all shall be well.*

Frank and Kate have passed through another archway. Ruth finds Frank gazing out at a tangle of trees and brambles. Kate is almost hidden in the waist-high grass.

'I think this must have been the churchyard,' says Frank, 'but it's so overgrown it's hard to see any gravestones. The woods have come right up to the walls.'

Ruth looks at the trees, their branches choked with ivy

and overhung with creepers. They look almost menacing, as if they are advancing on the church and mean, one day, to take it over forever.

'Is there a rowan?' she asks.

'What?' Frank is pulling aside a curtain of leaves. Kate, a few feet below, is digging enthusiastically.

'Rowan trees are traditionally found in graveyards. They're meant to ward off evil spirits.'

'Are you thinking of Jemima's diary? *I shall lay him with Emily and Susannah, where Rowan will stand guard.*'

'Yes,' admits Ruth. 'It occurred to me that she might have buried him here.'

'There haven't been any burials here since the 1600s.'

'Official ones, that is. And who were Emily and Susannah?'

'I think they may have been Jemima's sisters who died in infancy. There's a mention of Emily somewhere.'

'Well, could they have been buried here secretly? I mean, the family probably couldn't afford proper funerals but they may have still considered this hallowed ground.'

'It's possible,' says Frank. 'Most people were buried at Nethergate – Jemima's parents' graves are there – but they could have buried the babies somewhere else. They may have thought that they'd be safe from the grave robbers here. It would have been an isolated place, even then.'

He looks as if he is about to say more but Kate calls excitedly. 'Look! Look!'

Ruth and Frank scramble down the slope to where Kate is crouching. Ruth feels her heart pumping. She doesn't know what she expects. A human bone? A shroud bearing the name 'Joshua Barnet'? But Kate is holding something small in the palm of her hand. 'Nail', she says importantly. For a moment Ruth thinks of a finger or toe but she sees that Kate is holding up a sturdy piece of metal that is almost certainly a coffin nail.

'Lovely,' she says. 'Shall we go and have lunch now?'

When Nelson suggests that she goes home early, Judy doesn't wait for him to make the offer twice. All morning she has felt as if she's moving underwater, going through the motions but feeling curiously detached from the world around her. The rest of the team are still fired up, frantically following leads, urged on by Nelson's constant reminders that 'there's a potential child killer on the loose'. But Judy finds herself asking people to repeat things and logging herself out of her computer because she can't think of her password. Only when she remembers holding Poppy in her arms does she feel some sense of urgency. Otherwise the events of yesterday seem as remote as a TV series, something grey and Swedish and ultimately unrealistic.

Clough and Tim follow up a sighting of the short-haired woman with the pram, which turns out to be a blameless down-and-out pushing his belongings around the shopping centre. Otherwise all their enquiries draw blanks. None of the neighbours saw anything that Sunday afternoon when Tanya and Judy were in the house and Poppy's abductor was apparently able to return her as easily as posting a card through the letterbox.

'That's the trouble with these posh houses with big gardens and long driveways,' said Nelson. 'Back home in Blackpool there wasn't a thing happened on our street without my mum knowing about it.'

'It's grim up north,' murmured Clough to Judy, their standard response to the boss's trips down Memory Lane, Lancashire.

But Judy was barely able to summon up a smile. Even talking was an effort. So now she ignores Clough's knowing glance and Tanya's pretended sympathy and heads for the door without giving Nelson the chance to change his mind. She'll collect Michael from the childminder and have a few blissful hours in front of children's

TV. Then she'll go to bed at eight and be fresh for the fray tomorrow.

'Must be great to be on part-time,' is Clough's parting shot but Judy hardly notices. She is on her way to Michael.

Ruth, Frank and Kate have lunch at the Mill Inn, a charming pub overshadowed by an immense mill tower. 'It's known as the Black Mill,' explains the barman. 'It was working right up to 2003, the only working mill in these parts.' But Ruth thinks there is something ominous, almost Tolkienesque, about the stark black tower reflected in the rushing water of the river. It's a reminder of another age, of hellish furnaces and backbreaking labour and nightmare machines that can bite off a woman's hand.

As Kate devours nuggets and chips (she rejects the salad with a shudder), Frank and Ruth discuss Jemima Green.

'I found her frightening,' says Ruth. 'All that stuff about the children being angels, laying them out and writing their names in the book.'

'She loved them,' says Frank mildly. 'What's wrong with that?'

'They weren't her children. Joshua Barnet had a mother. I felt that Jemima wanted them all for herself. I mean, not letting Joshua's mother have his body. No wonder she was furious.'

'Jemima may have had her reasons for not trusting Anna Barnet. She made some terrible allegations at the trial, that Jemima was a witch and that she used the children for human sacrifices.'

'She was grieving. And there *was* some mystery about the bodies. Why did Jemima talk about giving them to Mr G? Was he a body snatcher?'

Frank nods, sprinkling salt on his chips. Ruth likes the way that he seems remarkably un-health conscious. 'I think so. I think he bought the bodies from Jemima and sold them to the medical schools. These children were the 'unclaimed poor', if you like. No-one was going to ask questions about them.'

'That doesn't make it OK.'

'Maybe not, but they were dead and Jemima used the money to care for the living. I think that was the bargain she made with herself.'

'Did Mr G give evidence at the trial?'

'No, he disappeared completely. Jemima and Martha both refused to answer questions about him. They were probably scared. Some of these resurrectionists were pretty unsavoury characters.'

'And she didn't give him Joshua's body.'

'No. She obviously couldn't bear to.'

'In the poem she says something about wanting to be buried with him.'

'Well that didn't happen,' says Frank. 'She was hanged and her body thrown into an unmarked grave. We don't know where Joshua was buried.'

There is a pause while Ruth tries not to eat too loudly. 'You sound sad about her,' she says.

'I guess I am,' says Frank. 'She was unjustly accused and I care about injustice. She was the victim of all sorts of prejudices, against the poor, against the disabled, against women who don't conform to society's idea of how women should look. Look at how they labelled her a devil worshipper because of that medal she wore. Pure ignorance.'

Ruth wonders if she too fails to conform to society's idea of how women should look. Tough, if so. But she feels slightly guilty about her instinctive distaste for Jemima Green. Well, she knows a way that she can make amends. 'About that medal . . .' she says.

Once again Debbie and the children are out when Judy knocks on the door, but as she didn't call ahead she can't feel too aggrieved. They are probably in the park again. She leaves her car outside Debbie's house and walks the

few hundred yards to the playground. It's a sunny afternoon so the swings and slides are crowded with children.
She soon picks out the identical Arsenal tops of Archie
and Tom as they play on the climbing frame. Where's
Michael? In the sandpit, excavating for treasure? Without
quite knowing why she starts to walk faster. Now she can
see Debbie. She's wearing a pink t-shirt and an inappropriately short skirt and is sitting on a bench watching
the boys.

'Debbie!' Now Judy is running, hurdling abandoned
scooters and dodging picnicking families. Debbie turns
round, her face blank with surprise.

'Debbie! Where's Michael?'

Debbie looks at her in concern.

'He's gone, love. Your friend came to pick him up. The
girl with the short hair.'

CHAPTER 25

Judy is amazed that her voice still works. In fact, part of her is surprised that she is still alive, that she hasn't fallen down dead on the spongy playground asphalt. Michael has gone. Isn't that what she has been dreading, in her most secret heart, as soon as she knew that Poppy was missing? And, if she is honest, hasn't she been expecting a disaster – cosmic retribution – from the moment that she looked into Michael's dark eyes and realised that he wasn't her husband's child?

'What friend? I didn't send a friend to pick him up.'

Now Debbie jumps up, hand to her mouth. 'But she had a note from you. She seemed to know Michael . . .'

Judy is fumbling for her phone. It takes her three attempts to find Nelson's number. Then, when he answers, the words won't come. Debbie has to take the phone from her. When she hears Debbie telling him what has happened, Judy really does fall to the ground. Then somehow she is lying face down next to the hop-scotch markings, whimpering like an animal.

'Judy? Judy!' Debbie is leaning over her. She is aware of other figures, shadowy forms in the background radiating concern and curiosity, of two little boys in Arsenal tops, of a hang-glider, high up in the blue blue sky.

'Judy. I've rung Darren. He's meeting us at the house. Come on, let's go.' Debbie pulls her to her feet and Judy finds herself holding a child's hand, Archie's or Tom's. Strangely, it is the contact with the child that keeps Judy going, she clings to the little fingers like a lifeline and the child – Archie or Tom – squeezes back as if he understands.

As they reach the house, two police cars are screeching to a halt outside. Nelson and Clough jump out of the first car. Nelson's face is pale but he's completely in control. He seizes Judy's arms and says, quite roughly, 'Judy, you've got to concentrate. The first hour's the most important, you know that. We can find this woman if we act fast enough.'

Judy nods and, still clasping the little boy's hand, she follows Debbie into the house. Nelson's talking on his phone and Judy recognises the code for high alert, all units converging on Castle Rising. Clough is speaking to Debbie, getting a description of the short-haired woman. A policewoman puts a cup of tea into Judy's hand and she smiles faintly, recognising her own role in so many such incidents.

'Have you got the note?' asks Clough.

Debbie fishes in her bag and hands it to him. Clough shows the piece of paper to Judy. It's headed 'Norfolk Constabulary: Our Priority is *You*'.

'It's not my writing,' says Judy.

'I didn't know,' Debbie sobs. 'I just s-saw the headed paper and I thought it was genuine. I'm s-so sorry.' She covers her face with her hands.

Judy stares at the childminder wondering if she ought to comfort her. Debbie's saying that it's all her fault but Judy knows that's not true. She knows whose fault it is. She's aware of a commotion outside and of Nelson coming back into the room with a man who looks vaguely familiar.

'Judy!' The man rushes over and kneels at her feet, wrapping his arms around her.

'Darren,' says Judy.

'Judy.' Now Nelson is speaking to her over Darren's head. Judy focuses on him with relief. She knows what to do now. She has to listen to the boss and everything will be all right.

'Do you recognise this woman?' Nelson is holding out a photograph.

'No.'

Nelson shows the picture to Debbie. She shakes her head, still sobbing quietly.

'Who is it?' asks Judy.

'Justine Thomas.'

Clough is talking on his phone. He turns to Nelson. 'Justine's at the Grangers' house looking after the children. Apparently she's been there all day.'

'Double check,' says Nelson. 'She may have gone out for an hour or so. She's got her own car.'

'Boss?' A policeman is hovering in the doorway. Judy doesn't recognise him.

'This was posted through the door.'

The PC is holding out a sheaf of free newspapers and flyers from Chinese restaurants. The sort of post that accumulates on every doormat. But on top is a sheet of A4 paper in a clear plastic folder. Nelson turns it so Judy can read the message.

I've taken him. The Childminder.

'Thank you for a lovely day,' says Ruth, rather awkwardly. They are standing in the car park by the Mill Inn. After lunch they went for a walk by the river but Kate was tired and inclined to be grizzly. Frank carried her back which made conversation difficult, Ruth trailing behind unable to keep up with Frank's long strides. Kate, though, cheered up enough to sing 'Wind the Bobbin Up' again.

'Interesting rhyme,' says Frank. 'Probably goes back to the Victorian textiles industry. They may have used children to wind the bobbins.'

Ruth looks back at the mill with its stark black tower. She doesn't like the thought of children – how old would they have been? eight? ten? – working in factories, though she knows it happened. Charles Dickens was working in the blacking factory at the age of twelve. Images come into her mind: brutal overseers, children forced to work thirteen-hour days, beatings and maimings and deaths.

'Children used to lead terrible lives,' she says.

'Still do,' says Frank putting Kate on her feet. 'There's still child labour in many parts of the world.'

This pronouncement seems to put a damper on them both. Ruth says again how nice it has been and thanks Frank for lunch (he had refused to let her pay half). He says that he's enjoyed himself. Kate, impatient with all this adult chat, rattles the car door and says, 'In!' Ruth settles Kate into her seat and turns to say goodbye to Frank. He extends his hand but, at the last moment, leans forward and kisses her on the cheek. 'Bye Ruth. Bye Kate.'

'Bye, bye, bye!' shouts Kate. Ruth contents herself with a small wave. She can feel that she's blushing.

Kate is asleep by the time they get home. Ruth carries her into the house, lays her on the sofa and goes into the kitchen. She knows that she has some silver cleaning stuff somewhere. Where is it? Eventually she finds the rusted can in the shed. Making herself a cup of tea she sits down by the window to clean Mother Hook's medallion. Flint jumps onto the table and sniffs at the cleaning fluid. Ruth pushes him aside.

'Go away stupid cat. It's bad for you.'

Flint purrs loudly.

After half an hour's vigorous cleaning Ruth is no wiser. The medal definitely shows two heads and one looks to be a child. The other could be almost anyone. Is it a woman or a long-haired man? Is that a halo or tiny horns? Ruth sighs. She feels exhausted. She wouldn't last a minute in a Victorian factory. She had wanted to be able to tell Frank that she'd solved one of the mysteries that surround Jemima Green but she has just added another layer of confusion. The tiny silver object gleams at her balefully. She'll have to see if she can get it X-rayed, which means explanations and possibly even apologies.

Even so, she's not sure that a radiograph will show anything. X-rays can be very helpful in detecting metal lodged within some other substance, stone or soil for example, but she is not sure how much help it will be with an object that has already deteriorated so much.

Ruth looks at her watch. Five o'clock. She should really wake Kate or she'll never sleep tonight. She is just about to start some gentle stirring when the phone rings. She has a crazy feeling that it will be Frank but the caller is entirely unexpected.

'Ruth? It's Dave Clough.'

'Clough!' Without thinking, Ruth calls him by his surname as Nelson does. Clough doesn't seem to notice.

'Ruth, could you possibly come over to Judy's? I think she could do with some support.'

CHAPTER 26

Ruth drives to Judy's house in a state of frozen shock. Even Kate, sitting in her car seat at the back, is silent. Under the circumstances, Ruth feels that it's tactless to bring Kate but what else can she do? There's no time to sort out a babysitter and, besides, after what she's heard Ruth never wants to let Kate out of her sight again. She still can't believe it. Judy's baby abducted. Michael taken by the same shadowy bogeyman who spirited away Baby Poppy. 'Looks to be the same person,' Clough said. 'Of course, we're not ruling anything out.'

Clough was still talking like a policeman but Ruth could hear the shock in his voice. They may have had their differences but Ruth knows that Clough cares about Judy. The whole team are close in a way that she can never understand, never really be part of. To use the cliché, they are a family. Nelson is the father, to be teased and grumbled about but always ultimately obeyed. Clough is the rebellious son, seeing just how far he can push the boundaries. Judy is the studious daughter, always doing what Daddy wants but somehow not quite as close to him as the wayward son. Tim is the newcomer, the golden boy, resented by both siblings.

And, now, tragedy has hit the whole family. Hang on, Ruth tells herself, taking the turn into Judy's road, a blameless suburban street now crowded with police cars and flashing sirens, it's not a tragedy yet. Poppy was found safe and well. The odds are that the same will happen with Michael. But if Ruth were Judy she would not be thinking about the odds. She would be thinking about her baby, lost in the dark and cold, away from her. Instinctively Ruth glances in the mirror. Kate is wide awake, gazing entranced at the pretty blue lights. 'Stars,' she says.

There's a helicopter hovering overhead. Is that searching for Michael too? It's flying so low that the rotors are stirring the privet hedges. There are policemen outside the red front door but they recognise Ruth and let her through. Carrying Kate, she walks into the sitting room to find Judy and Darren sitting on the sofa, both of them staring straight ahead, not speaking.

'Judy.' Ruth puts Kate down and tries a hug. Judy doesn't respond at all, her body as stiff and cold as a statue. Darren, though, stands up and shakes hands awkwardly.

'Thanks for coming, Ruth.'

'Clough told me. I just came to see if there was anything I could do.'

'That's kind of you, Ruth,' says Judy politely, 'but there isn't anything anyone can do.'

'Both sets of parents wanted to come over,' says Darren, 'but Judy wouldn't let them.'

'Can I make you a cup of tea?'

Judy laughs hollowly. 'If I drink another cup of tea I think I'll be sick.'

'Everyone's been very kind,' says Darren. 'Nelson's here now. He's just making a phone call.'

Despite everything, Ruth is still capable of feeling disconcerted at this news. She has only been thinking about Judy and Michael. She hadn't considered that she would have to face Nelson though, of course, it's inevitable that he would be here. This is a serious crime, on his patch, and involving one of his officers. Will he be pleased to see her or will he think that she's in the way or, worse, pushing herself forward, wanting to be involved in the crisis? Stop it, she tells herself. It doesn't matter what he thinks about you. It's only Michael that matters.

Ruth sits down on a chair opposite the couple. Kate climbs into her lap. She has no idea what to say or do. Why on earth did Clough think that she'd be any help? Judy obviously doesn't want support of any kind. She sits rigidly on the sofa, staring into space. Darren, on the other hand, seems to appreciate having someone to talk to.

'Nelson says that this Childminder person will look after Michael,' he says. 'After all, they looked after Poppy didn't they?'

'Of course they did,' says Ruth, not daring to look at Judy.

'Nelson says that it's probably someone who wants to look after children,' he says. 'It's just that they're a bit . . .' His voice tails off and Ruth knows that he's trying to avoid saying the words 'mad' or 'deranged'. She hurries into the gap.

'I'm sure he's right,' she says. 'Nelson knows what he's doing. And they've got the note, haven't they? They've got clues.'

'They've got fuck all,' says Judy. It's the first time that Ruth has ever heard her swear and the words effectively cast a spell of silence on the room.

*

When Nelson comes in, they are all still sitting there, Darren and Judy on the sofa, Ruth in the chair. No-one is speaking. Kate is asleep on Ruth's lap. It's nearly seven but still light outside. They can hear children playing in the street. 'You're it.' 'No, you're it.' 'Ip dip sky blue . . .'

'Right,' Nelson is saying, 'we're pretty sure that the handwriting's the same . . .'

He stops. 'Ruth. What are you doing here?'

'Clough called me.'

'He's meant to be coordinating the door-to-door,' Nelson looks irritated. 'Why did he ring you?'

'I think he thought I could . . . help.'

'Isn't it past Katie's bedtime?'

As her daughter is snoring quietly there is nothing Ruth can say to this. Darren leans forward, 'You can put her down in Michael's cot . . .' He stops, looking at Judy.

'It's OK,' says Ruth hurriedly. 'She can sleep here. Or I can put her on a bed somewhere.'

'She might fall off,' objects Nelson.

'It's OK,' says Ruth again. She wishes that Nelson would stop going on about Kate. She feels guilty enough that she has her child alive and well and sleeping on her lap when Michael is . . . well, who knows where Michael is and where he is sleeping? Nelson seems to realise this too because, with one distracted glance at his daughter, he turns back to Judy.

'We've got all units out,' he says. 'We'll find her, I promise. She can't have gone far.'

'She?' says Judy. Her voice is hard, professional.

'The handwriting expert thinks it's a woman,' says Nelson.

'Experts are crap,' says Judy.

Nelson looks surprised, though Judy is probably just repeating one of his opinions. He looks at Darren as if asking for help. Darren puts his hand on Judy's arm. She shakes it off.

'We'll find Michael,' says Nelson again. He crouches down in front of Judy. 'Judy? I promise you, we'll find him.'

Judy looks at him with something like contempt. 'That's what you said about Scarlet.'

Nelson stands up. For a second Ruth thinks that he is close to tears, but when he turns to her his voice is as brusque as ever.

'Give Katie to me, Ruth. I'll put her on the bed.'

Ruth follows Nelson upstairs. He lies Kate on what is obviously the matrimonial bed, large and comfortable, covered with what looks like a wedding present duvet in shades of taupe. There's a photo of Darren and Judy on the bedside table. She is radiant in a red dress, he is looking at her proudly.

Nelson pulls the duvet over Kate. 'Do you think she'll be too hot?'

'No. She'll be fine.'

It feels strange to be with Nelson, looking down at their sleeping daughter. Strange but oddly sweet. Sometimes it makes Ruth sad to think of all the things that she, Nelson and Kate will never do together – go on holiday, have breakfast in bed, visit grandparents. She wonders if Nelson also thinks about this. But now he has something else on his mind.

'Ruth, do you think we should tell Cathbad?'

Ruth has never known whether Nelson suspects that Cathbad is Michael's father. He's not given to gossip, and deep down he's pretty strait-laced. Even so, he must know that people have affairs. After all, didn't he have one himself?

'Why should we tell him?' she counters.

'Well, he and Judy are pretty close,' says Nelson. 'And you know how he likes to know everything.'

Ruth stares at him. What is Nelson really saying here? Does he really think that Cathbad and Judy are just friends and that Cathbad would like – in some vaguely interested way – to know what's going on? Or is he suggesting something else?

'He usually knows without being told,' she says.

Nelson turns away to straighten the duvet over Kate. Ruth thinks that he looks embarrassed.

'That's just it,' he says, not looking at her. 'Cathbad always just appears and things usually turn out all right if he's here.'

Now Ruth really is astonished. Nelson seems to be suggesting that Cathbad has some magical power, that he is, in some way, *necessary*. Of course, other people have claimed that Cathbad is magic but Ruth never thought that Nelson would turn out to be one of the believers. She thinks of the times that Cathbad has just appeared – leading the way across the marshes, materialising out of the snow, climbing the highest roller-coaster in Europe to save Kate. But, if she calls him now, he'll come down like an avenging angel and throw this whole house of cards into the air. She thinks of Darren downstairs. 'Our little champ will be all right,' he had said to her earlier. 'He's a toughie, our Michael.' What if the sight of Cathbad makes Judy blurt out the whole thing, that Darren's little champ is someone else's child? But, then again, doesn't Cathbad have a right to know what has happened to his son?

Ruth is about to speak when a pounding on the door makes them both jump. Ruth hears Judy cry out and Darren run towards the sound. Ruth is sure that he's imagining a kindly policewoman with Michael in her arms. She looks at Nelson and knows that he's seeing a different image altogether.

She goes to the top of the stairs and, through the glass panel in the door, she sees a flash of purple.

Seconds later a cloaked figure strides into the house.

'Where's Judy?' says Cathbad.

CHAPTER 27

Cathbad looks exhausted, his face grey, his eyes shadowed. He has also lost about half a stone since last summer and let his hair grow. This, together with the cloak, gives him a rather desperate appearance. Ruth doesn't blame Darren for backing away and looking round for help.

It's Nelson, though, who speaks first. He comes bounding down the stairs.

'What are you doing here?'

Cathbad looks at him. 'Where's Judy?' he repeats.

Judy appears in the background. The little hall now seems uncomfortably crowded. Ruth is happy to stay out of sight on the stairs. In fact she wishes she was further away still. Edinburgh would be nice.

'Cathbad,' says Judy.

Cathbad almost pushes Darren out of the way. He comes up to Judy and puts his hands on her shoulders.

'It'll be OK,' he says. 'They'll find him.'

This seems to have a far better effect than Nelson's earlier reassurances. With a sound halfway between a sob and a scream, Judy throws herself into Cathbad's arms. Ruth and Nelson look at each other.

Still standing by the door, Darren says, 'She hasn't cried since she heard.'

'It's the shock of seeing Cathbad,' says Nelson breezily. 'Let's all have a nice cup of tea shall we?'

Nelson and Ruth almost fight over making the tea, anything to avoid the threesome in the sitting room. Ruth wins but, to her surprise, Cathbad soon joins her in the kitchen.

'Hi, Ruthie.'

'You look terrible.'

'I've been driving for four hours. I came as soon as I heard.'

'How did you hear?' Ruth doesn't know what she's expecting. That the druid grapevine has been in action, that Harry Potter sent an owl, that Cathbad read the news in the tea leaves. But the truth is far simpler.

'Judy told me,' says Cathbad. 'She rang almost as soon as it happened.'

Ruth can believe this and it confirms what she has already suspected: Judy is sure that Cathbad is Michael's father.

'I'm sorry,' she says now.

Cathbad looks at her. His thin face makes his eyes look unfathomably dark. 'We'll find him,' he says. 'The spirits are so strong in Michael. They'll protect him.'

Ruth is glad that Cathbad has this certainty to comfort him. If Kate were missing and someone told her that the spirits were protecting her, she'd hit them, but maybe Judy doesn't mind this kind of stuff. She certainly didn't seem to have much patience with Nelson's more practical approach.

'I'm worried about Judy,' she says. 'She seemed to be almost in a trance until you came.'

'She's gone into herself,' says Cathbad. 'She's trying to keep it together for Michael's sake.'

'Darren's been trying to look after her,' says Ruth. She wants to ask Cathbad to be kind to Darren, to respect his relationship with Judy – and with Michael – but she doesn't seem to have the words. Luckily Cathbad's sixth sense is still in working order.

'I won't rock the boat,' he says. 'If that's what you're thinking.'

'Good,' says Ruth. A thought strikes her. 'Where's Thing?'

'In the car,' says Cathbad. 'I'll get him in a minute.'

That's all the house needs, thinks Ruth, a mad bull terrier. But Thing is actually the sweetest of dogs and, who knows, he might give them all something to talk about. She pours milk into the cups. The tea looks odd, muddy and almost opaque. Still, she doesn't suppose for one second that anyone will drink it.

'Where's Hecate?' asks Cathbad, taking the tray from Ruth.

'Asleep upstairs.' For once, she doesn't correct Cathbad about the name. If Michael is found, she thinks, she'll never worry about such trivial things again.

Nelson leaves soon afterwards. He is needed at the station but promises to call back later. He also says that Michael's disappearance will be covered on all news channels.

'That's good,' says Darren. 'The more publicity the better.'

'More limelight for Tim,' sneers Judy.

'Tim's with the search team,' says Nelson. 'I'll do the TV.'

At nine o'clock, Clough drops round to report on the search. He too looks exhausted, barely pausing to exchange greetings with Ruth (who answered the door) before hurrying into the sitting room. He shows no surprise at seeing Cathbad, or Thing, who jumps to his feet, tail wagging.

'All right, Michael?'

Ruth had forgotten that Clough always calls Cathbad by his given name. Darren gives a start.

'Michael?'

'It's my baptismal name,' says Cathbad. 'No-one really uses it anymore.' He glares at Clough.

Judy, though, is oblivious to anything but the news. She questions Clough intently. The house-to-house team have come up with nothing but there was one sighting of a short-haired woman putting a child in a car. The witness gave the car colour and make but couldn't come up with a number-plate.

'Are all units on to it?'

'Top priority,' promises Clough. 'We'll find them.'

Judy says nothing. She must knows the odds of this better than anyone. She asks complicated questions about funding and man hours. Clough tells her that the helicopter search will begin again at first light. It's the first time that anyone has suggested the possibility that Michael will still be missing in the morning. Darren covers his face with his hands. Judy doesn't react at all. She has shown no emotion since the storm of weeping in Cathbad's arms.

'We can get local search teams going too,' says Clough. 'People will want to help now it's been on the news.'

'What about a psychic?' asks Cathbad. 'Have you consulted a psychic?'

'No,' says Clough with exaggerated patience. 'We haven't contacted a psychic.'

Judy turns on him, eyes flashing. 'Well, do it! I thought you said you wouldn't leave any stone unturned.'

'OK, Judy,' says Clough. 'Anything you want.'

'Madam Rita from Yarmouth is very good,' says Cathbad.

Ruth leaves at ten. There's nothing she can do for Judy, who seems oblivious to everyone, except perhaps Thing, who is now sitting beside her with his head on her lap, eyes liquid with sympathy. Nelson is due back in an hour and Ruth thinks she should remove Kate before he starts lecturing her about bedtimes. Cathbad helps carry Kate to the car.

'I'll call in the morning,' says Ruth.

'I'll let you know anyway as soon as we have news.'

Ruth looks at Cathbad, impressed, despite everything, by his certainty.

'Please do,' she says. 'I'll be . . . I'll be thinking of you.'

Cathbad smiles as if this isn't the worst cliché in the world. 'I know you will, Ruthie. Thank you.'

'Bye Cathbad.'

The drive home is quiet and oddly comforting. Safe in her car, with Kate sleeping in the back, Ruth doesn't feel that she has to think about Judy or Cathbad or Michael or what will happen if the search teams fail to find the abductor. She only has to think about changing gear and turning the wheel. New Road is pitch black but, as she gets closer to her house, she thinks that she sees some little lights far out towards the shore. They are moving in a wavery, uncertain way, first this way and then that. Cockle pickers? Druids celebrating the solstice six days too late? Or just the last vestiges of the June sun? 'The west yet glimmers with some streaks of day.' Where's that from? *Macbeth*, she thinks, a play far too full of bloody babes and murdered children for her liking.

The security light comes on as she carries Kate to the front door. Tonight, though, Ruth finds herself disliking its searchlight glare. She preferred the darkness in the car. While it's still night there is still a chance that they will find Michael. Morning will bring the helicopter and the house-to-house search and heartbreak for Judy.

Putting Kate down on her bed Ruth finds herself

envying her parents. They would know what to do in these circumstances. They would kneel down and pray. They would ask God to protect Michael and restore him to his parents, all three of them. But Ruth can't do this. She wants to, she wants to so badly that she actually kneels down on the floor of Kate's bedroom next to the building bricks and discarded teddies. She wants to pray but she can't because of the little niggling reason of not believing in God. Ruth doesn't believe that a benevolent power is shaping her destiny. She doesn't believe in anything much apart from nature. Cathbad would say that Nature herself is a kind goddess but Ruth doesn't agree. Erik used to quote a poem about seeing rocks ground into powder and seas sucked dry. Ruth didn't know what he meant at the time but she thinks she does now. Everything, in the end, turns to dust.

Ruth gets to her feet, covers Kate with a blanket and tiptoes into her own room. She lies down on her bed but doesn't feel like sleep. She listens to Radio 4 for a while but even *Today in Parliament* has lost its power to soothe. Eventually she picks up the book beside her bed. *Poems* by Alfred Lord Tennyson. 'To Ruth,' reads the inscription, 'with very best wishes from Frank Barker.'

Ruth opens a page at random.

The hills are shadows, and they flow
From form to form, and nothing stands:
They melt like mist, the solid lands,
Like clouds they shape themselves and go.

'The hills are shadows,' Ruth repeats. She has no idea what it all means or why Frank gave her this book 'with very best wishes'. All she can do is hope and pray to the uncaring goddess that Michael will come home safely.

CHAPTER 28

Ruth is woken by a pounding on the door. In her sleep-fuddled state she thinks it must be Cathbad, coming to look for Michael, or Nelson asking for safe passage across the marshes. 'I'm coming,' she mutters, feeling for her slippers under the bed. She pads downstairs and opens the door and sees, not a wild-eyed druid in a cloak, but a balding middle-aged man and two boys carrying sleeping bags.

'Say hi to Auntie Ruth,' says Simon.

Ruth gapes at him. In the horror of Michael's disappearance she has completely forgotten her alter-ego as Auntie Ruth. Is it really Tuesday already? She asks Simon the time.

'About eight, I think. We started at four a.m.' he adds, as if this is normal behaviour.

'Well, you must be starving,' says Ruth, making an effort. 'Come in and have some breakfast.'

'Where's Kate?' asks Jack, her younger nephew. Ruth is grateful that he, alone of all her family and friends, seems capable of getting her name right.

'She's normally awake by now,' she says, 'but she had a bit of a late night. We both did.'

'Been out partying?' asks Simon. He is wearing a huge backpack that makes him looks like a snail. Maybe he too is carrying all his worldly goods with him.

'Not quite,' says Ruth.

She takes Jack upstairs. Kate is sitting up in bed and seems enchanted to see her cousin. She last saw him at Christmas and Ruth is surprised that his name comes so readily to her lips.

'Jack,' she beams. 'My Jack.'

'Hi, Kate,' says Jack from the doorway. It's quite sweet really.

Ruth and the children come back downstairs to find that Simon has filled the sitting room with camping equipment. There's a tent, two more rucksacks, two cold boxes and what looks like an inflatable football pitch.

'Thought we could have some footie games on the beach,' says Simon. 'It's quite small in here, isn't it?'

'Yes,' says Ruth. She goes into the kitchen to make breakfast. She's pretty sure that Simon will expect the full English. It's a concept which, like footie, is almost entirely alien to her.

She puts bacon under the grill, listening to Jack and George teaching Kate how to blow up a beach ball. Without thinking she switches on the radio.

'Police in Norfolk are still searching for Michael Foster, the one-year-old boy abducted yesterday. Michael was taken from his childminder's house in Castle Rising by a woman claiming to have authority from his mother. Childminder Deborah Squires described the woman as being in her twenties or early thirties with short, dark hair. Police are also searching for the owner of a white Skoda seen in the area yesterday. Detective Chief Inspector Harry Nelson of the Norfolk CID called on the public to come forward if they have any knowledge of the woman or the car. The parents are desperate. They love Michael and just want him back safely.'

It sounds so unreal, hearing it on the news. She didn't even know that Michael's surname was Foster. And Detective Chief Inspector Harry Nelson of the Norfolk CID sounds like a stranger, not the man she saw yesterday, worrying that Kate would be too hot under the wedding-present duvet. She's so deep in thought that she doesn't notice Simon appearing in the doorway. He's still wearing his backpack.

'We heard that on the radio coming up,' he says. 'About the little boy being abducted. Terrible isn't it?'

'It's my friend's baby,' says Ruth. 'My friend's baby is missing.'

Simon stares at her as the kitchen fills with the smell of burning bacon.

Nelson has never known the team so subdued. In any case that involves children the black humour and cheerful callousness that usually accompanies police work vanishes overnight, but the abduction of Michael is something else altogether. Clough is close to tears. 'I just saw the little fellow last week,' he keeps saying, as if this is relevant to anything. Even Tim, who hardly knows Judy, looks haggard. He has worked all night with the search teams and is now collating the reports. Tanya offers to go over to see Judy, 'just for support.' 'No,' says Nelson, 'I need you here.' He knows that Tanya is the last person Judy would want to see. The trouble is, the best officer at all that touchy-feely stuff is Judy herself.

Nelson begins the briefing by showing a map of the King's Lynn and Castle Rising area.

'The playground is here. The car was seen here. Judy lives here, the Grangers' house is here. It's likely that the abductor lives or works in easy reach of these places. I'm starting a fingertip search this morning. But we have to think: is there anything that links Judy and the Grangers, apart from geography?'

'The abductor may have known that Judy was part of the team looking for Poppy,' says Tim.

'She wasn't high profile,' says Clough. 'She didn't do the TV appeal.'

'Yes, but when they brought Poppy back they could have looked in and seen us in the house,' says Tanya, not without a certain self-importance.

'But how would they know that Judy had a child?' says Clough. 'They knew the childminder and everything.'

'It would be fairly easy to find out,' says Nelson. 'We know that this person plans ahead.'

'I checked Justine Thomas again,' says Clough. 'She went out with the kids twice, once to the park by The Walks and once to pick the eldest up from school – what's his name, Bailey. It's hard to see how she can have found time to abduct Michael.'

'Even so,' says Nelson, 'she fits the description. What sort of car does she drive?'

'Sporty little Golf. Silver.'

'That's pretty close to white. We're looking for a white car.'

'But a Golf's not a Skoda,' objects Tanya.

'The public always gets cars wrong,' says Nelson. 'Actually they're pretty similar. Volkswagen owns Skoda. Either way, we should keep her under surveillance.'

'There could be a link with the Donaldson case,' says Tim. 'Justine Thomas gave information that helped us charge Bob Donaldson. Judy was closely involved in the case.'

'Good point,' says Nelson. 'Let's check on Bob's movements. He's out on bail.' This is a sore point as Nelson opposed bail, but Nirupa Khan had prevailed.

'I thought we were looking for a woman,' says Clough.

'A slight man could be mistaken for a short-haired woman,' says Nelson. 'Bob had reason to resent both Justine and Judy. Follow it up, can you Tim?'

'Sure,' says Tim. 'I think this whole Childminder thing is key. Maybe we're looking for an ex-childminder or someone wrongly accused of abusing a child in their care.'

'You sound like Madge Hudson,' says Nelson, but he has to admit that Tim has a point. Madge's (unsolicited) opinion is that the capital C in Childminder implies that this is the abductor's whole identity. 'It's as if they're a superhero, like Batman or Zorro. Someone righting wrongs whilst in disguise.'

'So we're looking for someone in a bat suit,' Nelson had said.

Madge had smiled tolerantly. 'The definite article is significant too. *The* Childminder. Like The Terminator or The Avenger. It's indicative of a monomaniacal sense of self-importance.'

'OK,' Nelson says now. 'Tanya, you do a trawl for any police cases involving childminders. Highlight anything in this area or anything involving abduction.'

'Right,' says Tanya. Normally she would complain about being given office-based work but today no-one is complaining.

'Cloughie, you check up on the door-to-door. Make sure the uniforms haven't missed anything.'

'OK, Boss.'

'Is anyone at Judy's house?' asks Tanya.

'The house is under surveillance,' says Nelson,' but I want police presence to be low-key. Remember the abductor returned Poppy at a time when the house was quiet. I'm hoping that they may do the same again.'

'We ought to see how she is,' says Clough.

'I will,' says Nelson. 'I'll call in now. After all, someone needs to keep Cathbad under control.'

*

But Cathbad is not at the house. He is sitting on a bench outside the Old Customs House with his daughter. As it's still early the only other inhabitants of the quay are an aged tramp and a woman who appears to be giving a solo aerobics exhibition.

'I couldn't do that,' says Maddie, as the woman bends backwards into a croquet hoop shape.

'Why would you want to?' says Cathbad.

'I'm not fit enough,' says Maddie. 'I used to do Tai Kwando every day.'

Cathbad doesn't think that Maddie looks strong enough for martial arts. She's too thin for a start. Cathbad is thin himself but he's wiry, he thinks of it as a typical Irish peasant's build. There's a frailty to Maddie, as if a strong wind would blow her down. As least she's eating, they stopped to buy croissants and hot chocolate on the way. Cathbad couldn't eat so Maddie demolished both croissants. She drinks her chocolate the way all teenage girls do, hunched over it like a vagrant. Cathbad is horrified to find himself wanting to tell her to sit up straight. Good God, he's turning into a fascist.

'Is there any news?' Maddie asks. 'About the little boy?'

Cathbad shakes his head. He, Judy and Darren stayed up all night, sometimes dozing in their chairs but always alert for that knock on the door, the knock that never came. At dawn Judy had become hysterical. Darren called the doctor who prescribed tranquillisers. Two pills washed down with coffee turned Judy back into a living statue, staring blankly out of the window. At eight Cathbad could bear it no longer. He had called Maddie and suggested a walk by the river. He hadn't meant to tell her about Michael – now isn't the time after all – but, draining the last of her drink, Maddie says, 'This little boy, the policewoman's son, is he yours?'

Cathbad nods. He doesn't trust himself to speak.

'So he's my half-brother.'

This aspect of things hadn't occurred to Cathbad. He ponders the self-obsession of teenage girls. Even in this situation, Maddie thinks of things only in relation to herself. But, then again, aren't we all like that really? It's just that as we get older we hide it better.

'Yes,' he says. 'He's your brother. I can't wait for you to meet him.'

To her credit, Maddie does not betray any unease at this remark. She doesn't look overjoyed at the prospect, it's true, but she doesn't seem to doubt that the meeting will one day take place.

'I've got enough brothers,' she says. 'I'd like a sister.'

'Do you still miss her? Scarlet?'

Maddie turns to look at him. He had forgotten about her extraordinary eyes. Photographs do not do them justice.

'What do you think?'

'If one should say to you that the soul perishes like the body, answer that the flower withers but the seed remains.'

'And that's meant to be helpful, is it?'

'You sound like Nelson.'

'I liked Nelson,' says Maddie. 'He was kind to me but he seemed sort of sad.'

'He's had a tough few years.'

'And I love Rebecca. We've become like sisters.'

Cathbad wonders if Maddie is going to spend her life in search of sisters. He says, 'Why did you come back here, Maddie?'

'You told me to speak to Nelson.'

'I meant on the phone. I didn't mean turn up and become one of the family.'

'Is that what he said? That I'm like one of the family?'

'I haven't talked to him about you. He's got other things on his mind at the moment.'

'Oh yes. Michael. Well . . .' She turns to Cathbad and he can see the sun gleaming through her hair. She looks like an angel. 'Well, I came because of Liz. I knew she was innocent, you see. And I suppose I always felt guilty about Liz. Because of Bob.'

'What do you mean, because of Bob?'

'Bob and I were lovers. Three years ago, when I was sixteen.'

CHAPTER 29

'Are you joking?'

Clough looks embarrassed, an expression that seems entirely wrong on him. He looks down. 'It's just that I promised Judy.'

'Judy wanted you to consult a psychic? *Judy?*'

'Cathbad was there. Michael Malone. It was his idea.'

'It would be. So when is this woman coming in?'

'This afternoon.'

'Well, you'd better deal with her. I haven't got the time to waste.'

'OK, Boss.'

They are standing by the river bank watching the search teams wade through the shallow water. It's a beautiful spot, the river winding into the distance, fields lush with summer grass, the castle in the background.

But neither Nelson nor Clough is getting any pleasure from the view. This is one of the grimmest parts of any search. The idea that a child may have wandered to an accidental death seems almost worse than the thought of a faceless abductor. If Michael is with The Childminder, there's a good chance that he's still alive. If he's here, on the other hand, his little body trapped in the reeds or floating unobserved out to the sea, that's too horrible to contemplate. But the search must be done. Tom Henty, the sergeant in charge, has made his report and is now preparing to brief the group of volunteers who have gathered on the bank, clutching rakes and hoes and anything else they think might be helpful. Nelson appreciates that they want to help but he can see an eagerness on some faces, a suppressed excitement, that makes him want to arrest the lot of them for wasting police time.

'Come on,' says Nelson. 'Let's get back to the station. We're doing no good here.'

'How was Judy when you saw her?' asks Clough.

'In a pretty bad way. She'd taken some tranquillisers. I couldn't get anything out of her. Darren was coping with everything. I only hope he doesn't crack up too.'

'Was Malone there?'

'Apparently he'd taken the dog out for a walk.'

Clough grunts, as if this unsupportive behaviour is only to be expected but, as they approach their car, they see Cathbad coming towards them.

Nelson thinks that Cathbad looks worse than ever. He's not wearing his cloak and, in jeans and a t-shirt, looks thin and unkempt, an impression only reinforced by the presence of a bull terrier on a string lead. Cathbad must really care about Judy, thinks Nelson, to look so utterly derelict.

'Hallo, Cathbad. Hallo, Thing.' Nelson tries to contain the dog's enthusiastic welcome. At least somebody's smiling, he thinks.

'Any news?' asks Cathbad.

Nelson shakes his head. 'We've got all teams on to it though. We'll find him.' If he keeps saying it, it must be true.

'I've contacted the psychic,' Clough cuts in. 'Can you tell Judy?'

The faintest trace of a smile crosses Cathbad's drawn face. 'I'll tell her. Thanks Dave.'

'Been out for a walk?' says Nelson.

'I met up with Maddie in Lynn,' says Cathbad. 'Just felt I had to get out of the house for a bit.'

'She's a nice girl, Maddie,' says Nelson. 'Michelle and I liked her very much.'

'She likes you too,' says Cathbad. 'Thanks for looking after her.'

There's a slightly awkward pause. A group of policemen pass by with German Shepherds on leads. Thing strains and pants, wanting to follow them.

'She did say one thing that disturbed me though,' says Cathbad. 'I think I ought to tell you. It's about Bob Donaldson.

'This is police harassment,' says Bob. 'I could sue.'

'I'm simply asking you to account for your movements yesterday afternoon,' says Tim. 'That's hardly harassment.'

'This is to do with that missing child, isn't it? You think I did it.'

'That's an interesting conclusion to jump to,' says Tim. 'Why would I think that?'

Bob looks away. They are sitting in his study, a room crammed with computers, speakers and sundry pieces of electronic equipment. Bob Donaldson has a disconcerting habit of looking at his laptop when he speaks, as if he's reading the words from the screen. Tim wonders whether this is a distancing device or if it means something more sinister. The laptop is on Bob's left and, according to a neuro-linguistic programming course that Tim once attended, looking to the left can indicate that the subject is lying.

'I know you've all got it in for me,' says Bob. 'You fitted me up for one crime, why not pin every child murder in the last twenty years on me?' His voice rises hysterically.

'That seems rather an extreme reaction,' says Tim. 'I just asked what you were doing yesterday afternoon.'

Bob sighs and his eyes flick up and left. 'I was here, working.'

'Anyone with you?'

'No. Aliona was at college.'

'What time did she get back?'

'She stayed over with a friend.' There's a pause and Bob frowns at the blank screen. 'These last few weeks have been hard on her.'

I bet they have, thinks Tim. Teenage girl shacks up with her lecturer to find that he's accused of child murder. He wonders whether Aliona will ever come back to the house in Pott Row.

'So you were on your own?'

'Yes. Do you want to search the house for the missing baby? Do you think I've buried him under the patio?'

'That's a very odd thing to say,' says Tim. 'What makes you think he's dead?'

'I know what you're doing,' says Bob. 'You're trying to

trap me. I've studied the lot of you. You're the clever one, the policewoman's the nice one and there's a thuggish one too. Then there's the boss, DCI Nelson.' Now there's real hatred in Bob's voice. 'It's Nelson who's really got it in for me. He's in league with her.'

'Who? Liz?'

'Liz? No.' Bob dismisses his former wife with a wave of his hand. 'Justine.'

'Justine Thomas? Why would she have it in for you?'

'Oh.' Bob's tone is almost careless. 'Because I dumped her for Aliona.'

Tim stares at the man opposite him, balding, slightly stooped, dressed in a beige cardigan and jeans that look as if they've been ironed. How come I can't get a girl-friend, he thinks, and this guy has them fighting over him?

Aloud he says, 'You had an affair with Justine?'

'Well, it wasn't really an affair. Just a few nights, you know.'

'But she took it badly when you left her for Aliona?'

'Yes. She kept saying that she felt guilty over Liz as if Liz was the only thing that kept us apart. So when I left Liz for Aliona, Justine was furious.'

'Did Liz know? About Justine?'

'God no! We kept it really quiet.'

But the partner usually does know, thinks Tim. Even if they don't know what they know.

'When you were,' he pauses to think of the right word, 'seeing Justine, did you get to know the children she was looking after?'

'Poppy and co?' says Bob. 'Yes, I met them in the park a few times. At least I never saw the older boy but I got to know the younger ones pretty well. Especially Poppy. I had a really soft spot for Poppy.'

Tanya gazes at the screen. Registered childminders, childminders' forum, how to become a childminder. Who knew there were so many of these people out there? She gets caught up in a long forum discussion between mothers complaining about childminders, nannies and nurseries. She wants to post a comment saying 1. learn to spell and 2. why have children anyway, but decides that this would probably be unhelpful. Tanya can't imagine ever having a baby. She wants to be Norfolk's first woman police commissioner and to have a penthouse apartment with white carpets and glass furniture. Neither of these ambitions would be compatible with becoming a mother. Luckily her boyfriend, a fitness instructor, agrees. Fatherhood is also not compatible with fourteen-inch biceps.

Despite all the complaints, there seem to be very few

cases of childminders actually charged with abuse. Eventually Tanya narrows it down to three in the East Anglia region. She wastes half an hour looking at a case where a teenage childminder testified against abusive parents before realising that it took place in Boston, Massachusetts and not Boston, Lincolnshire.

Tanya arranges her three cases in the list format preferred by Nelson.

1. Norwich 2008. Childminder accused of abusing her charges by leaving them outside in the garden as punishment. Margaret Rogers, aged 50, was given a suspended sentence and barred from working with children.

2. Cambridge 2009. Childminder Sally Fisher went on the run with a four-year-old child in her care. She claimed that the child's Turkish parents wanted to take him out of the country. Given a three-year sentence for child abduction.

3. Chelmsford 2010. Boyfriend of childminder Vicky Lomis found to have previous conviction for sexual abuse. No question of him abusing any of Ms Lomis's charges but Ofsted were criticised for not investigating his background.

She doesn't think that any of these will yield useful leads but at least she has something to show for the morning's work. She sighs. She often finds Judy exasperating (Tanya likes rules as much as the next person but Judy is *obsessive* about procedure) but the thought of something happening to her baby is just too horrible. That's another reason for remaining childless, thinks Tanya as she prints out her list, it saves you a whole lot of heartbreak.

Madame Rita turns out to be a sensible-looking woman in her mid fifties. She places a large handbag on the desk and puts on a pair of bifocals.

'Did you get my message? Have you got something that belongs to the little boy?'

Clough hands over a cuddly giraffe. He hadn't wanted to ask Judy for one of Michael's possessions so had phoned Cathbad, who turned up at the station an hour later with the giraffe in a plastic bag.

Madame Rita holds the toy to her chest and closes her eyes. Clough watches her nervously. Is she about to go into a trance and start frothing at the mouth? They are in Nelson's office so at least they haven't got an audience, but who's going to help him when she starts speaking in a guttural voice and rolling her eyes? He's seen *The Exorcist*. He knows what to expect.

'Why are you looking so nervous?' Madame Rita has opened her eyes and is regarding him with amusement.

'Nervous? I'm not nervous.' Clough attempts a laugh.

'It's nothing to be afraid of, you know.'

Clough doesn't dignify this with a response. Still smiling, Madame Rita closes her eyes again. Clough looks at his watch. Nelson will want his office back for the team briefing at four.

'He's still alive,' says Madame Rita.

Despite his scepticism, Clough finds himself exhaling with relief.

'Are you sure?'

'Absolutely sure. His life force is strong.'

'Do you know where he is?'

'He's close by. An old place. Full of ghosts.'

'No address? Nothing useful like that?'

'The spirits don't deal in addresses, love,' Madame Rita explains kindly.

'Can you tell us anything else? Anything that might actually help?'

'He's with a woman from the spirit world. She's looking after him. She loves little children.'

'Any clues from our world? The one we're living in?'

Madame Rita strokes the giraffe. 'He's in a room with

low ceilings. I can see a tower. Look for a red heart and a white lady.'

'A red heart and a white lady?'

'That's as specific as I can be.'

Nutcase, thinks Clough. 'Well, thank you very much Mrs . . . Madame Rita.'

Madame Rita picks up her bag. 'He's alive, Sergeant Clough, but be quick. She can't protect him forever.'

Smiling gently, she places the toy giraffe in his arms.

'A tower? Where could that be?'

Clough is amazed that the boss is taking the psychic's remarks this seriously. Perhaps it's a sign of how few leads they have. Anything, even the ravings of a mad-woman, is better than nothing.

'There's Cow Tower by the river,' he says. 'It's a bit out of the way though.'

'There are lots of church towers in the old town,' says Tanya.

'Yes,' says Clough. 'There's that famous one in Tomb-lands. St George's. I went to a wedding there once.'

Nelson sighs. 'It might be worth checking out. Just have a look at any houses that overlook the towers. But not a word to the press, mind. We don't want to look desperate.'

No-one makes the obvious comment. 'Maybe we're taking it too literally,' says Tim. 'She could mean a tower block, or a pub called the Tower.'

'You know all the pubs, Cloughie,' says Nelson. 'Is there one called the Tower?'

'Not that I know of. You need Irish Ted. He knows every pub that ever sold a pint.'

'Give him a ring. He knows the area too. Don't mention the psychic. Just ask for his help.'

'OK, Boss.'

'Right.' Nelson pulls his notes towards him. 'We're still looking for the white Skoda. We've followed up all possible sightings but they all check out. Tanya, did you have any luck with the childminders?'

Tanya hands him her list. Nelson grunts with approval. 'Nicely arranged, Fuller. Sally Fisher's the one that fits the profile best. Is she still inside though?'

Tanya shakes her head. 'She got out earlier this year. Released on license.'

'Might be worth checking to see if she has any links with the Grangers or with Judy. I can't see it though. There's a difference between abducting a child you know and love and snatching random children.'

'There are lots of childminding forums,' says Tanya. 'I could keep a watch. See if anything weird crops up.'

'Good idea,' says Nelson. 'Might even be worth posting something yourself about this case. Be careful though, we don't want to be done for entrapment.' He turns to Tim. 'What did you get from Bob Donaldson?'

'Well, he hasn't got an alibi for yesterday afternoon. He seemed very hostile but perhaps that's only to be expected. I can't see a link to Judy but there is a connection with Justine Thomas.' He explains.

'Bloody hell,' says Clough. 'What the hell do all these women see in him?'

'My thoughts exactly,' says Tim.

'People say that about Michelle and me,' says Nelson. 'Sometimes beautiful women like ugly men.'

He thinks that Tim is looking at him rather oddly. Probably thinks that his tone is too light-hearted. If only he knew how heavy his heart was.

'And there's something else,' says Nelson. 'Maddie Henderson had an affair with Bob when she was only sixteen'

'That's not relevant to this case, though, is it?' says Tim.

'Shows you the kind of guy he is,' says Clough. 'I wouldn't trust him further than I could throw him. Which might be a long way, the bloody wimp.'

'I agree with Cloughie,' says Nelson. 'He took advantage of Maddie when she was most vulnerable, just after her sister died. He took advantage of Justine but never planned a future with her. Both these women were connected to young children. I think we should search his house.'

'Nirupa Khan will be on our case,' warns Clough.

'Let her make a complaint to me,' says Nelson. 'I'll tell her where to get off. This is a child abduction case, we can't discount anything or anyone. And time's running out.'

Unconsciously he looks at the clock over the door. The other officers follow his gaze. Five o'clock. Michael has been missing for more than twenty-four hours.

CHAPTER 30

Ruth is sitting in the garden with her brother sharing a bottle of wine. This situation is rare enough to seem almost surreal. Ruth can't remember the last time that she sat down with Simon, just the two of them – not since he married Cathy anyway. And despite the ever-present gnawing anxiety over Michael, she has to admit that it's rather pleasant. Kate has pitched her tepee next to the giant blue tent which now takes up most of the garden and the cousins are playing a very complicated game called 'Squeak piggy squeak'. There's no doubt that Kate is doing most of the squeaking. Her squeals of delight would be deafening the neighbours, if Ruth had any. As it is, Flint has retreated in high dudgeon to the top of the apple tree, where he sits like a disgruntled owl, gazing at Ruth reproachfully.

'Kate's having a brilliant time,' says Ruth. 'Jack and George are really kind to spend so much time playing with her.' It's true that the boys have been kind, going into the sea with Kate – holding her hands, one either side – playing football on the beach with her and swinging her along on the walk home. The trek back from the beach, which often ends in tears, today was pure joy.

Simon watches his sons, eyes screwed up against the setting sun. 'They're good boys,' he says. There's a pause, during which Kate's shrieks rise to new levels, and then he says, 'I've left Cathy.'

Ruth, who has by now guessed as much, says, 'Why?'

Simon spreads out his hands. The gesture would look melodramatic were it not for the expression of acute misery on his face. 'I don't know, Ruth. It's just . . . I'm forty-five and I've started thinking is this all there is to life? A boring job, a three-bedroom house on Shooter's Hill, golf on Saturday, roast meal on Sunday. I mean, what's it all for?'

Ruth can't answer this one. She has never lived the kind of life described by Simon, though she has sometimes wanted to. Also, she's not the biggest fan of her sister-in-law, but it seems a bit harsh that she should bear the brunt of Simon's existential mid-life angst.

'But that's not Cathy's fault, is it?' she says. 'Have you talked to her about how you feel?'

Simon takes a slug of wine. 'Oh yes, I've tried to talk to her but you know Cathy. As long as she's got a nice house and a nice car and the latest cupcake-maker, she's happy. She told me that I was just being stupid.'

Ruth can't understand the latest craze for dressing up like a Fifties housewife and making cupcakes (though she can understand eating them), but she still feels that this is a rather patronising statement. She decides that Simon needs shaking up a bit.

'Have you told Mum and Dad?' she asks.

Simon groans. 'No. They just think that I've taken the boys on holiday. Cathy won't tell them because she thinks I'll come to my senses. It'll kill them.'

Ruth says nothing. The news won't kill her parents but there's no doubt that it will come as a body blow. Their favourite child; perfect Simon with his perfect marriage and perfect children. A tiny ignoble part of her can't help feeling slightly pleased that she'll no longer be the family black sheep. In fact her life (no husband but no divorce either) might seem almost virtuous by comparison. Another, even smaller, part of her thinks: what if Nelson woke up one morning and realised his marriage was over? He too seems to live a suburban half-life, especially now that his daughters have left home. What if he, too, thought, 'Is this all there is?'

'What are you going to do?' she asks at last.

'Find somewhere on my own,' says Simon. 'Think about things. Maybe travel a bit. Do you know, I've never been anywhere. Just Spain and Greece on holiday. I've never been to America or China or Russia. I've never climbed a mountain or swum with dolphins.'

Again, Ruth feels slightly impatient. A sudden urge for world travel is fine for an eighteen-year-old. Ruth had it herself and remembers her mother's horror at her backpacker trips with her university friends, contrasting them with Simon's carefully organised package holidays. But Simon isn't eighteen. He's a forty-five-year-old man with two children.

'What about the boys?' she says. 'What are they going to do when you disappear to a kibbutz for a year?'

'Who said anything about a kibbutz?' says Simon. She'd forgotten how maddeningly literal he was. 'I just want to have some fun.'

Fun. There's that word again. Why does everyone suddenly think that they're entitled to have fun all the time? Ruth thinks of Judy, sitting in her little house waiting for the phone to ring. She doesn't want to have fun, she just wants her child to be alive. The thought makes her voice harsh.

'Can't you wait until the boys are grown up?' she asks. 'Then you and Cathy can go and climb Mount Kiliman-jaro together, or whatever it is you want to do.'

Simon laughs hollowly, draining the last of his wine. 'Can you imagine it? When we went to Center Parcs, Cathy wouldn't come on a bike ride in case it messed her hair up. I can't exactly see her on a Polar expedition.'

Mount Kilimanjaro's in Africa, thinks Ruth. She seems to remember that Simon didn't take geography O-Level. In fact it wasn't long after O-Levels that Simon met Cathy, even then not a girl known for her adventurous instincts. Ruth remembers how shocked she was when she heard Ruth, aged sixteen, talking about going to a music festival. 'They haven't got proper toilets in those places,' Cathy had warned. 'And there's nowhere to plug in your hair dryer.'

'But you've always known what she's like,' she says now. 'It's not fair to blame her for being the way she is. She hasn't changed.'

'She hasn't changed,' says Simon. 'But I have.' Ruth has no answer to this and is relieved when the boys come over and nag their father to start the barbecue.

*

Cathbad holds Judy in his arms while Darren watches. It's like the realisation of all his darkest fantasies. Except that Judy is sobbing about wanting to be dead, both Cathbad and Darren are crying and Thing is whining to be let out.

'Nelson says there's still a good chance they'll find him,' says Darren, for the hundredth time.

Judy turns her head. Her face is a mask of anger. 'For Christ's sake, Darren. Nelson is full of *shit*. He doesn't know anything.'

Cathbad has noticed before that Judy's anger seems particularly directed towards Nelson. He's not sure why this is unless, on some level, Judy expected Nelson to be able to protect her and, by extension, Michael. But he does know that Judy is feeling guilty. He can feel the negative emotion everywhere. It's poisoning them all, he thinks.

'She kept Poppy alive, she'll keep Michael alive,' Darren says desperately.

'Shut up!' screams Judy. She collapses onto Cathbad's chest.

Cathbad looks at Darren over Judy's head. 'I'm sorry,' he says.

CHAPTER 31

'Norfolk police are still searching for one-year-old Michael Foster who was abducted from his childminder's house on Monday afternoon. Police search teams and local volunteers worked through the night in the village of Castle Rising, near King's Lynn, but no traces of the missing child have been found. The detective in charge of the case, DCI Harry Nelson, said that he was still hopeful of a positive outcome. He wouldn't comment on similarities to the abduction, just two days earlier, of fourteen-month-old Poppy Granger. Poppy's disappearance led to another extensive police search but she was returned anonymously to her family.'

Ruth reaches out a hand and switches off the radio. She doesn't want to hear any more. Although she knows that Cathbad would have called her if there had been any developments, she had still hoped to wake to good news. She thinks how alien it all sounds: 'police search teams', 'detective in charge', 'returned anonymously'. But she knows the truth. She has seen the desperation – and, worse, the resignation – in Judy's face. She has sat in the house with Michael's parents, listening for the knock at the door. And she knows the detective in charge intimately. She can see beneath the policeman's phrase 'still hopeful of a positive outcome'. She knows that Nelson won't be hopeful, there is a deep vein of pessimism in him, but she also knows that he'll never give up. He won't rest until Michael is found, alive or dead. And, if it's the latter, if Nelson has to return Michael's body to Judy, she thinks it may well kill him.

She had set the alarm for six. She hadn't wanted to waste any time not knowing. All last night, while Simon burned sausages and the boys tried to build a tree-house, her mind kept going back to the little house in Castle Rising. When she finally carried an exhausted Kate up to bed, she had looked at her phone for the hundredth time. No news. A second night with Michael out there somewhere in the dark. She gets up and goes into Kate's room. Her daughter is still asleep, arms and legs splayed out in abandonment. She doesn't know that Michael (her future husband, according to Cathbad) is still missing. Ruth looks out of the window at the blue tent squatting in the garden. Simon might say that his life is empty and has no meaning (two phrases that kept recurring well into the second bottle) but does he know how lucky he is, just to be sleeping with his sons at his side?

But Simon isn't sleeping. To Ruth's surprise, when she comes downstairs, he's already up, drinking tea and reading through her proofs.

'I still can't believe that you've written a book,' he says.

'Can't you?' says Ruth airily. She finds it pretty hard to believe herself.

'Mum and Dad are really proud of you, you know.'

'Are they?' Now this *is* a surprise.

'Yes. Mum tells everyone about it. It's embarrassing sometimes, the way she shoehorns it into the conversation. "Do you want your windows cleaned, madam?" "No, but did you know my daughter's written a book?" Goodness knows what she'll be like when the book actually comes out. She'll probably wear it round her neck like a pendant.'

Ruth laughs. Simon could always be funny, she remembers now. It's a bigger shock to know that her mother's actually proud of her, actually shows off about her to other people. She's so used to thinking of herself as a disappointment to her parents that this new perspective will take some adjustment. To give herself time she asks Simon if he'd like another cup of tea.

'I've made a pot,' he says. 'It should still be hot.'

A pot? Ruth didn't know that she actually owned a teapot.

'Mum always makes a pot,' says Simon now, half-laughing and half-defensive.

'God, Simon. It's true what you said last night. You really do live on the edge.'

Ruth pours her tea, thinking that this is easier than she thought, sharing the little cottage with Simon and the boys. Still, it probably helps that they're sleeping in the garden and that it's only for a few days. This reminds her of something. She goes back into the sitting room.

'Do you think you'd be able to look after Kate tonight, Simon? I've got to go out. It's to do with work.'

Simon looks pleased. 'Of course. I'm glad to be able to help. What are you doing?'

'Well, there's this TV programme, you see . . .'

When she woke up, Ruth had found a text message. Not from Cathbad but from Frank. *Looking forward to seeing you tonight.* Of course, the night filming at the castle. Ruth had looked down at her phone, feeling both pleased and slightly shocked that Frank could send such a message at such a time. But of course Frank doesn't know about her link with Judy even if he has heard about the abduction on the news. *Looking forward to seeing you tonight.* What an inappropriately cheery sentiment. And what does he mean by it anyway?

Simon, though, is impressed. 'So we're going to see you on TV? Wow. Wait till I tell Mum.'

'I'll probably only be on screen for half a second,' warns Ruth, but she too is rather pleased at the thought of more maternal approval.

'I'll tape it and play it back on a loop,' says Simon.

Ruth is about to say something – something about mothers and families and how nice it is, despite everything, to have the prospect of a day together – but Kate calls her and the moment is lost. Just as well, thinks Ruth, as she climbs the stairs. One of the few things she and Simon have in common is an extremely low embarrassment threshold.

Clough never thought that he'd feel guilty about being in a pub but he does. He can just see how it would look: *Callous copper in boozer while his colleagues hunt for missing baby.* And it's so early, barely eleven o'clock. Even Clough, who holds the station's record for downing pints, doesn't feel like a drink at this hour. But Ted, who requested the meeting place, orders a pint of Guinness and a chicken and ham pie.

'Are you sure? They do good beer here.'

'No, you're all right. I might have a pie though.' However bad things are, Clough can always eat.

The pub is almost empty although the two old men in the corner look as if they've been there for several days. Clough wonders if he should check them for signs of life. Ted, on the other hand, looks around him with every appearance of pleasure.

'Great place, this. Hasn't been dolled up too much.'

'You can say that again.'

Ted takes a long draught of beer. Despite himself, Clough feels his throat contracting. Maybe a half wouldn't hurt.

'So, what did you want to ask me?'

'I'm looking for a pub called the Tower or Towers. Do you know anywhere like that?'

Ted leans back, thinking. He's a big man, bald and burly with tattooed forearms. Clough has to admit that he doesn't look like an academic. If he had to place Ted he'd say builder or farm worker. Or a criminal.

'I don't think so,' Ted says at last. 'It's not a very common pub name. There's the Rook near Downham Market. I think that refers to the chess piece.' He sees

Clough's blank expression and explains. 'The castle in chess is sometimes called a rook.'

'What about other towers? Church towers, water towers. That sort of thing.'

Ted looks at him curiously. 'Is this about the little boy that's missing?'

'I can't tell you any more,' says Clough. 'But it's important.'

'There are a few towers around the city walls, the remains of the old fortifications. Cow Tower's one of those. Then you've got the church towers like St Giles in Norwich. Cromer Church has a famous tower too.'

'We've thought of all those,' says Clough. 'I just wondered if you could think of anything . . . unusual.'

'Well, there's The Devil's Tower, of course.'

'What?'

'Out Carrow way, by the bridge. There's a famous painting of it. You must have seen it.'

'Don't go much on paintings myself.'

'No-one knows why it's called The Devil's Tower. It may be one of those devil-crossing-the-bridge stories. You know, the devil demands a forfeit for crossing the bridge. Sometimes it's gold, sometimes it's your immortal soul, sometimes it's your first-born child.'

Michael is Judy's first-born, thinks Clough. Somehow he doesn't fancy his pie any more.

'It looks bad, Harry. Surely you can see that.'

Nelson counts to ten, and when that's not nearly enough starts again. It's bad enough that he has to waste valuable time having a meeting with his boss but now Whitcliffe seems to be implying that the loss of Judy's child is a public relations disaster for the force.

'It is bad,' agrees Nelson. 'Especially for Judy.'

'Indeed.' Whitcliffe puts on his caring face. He is tanned and handsome from the Tuscan sun and Nelson is hating him more than ever.

'But the fact is,' Whitcliffe is already moving on, 'we've had two child abductions in a week and we're no nearer to finding the perpetrator.'

'We got some leads,' says Nelson. 'A description, the car, the babygro.' They have traced the pink babygro worn by Poppy to a smart shop in Thetford. This is as far as their luck goes, the owner of the shop was unable to add much to their identikit. 'I think she was youngish. I think she had short hair.'

'Not enough, Harry,' says Whitcliffe. 'What are your guys doing out there? I heard that Sergeant Clough had consulted a psychic.'

Cursing Clough, Nelson says, 'That was a favour for Judy. We're not placing any reliance on anything the woman said.' He prays that Whitcliffe doesn't look up and see the words 'tower, red heart, white lady' on the whiteboard.

'I'm glad to hear it. What if the press got wind of it?'

'They won't.' He crosses his fingers behind his back.

'Well, we need to get out there and reassure the public that we're doing our best.'

'I'll make another statement.'

'No,' Whitcliffe starts fiddling with the silver paper-knife on his desk, always a sign that he's feeling uncomfort-able. 'I think Tim should do it. You always look as if you're about to head-butt someone.'

'Fine by me.'

'No offence, Harry, but you're not exactly a TV natural.'

'None taken.' Nelson doesn't give a toss about TV. He knows that he doesn't come across well and that Tim does. All that matters is that someone may be watching, someone who knows something about Michael. And if that person is influenced by hearing an appeal from a handsome policeman, let's get Tim into make-up at once.

'We haven't had much reaction to the parents' TV appeal. We need to get them to do another one. The trouble was, Judy looked too calm.'

Nelson grinds his teeth. 'She was trying to hold it together, for God's sake. Can't you see that?'

Whitcliffe smiles understandingly. 'You're very closely involved, Harry. I respect that. But if Judy could just show a little more emotion for the cameras . . .'

'If she cracks up altogether, will people prefer that?'

'Of course not,' says Whitcliffe. 'But people need to feel involved. They need to feel that they have a personal stake in finding Michael.'

'We've had lots of volunteers for the search.' Bloody rubberneckers, he adds to himself.

'That's good,' says Whitcliffe. 'But we need a breakthrough. Time's running out.'

Does Whitcliffe think Nelson doesn't know this? 'If it's the same person that took Poppy Granger,' he says, 'there's a good chance that they'll be looking after him.'

'But crimes escalate, Harry. You know that. This person abducted a child and got away with it. Next time they take it further. I think we have to prepare ourselves for some bad news management.'

Nelson looks longingly at the paper-knife.

Ruth and Simon have taken the kids to Yarmouth. The boys expressed a desire for 'amusements' and Ruth felt that this was the nearest place that provided anything

close to Thorpe Park or Alton Towers (two venues mentioned with enthusiasm). She was right in one way. Jack
and George made approving noises as soon as the pier
and rollercoaster came in sight. Kate, though, is another
matter. As soon as she sees the flashing signs exhorting
her to try the Silver Falls and the Wacky Racers and the
Ride of Death, she starts to cry. Ruth had forgotten how
much the place modelled itself on Blackpool.

'It's OK, Kate,' says George. 'You're too little to go on
anything really scary.'

But Kate just stands in the middle of the Golden Mile
and howls. Fellow holiday-makers regard her with mingled sympathy and irritation. The boys fidget with
embarrassment. Jack puts on his dark glasses.

'What's the matter with her?' asks Simon.

'We went to Blackpool last year,' says Ruth. 'She was
frightened by something that happened on the Pleasure
Beach.' This doesn't really do justice to the horror of that
day but Ruth can't bring herself to tell the whole story
to Simon.

The word 'beach' gives her an idea. Beyond the iron
monsters of the roller coaster and the Waltzer and the
bumper cars is the sea, miles of flat grey sand filled with
more traditional seaside entertainments.

'Come on sweetheart,' says Ruth, 'Let's go and find some lovely donkeys.'

Leaving Simon and the boys queuing up for the roller-coaster, Ruth and Kate go in search of donkeys. Soon Kate is swaying happily on a dun-coloured steed called Kevin and Ruth is running along behind, trying not to lose her shoes in the sand.

'Look at me, Mum!'

'I am looking,' pants Ruth. She ought to take a photo. Oh hell, where's her phone?

When they get to the pier the donkeys turn round and Ruth gets her picture: Kate grinning happily, all tears forgotten, sun hat over one eye. The sky is the kind of blue that you associate with Italy, not Norfolk. Suddenly Ruth feels like crying. It's not fair that she has Kate in her Little Miss Sunshine top and pink sun hat. Judy should have Michael. They should all be here together – Nelson, Cathbad and Darren too – in a happy dysfunctional family.

'Keep looking, Mum!'

'I can see you,' shouts Ruth, wiping away tears and falling over a sandcastle.

Judy is lying down. People keep telling her to lie down, try to get some sleep, so it seems less trouble just to do what they want. It's odd how people think that being horizontal will somehow take away the pain of losing her only child. And she has lost him, she's sure of that. If a missing child isn't found in the first few hours, the prospect is always bleak. Poppy was a miracle and miracles don't happen twice. It's funny, she feels completely calm now. She has faced the worst that can possibly happen and honestly doesn't care whether she lives or dies. In a strange way it makes her feel strong, invincible. She could jump out of the window and maybe she would fall to her death and maybe she would fly. It doesn't really matter which.

She can hear Cathbad and Darren talking downstairs. It doesn't even feel odd any more to have them both in the house. In a strange way, it seems right that they should both be here. She's dimly aware of feelings drifting under the surface. She knows that though no-one can actually comfort her, being with Cathbad makes things marginally less terrible. She knows that guilt about Darren is adding to her guilt about Michael. She knows that Cathbad knows this. She doesn't worry about the future because, without Michael, there will be no future.

She shuts her eyes and actually falls into an uneasy, fluttering sleep. She dreams of Michael, and even in her dream she knows this is a privilege – to see and hear him, she even imagines that she can feel him, the firm softness of his cheek, the feathery warmth of his hair. She is in the park, pushing Michael on the swings, higher and higher. A seagull is hovering overhead, crying and calling. Then the seagull turns into a man with huge, white wings. He swoops down on Michael and they fly away together. Michael is calling 'Mummy! Mummy!' Judy wakes with a start.

There's someone at the door. She hears the words 'found something' and she forgets that she is resigned to the worst, that nothing bad or good can ever happen again, and she runs downstairs, her heart beating a timpani of hope and fear.

'Have you found him?'

CHAPTER 32

It's Nelson. He makes a gesture as if warding something off.

'I need you to be calm, Judy. This might not mean anything bad.'

Judy is aware that Cathbad and Darren are standing on either side of her.

'Have you found him?' she asks again, her voice completely steady.

'No but . . .' Nelson takes a step nearer and holds up a plastic bag. Inside is a blue-and-white-striped t-shirt. Darren lets out a strangled sound.

'It was found in the river,' says Nelson. 'It had floated downstream to Keeper's Wood. It's his then?'

In answer, Judy reaches out to snatch the bag. She holds it to her chest.

'We'll need to take it to the lab,' Nelson says gently. 'Just to do a few tests. Then you can have it back, I promise. And, remember, the abductor changed Poppy's clothes. Ten to one they'll have done the same with Michael.'

Darren clears his throat. 'Did you . . . did you find anything else?'

Nelson shakes his head. 'But we're still looking. We've got a full description of what he was wearing.'

Judy says, 'She's got his bag too. It had a change of clothing in it. Debbie gave it to her.' She tries not to blame Debbie but this is particularly hard, imagining the childminder happily handing over Michael and his precious day-bag.

Nelson holds out his hand and, slowly, Judy passes over the T-shirt in its bag.

'We'll find him,' he says, speaking directly to her. 'We'll find him if it kills us.'

Judy doesn't explode as she usually does with Nelson's promises. She looks at him almost as if she feels sorry for him. 'Goodbye,' she says. And she turns and goes back into the house.

By six o'clock Ruth is ready to drop. She is in her room, supposedly getting ready for the night shoot, but all she can think about is how good it would be to collapse on her bed and go to sleep. She doesn't dare even sit on the bed, partly because of the temptation to shut her eyes and partly because it's freshly made. Jack and George are going to share the double bed tonight and Ruth is going to sleep in Kate's room. Though neither of them actually mention the child abductions there's a general feeling that it would be better to have everyone sleeping in the house. Simon insists that he'll be quite happy on the sofa. Ruth can hear him downstairs. He's making spaghetti bolognaise, assisted by all three children. Ruth hadn't realised just how domesticated her brother was but it appears that he can cook, put up tents and make a dozen pots of tea a day. Cathy should try to hang on to him, she thinks. But presumably Cathy is trying to do just that in the only way she knows how; by pretending that nothing's happening. Simon hasn't mentioned his domestic arrangements again but Ruth knows this whole trip is part of his rebellion against his wife. What would Cathy really hate? Simon getting on with his snotty sister, that's what.

And they are getting on well. They have had a great day. The boys loved Yarmouth and Kate was even persuaded to go on some of the gentler rides with them. They all ate fish and chips on the pier and the children made a giant sandcastle on the beach. Simon was an undemanding and tactful companion. He understood both that Ruth was sad about Michael and that she didn't want to talk about it all the time. He entertained the children and was prepared to carry Kate when she got tired. Seeing Kate on her uncle's shoulders reminded Ruth of Frank and their walk along the river at Saxlingham Thorpe. She has had another message from him. *See you later. Frank.*

Now she checks her phone again. No message from Cathbad. Is she really expecting to hear that Michael has turned up, safe and well? She can't help hoping. They listened to the five o'clock news in the car. 'Police are still searching . . .' Ruth thought of Nelson, Clough and Tanya, how desperate they would be by now, how frantically they would be following up the smallest lead. Do they have any more leads, apart from the 'Childminder' letter? Ruth types 'childminder' into her phone. Like Tanya earlier, she gets a string of results: forums, helplines, horror stories from the past. Where would you start? Presumably Nelson has police files and past cases at his disposal, but how do you find someone who wants to stay hidden? How do you find a child when the world is full of children?

Looking at herself in the mirror, Ruth thinks of Mother

Hook. Was she Frank's wronged woman or something altogether more sinister? Does the so-called Childminder honestly think that they are looking after Michael? In a way Ruth hopes so, because that way he will stay safe. But if whoever it is wants Michael that much, maybe they'll never give him back. All day some lines from the terrible Book of Dead Babies have been echoing in her head.

You never spoke yet we miss your silence

You never walked but we miss your step.

Is this what Judy is condemned to? A lifetime of remembering? Ruth looks at her stricken face in the glass. How on earth are they all going to get through this night?

It's nearly eight when she arrives at the castle. Filming is due to start at nine. It's still light but the air has that charged feeling that you sometimes get at twilight, as if every object has been outlined in pencil. She can see lights being set up on the battlements and tents being erected in the castle grounds. It looks like the beginning of a siege.

Aslan is waiting for her in the car park.

'Dani says can she have a word? In the truck.'

Ruth remembers how, on the first day of filming, she'd been surprised that people like Dani and Corinna didn't have trailers, places where they could receive visitors while lounging on sofas surrounded by flowers. She began to realise that *Women Who Kill* was being filmed on a pretty strict budget. The cameramen travel with their equipment in a truck and, for longer shoots, there's a catering van and a portaloo. Most meetings seem to be held in Corinna's hotel room, which is apparently the biggest. Ruth remembers her embarrassment at the only meeting that she attended, to find herself sitting on the double bed wedged between Dex and Frank while Aslan crouched in the en suite bathroom.

Now, in the back of the truck, Corinna looks furious to find herself perched on a packing case with a tripod in her ear. Frank is leaning against the door, obviously enjoying himself. Aslan ushers Ruth up the ramp like someone loading a horse into a trailer.

'Where's Dani?' Corinna is demanding. 'It's bloody rude keeping us waiting like this. Night air is very bad for me, I have to be very careful of my chest.'

Ruth can't prevent an involuntary glance at Corinna's chest, magnificently exposed in black velvet.

'Shall I get you a coffee?' asks Aslan. This, after all, is what he does best.

'No thank you, darling,' says Corinna, with dangerous silkiness. 'I just want to see our bloody director.'

'Now you see me,' comes Dani's voice. She bounds up the ramp carrying a clipboard. She's wearing jeans and a thin T-shirt. Her only concession to the evening chill is a woolly cap.

'Just want to give you a few notes,' says Dani, ignoring both Corinna's hostility and her ostentatious shivering.

'We've got a lot of extras in,' she says. 'So I'd like you, Ruth, to brief them.'

'Brief them?'

'Tell them the right way to hold a trowel, that sort of thing. Nearest most of them have ever come to digging is on Cromer beach.'

'Couldn't Phil do it?' says Ruth. 'He said he was coming tonight.'

'No,' Dani shakes her head authoritatively. 'I get the impression that Phil doesn't get his hands dirty too often.'

Frank laughs. 'And Frank,' Dani whirls round. 'I want a scene of you talking about the hanging. We can make those signposts look like gibbets. I want you to say that an innocent woman may have been killed.'

'Excuse me,' Corinna tosses her head. Ruth finds herself looking at the cascading curls and wondering if she can see the join. The metal truck positively reeks of expensive scent. 'Excuse me, but I'm going to take advantage of the night setting to give a bit of *atmosphere*. The sort of atmosphere for which *Women Who Kill* is rightly famous.'

'Are you going to mention the hook?' asks Ruth.

'Yes, Ruth.' Corinna turns on her. 'Our viewers will have tuned in to see a programme about one of the most evil women who ever lived, a woman who had a hook for a hand. So, yes, I am going to mention the hook.'

'And Frank is going to mention that she may have been innocent,' says Dani. 'It'll make good TV. Dex, is that you?' The lead cameraman has appeared at the truck door.

'Yes, Captain.' The crew sometimes treat Dani the way Nelson's team treats him.

'A word.' And Dani sweeps out of the truck.

'Frank!' calls Corinna without looking at Ruth.

'Coming ma'am.' Frank levers himself upright.

'Can you give me your arm to make-up, there's a darling? The ground's wretchedly uneven.'

'Sure,' says Frank, proffering his arm. 'Will you be OK, Ruth?'

'Yes, Ruth,' says Corinna over her shoulder. 'Don't forget to visit make-up yourself, dear. You could do with a bit of toning down.'

*

Ruth decides to give Corinna time to get through make-up. She also wants to give her decidedly flushed face a chance to tone itself down. She sits on the bank below the castle and watches as the sound engineers unload their equipment. Tents are being set up on the grass and she can see a sign saying 'Extras. Queue Here.' The castle is obviously expecting an invasion. She checks her phone. No message from Cathbad.

'Hi, Ruth.'

It's Dex, the friendly cameraman. As usual he looks perfectly relaxed, Styrofoam cup in hand, camera on shoulder.

'Looking forward to tonight?' he asks.

'Not particularly.'

'It'll be all right. Corinna will put in a command performance.'

'That's what I'm afraid of.'

'You mustn't mind Corinna. She's had a tough life.'

'She has?' A successful acting career followed by being a full-time mother to two supremely gifted children doesn't seem exactly roughing it to Ruth.

'Yes. Her husband left her a few years ago. She practically had a nervous breakdown.'

Was this when she lost her hair, wonders Ruth. She wonders about the nature of Dex's relationship with

Corinna. On set, they often argue but they are also often to be seen deep in discussion. Could Dex have consoled Corinna after her husband left? He's curiously ageless with his shaven head and earrings but they could be almost the same age.

'I don't think I'll have much more to do with Corinna,' she says. 'I'm just digging today.'

'That's right,' says Dex. 'You concentrate on the archaeology. It's safer that way.'

Ruth looks up at the cameraman. His face is in shadow and, just for a second, the camera on his shoulder gives him a monstrous misshapen look. Richard the Third, the bottled spider.

Then Dex smiles and the shadow passes. 'Have fun,' he says.

The hair and make-up area has been set up in a little room at the front of the castle usually used for lockers. Ruth sits feeling uncomfortable as the make-up artist, a kindly woman called Mary-Anne, puts rollers in her hair. The windows are leaded so it's hard to see out but she can hear people going past all the time. Mary-Anne is being driven distracted by extras coming in and wanting her to powder their noses.

'You can finish with me,' says Ruth. She hates people

fiddling with her hair and face. She has her hair cut once every six months and often trims the ends herself. She remembers being excruciatingly embarrassed throughout her one and only visit to a spa (to celebrate one of Shona's thirty-ninth birthdays). Besides, it's torture to sit still when all the time she's longing to check her phone. It feels so wrong to be sitting here in this scented room with a towel round her shoulders while Judy is . . . but Ruth can't even imagine what Judy is doing.

'No, I've got to have you looking beautiful,' says Mary-Anne seriously, slathering on orange foundation. 'Dani says there are going to be some close-ups.'

Take more than a bit of foundation, thinks Ruth.

'Hi, Ruth.' Frank appears in the doorway.

'Hi.' Instinctively Ruth raises a hand to her hair but Mary-Anne gently pushes it away.

'Hallo, Frank,' says Mary-Anne. 'Come for some make-up?'

'One of your colleagues has just offered to take some of the grey out of my hair,' says Frank, sitting beside Ruth.

'Grey's OK on a man,' says Mary-Anne. 'Silver fox and all that.'

Ruth notices that Frank doesn't seem to mind this description. She also muses that there isn't a female equivalent to 'silver fox'. 'Grey-haired old bat' doesn't cover it somehow.

Frank is lounging beside her, watching her reflection in the mirror. He has this in common with Nelson, if nothing else; when Frank is in a room it instantly feels smaller. Ruth feels nervous, acutely conscious of the curlers and her orange skin. Frank seems to feel no need for conversation. Mary-Anne is humming along to the radio, a cheery little Lana Del Ray number. 'Video Games'.

'Is Phil here?' asks Ruth at last.

'Yes,' says Frank. 'Wafting around looking very pleased with himself. I bet he's already made the trip to make-up.'

'He spent about an hour in here,' says Mary-Anne. 'He was very particular about the bags under his eyes.'

'Man's a complete asshole,' says Frank. 'What does his girlfriend see in him? I mean, she's gorgeous.'

Ruth is used to men reacting to Shona in this way. Cathbad, for example, exempts Shona from all Phil's idiocies. 'Poor Shona,' he'd comment. 'He probably made her do it.' But Shona, as Ruth knows, is tougher than she looks.

'She loves him,' she says now. 'God knows why.'

'Well, love is hard to explain,' says Frank. There's another awkward silence while Lana sings about heaven and bad girls and the blue dark. Mary-Anne is taking out the rollers, which seem attached to Ruth's skull by tiny wires.

'I can't believe how many people are here tonight,' says Ruth, wincing.

'Yeah. The production company are really pushing the boat out. I'm surprised. Must be costing them a fortune. The crew'll be on golden time. That's why they're all so cheerful.'

'Who do you think will win? Corinna's "most evil woman who ever lived" or Dani's "she was innocent all along"?'

Frank grins. 'Dani. After all, she'll be the one doing the editing. And she's determined, Dani. She usually gets what she wants. '

'But you think Jemima Green was innocent too.'

'You bet. That's another reason why our version will win. Because I'll be better than Corinna.'

He grins again but Ruth can see something rather steely in the blue eyes reflected in the mirror. She thinks that Frank, too, is used to getting what he wants.

'It's a pity that we haven't got any hard evidence,' says Ruth. 'If we could only find Joshua's body . . .'

'We'll have to go on another trip,' says Frank. 'How's Kate?'

'She's fine,' says Ruth. 'We went to Yarmouth today. With my brother and his children.'

'Oh, you said your brother was coming to stay. Must be good to catch up, huh?'

'Yes,' says Ruth. 'It has been good.'

'Are the two of you close?'

Ruth hesitates. Are she and Simon close? They are close in age, they have endured a childhood characterised by their parents' religious certainties. They share both a defensiveness about their lower-middle-class origins and a desire to escape them. They are both intelligent, cynical and somewhat insecure.

'We haven't seen that much of each other recently,' she says. 'But we are close. Yes.'

'I'd like to meet him.'

Ruth finds herself blushing again. She imagines the pink clashing horribly with the orange. What does *that* mean? That Frank wants to get to know her family? That he likes spending time with random English people? Maybe he's just missing his own children. As she thinks this, she sees Kate on her donkey and has a sudden excruciating pang for Judy. She simply must check her phone.

'Are you OK?' asks Frank. 'You look a bit worried.'

Ruth opens her mouth. She wants to tell Frank that she's tired and sad, that she can't work up any enthusiasm for night digs or Mother Hook while her friend's baby is missing. But just as she is about to speak, Mary-Anne removes the towel with a flourish.

'There you are, Ruth. All finished.'

'Come on,' says Frank. 'Let's go and join the action.'

Outside, the excitement is mounting. The arc lights make the castle look unreal, like a stage set. Ruth thinks again of a siege. The shadowy figures scurrying across the bridge could be an army ready to attack, the giant wheeled cameras battering rams and trebuchets. Ruth wonders if the castle has seen anything like this in all its nine-hundred-year history. Surely William Rufus and gang can never have imagined a time when their fortress would be invaded by make-up artists and sound systems engineers. The medieval overlords who turned the place into a prison could never have thought that the mere memory of one of those prisoners would be enough to create this jamboree, this modern *son et lumière*.

She checks her phone. No messages.

By the castle wall Corinna, wearing a black hooded cape that makes her look like a Scottish Widow, is being filmed talking straight to camera. Ruth can't hear what she's saying but she's got a good idea that it will include the words 'horror', 'evil' and 'monstrous.' Frank watches with a half smile on his face. They cross the bridge and approach Dani's dig. It's being set up near the seating area where the service for the Outcast Dead was held, but now the space has been transformed into an arena of bright lights and white tents. The finds are going to be examined live on camera. 'What if there aren't any finds?' Ruth had asked earlier. 'Your friend Phil has brought some coins and stuff over from the university,' said Dani. Phil is now standing by one of the tents being briefed by Dani. Ruth can sense his excitement from a hundred yards away. Shona, in her mini skirt, is standing at Phil's side flicking back her hair.

The extras are gathered by the trench, milling around and tripping over cables. Ruth recognises a couple of faces from local archaeology groups – they will certainly know how to dig – but the others are a motley collection of history buffs and people who just fancy being on television. Some of the older ones have brought shooting sticks and thermos flasks, obviously used to the rigours of filming. The younger ones are taking photos of each other and squealing whenever a furry microphone goes past.

Dex appears, camera on his shoulder like a monkey. 'What a circus,' he says.

'How's it going?' asks Frank.

Dex shrugs. 'All right. Dame Judi Dench over there is giving a command performance.'

Ruth guesses that he's talking about Corinna. There's no sign now of any special understanding between the two. 'How much more is there to film?' she asks.

'Just the digging scene, your mate in his tent and then Frank's words of wisdom.'

Ruth wants to tell him that Phil's not her mate. Before she finds the words, Dani prances over, carrying a megaphone.

'All right Ruth?' Without waiting for answer. 'Let's get this show on the road.'

Dani needs to stand on a box to be seen. Watching her, Ruth thinks of a boy prince leading his army into battle.

'Right everyone,' she shouts. 'I'm going to film you digging this trench here. This is Ruth. She's a famous archaeologist.' Ruth is glad that it's too dark for anyone to see her blushing. 'She's going to tell you how it's done.'

Ruth does her best: she tells them not to sit on the side of a trench, to trowel back carefully and to keep the sides of the the trench sharp and clean. She explains that digging is both methodical and incremental. 'Everything has to be done with the utmost care because every little piece helps put the picture together.'

Two runners divide the extras into groups. One set is told to get into the trench, the other is led away to work in Phil's tent. Ruth can hear Phil shouting, with no need for a megaphone. 'Now folks, look at me . . .'

Ruth prepares to climb into the trench. Normally she'd be wearing coveralls but she was pleased when Dani said that this wouldn't be necessary. All the same, it's getting chilly, maybe she should put on her new cagoule. She runs her hands through her hair, which has already lost its careful curls. Oh well, with any luck it'll be too dark to see her properly. Ruth pulls the cagoule over her head. While she's still struggling to free herself from its waxy folds, a voice says, 'Ruth?'

Ruth forces her head out through the top. Her hair is now completely ruined. A woman is standing in front of her. She looks vaguely familiar, tall and attractive with a fashionable elfin haircut.

'Ruth Galloway? I'm Liz Donaldson.'

Donaldson? For a moment Ruth's mind is blank and then she remembers. Liz Donaldson. Cathbad's friend. The woman wrongly accused of killing her babies.

'I just wanted to thank you for trying to help me,' Liz Donaldson is saying.

'I didn't do anything much,' says Ruth, 'but I'm glad it worked out in the end.' She winces, thinking that this is a poor way to describe Liz's husband being charged with the murder of their child. But Liz doesn't seem to notice, 'Cathbad's told me all about you,' she says. 'I came here especially to meet you.'

This seems slightly strange to Ruth but she smiles politely. In the distance she can hear Phil asking for 'complete silence please'.

'Cathbad says that you're close to DCI Nelson,' says Liz.

'I know him,' says Ruth cautiously.

Suddenly Liz leans forward. Just for a second, her face changes completely, as if she has pulled on a mask. 'Well, tell him this. He'll never know the truth. And he'll never know the truth about baby Michael either.'

And she turns and disappears into the crowd.

CHAPTER 33

Nelson is on his way home when Ruth calls. He doesn't really want to go off-duty, not with Michael still missing, but he has to get some sleep or he'll crack up. He was up all last night and he knows that soon he'll reach that pitch of tiredness when he'll start making mistakes. But at the moment he feels hyper-alert, as if every nerve is tingling. His skin feels prickly and loud noises make him jump. When he got into his car the door gave him an electric shock and it's as if the volts are still surging through his bloodstream.

His phone is on hands-free but he still swerves into the road when it rings.

'What is it? Is Katie OK?'

'She's fine. She's with Simon.'

'Simon?'

'My brother.' Impatiently. 'Look Nelson, I'm at the castle doing some filming. I've just seen Liz Donaldson and she said something a bit weird. It might be nothing but, then again, it might not.'

'I'm on my way,' says Nelson. He's already looking for a place to do a U-turn.

Liz Donaldson. She is linked to both Justine Thomas and to Judy. Judy was the lead officer on her case and made an effort to bond with her. Clear as day, Nelson can see Liz leaning towards Judy in the room smelling of lilies and death: *Do you have children? Keep him safe.* Liz knew that Judy had a child. She may have resented him – and Poppy too – simply for being alive. He can see Liz as if she's still sitting in front of him. The intelligent eyes and strong jaw. The short hair.

He calls the station to ask for backup.

Ruth puts away her phone, thinking hard. She can no longer see Liz Donaldson amongst the crowd of extras. It's completely dark now and the arc lights are illuminating the castle battlements. They are rather sinister, these powerful beams of light shooting into the darkness, they remind Ruth of a Nazi rally. The areas that escape the searchlight seem doubly dark. Ruth climbs into the trench, feeling uneasy.

'Come on Ruth,' shouts Dani. 'Let's have you at the front.'

Ruth takes up her position and starts to dig. Where is Liz? Is she in the trench behind her or has she melted away, having said what she came to say. Was Ruth mad to call Nelson? Liz has every excuse for seeming slightly unhinged, after all. It's just . . . Ruth had expected to *like* Liz Donaldson. Several people had told her that she was a lovely person, but she hadn't liked her. She had found her odd and scary. *He'll never know the truth. And he'll never know the truth about baby Michael either.* Is it possible that Liz has abducted Michael? Maybe she wants, in some deranged way, to replace her lost baby. On paper, Ruth would feel sorry for any woman driven to do something so desperate. But she hadn't felt sorry for Liz. She had been afraid of her.

The scene seems to go on forever, but eventually Dani yells 'Cut' and Ruth climbs stiffly out of the trench. The summer night has turned cold and she pulls up the hood of her cagoule. She looks around for Nelson but there's no sign of him in the shifting crowds. Is he coming or has he decided that she's just a hysterical woman, seeing things in the shadows? 'I'm on my way' he'd said. She doesn't like to admit it but the sight of Nelson steam-rolling his way through the extras would be incredibly comforting right now. She checks her phone. No new messages.

'Ruth!' She looks up to see not Nelson but Frank, emerging from the huddle around the catering van. His hair gleams silver in the moonlight. He is welcome too, especially as he's carrying two Styrofoam cups of coffee.

'Gosh, thank you,' she says. 'You're an angel.'

'Am I?'

He says this seriously, as if making a genuine academic query. Ruth covers her confusion by taking a long swig of coffee. She chokes.

'The angel will now administer first aid,' says Frank, patting her on the back.

'Thank you,' Ruth mops her streaming eyes.

'Crying Ruth?' says a voice. 'It's not as bad as that.'

Dani has joined them. Ruth has noticed before how she often defers to Frank on set. Now she's asking him what he thought of the earlier segment with Corinna. 'I thought it was quite good.'

When Dani has darted away, in a hurry as always, Frank turns to Ruth. 'When Americans say something's 'quite good' they mean that it's very good, when Brits say it, they mean 'so-so'. That had me confused for years.'

Something clicks in Ruth's brain. A tiny piece of a puzzle begun long ago.

'Is Dani American?'

'Yes,' says Frank. 'She's from Boston originally.'

Ruth puts down her coffee and fumbles for her phone. 'No mobiles on set,' shouts someone but Ruth ignores them. She's not particularly good with smart phones at the best of times and now her fingers are almost too cold to type. It's dark too and the screen keeps going blank. She almost cries with relief when a beam of light illuminates the keypad. She looks round to see Frank shining a torch at her.

'I always carry one on night shoots,' he explains.

Perhaps he really is an angel, thinks Ruth. Painstakingly she types 'childminders' into 'search', trying to find the sites that she visited a few hours earlier. Where the hell is it? Why are there so many bloody childminding forums? Oh God, she's scrolled forward instead of back. Has she gone too far? No, here it is.

It's a case from fifteen years ago.

Teenage childminder Danielle White was a key witness for the prosecution in the case of Boston lawyers Charles and Maddison French accused of killing their eighteen-month-old son Jackson. Miss White testified that she had often seen bruises on Jackson's body and had been worried enough to call the police. 'They didn't listen to me,' she says, 'I was only the babysitter. If they had, it might have saved Jackson's life. I'm heartbroken. I really loved that little guy.'

She remembers her birthday dinner. 'Lots of childminders really care for the kids they look after,' Dani had said. She had cared but she hadn't been able to save Jackson. Dani doesn't have children of her own, she knows. Does she feel it's her duty to protect the babies of working parents like Charles and Maddison French?

'Can you put that phone away?' It's Martin, the assistant director.

Ruth looks up wildly. 'Where's Dani?'

'She had to go back to her digs,' says Martin. 'I'm in charge now. I want to shoot the trench sequence again.'

Clough is now seeing towers at every turn. Nelson sent him off duty at six but, instead of going home, Clough embarked on a tour of the places mentioned by Irish Ted. It's madness, he tells himself, I'm becoming as weird as Cathbad. But what if the lunatic psychic woman was right? What if she really did know where Michael was hidden? *He's alive, Sergeant Clough, but be quick. She can't protect him forever.* Time's running out, you don't need to be a psychic to know that. His colleague's baby is lost and Clough can't just stay at home watching *Top Gear* with a microwave meal. He has to do something.

So Clough drives to Cow Tower and The Devil's Tower and several piles of rock along the old city walls that look more like rubble than fortifications. He checks all these places for white Skodas and short-haired women until he's seeing both in the shadows. Eventually, he gives up and heads back to the A147. Driving down Riverside Road he sees the castle on his right, lit up like Christmas. What's going on there? He vaguely remembers Nelson telling him about some filming at the castle. One of those historical programmes. He thinks that Ruth is involved somehow.

Stuck at the lights, he looks across at the floodlit battlements. Despite living in Norfolk all his life, Clough has never been in the castle. He even managed to avoid the obligatory school trip to learn about Boadicea. But now, looking at it, he's struck by how *castle*-like it is. Just what a kid would draw. A big square like a giant tower.

A giant tower.

Clough performs a screeching hand-brake turn worthy of the boss himself. How the hell is he going to get near the bloody place? Everything's pedestrianised and cobbled and shut off with bollocking bollards. After driving into two dead-ends he stops, frustrated, in the middle of the road. He's in the historical centre of Norwich, all boutiques and oldy-worldy pubs. He's practically parked in the front porch of one such place, a crazy lop-sided building, criss-crossed with ancient beams. A woman is glaring at him from the doorway. Clough raises his hand in apology and starts to back out. As he does so, he looks up at the sign. It shows a deer-like creature bearing the pub's name upon its curly horns.

The Red Hart.

'I've got to go,' says Ruth.

Frank stares at her. 'You can't. Martin wants to shoot the sequence again.'

'I've got to. I can't explain but it's about the missing child. My friend's child. Do you know where Dani's staying?'

'Dani? No. Why?'

'Who would know? Please Frank . . .' Suddenly she realises that she's holding his arm, squeezing it tight. 'Please. It's important.'

'Aisling would know.' Aisling is Dani's assistant.

'Where is she?'

'Up at the castle I think.'

Ruth is running through the crowd of extras, oblivious to Martin's furious shouts. She runs back along the bridge and arrives panting at the castle doors. Where can Aisling be? She's usually one of those people who's everywhere at the same time, popping up at Dani's shoulder with briefing notes, shooting schedules, cold drinks. How can she have chosen this moment to disappear?

'She'll be in the production office,' says a voice behind Ruth. She hadn't even realised that Frank had followed her.

'It's along here. By the make-up room.'

He leads the way into the castle.

Nelson hoots his horn impatiently. In defiance of all the signs telling him not to, he has driven across the bridge – scattering startled extras – and has parked in front of the castle entrance. A sign on the wooden door says, 'Silence. Filming in progress.' Nelson gets out of the car and looks around disapprovingly. The place seems to have been transformed into bloody Disneyland. There are lights and cameras everywhere. The castle grounds are full of people. Someone is selling drinks and burgers from a van. It's like the Golden Mile. Don't they know that there's a child missing?

'Excuse me,' says a voice. 'You can't park here.'

Nelson wheels round. An earnest-looking youth with a clipboard is looking at him rather apprehensively.

'Police,' says Nelson briefly. 'Who's in charge?'

The youth now looks terrified. 'Martin. He's the assistant director. But you can't just . . .'

'Take me to him,' says Nelson.

Ruth doesn't think she has ever run so much in her life. Not since, as an extremely reluctant schoolgirl, she was forced to go on cross-country runs in Eltham Park. She pounds back over the bridge with Frank at her side (not even out of breath, she can't help noticing) and into the Castle Mall, the modern shopping centre that has sprung up beside the fortress.

'Shall I get my car?' Frank had asked.

'No,' said Ruth, 'we'll be quicker on foot. I know where it is.' But now she wonders if she spoke too soon. Norwich town centre is a mixture of old and new, the streets turning back on themselves, ancient timbered houses crammed next to modern shop fronts. The shops are shuttered now and the streets are empty apart from a couple of rough sleepers who look at them curiously. Ruth jogs on, looking down at Aisling's scribbled directions. The Red Hart, near Maddermarket.

They are going uphill now. Who said there were no hills in Norfolk? Ruth stops, clutching her side.

'We should be close,' says Frank. 'She said it was in the old part. These look like fourteenth-century gables. Beautiful.'

But just at the moment Ruth can't see anything beautiful about the old city. The jutting gables seem oppressive, the little alleyways dark and sinister. She imagines it in the time of the plague, raw sewage running in the gutters and doors marked with a red cross.

'I think it's this way,' she says.

Another cobbled street but this one is blocked by a car parked diagonally across the road. Ruth swears, trying to edge past it but Frank grabs her arm.

'Ruth! Look!'

He's pointing. Shining his torch on an inn sign creaking in the breeze above them.

The Red Hart.

They burst into the reception area and there, clearly berating the woman behind the desk, is a dark heavily built man.

'Clough,' says Ruth. 'What are you doing here?'

Clough hesitates and, not waiting for a reply, Ruth rounds on the receptionist.

'Have you got a Dani White staying here? Danielle White?'

'White?' says Clough sharply.

'Yes,' says Ruth. 'Dani White. I think she's got Michael.'

'I can't just show people into guests' bedrooms,' says the receptionist.

Clough gets out a card. 'Police. Open the room. Now.'

The woman looks absolutely terrified but she takes a key from a drawer and leads the way towards a staircase.

'Isn't there a lift?' asks Clough.

'It's a listed building.'

They follow her up three twisting, uneven flights. Clough takes the stairs two at a time but Ruth is out of breath long before they get to the top. Frank is still following her. On the landing, the receptionist fumbles for the right key. 'Hurry!' says Ruth. 'Please hurry.'

Finally the room is open. Clough and Ruth burst through the door, Frank and the receptionist following. The room is low-ceilinged and attractive, with mullioned windows and floral wallpaper. It also contains a baby's cot, a four-poster bed and a reproduction of John Sell Cotman's famous painting 'The Devil's Tower.'

CHAPTER 34

Clough turns on the receptionist. 'So there is a baby staying here.'

The receptionist backs away. She's young, barely more than a teenager. 'She said he was her nephew. She was looking after him for a few days.'

'Don't you know that a child went missing three days ago? Don't you read the papers? Listen to the news?'

The girl puts her hand to her mouth. 'Was that the baby . . .'

'Didn't you ask how she suddenly came to have a child?'

'It couldn't be her,' the girl says, 'I mean, she's to do with TV, isn't she?'

Not for the first time Ruth reflects on the corrosive magic of TV. Dani was trusted implicitly by the hotel staff, just because she was bathed in its reflected glow. Clough looks as if he has more to say on the subject but suddenly Frank shouts, 'Ruth!'

They all turn towards him. He's pointing out of the window. Ruth, peering round Frank's arm, sees a courtyard, obviously now a car park, and a woman putting a baby into the back of a white car. The woman is wearing a jaunty woollen cap.

'It's her,' says Ruth.

'Come on,' Clough bounds out of the room, Ruth on his heels.

Outside, they are just in time to see the white car disappearing around the corner. Clough leaps into his car and Ruth runs around to the other door. 'Call the boss,' says Clough, starting the engine. Ruth hasn't given a thought to Frank but, suddenly, there he is, opening the back door and throwing himself onto the seat as the car lurches forward. 'Who's that?' asks Clough, not looking round.

'He's a historian,' says Ruth.

Clough laughs. 'Just what we need. A bloody historian.'

Nelson is having a trying time up at the castle. The man called Martin, a nervous bearded type, denies any knowledge of Liz Donaldson.

'I don't know the names of all the extras. There must be hundreds here tonight.'

'Someone must know. Isn't there a list?'

'Aisling's got a list. Aisling!' He looks around rather helplessly. 'Aisling!'

A woman emerges from the scrum of cameras and people carrying trowels. Nelson recognises her but without much enthusiasm. It's Shona, Ruth's nutty friend, wearing an extremely short skirt and and expression of avid curiosity.

'DCI Nelson! What brings you here?'

'Business,' says Nelson shortly. He's never had much time for Shona and he can see her loser of a boyfriend hovering about in the background. Still, Shona might at least know where Ruth is. He asks. Shona responds with a laugh and a hair toss.

'Ruth? Oh she was around here somewhere but I think she's gone off with her boyfriend.'

'Boyfriend?'

'Frank, the historian. Have you met him? He's charming. You'd like him.'

Nelson is wondering how to disabuse her of this notion when his phone rings. Ruth. Thank God for that.

'Ruth! Where the hell are you?'

Ruth's voice sounds tight and strained. 'Nelson, we

think we've found Michael. Dani's got him. The producer. We're chasing them now.'

Nelson leaves Shona standing and starts to run back towards his car. Why the hell did he leave it at the end of the bridge? Once again, he scatters film people right and left. Someone swears as they almost drop their camera.

'Who the hell's "we"?' he pants into his phone.

'Me and Clough. Oh, and Frank.'

'Put Clough on the phone.'

'He's driving.'

'OK. I'm on my way. Where are you heading?'

'Towards King's Lynn.'

'Tell Clough to put his tracker on.'

Nelson has reached his car. He is about to put on the siren but has another thought. He calls Ruth back.

'Ruth, tell Clough to keep it low key. No sirens. It's just possible this woman may be returning Michael to Judy, like she did with Poppy. We don't want to spook her.'

There's a muffled consultation. Then Ruth says, 'Clough says he doesn't think she's spotted us.'

'Good. Keep me updated. I'll pick up your route and follow.'

Nelson drives back across the bridge. Parked by the grass he finds the two squad cars that answered his earlier call for backup. Nelson dispatches them both to Castle Rising but tells them not to approach Judy's house. 'Just lie low until you hear from me.' He's finding these precautions very irksome. His instinct is to get into his car and scorch after the suspect. But it's over an hour's drive from Norwich to King's Lynn, if that's where they're heading. He has some time and he must use it. He can't afford to get this wrong.

Luckily Clough's car is one of the few in the force equipped with a tracking device. Nelson gets the co-ordinates from the station and sets off in pursuit. Ruth's right. They've taken the main King's Lynn road. Using his hands-free, he calls Tanya. He tells her to go to Judy's and prepare her for some news. He knows it's a risk sending a police officer to the house because it could spook Dani if she's watching, but, after all, both Judy and Tanya were present when Poppy was returned. Maybe it's a good omen.

Once he's clear of Norwich, the roads are dark and mercifully empty. It's only eleven o'clock but people go to bed early round here. At this rate he'll catch up with Cloughie. God, he wishes he was the one doing the chasing. And what will happen when they catch up with the woman? Who's going to talk her down, persuade her to hand Michael over? Clough's a good copper but subtlety isn't his strong point. And he'll be hampered by the presence of Ruth and Frank. Why the hell has Ruth brought that bloody TV bloke with her? Why is she even bothering with all this TV stuff when she should be staying at home and looking after Katie? It's irresponsible, that's what it is, gallivanting about with Americans, leaving her daughter with that nutty Clara (Nelson has reasons of his own for disliking Clara).

He jumps guiltily when Ruth's name appears on his incoming calls.

'She's taken the turning for Castle Rising.'

So Dani is taking Michael home. As long as nothing happens to make her change her mind. Nelson presses down on the accelerator.

Cathbad, Darren and Judy are watching television. Thing lies at their feet, occasionally sighing heavily. Thing has developed a real passion for Judy, watching her all the time and whining whenever she leaves the room. Really, thinks Cathbad, he has heard of familiars acting out their master's wishes but this is ridiculous. He himself is careful never to be alone with Judy. He even tries not to look at her too much but he's conscious of her all the time. Now the space between them on the sofa seems charged. Cathbad almost imagines that he can see little pluses and minuses hovering in the air. He knows that if he were just to stretch out his hand he could touch her hair, that strand that has escaped from her ponytail, he could . . .

He jumps up. 'Anyone want a cup of tea?'

It seems that over the last three days they have done nothing but drink tea and watch television. The mere action of filling the kettle is comforting, giving the impression that something, at least, is being achieved. Liquid is reaching boiling point, hot drinks are being made. Setting out the cups, finding sugar for Darren, waiting for the water to boil; in those minutes Cathbad allows himself not to think, except about whether he should bring in a plate of digestives. Even being in a separate room is a relief. The kitchen, with its shiny new cabinets, is pleasantly sterile in contrast to the teeming emotions in the rest of the house.

And the television is a life-saver. Sitting in front of the news or a turgid sitcom they don't have to speak. They watch late into the night – nature programmes, re-runs of *My Family*, Open University tutorials, political discussions, ancient horror films. Cathbad knows that, for himself, they all merge into one, a ghastly stream of consciousness involving Robert Lindsay chasing vampires through the *Question Time* studio. But it's a hell of a lot better than having to talk. Darren seems to accept Cathbad's presence in the house without question. In fact, the whole situation is so horribly surreal that it doesn't even seem odd that the three of them are there together, sitting side by side, watching endless television. Darren doesn't seem jealous of Judy's relationship with Cathbad but, Cathbad reflects sadly, there's really nothing to be jealous of. Apart from that first moment when Judy had flung herself into his arms she has treated Cathbad exactly as she treats her husband – as if he's not there. Thing is the only one that she treats with any affection and he responds in kind, leaning against her legs and looking up into her eyes. Most of the time he ignores Cathbad completely. Cathbad feels that he deserves this but it's hurtful all the same.

The kettle has done its stuff and Cathbad carefully pours the water into the cups. He's always very careful with his choices. The best mug, bone china with hollyhocks, for Judy, a suitably macho choice for Darren (Norwich City or Union Jacks) and the worst cup for himself, as a sort of penance. Sometimes he torments himself further by looking at the other items in the cupboard: the Thomas the Tank Engine bowl, the yellow beaker with two handles, the sterilised milk bottles. He doesn't do this now, he knows that he wouldn't be able to bear it. This is the third night and even his faith is starting to wane. Stay strong, he tells himself, stay strong for Judy. The spirits are protecting Michael. But, tonight, his trust in the spirits is beginning to fail. From the sitting room comes the sound of laughter from the *Friends* studio audience. Lucky them. Cathbad doesn't think that he'll ever laugh again.

A knock at the door. Cathbad drops a mug (Darren's) and darts forward. He collides with Judy and Darren in the hall. Cathbad wins the race for the door. Outside is a strange woman in jeans and a dark jacket. She has a lean, sporty look, like a greyhound. Judy seems to recognise her.

'Tanya,' she says without enthusiasm.

'Can I come in?' says the woman called Tanya. 'We think there's been a development.'

'She's not going to Judy's,' says Ruth. It seems like the first time that anyone has spoken for a long time. For the last hour they have all been leaning forward, eyes fixed on the white car in front. Clough is careful to keep as far back as he dares. He doesn't want to alert Dani to the possibility of being followed. At one point it seemed that they had lost her altogether but then Ruth spotted a white shape moving between overhanging trees. 'She's taken a side road.' Clough swerved to follow. 'Thank God it's a white car,' he said.

There are no other vehicles on the Castle Rising road but it's dark and Clough doesn't put on his beam. Dani is driving fast but not too fast. Ruth wonders if this too is part of her mad logic, wanting to care responsibly for the child whom she has snatched from his mother. The castle looms above them behind its high earth wall, square and forbidding. Ruth seems to remember that, like most castles, it has a rather nasty history. Wasn't a queen locked up there once? She'll have to ask Frank. But not now. Now only Michael matters.

Dani drives past the turning to Judy's house, following the castle walls.

'Where is she going?' mutters Clough. Dani has slowed down though and he too kills his speed. What was that thing you learnt in your driving test, thinks Ruth. Only a fool breaks the two second rule. She finds herself saying it under her breath. Only a fool breaks the two second rule. Only a . . .

'She's stopping,' says Frank.

Mirror, signal, manoeuvre. Dani parks carefully by the side of the road. It's dark, open country all around. Clough stops in the shade of an overhanging tree.

'Wait,' he tells the others. 'Don't move.' Ruth hears

him radioing in to Nelson. 'She's stopped. Castle Rising, just beyond the village. Yeah. I will. Yeah. OK Boss.'

Ruth watches as Dani gets a pushchair from the boot of the car. She must have bought it specially, she thinks. She lifts Michael out of the car and straps him into the chair. He's not moving but maybe he's asleep. Ruth's heart is pounding. She wants to jump out and snatch Judy's child back. He's so close. She can see his dark hair and the white blur of his face. But Clough's voice holds her back. 'Wait. Don't move.'

Dani sets off at a brisk pace over the field. Clough swears. 'I'm going to follow,' he says. 'You wait here. The boss is on his way.'

Clough gets out of the car and sprints over the grass after Dani, surprisingly light-footed for such a big man. Ruth watches his white shirt disappearing into the trees. She gets out of the car.

'He said to wait,' says Frank uncertainly.

'You wait,' says Ruth.

She hasn't gone a few hundred yards when she realises Dani's destination. There's a children's play area in the shadow of the castle mound, swings, slides, a roundabout turning slowly in the slight breeze. Calmly Dani lifts Michael from the pushchair and puts him in one of the baby swings. Ruth can hear her singing as she pushes him to and fro. Perfectly normal behaviour, mother and child playing on the swings. Except that it's nearly midnight. And Michael is someone else's child.

Ruth catches up with Clough, who is concealed behind a tree.

'Clough.'

'What are you doing here?' he hisses. 'I told you to wait.'

'I know. Clough, let me talk to her. I know her. You don't. I can persuade her to give Michael back.'

Clough looks at her doubtfully. He's obviously weighing things up. Maybe Ruth would be better, she's a woman after all. And a mother. But what would the boss say? While he's still thinking, Ruth steps forward into the playground.

Dani doesn't even notice at first, she's so intent on Michael. 'Swing low sweet chariot,' she's singing. A very scary song, Ruth has always thought, isn't it all about dying?

'Swing low sweet chariot, coming for to carry me home.'

'Dani!'

Dani glances up. She looks the same. A wiry, nononsense professional who can also look disconcertingly like a little girl. Ruth finds it almost impossible to equate TV Dani with the woman who could do something like this. The Childminder.

'Hi Ruth,' says Dani. 'Has the filming finished?'

This simple query takes Ruth completely by surprise.

'Yes,' she says. 'No. I don't know.' She is aware that, to the listening Clough, she is hardly coming across as a silver-tongued orator.

'Is that Michael?' she says. She is relieved to see that Michael seems alert and quite happy. He is looking up at the dark trees, a strange little smile on his face.

'Yes. This is my Michael.'

My Michael. This throws Ruth for a moment and it's Michael himself who saves her. 'Kate,' he says loudly and clearly. He waves at her, beaming.

'Who's Kate?' asks Dani sharply.

'My daughter.'

'Do you know Michael then?' She looks down at the little figure on the swing as if surprised that he can have a life that doesn't involve her.

'His mum's a friend of mine,' says Ruth.

Dani makes a sound that is almost a hiss. 'His mother. She doesn't love him. She doesn't care for him. She just leaves him with a childminder.'

Ruth tries to keep her voice calm. 'She does care. She loves him very much.'

'I heard her that night in the restaurant,' says Dani. '"It's good experience in socialising."' She puts on a mocking, high-pitched voice. 'Socialising! Children don't need to socialise. They need *looking after*.'

'You've certainly looked after Michael well,' says Ruth.

'Yes,' says Dani. 'I looked after the other one too, the little girl. Poppy. It was Judy who told me about her too. The family that never saw their children. So I decided to take Poppy for myself, to look after. It was so easy, I just walked into the house. The door was unlocked. The parents were downstairs, completely ignoring their babies. I just went upstairs, and took Poppy out of her cot. I'd bought a buggy and we walked to my hotel. I was staying at a different place then. They didn't ask questions because I'm so good with children. No-one ever asks questions. Michael's childminder just handed him over to me. I had the letter, you see. The letter on police paper. Remember the letter I had giving authorisation for the filming? I used the letterhead.'

'Very clever,' says Ruth, edging forward.

'Poppy loved being with me,' says Dani and her voice is soft with reminiscence. 'But then I saw the mother on television and she did look sad. So I gave her another chance. I gave Poppy back to her.'

'Are you going to give Judy another chance?' asks Ruth. She is near enough now to touch the tip of

Michael's foot as he swings towards her. 'She's completely devastated.'

'No,' says Dani. 'I saw her on TV and she didn't look upset at all. I'm going to keep Michael with me forever.'

Nelson sees Clough's car parked by the trees. A tall grey-haired man is standing beside it. He recognises the man as the TV guy – Frank – but now he looks different. All his self-assurance (cockiness, Nelson calls it) has vanished. He looks worried and rather scared. As Nelson approaches, Frank says, 'Are you the boss? They're over there.' He points towards the open ground. Nelson can hear voices and what sounds like the creak of a swing.

'They?'

'Ruth and Clough.'

'What's Ruth doing getting involved in this?'

The man shrugs as if implying that he has no control over Ruth. Nelson knows the feeling. He stomps away angrily. After a few yards he finds Clough hiding behind some trees.

'She's over there. Child looks in good health. Ruth's talking to the woman.'

'Why?'

Clough doesn't answer. Nelson imagines that Ruth didn't wait for his permission. Even so he feels angry.

Ruth could be putting herself in all sorts of danger. Still, the voices don't sound angry exactly.

'Come on,' he starts to edge nearer.

Tanya puts her phone away. Three people are staring at her intently but she addresses herself to Judy.

'He's here. In Castle Rising. At the park. He's fine. It's all under control. But Nelson says to stay in the house. He doesn't want a lot of people there. It's a delicate situation, he says.'

In answer, Judy pushes past Tanya and out of the door. Darren, Cathbad and Thing follow.

'Come back!' Tanya yells. 'You could jeopardise the whole operation.'

But Judy is far away, running as if her life depended on it.

Ruth is near enough to catch Michael as he swings towards her. Should she grab him? Clough is nearby, she could call for his help. But then Dani might get away. And what if she's armed or something awful? Instinct tells her to keep playing the game. She propels Michael back towards his abductor. For a few minutes they swing him to and fro in a ghastly parody of a happy family. Ruth can hear rustling in the bushes. The police must be getting closer.

'I'd better take him home soon,' says Dani. 'It's getting late.' She says this as if it's nearly teatime, not one a.m.

'I could take him home,' says Ruth. 'It's just round the corner. Honestly, it's no trouble.'

Dani's face darkens. 'I know she lives round here. That's why I brought him to this park, I thought it would be familiar. He used to come here with his childminder. I watched them. Nice girl. She cared for him, I know.'

'She's very upset,' says Ruth. 'She blames herself.'

For the first time, Dani seems to falter. 'Does she? She mustn't do that. I blamed myself for Jackson. But it wasn't my fault. Everyone said it wasn't.'

'Of course it wasn't,' says Ruth. She stops the swing, holding on to both sides. 'it must have been awful for you.'

'Everyone always blames the childminder,' says Dani. 'Just like everyone blamed Jemima Green. That's why I wanted to make this film. To set the record straight.'

Ruth lifts Michael out of the swing, holding him close. 'Poor Jemima,' she says, backing away. 'Frank says he can prove she was innocent.'

'Good old Frank.' Suddenly Dani seems to realise what Ruth is doing. 'Hey!'

Then several things happen at the same moment. A white dog comes bursting through the undergrowth and hurls itself on Dani. Two large men appear from behind the trees. A female whirlwind comes blazing over the grass and snatches Michael from Ruth's arms. And Michael looks up and says 'Daddy' as Cathbad and Darren come panting around the corner.

CHAPTER 35

'My baby. My baby.' Judy and Michael lie on the grass, inextricably entangled. Clough has tackled Dani and they, too, are on the ground. Nelson is restraining Thing, who seems intent on licking him to death. Other police officers emerge from the shadows and take charge of Dani. Ruth sees her being led away. Darren and Cathbad kneel either side of Judy, both weeping. It's an oddly religious image, the kneeling men, the mother and child. Ruth finds that she, too, is crying.

'How the hell did you get involved?' This, of course, is Nelson, still holding Thing by the collar.

'Don't you mean "thank you"?' says Ruth, wiping her eyes.

'Thank you. How the hell did you get involved?'

'I suddenly realised about Dani. It was a case I'd read

online, about a childminder in Boston. So I went to her hotel and Clough was already there.'

'I read about that case.' Tanya has joined them, out of breath and rather disgruntled.

'But you didn't make the link, did you?' says Nelson.

'It was in America!'

'Dani's American,' says Ruth. 'That's what made me think. She was a childminder for a baby that died. The parents were found guilty of murder. It made Dani resent all working parents.'

'So, years later, she started snatching babies,' says Nelson. 'Why now? It doesn't make sense.'

'I don't know,' says Ruth. Suddenly she feels very tired. 'I think it may have had to do with Jemima Green. Mother Hook, you know. Dani really wanted to make this film about her, to prove she was innocent. It must have brought it all back.'

Thing barks ecstatically. Judy is on her feet, walking towards them, holding Michael so tightly that he seems almost part of her body. Ruth goes over and hugs them both.

'I'm so glad he's OK,' she says.

'Thank you,' says Judy. 'Thank you, Ruth.'

'I didn't do anything really.'

'You found him!'

ELLY GRIFFITHS

'Clough found him too.'

Hearing his name, Clough ambles over. He is covered in bits of grass and grinning broadly.

'How is the little fella?' He ruffles Michael's hair.

'He's fine,' says Judy. She reaches up to give her colleague a kiss. 'Thank you, Dave.'

Even in the dark, Ruth can tell that Clough is blushing. 'Just glad it worked out,' he says gruffly.

'One thing I don't understand, Cloughie,' says Nelson. 'What made you go to that woman's hotel in the first place?'

'You'll never believe me even if I do tell you,' says Clough.

Cathbad, who has been enfolding Ruth in a fierce hug, suddenly gives a shout of laughter. 'I know. It was the psychic wasn't it? It was Madame Rita. She gave you the clue.'

'Of course she didn't,' says Clough.

'Well, all this can wait,' says Nelson. 'Let's get this little boy home. Here, Cathbad, take your dog. He's a complete nutcase, like you.'

Cathbad grabs hold of Thing's collar. Darren takes Judy's arm and they start to walk away. As Judy passes Nelson, she says, 'Thank you, Boss.'

*

Suddenly the little park seems full of people. More uniformed policemen are looming up behind the swings and the climbing frame. Ruth can hear Nelson barking orders. Judy, Cathbad and Darren are making their way across the grass. Darren is now carrying Michael. Ruth sees Judy and Cathbad touch hands, just for a second, before Thing jumps jealously between them. At the edge of the crowd, she finds Frank.

'All's well that ends well?'

'Yes,' says Ruth. 'Michael's back with his parents.'

Frank shakes his head. 'It all seems totally unreal. Why would Dani do something like that?'

'I don't know,' says Ruth. 'Why does anyone do anything?'

Back at the cars they find Clough deep in conversation with Nelson. Ruth just hears the words 'heart' and 'tower.' Nelson looks up as they approach. Ruth thinks that he seems irritated about something. 'I'll get a car to drive you home, Ruth. And you,' he adds as an afterthought to Frank.

'I need to go back to Norwich and pick up my car,' says Ruth.

'I'll have someone collect it in the morning,' says Nelson. 'Right now, you need to get back to Katie.'

Ruth opens her mouth to protest, then shuts it again.

After all, it must be nearly two and she does need to get home. And Nelson has returned a missing child to its mother, why choose this moment to complain about his dictatorial tendencies?

'I do need to get back to Norwich, I'm afraid,' says Frank. 'My car's there and I have to drive home to Cambridge tonight.'

'Cloughie'll take you,' says Nelson. 'I must get back to the station.'

And he gets into his car without saying goodbye.

Nelson drives back to the station wondering if he's ever felt so many emotions at the same time. There's relief – of course that's uppermost – utter joyous relief that Michael has been found safe and well. He will never forget the sound that Judy made as she sprang though the trees to launch herself on her son. It was almost inhuman, a moan of anguish and happiness and undiluted mothering instinct. Who would have thought that self-contained Judy could ever make a noise like that? Michael is back home and, whatever's going on with Judy, Cathbad and Darren, he's sure they'll sort it out. Whitcliffe will be pleased, a good news story at last, and Nelson will skim over the combination of luck and voodoo that took Clough to Dani's hotel in the first place.

He is still disturbed by the idea that his stolid sergeant not only consulted a psychic but actually acted on her words. It's pure codswallop of course, but Clough seemed really shaken by the combination of towers, hearts and white women. 'That was her name, you see, Boss. Danielle White. And Madame Rita told me to look out for a white lady. You see? Danielle White. White lady.'

'I get it, Cloughie, but it's just a coincidence.'

'What about the tower? There was a picture of The Devil's Tower in the bedroom. And the hotel overlooked the castle. And it was called The Red Hart. That's what Madame Rita said, a red heart. Of course I thought she meant a heart like in your body . . .'

'You did well, Cloughie,' Nelson had interrupted him. 'Go home and get some rest now.'

Now, as he negotiates the familiar roads, he asks himself if he is jealous that it was Clough (supernaturally inspired or not) who made the final breakthrough. He doesn't think that he is. Maybe it's a sign of arrogance but he usually takes good work by his officers as a compliment to the team – and, by extension, to himself. He trained them, after all, and Clough is, in some ways, the officer closest to him. No, he doesn't resent the role that Clough played in the rescue. He is proud of the fact that Clough both trusted to his instincts and had the sense not to race after Dani with all guns blazing. Clough is growing up at last.

It's Ruth's part in the whole thing that bothers him. Why did she have to be there and why did she have that American bloke with her? Is he really her new boyfriend, like Shona said? In one part of his mind he accepts that Ruth might find a new boyfriend – in his more rational moments he even hopes that this will happen – but a far greater part of him wants her to forswear men altogether and concentrate on Katie. It's unfair, he knows. He's married, why shouldn't Ruth have a partner? But, in his heart, he likes it the way it is. He has both women, all three children. Michelle is his wife and he will never leave her, but over the years Ruth has somehow become essential to his happiness. It's not right, he knows that. Nelson isn't a Catholic for nothing. He knows that someone has to pay, and in the last few days he has sometimes wondered whether, in some ghastly Old Testament way, Michael was taken as a punishment for Nelson's sins.

But it's all right. God has forgiven them all. Michael is safely home with his mother. But Nelson had better stop pushing his luck. If Ruth wants to start a relationship with a smug-looking American, he has to let her. Maybe that's his punishment. As he parks outside the station he considers that he'd give almost anything – barring his children – for a good night's sleep.

Ruth opens her front door, trying not to make any sound. The house is quiet but there's a heap of blankets breathing gently. Ruth looks down at her brother. In sleep he looks much younger, his thinning hair ruffled, lips pursed slightly. A memory comes back to her. Looking down at Simon from her vantage point of the top bunk in the caravan. He would always fall asleep first and Ruth, who often used to feel frightened at night, was always comforted by the thought of the sleeping presence below her. It was kind of him, she thinks now, to let her have the top bunk. He's not that bad, as brothers go.

Ruth smiles as she climbs the stairs. Just now, she loves everyone. She could even be pleasant to Phil (though she wouldn't kiss him because he's grown a horrid little beard). Bloody hell, is this what her parents are always talking about? Heavenly bliss and all that. She doesn't know about heaven but this world is looking very good just at the moment. She bends to kiss the sleeping Kate, reflecting that Judy will now be able to do the same with Michael. In her own bedroom, she opens the Tennyson book, now a night-time ritual.

'Peace and goodwill,' she reads, 'goodwill and peace
Peace and goodwill to all mankind.'
You said it Alfie, thinks Ruth, shutting her eyes.

Nelson is woken from the sleep of the just by his ring
tone. Instinctively he stretches out an arm but Michelle
isn't there. Nelson reaches for his phone. The digital
clock says 9.10. Bloody hell, it's been years since he's slept
this late. A message flashes: Maddie Henderson calling.
'Hi Maddie. What's up?'
'Nelson, you'd better come. I'm at Liz's house.'

CHAPTER 36

Liz Donaldson is dead. Nelson knew as soon as he entered the room, in fact as soon as he entered the house. He'd arrived to find Maddie sitting on the wall outside. Like her father, she doesn't waste much time in pleasantries.

'Something's wrong, Nelson. I know it. I arranged to meet her here at nine but there's no answer. I know she's inside. Her car's parked on the road.'

Nelson peered through the window. The immaculate front room was the same, minus the cards and the flowers. Nothing out of place, no newspapers on the table, not a spare cardigan on a chair, cushions neatly plumped and standing on their points like ballet dancers. Nelson couldn't say why, but the perfect room struck a chill to his very soul. He turned to look at Maddie, who, despite the warmth of the summer day, was huddled in her green jacket, looking a lot younger than nineteen.

'Could she have just popped to the shops?' he asked.

'She could but I don't think so. She was very particular about me getting here exactly at nine. Kept saying "you will be here won't you?" I thought then that she sounded odd.'

Nelson hammered on the front door and the sound echoed up and down the street. No-one came to investigate the noise. It was nine-thirty on a Thursday morning. All the inhabitants of the neat terraced houses were either at work or involved in some equally respectable activity.

'Have you called her?' he asked Maddie.

'Loads of times.'

Sighing, Nelson set his shoulder to the front door. It gave way easily. After a quick look around the sitting room and kitchen, he took the stairs two at a time, Maddie following.

Liz Donaldson is lying on her bed. She is fully dressed, hands clasped on her chest. On the table next to the bed stands an empty pill bottle and a letter addressed in heavy black ink, 'To the police'.

Nelson calls an ambulance but he knows, and he suspects Maddie knows too, despite her rather half-hearted attempts at mouth-to-mouth. He takes Liz's wrist in one hand and, with the other, pats Maddie on the back. 'She's gone, love.' Maddie nods, her mermaid's eyes full of tears.

They wait in silence for the ambulance. Nelson calls the station and asks for a SOCO team. He doesn't think that a crime has taken place but he knows that in this house and with this woman he has to go by the book. He doesn't touch the letter. He is grateful that Maddie doesn't speculate why or how Liz took her life. They sit either side of the bed as if they're visiting a patient in hospital. Nelson finds it unbearably poignant that Liz took off her shoes before climbing onto the bed.

The paramedics pronounce Liz dead at the scene. They can't take a dead woman in the ambulance so they call for the coroner's van. The SOCO team arrive and begin dusting the room down. Nelson and Maddie wait in the silent sitting room which still, somehow, smells of lilies.

'Air freshener,' says Maddie when Nelson comments on this fact.

He is more relieved by this explanation than he cares to say. He asks Maddie if she has phoned Bob. What did Cathbad say about Maddie and Bob? It all seems so long ago.

'I left a message on his answer phone,' says Maddie.

Bob and the coroner's 'private ambulance' arrive at the

same time. He stands back to let the covered stretcher go past.

'What's going on?' he sounds very scared.

Maddie puts an arm round him and leads him back into the house. They sit side by side on the sofa, disturbing the cushions.

'Liz's dead. I'm so sorry, Bob.'

'Dead?' Bob looks accusingly at Nelson. 'Dead? How? I don't understand.'

'It's looks as if she killed herself,' says Nelson. 'I'm sorry, Mr Donaldson.'

Bob's reaction is depressing but not, to Nelson, unexpected.

'You see,' he says. 'She was guilty all along.'

Judy, Darren and Michael are on the way to Southwold. There has been so much press interest in the case that Nelson has advised them to get away for a few days. Darren's parents, delirious with relief and also desperate to help, were only too happy to invite them to stay. Humans, thinks Judy, are remarkable creatures. She and Darren have just been through the worst experience of their lives. She feels as if she has plumbed the very depths of the human soul but here she is, sitting in the family car listening to Radio 2 with Michael in the back, almost as if nothing has happened. Michael seems quite content, holding his toy giraffe and humming to himself, just as if he hasn't spent three days being kept prisoner by a mad woman. Will he remember it? Judy wonders. Will the experience leave him scarred for life? Will it leave him with a terror of swings and a hatred of Chanel N° 5? She remembers how it had felt last night, smelling Dani's perfume on her baby. When they got back to the house, the first thing she had done was to give Michael a bath. Then she had thrown the clothes he was wearing into the bin and dressed him in his well-worn blue pyjamas. Then she, Darren and Cathbad had watched their baby sleep.

'I was surprised that Cathbad said he was leaving,' Darren says as they drive along the seafront. 'What do you think he'll do now?'

'I don't know,' says Judy. 'He's a free spirit, Cathbad.'

'Has he still got a place in Norfolk?'

'He's got a caravan in Blakeney,' says Judy, 'but I don't think he'll go there.'

'He's been a real support over the last few days.'

'Yes, he has.'

'Maybe he'll catch up with that daughter of his?'

'Maybe.'

'Things like this,' says Darren, 'they make you appreciate your family more.'

Judy agrees that this is true and they drive in silence past the lighthouse and the pier and the multi-coloured bathing huts.

Cathbad and Ruth are also by the sea. Simon has taken the boys to see the seals at Blakeney and Ruth was alone when Cathbad appeared at her door just after nine. 'You look exhausted,' she said. 'Why don't you have a few hours' sleep? The spare bed's made up.'

'I can sleep on the beach,' said Cathbad. 'Right now I need fresh air.'

So they had taken the path through the marshes to the sea. And now Cathbad lies stretched out on a blanket watching Kate build an elaborate sand monolith.

'It's positively Neolithic,' he says.

'It's a tower,' says Kate. 'Like in Rapunzel.'

'I used to have long hair like Rapunzel,' says Cathbad.

'Silly,' says Kate, not looking up. 'You're a boy.'

Ruth looks out to the sea where a single windsurfer is tacking across the horizon. She wants to ask Cathbad whether he's going back to Lancashire and what is happening with Judy. So far they have only talked about Michael, about how he appears to have emerged from the ordeal unscathed, albeit with two new words, 'Kate' and 'Daddy'. Ruth wants to ask which Daddy Judy will choose but she doesn't want to spoil the peace of the morning. Luckily, Cathbad's sixth sense is still in working order.

'It's up to Judy,' he says now, shutting his eyes. 'She's not happy with Darren but she feels guilty about him.'

'But . . .' Ruth struggles to find the words. 'Do you want her to leave Darren? Do you want to . . . to set up home together?' She can't imagine Cathbad in a nuclear family: Druid, mother and child. But Cathbad sits up and turns to her, his face touching in its intensity.

'It's *all* I want. I want us to live together as a family. Me, Judy and Michael.'

'And Thing.'

'And Thing, of course.' They have left Thing behind in the cottage as people on the beach tend to get twitchy about dogs, particularly bull terriers.

Cathbad flops back down on the blanket. 'Talk to me Ruth. Take my mind off it. Tell me a story.'

So Ruth tells him about Mother Hook, about how she was convicted of killing the children in her care. She tells him that Frank thinks she was innocent and the tension on set between Corinna's 'black as midnight hag' and Dani's wronged childminder. Cathbad listens intently, propped up on one elbow, his eyes on her face. Kate, recognising Ruth's story-telling voice, stops building and comes to sit on her lap.

Ruth tells Cathbad about the medallion, at present residing on her bedside table. She tells him about the diaries and The Book of Dead Babies. When she gets to the bit about 'Rowan will stand guard', he says, 'The rowan. The witchbane. The whispering tree. It's said to guard against vampires.'

'That's all very well,' says Ruth, 'But which rowan? There must be rowan trees everywhere.'

'There's a Saint Rowan too,' says Cathbad, who is always well informed about the saints. 'It's an anglicised version of the Gaelic name Ruadhan. It means 'little red haired one'. I wonder if Joshua was red haired.'

'I don't know,' says Ruth. 'Jemima doesn't say. Actually she may have meant the saint because she mentions Saint Michael too.'

'A fellow close to my own heart,' says Cathbad. 'Is there a place where the saints could be watching over Joshua?'

And Ruth thinks of the church at Saxlingham Thorpe and the stone saints, their faces worn away by the years.

When Forensics release Liz's letter, Nelson takes it to his office to read. It's a quiet day at the station. Judy is still on compassionate leave and Nelson has given Clough the day off. There's only Tanya, sulkily writing up case notes, and Whitcliffe, wafting around on a high from so many press conferences. Tim, slightly put out at missing last night's action, has been on TV and radio all morning.

Nelson sits down at his desk and unfolds the single sheet of paper.

To whom it may concern (he reads),

I killed David. I couldn't bear life without Bob. I wanted him to come back to me. I thought that if David died Bob would come back because he felt sorry for me. So I put David down in his cot and I held a pillow over his face. It was all over so quickly and he looked so peaceful afterwards. But Bob didn't come back and now I know that I'll go straight to hell. I'll never see my babies again because they'll be in heaven. I didn't kill Samuel and Isaac. They were tragedies and everyone feels sorry for you when you've had a tragedy. I wanted Bob to feel sorry for me. I put the message on his Facebook because I wanted it to be true. I wanted us to be together. I guessed his password because it was her name. I can't expect forgiveness but I'm sorry. For everything.

Liz Donaldson (Mrs)

Liz Donaldson (Mrs). When it came down to it, that was all Liz had wanted to be: Mrs Liz Donaldson. It was all about the husband after all. Like Tim before him, Nelson can't see what there is in the colourless computer programmer to incite so many women to passion, even, it seems, to murder. But there must be something, because Liz Donaldson killed her child in a desperate attempt to regain her husband's love. Justine was prepared to denounce her former lover, maybe motivated by thwarted passion, and even Maddie, a young and beautiful schoolgirl, had succumbed to the unlikely lure of Bob Donaldson. He wonders what Liz meant by 'her' name: Aliona or Justine or Maddie? And there was something odd about Liz's choice of Maddie as the person to discover her body, because that was surely what the early morning tryst was all about. Was this a way of punishing Maddie for her affair with Bob or simply because Liz had fond memories of the family for whom she used to babysit? Well, they'll never know now. Nelson sighs. They'll have to drop charges against Bob and Nirupa Khan will probably threaten to sue. They'd better release a statement today while everyone is still euphoric over Michael.

Nelson looks back at the letter. He was right about Liz Donaldson. There was a side to her that enjoyed her role as victim, as the blameless recipient of sympathy. He was also right about religion. It's there in every line of the letter, in the references to heaven and hell and forgiveness. He thinks of David, the little boy who was just learning to crawl. Never has being right given him less satisfaction.

Judy and Darren are on Southwold pier. Michael is at home with his doting grandparents. All around them, families are enjoying the old-fashioned delights of the penny arcade and the water clock. It's like a day trip to the Fifties, a homage to family fun. But Judy has brought Darren here to break up their family. He seems to know that something is wrong because he doesn't suggest a cream tea or a go on the coconut shy, he just shuffles along with his head down.

'Darren,' Judy grabs his arm. 'I've got to talk to you.'

'Fancy some candyfloss?' he says desperately.

'Darren. I'm sorry. I'm in love with someone else.'

They have reached the end of the pier and they stand in silence, watching fathers and sons fishing for crabs.

'Who is it?' Darren asks at last.

'Cathbad.'

'*Cathbad*,' Darren repeats incredulously. 'Are you sure?'

Judy almost laughs. 'Of course I'm sure.'

'Cathbad. I knew it was someone but I never thought . . .'

Judy stares at her husband. 'What do you mean, you knew it was someone?'

'I knew there was someone else,' says Darren. 'Even before we got married, I sensed it. I knew you didn't feel the same about me anymore. I just hoped that it would fizzle out. And then, when you got pregnant, I thought it was a second chance for us. Then, when I saw little Michael . . .'

'You knew he wasn't yours?'

Darren winces. 'I wasn't sure. But he doesn't look like me, does he?' He makes a gallant attempt at a joke. 'He's much better looking than me. And he's not ginger.'

'I don't know about Michael,' says Judy. 'I can't be sure . . .'

'I'll always love him,' says Darren. 'You know that, don't you?'

'I know.'

They are silent for a few more minutes. The sea is as calm and still as glass.

'If you didn't think it was Cathbad,' says Judy, 'who did you think it was?'

Darren looks away, his voice muffled. 'I thought it was Dave Clough.'

'*Clough*?' Now it's Judy's turn to sound astonished. 'You thought I was in love with Clough?'

'Well, you seemed so close. You were always working late with him. And he's always been really interested in Michael. And Michael's dark, like him.'

'Clough's a friend,' says Judy, 'no more.' She reflects that even a few days ago she would have hesitated before calling Clough a friend.

'So,' says Darren, turning to look at her. She knows that his face at this moment will haunt her for the rest of her days. 'Do you want to live with Cathbad?'

'I'm sorry,' says Judy. 'If I could forget Cathbad, I would. God knows, I've tried. I'll always love you, Darren. You're my best friend. But I can't live without Cathbad. I've tried and it's killing me.'

'Does he love you?' asks Darren.

'Yes,' says Judy. 'Yes he does.'

'What about Michael?'

'You'll always be his father,' says Judy. 'Cathbad understands that. He'll have two fathers.'

'Oh my God,' Darren turns away, half-laughing, half-crying. 'What are my parents going to say?'

What's everyone going to say, thinks Judy. Not only the two sets of grandparents but her colleagues, Nelson, Ruth. They'll all think she's gone mad. But she fixes her eyes on a future with Cathbad and Michael. It is all that has kept her sane over the last few days.

'It'll be horrible,' she says now. 'But they'll accept it in the end.'

'I don't want to worry about what people will think,' says Darren quite aggressively, 'I'm not that sort of person.'

'No,' says Judy. 'You're not.'

'It's just . . .' He looks at her, his eyes transparent with tears. 'I'll miss you both so much.'

And now Judy cries too. They stand on the pier, holding each other and crying, as the happy families trail past them.

CHAPTER 37

'Thanks for having us,' Simon says. 'It's been great.'

'We've enjoyed it,' says Ruth. And this is no more than the truth. The last week of Simon's visit, with the knowledge that Michael is safe, has been really enjoyable. Fun, for want of a better word. They have visited Norwich castle and paid their respects to Boadicea. They have been on a wherry and have caught a train over the beach at Wells. The boys have been body-boarding and horse riding. Kate now knows all the words to 'Glory Glory Man United' (for some reason both Simon and his sons, neither of whom have ever been north of Birmingham, support this team). Simon and Ruth have shared several more bottles of wine. Ruth has told Simon about the Bronze Age and he has tried to teach her about computers.

'I wish we could stay longer but I promised Cathy that we'd be back today.'

It was only yesterday that Simon told Ruth, rather shamefacedly, that he was going back to his wife. 'I'm glad,' she had said. 'I'm really glad.' 'You must think I'm an idiot,' said Simon, looking so like his ten-year-old self that Ruth had almost laughed. 'We're all idiots,' she said, 'isn't that what it's all about?'

The holiday in Norfolk has apparently shown Simon that he needs to change himself before he changes his life. He's going to get another job, learn Spanish, go on a creative-writing course. Ruth wonders what Cathy will make of it all. 'She's all for it,' Simon said. 'She's going to do an Open University degree.' Ruth wishes them all the luck in the world but she can't help hoping that her sister-in-law doesn't turn up at one of her summer schools.

'Bye Kate,' says Simon, kissing her. 'See you soon.'

'Clara's coming,' Kate informs him. The boys are pulling monkey faces from inside the car.

'Who's Clara?'

'My babysitter. She's coming tonight.'

'Going out on the razz as soon as we leave, eh?' Simon might be a much improved version but he still sometimes says things like 'out on the razz'.

'I'm going to a ruined church to exhume a body,' says Ruth.

Judy and Cathbad are also on their way to the church. Michael is with Darren – one of his two fathers. The last week has been hellish. Darren moved in with his parents, who were at first fairly understanding, attributing Judy's behaviour to delayed shock about Michael's abduction. Now, as their daughter-in-law's resolve to end the marriage shows no sign of weakening, Judy is sure that their tolerance is wearing thin and she doesn't blame them. God knows what they'll say when she moves in with Cathbad. Judy and Darren are agreed that they want to sell the house in Castle Rising. For her part Judy never wants to set foot in the place again. It will always be associated with those nightmare days of Michael's absence, watching endless television and waiting for the Grim Reaper to knock on the door.

Cathbad says that he'll sell the caravan and buy a house. He's got some money saved, he says. Judy can't really imagine Cathbad owning a house but she goes along with the suggestion is the same dream-like way that she has been acquiescing with everything recently. 'Are you sure you're OK?' said Nelson, when she explained the situation to him. 'You seem in a bit of a trance. Not that I blame you, mind.' Nelson had been kind. He had even (looking acutely uncomfortable) suggested counselling. 'You've been through a lot. It might help.' 'You think counselling would stop me being in love with Cathbad?' asked Judy. Nelson had smiled, though Judy thought he had looked rather sad. 'There's a limit to what counselling can manage,' he'd said.

In fact Cathbad and Judy have seen very little of each other since Michael's return. This gives the evening's expedition a rather holiday-like air. 'Our first date,' said Cathbad, 'and it's to an exhumation. Something to tell the grandkids.' Judy ponders these words as she takes the road for Saxlingham Thorpe (she might love Cathbad but she doesn't trust his driving). It's funny to think of them being on a date. She and Cathbad seem to have been through heaven and hell without ever having done any of the bits in-between. They have never had a meal in a restaurant, been to the cinema or shared a holiday. They have a child, though, and as Judy parks by the Mill Inn she thinks about the other implications of Cathbad's remark. Grandchildren? Does he mean Michael's children or the descendants of the hypothetical children still to come? The thought that they might have more children together makes her suddenly feel dizzy with emotion. As they get out of the car and walk towards the wood, she reaches out and holds Cathbad's hand.

Exhumations are usually done at night says Kevin Davies, a local undertaker (and acquaintance of Nelson's). 'It's to show respect, you see.' Nelson says it's more about avoiding unnecessary publicity. But when Ruth mentioned this tradition to Martin, the new director, he had been wild with enthusiasm. The moonlight, the abandoned church, ruined walls rising out of the shadows, it would all make perfect television.

The *Women Who Kill* episode has survived the arrest of its director, but only just. Corinna walked out as soon as the facts were known. 'I can't stand cruelty to children. I'm funny that way.' Martin, as assistant director, had a series of crisis meetings with the producers and the television company but, in the end, it was decided to continue with the programme. Now Martin is in the process of re-shooting all the early scenes with Frank as the main presenter. Much to her embarrassment, Ruth has also been given a much enlarged role. She thinks cynically that the extra publicity won't hurt the ratings.

Now Martin is getting ready to shoot the midnight dig. There was a lot of discussion about whether to allow the

TV crew to film the exhumation. Eventually Nelson gave the go-ahead, subject to a few conditions: Martin mustn't film the bones themselves and the footage must be given to the police for approval. As Ruth approaches she sees that the cameras have already been set up. The space between the crumbling arches already seems full of people. As well as the film crew there is Irish Ted, who's going to do the actual digging, several other members of the field team and, standing hand in hand, Cathbad and Judy. Next to them is an elderly man wearing a clerical collar. And with a lurch of the heart, Ruth sees Frank talking to Dex the cameraman.

Cathbad waves and Ruth makes her way over to him. Cathbad introduces the clergyman as Father Tom Douglas. 'Father Tom's just going to say a few prayers over the body.'

Ruth doesn't question why Cathbad has decided to bring along a priest – or a vicar, whichever he is. It's typical of Cathbad to introduce an element of mysticism but not, Ruth acknowledges, entirely inappropriate.

'If we find a body,' she says.

Ted starts to trowel. The last two days have been wet and the earth crumbles easily. A yellow moon appears fitfully from behind the clouds and somewhere nearby an owl hoots.

'Bloody hell. That scared the hell out of me,' says Ted cheerfully.

Cathbad has identified Saint Rowan as the statue with a faint tracery of leaves around its brow. Ruth has found the same adornment on the head of the figure in the medallion. Saint Rowan holding a child. Why did Jemima Green have such a fondness for this particular saint? Was it because of the statue here, in the ruins of her parish church? Did someone tell her that Saint Rowan would protect the dead children, like Jemima's little sisters who are also (they assume) buried in his shadow?

'Cut!' shouts Martin. 'Can I have a close-up of Ted's face?'

'Fame at last,' says Ted.

It's ironic, thinks Ruth, watching an assistant holding a light-meter next to Ted's gleaming bald head, the programme is now the one that Dani always wanted to make. Frank will sift the evidence and come to a considered historian's conclusion. There will be no melodrama and no hook-handed monster. Even so, this scene, with the silhouetted figures digging in the shadows of the old church, will add a Gothic touch to the proceedings. Ruth wouldn't put it past Martin to add spooky sound effects either. And *Carmina Burana* in the background . . . 'I think we've got something,' says Ted. 'Over to you, Ruth.'

Ruth climbs into the trench and sees the little bones
– so fragile and white – outlined in the dark soil. She
works slowly to expose the skeleton, conscious of all the
eyes (not to mention the cameras) upon her.

'It's a child,' she says.

'How do we know it's not one of the sisters?' asks
Martin.

'We can't be sure yet,' says Ruth. 'With pre-pubescent
skeletons it's hard to determine gender. We may be able
to get some DNA from the bones though.'

Even after this note of caution, the atmosphere around
the grave is tense. Ruth has already recorded the skeleton
in plan. Now she excavates the bones one by one, placing
them in marked plastic bags. Ted fills in the skeleton
sheet. The only sounds are the scratch of Ruth's trowel
and the night noises in the woods behind them.

'Father Tom,' says Cathbad. 'Could you say a few
words?'

Father Tom steps forward. For such an elderly man his
voice is surprisingly powerful. It echoes around the
shadowy stones. The sky above is clear and full of stars.

'Lord, you told us that not a sparrow falls without Our
Father in Heaven knowing.'

Ruth is surprised to recognise the words from the service for the Outcast Dead. She supposes that these are

all-purpose prayers for bodies in unmarked graves. Even so, they seem particularly appropriate here.

'We pray for the souls buried beneath this soil. We know that they are known to you and loved by you.'

They were certainly known and loved by Jemima Green, thinks Ruth, lifting the little skull from the earth. She thinks of Jemima's poem.

And when the good Lord calls me from this life of pain
I will lie beside you and hold you in my arms again.

Frank wants the posthumously pardoned Jemima Green to be re-buried in consecrated ground. Perhaps Joshua – if this is Joshua – could be buried with her? But then Ruth thinks of Anna Barnet, Joshua's mother. Is it fair that she should lose her son to Jemima Green for a second time? Surely Joshua belongs with his mother, presuming they can find her grave. Ruth makes a silent promise to the ghost of Anna. If I can find you, I'll reunite you with your son. It wasn't Anna's fault that society wouldn't let her bring up her own child. And she hadn't given him up for adoption. She had always meant to come back for him.

'I am the resurrection and the life says the Lord. He who believes in me will live, even though he dies.'

Ruth thinks of the Resurrection Men, of Mr G, cheated of this body at least. Why does it matter what happens to our bodies when we die? Surely Ruth, as a good atheist, should be happy to leave her body for medical research? But Ruth knows that, if she wants anything for her remains, it's this – a lonely churchyard where Kate and her children can visit and bring flowers. Bloody hell, what a morbid thought. She's been seeing too much of Cathbad.

At last the exhumation is complete and Ted's 'Amen' is ringing into the night. Ruth climbs out of the trench and takes off her coveralls. She feels the need for some space and walks a little way away from the group around the skele box. She jumps when a tall figure appears next to her. It's Frank.

'You OK?' he asks.

'Fine,' she says. 'I hope it's him. Joshua, I mean.'

'So do I,' says Frank. 'I think it is, don't you?'

'Yes I do.'

'Another lost child found.'

'Is that what you're going to say in your voice-over?'

Frank laughs. 'I'm not always practising my lines, you know, Ruth. There are some things I mean.'

'Like what?'

'Like I'd like to see you again. Before I go back to the States.'

Ruth feels her cheeks lifting in a smile but, before she

can speak, Nelson comes striding through the derelict archway.

'Are you two planning to stay here all night?'

Frank grins. 'It's a thought.'

Nelson scowls. Behind him Martin is still filming spooky shapes and ghostly sound effects, Ted is drinking from a hip flask, Cathbad and Judy are laughing softly together.

'I need to get back to Kate,' says Ruth.

EPILOGUE

Six months later

'So we can say, with ninety percent certainty, that the bones are those of a pre-pubescent boy who died about a hundred and fifty years ago. His body shows no signs of trauma and it is likely that he died of natural causes.'

The monstrous creature looms out of the screen. Ruth shrinks back in her seat. She thought the camera was meant to put on ten pounds. Elephant Woman up there looks about three stone heavier than Ruth. It's the last five minutes of the *Women Who Kill* screening. Ruth has enjoyed a few scenes: Ted sitting on the edge of a trench like Humpty Dumpty; Phil in a dazzling white coat asking her about Carbon 14; a moody shot of the castle with the English Heritage sign creaking like a gibbet. She is less sure about the decision to use actors to tell the story. The woman playing Jemima Green is far too glamorous. She wields her hook like a fashion accessory. The actor playing Mr G is suitably sinister though.

Thankfully the camera pans away from the huge figure in the laboratory. Now it is following Frank as he walks along the bridge to the castle.

'So Jemima Green, the woman who so loved the children in her care, is on her way to a posthumous pardon. Little Joshua died from natural causes and Jemima's only crime was to bury him in a secret place, away from the clutches of the Resurrection Men. Jemima was condemned by her appearance. Put simply, she looked like a murderess, and for over a hundred years we have believed her to be one. Now, perhaps, the legend of Mother Hook can die and the story of Jemima Green can take its place. The story of a woman, disabled in a dreadful accident, who made a new life caring for the abandoned children of Norwich. She clothed them, fed them and loved them. And if they died – as children did tragically often in those days – she wrote poems for them and treasured their memories. Perhaps she will be remembered as the first modern childminder, who really tried to create a loving home for her charges. She will be buried next to her parents in the beautiful countryside that she loved so much. There, Jemima Green can rest in peace at last.'

He smiles sadly into the camera as it backs away. And now the screen is full of the beautiful Norfolk countryside: wide beaches, meandering rivers, crumbling red cliffs, cows knee-deep in green pastures. The credits go past so quickly that Ruth hardly takes them in. Directed by Danielle White and Martin Glover. Presented by Dr Frank Barker. Special thanks to Dr Ruth Galloway and Dr Phil Trent from the University of North Norfolk. Across the aisle she can see Phil swelling with pride. The small audience in the lecture theatre bursts into spontaneous applause. Phil rises in answer to a non-existent call for a speech and talks for ten minutes about his contribution to the film. He does mention 'our Ruth' in the way that politicians mention their pets, expecting an indulgent laugh. Some of Ruth's friends cheer ironically. Then, mercifully, the doors are open and Ruth can escape.

Outside it's cold and bright. It's two weeks before Christmas and the campus is strewn with the relics of end-of-term parties. Streamers hang from the trees around the lake and the statue of Elizabeth Fry is wearing a fetching paper crown. People are standing around talking and laughing, their breath billowing around them. Ruth can see Shona, wearing what looks like a real fur jacket. Irish Ted is also there, she can hear his laugh from across the quad. She thinks that she can see Maddie Henderson standing with a slim, short-haired girl. Maddie must be back for the holidays. She wonders if that's Justine Thomas with her. According to Judy, Justine is now living with Bob Donaldson.

Shona waves and beckons. Ruth's also dimly aware that colleagues who wouldn't have given her the time of day before now seem anxious to talk to her. She supposes that now she's been on TV she's a woman of substance. You can say that again, she thinks with a shudder. Putting up her hood, she sets off for the car park. She's halfway there when she hears footsteps behind her.

'Ruth!'

Ruth turns. It's Janet Meadows, resplendent in a patchwork coat.

'Rushing off?'

'I need to get home.'

'Can I walk with you?'

'Of course.'

They walk past the Natural Sciences block. Someone has sprayed 'Happy Xmas' on the double doors but the X has already disintegrated. Janet says, 'I enjoyed the film.'

'I enjoyed it except when I was on screen,' says Ruth.

'I looked like I'd escaped from one of those documentaries. "The World's Fattest Academics."'

Janet laughs but doesn't exactly disagree. 'I hate seeing myself on TV,' she says. 'I did a local history series once and I looked just like Alan Rickman.'

Ruth rather fancies Alan Rickman but she can see why Janet, a male-to-female transsexual, might not like the comparison.

'What happened to that poor woman?' asks Janet. 'The director.' Dani's arrest was front page news for a while but now seems to have been forgotten. The local papers have been full of flooding in Lowestoft and the possibility of snow at Christmas. Ruth imagines that they'll regain their interest when the case comes to trial in the spring.

'She's pleading guilty,' she says. 'I think there are a few mitigating circumstances. Judy and Darren have been really forgiving. Cathbad even went to see her in prison.'

As time has gone on, Judy, who once would have torn Dani's heart out of her body, has softened considerably. 'After all,' she said to Ruth, 'Dani did look after Michael really well. I feel sorry for her, I really do. Cathbad says it's all to do with karma.'

'Are Judy and Cathbad living together now?' asks Janet. She knows Cathbad of old.

'Yes,' says Ruth. 'They seem really happy.'

'Well, Dani made a good film,' says Janet. 'I'm glad that Jemima Green's name has been cleared. It's so terrible to think of her being hanged for a crime that she didn't commit. I hope her soul can rest in peace now.'

Ruth thinks of a strange conversation she had with Clough a few weeks ago. It was at Judy and Cathbad's Hallowe'en party. Cathbad has sold the caravan and bought a cottage in Wells-next-the-Sea. Ruth knows that he came into some money last year but was surprised to see him spending it on something as conventional as a mortgage. Still, it was good to see him celebrating All Hallows Eve in the traditional way. Ruth has quite a fondness for the day as it was on Hallowe'en that she went into labour with Kate. Even so, she was glad that Kate held out for November 1st, All Hallows itself. A far more respectable birthday.

This party was, in itself, fairly conventional. Lots of beer and mulled wine, very little communication with the dead. At the end of the evening, Ruth got trapped with Clough on the sofa. Ruth was too tired to move and Clough seemed set in for the night. They were watching Cathbad showing Michael the bonfire in the garden (Cathbad hasn't changed in this respect; he still loves lighting fires). Michael had just woken up and Cathbad had brought him down to 'commune with the friendly spirits'.

'Hope the spirits don't get too friendly,' said Ruth, reflecting that she would probably have put Kate back in bed. What a kill-joy parent.

'There's more in this spirit bollocks than you realise, Ruth,' said Clough, looking into his glass. 'More than you'll ever know.'

'What do you mean?'

'You know when Michael was missing?' He pointed at the little boy laughing delightedly at the flames. 'Well, I consulted a psychic. Judy asked me to. I thought it was odd at the time but if she was involved with Malone it makes sense. Anyway, I saw this woman, Madame Rita her name was, and she told me to look for a red heart and a white lady. Well, you know where we found him? In a pub called the Red Hart. And he was with a woman called White, Danielle White.'

'I did hear some of this,' Ruth admitted. Nelson has succeeded in keeping the psychic out of the papers but couldn't resist telling the story to Ruth.

'But you didn't hear this,' said Clough, 'because I've never told anyone else. Madame Rita said that Michael was with "a woman from the spirit world". She said that this woman loved children and was looking after him. Well, when I heard about your film I thought it might be her, Mother Hook, Jemima Whatsit. Nelson says that you've proved that she was a goodie all along.'

Was Jemima Green looking after Michael? On one level, Ruth doesn't believe a word of it. Jemima Green is dead, and if Frank has saved her reputation that's satisfying to him but not much good to the woman hanged outside Norwich Castle a hundred and fifty years ago. But, on another level . . . She thinks of the lights on the Saltmarsh at night, of the time when Cathbad claimed to have visited the underworld in a dream, of the saints and the spirits, of the many times when her foolish heart has overruled her scientific head. The best that she can say now is that she isn't sure. About anything.

'The guy in the film,' says Janet. 'The dishy American. Someone said that you were seeing him. Is that right?'

'He's gone back to the States,' says Ruth evasively.

There's some talk of making another film about Jemima Green. Martin has even suggested that Frank and Ruth 'team up' to film a series about the lost kings of England, starting with King Arthur and ending with Richard III. She will see him again, there's no doubt about that. As to whether she's 'seeing' Frank, that's altogether a harder question to answer. One way or another, she doesn't really know if she's in a position to see anyone, at least not until Kate starts school. She may be a working mother, but it seems that these days she's a mother before she's anything else.

'There's plenty of time,' says Janet comfortably.

And that, Ruth muses, as she gets into her car, is certainly true. One thing you learn as an archaeologist; there's always plenty of time.

ACKNOWLEDGEMENTS

Norwich Castle, a magnificent building that dominates the city's skyline, was once a prison. During the nineteenth century hangings took place on Castle Hill, with the 'new drop' gallows erected on the bridge. For details of these terrible events I am indebted to Neil R Storey's fascinating book *Hanged at Norwich*. Mother Hook and her crimes are fictional though there were many similar cases in Victorian times. Grave robbing was also a real fear. I was lucky enough to see a wonderful exhibition about the Resurrection Men at the Museum of London.

The ruined church at Saxlingham Thorpe is also real – and well worth a visit – but Jemima Green and her family are fictional. There is no such programme as *Women Who Kill* and its cast and crew have no counterparts in real life.

Every year at Cross Bones Graveyard in London a service is held for the 'outcast dead' buried in what was once a communal grave for 'single women' and paupers. This seemed such a lovely idea that I have transported it to Norfolk. The University of North Norfolk is purely fictional. For real-life archaeological information I am indebted to my husband, Andrew Maxted. Thanks also to Dr Frauke Dingelstad for answering all my medical questions. However, I have only followed the experts' advice as far as it suits the plot and any subsequent mistakes are mine alone.

This book is set in 2011. The Campbell's Soup tower in King's Lynn was demolished in 2012, thus depriving Nelson of a useful landmark.

Finally, special thanks to my children, Juliet and Alex, who first had the idea which became *The Outcast Dead*. This book is for them.

Elly Griffiths, January 2014

Read on for a preview of the
next Dr Ruth Galloway novel

The Ghost Fields

as well as exclusive insights from author
Elly Griffiths into her own life,
the inspiration for Ruth Galloway,
and the historical and personal roots
of *The Outcast Dead*.

I hate the dreadful hollow behind the little wood,
Its lips in the field above are dabbled with
   blood-red heath,
The red-ribb'd ledges drip with a silent horror of
   blood,
And Echo there, whatever is ask'd her, answers
   'Death'.

ALFRED TENNYSON, *Maud*

PROLOGUE

July 2013

It is the hottest summer for years. A proper heat-wave, the papers say. But Barry West doesn't pay much attention to weather forecasts. He wears the same clothes winter and summer, jeans and an England T-shirt. It's sweaty in the cab of the digger but he doesn't really mind. Being a man is all about sweat, anyone who washes too much is either foreign or worse. It doesn't occur to him that women don't exactly find his odour enticing. He's forty and he hasn't had a girlfriend for years.

But he's content, this July day. The Norfolk sky is a hot, hard blue and the earth, when exposed in the jaws of the digger, is pale, almost white. The yellow vehicle moves steadily to and fro, churning up the stones and coarse grass. Barry doesn't know, and he certainly doesn't care, that people have fought hard over this patch of land, now scheduled for development by Edward Spens and Co. In fact, the Romans battled the Iceni on these same fields and, nearly two thousand years later, Royalist forces engaged in bitter hand-to-hand combat with Cromwell's army. But, today, Barry and his digger are alone under the blazing sun, their only companions the seagulls that follow their progress, swooping down on the freshly turned soil.

It's hard work. The land is uneven – which is why it has lain waste for so long – pitted with craters and gullies. In the winter these fissures fill with water and the field becomes almost a lake interspersed with islands of grass. But now, after a month of good weather, it's a lunar landscape, dry and desolate. Barry manoeuvres the digger up and down, singing tunelessly.

It's at the bottom of one of these craters that the digger scrapes against metal. Barry swears and goes into reverse. The seagulls swirl above him. Their cries sound caustic, as if they are laughing. Barry gets out of the cab.

The sun is hotter than ever. It beats down on his baseball cap and he wipes the sweat from his eyes. An object is protruding from the ground, something grey and somehow threatening, like a shark's fin. Barry stares at the obstacle. It has a look of permanence, as if it has lain in the earth for a very long time. He bends down and scrapes some soil away. He sees that the fin is part of a larger object, far bigger than he imagined at first. The more earth he removes, the more metal is revealed. It gleams dully in the sun.

Barry stands back. Edward Spens wants this field cleared. Barry's foreman stressed that the work needs to be done as soon as possible, 'before the crazies get wind of it'. If he carries on, his digger will tear and crush the metal object. Or the unseen enemy will defeat him and the digger (property of Edward Spens and Co.) will be damaged. Suddenly, unexpectedly, Barry remembers a book that was read to him at school about a vast man made of iron who is found in a junkyard. Just for a second he imagines that, lying beneath the soil, there is a sleeping metal giant who will rise up and crush him in its digger-like jaws. But wasn't the Iron Man in the story a goodie? He can't remember. Barry stoops again and clears more earth. The metal goes on and on, but Barry is persistent and he labours away, his T-shirt sticking to his back, until he reaches something else, something even bigger. Breathing heavily, he digs with his hands like a dog. Then he encounters something that isn't metal. It's glass, clogged with dirt and almost opaque. But Barry, driven by something which he doesn't quite understand, clears a space so that he can peer through.

A scream makes the seagulls rise into the air. It is a few seconds before Barry realises that he was the one who had screamed. And he almost does so again as he stumbles away from the buried giant.

Because, when he looked through the window, someone was looking back at him.

Not far away, across the fields where the Romans marched in orderly lines and the Royalist troops fled in disarray, Ruth Galloway is also digging. But this is altogether a more organised process. Teams of students labour over neatly dug trenches, marked out with string and measuring tape. Ruth moves from trench to trench, offering advice, dusting soil away from an object that might be a fragment of pottery or even a bone. She is happy. When she started this summer dig for her students she was aware of the area's history, of course. She expected to find something, some Roman pottery maybe or even a coin or two. But, two days into the excavation, they made a really significant discovery. A body which Ruth thinks might date from the Bronze Age, some two thousand years before the Romans.

The skeleton, buried in the chalky ground, isn't preserved as bodies found in peat are preserved. Five years ago, Ruth found the body of an Iron Age girl buried in the marshy soil near her house. That body had been almost perfect, suspended in time, hands bound with mistletoe rope, head partly shaved. Ruth had been able to look at that girl and know her story. This body is different and Ruth can't be sure of its age (she has sent samples for Carbon 14-testing but even that can be skewed by as many as a hundred years) but the skeleton is in the crouched position typical of Bronze Age burials and there are fragments of pottery nearby which look like examples of so-called Beaker ware. Beaker burials, which date back about four thousand years, are often distinguished by rounded barrows but there have been examples of flat grave sites too. Besides, the mound could easily have been destroyed by ploughing.

She excavated the body yesterday, after photographing the skeleton in plan and filling in a skeleton sheet for every bone. From the pelvic bones she thinks that the body is female, but she hopes to be able to extract enough DNA to make sure of this. Isotopic testing will determine the woman's diet, her bones and teeth will tell the story of any disease or periods of malnutrition. Soon Ruth will know some of the answers but she already feels a link with the woman who died so long ago. Standing in the field with the air shimmering in the heat, she thinks of the location. The marsh where the Iron Age body was found is only a few miles away and, on a beach nearby, a Bronze Age henge was discovered fifteen years ago. Discovered, in fact, by Ruth's mentor, Erik Andersen. Could the body and the henge be linked? She hears Erik's voice, that wonderful Scandinavian sing-song, 'This is sacred land, Ruthie, everything is connected.'

'Ruth!' A far less musical voice. But Ruth is in a good enough mood for it not to be dented by the appearance of her boss, Phil. Even though he's wearing safari shorts.

'Hallo, Phil.'

'Found anything else?'

Honestly, isn't one Bronze Age body enough for him? It's one more than he has ever discovered. But, despite her irritation, Ruth secretly shares his hope that there might be more bodies buried under this soil. The position of the skeleton and the presence of pottery shards indicate that this was a body buried with some ritual and ceremony. Was this a grave site? If so, there will be others.

'Not yet,' says Ruth. She takes a swig from her water bottle. She can't remember a hotter day in Norfolk. Her cotton trousers are sticking to her legs and she is sure that her face is bright red.

'Anyway,' says Phil, 'I've had a thought.'

'Yes?' Ruth tries not to look too excited at this news.

'You know the English Heritage DNA project?'

'Yes.'

'Well, why not get them to include our body? We could test all the locals to see if they're any relation to him.'

'Her.'

'What?'

'Remember I said I thought it was a woman's skeleton?'

'Oh yes. Anyway, what do you think? It could really put UNN on the map.'

Putting UNN, the University of North Norfolk, on the map is an obsession with Phil. Privately, Ruth thinks that it would take more than a bit of Bronze Age DNA. But it's not a bad idea. The DNA project has been set up to discover if there are any links between prehistoric bodies and the local population. Norfolk, where – according to DCI Harry Nelson – the locals move around as little as possible, would be the ideal testing ground.

'It's a thought,' says Ruth. 'Do you think they'd be interested?'

'Well, I spoke to someone from English Heritage this afternoon and they seemed keen.'

It is typical of Phil that, whilst ostensibly asking Ruth's

advice, he has already set the plan in motion. Still, a hunger for publicity is not a bad attribute in a head of department.

'Do you want to have a look at today's finds?' asks Ruth. She excavated the skeleton yesterday and bagged up the bones herself, but there are still a few interesting objects emerging from the trench.

Phil pulls a face. 'It's awfully hot,' he says, as if the weather is Ruth's fault.

'Is it?' says Ruth, pushing back her damp hair, 'I hadn't noticed.'

Phil looks at her quizzically. He doesn't always get irony unless he's concentrating. Ruth is saved from elaborating by the buzz of her phone.

'Excuse me.'

When she sees 'Nelson' on the screen her heart beats slightly faster. It's because I'm worried that it'll be about Kate, she tells herself. You can believe anything if you try hard enough.

'Ruth.' Typically, Nelson does not waste time on the niceties. 'Where are you?'

'Near Hunstanton.'

'Oh good. You're in the area. That's handy.'

For whom? thinks Ruth but Nelson is still talking. 'Some builder has found a plane buried in a field near there.'

'A plane?'

'Yes. Probably from the Second World War. Apparently there are a few old RAF bases around here.'

'Well, you don't need me to dig out a plane.'

'The thing is, the pilot's still inside.'

A few minutes later, Ruth is driving along the Hunstanton road with Phil at her side. She can't remember asking her head of department to join her but, somehow, there he is, wincing when Radio 4 blares out from the radio and asking her why she can't afford a new car. 'After all, your book was quite a success. Haven't you got a contract for another one?' Ruth's book, about a dig in Lancashire, came out last year and has indeed attracted some praise in the scholarly journals. It was very far from being a bestseller, though, and – after the advance has been earned out – her royalties will hardly contribute anything to her income. The book has made her mother proud, though, which is a miracle in itself.

'I like this car,' she says.

'It's a rust bucket,' says Phil. 'Why don't you buy one of those cool Fiat 500s? Shona's got one in ice-blue.'

Ruth grinds her teeth. Fiat 500s are undoubtedly cool and Shona probably has one to match every one of her retro Boden frocks, but she's quite happy with her old

Renault, thank you very much. Who asked Phil to sit in it anyway?

She can see the field from a long way away. The digger perches precariously on a slope and next to it stand three men one of whom is, unmistakably even from a distance, Nelson. Ruth parks the rust bucket by the gate and walks across the baked earth towards the group. Phil follows, complaining about the heat and people who are selfish enough to have cars without air-conditioning.

Nelson sees her first. 'Here she is. Why have you brought Phil with you?'

Ruth loves the way he puts this. Phil would undoubtedly believe that he brought Ruth with him.

'He didn't want to miss the fun. Is this it?'

Her question is superfluous. Three-quarters of a wing and half a cockpit lie exposed at the bottom of the shallow pit.

'American,' says Nelson. 'I can tell by the markings.'

Ruth shoots him a look. She thinks that Nelson would have been just the sort of boy to collect models of World War Two fighter planes.

'There was an American airbase near here,' says one of the other men. 'At Lockwell Heath.' Ruth recognises this man as Edward Spens, a local property developer whom she encountered on an earlier case. Spens is tall and good-looking, his air of authority only slightly dented by the fact that he's wearing tennis clothes. The third man, dressed in jeans and a filthy football top, stands slightly aside as if to imply that none of this is his fault. Ruth guesses that he must be the digger driver.

She looks at the exposed soil. It has a faintly blue tinge. She kneels down and scoops some earth in her hand, giving it a surreptitious sniff.

'What are you doing?' asks Phil. Clearly he's terrified that she's going to embarrass him.

'Fuel,' she says. 'Can't you smell it? And look at the blue marks on the soil. That's corroded aluminium. Did you have any idea that this plane was here?'

It is Edward Spens who answers. 'Some children found some engine parts in the field long ago, I believe. But no one had any idea that this was buried here, almost intact.'

Ruth looks at the cockpit. Although dented and corroded, it looks remarkably undamaged, lying almost horizontally at the foot of the crater. She's no geometry expert but wouldn't you expect the prow of a crashed plane to be at a steeper angle?

'Where's the body?' she asks.

'Sitting in the cockpit,' says Edward Spens. 'It gave Barry here quite a turn, I can tell you.'

'Still got his bloody cap on,' Barry mutters.

Ruth kneels down and peers through the cockpit window. She can see exactly why Barry had such a shock. Sitting in the pilot's seat is a perfect skeleton, like some ghastly joke about a delayed flight. Perched on the skull is a cap, the material has almost rotted away but the peak remains.

Ruth sits back on her heels.

'It's odd,' she says, almost to herself.

'What's odd?' asks Nelson. Alone of the men he doesn't seem to be suffering from the heat though he is wearing his usual working clothes of open-neck shirt and dark trousers. Ruth, who hasn't seen him for a few weeks, thinks that he looks almost insultingly well, as if finding a body entombed in a plane is the ideal way to spend a summer day. She wonders if he's going away on holiday this year. That's the other part of his life; the part she can never really know.

'The soil is loose,' says Ruth. 'As if it's been disturbed recently.'

'Of course it's been disturbed,' says the driver. 'I drove a bloody digger through it, didn't I?' Spens makes a move as if to disassociate himself from the bad language, but it takes more than that to offend Ruth when she's in her professional mode.

'The layers have been disturbed lower down,' she says.

'It's hot, not much rain, you'd expect the particles to be packed close together. And that's another thing. The topsoil is clay but there are chalk layers below. Chalk is destructive to bone but this skeleton looks perfectly preserved. The way the pilot's sitting too, hands on the joystick, it's almost as if he's been posed.'

Ruth leans in closer. She doesn't want to touch anything until they can do a proper excavation. Behind her she can hear Nelson telling Spens that the field is now a crime scene.

'The thing is,' says Spens in his most confidential voice, 'we're rather up against it here. There's been a bit of ill-feeling about this location and I'd like to get the land cleared as quickly as possible.'

'I can't help that,' says Nelson. 'I have to get a SOCO team here and Doctor Galloway will need at least a day to excavate the body. Isn't that right, Ruth?'

'Scene of the Crime team?' says Spens. 'Isn't that going a bit far? I mean the poor chap obviously crashed his plane into this field during the war, seventy years ago. Must have landed in the chalk pit and been covered by a landslide or something. It's not as if there's been a crime or anything.'

'I'm afraid you're wrong,' says Ruth, standing up.

'What do you mean?' says Spens, sounding offended.

'I think a crime may have taken place.'

'What makes you think that, Ruth?' asks Phil implying, by his tone, that he is likely to side with the local captain of industry rather than his colleague.

'There's a bullet hole in his skull,' says Ruth.

CHAPTER 1

September 2013

'Just one more picture.'

'For God's sake, Nelson, she'll be late for school on her first day.'

But Nelson is focusing the camera. Kate stands patiently by the fence, neatly dressed in her blue school sweatshirt and grey skirt. Her dark hair is already escaping from its plaits (Ruth isn't very good at hair). She holds her book bag in front of her like a weapon.

'First day at school,' says Nelson, clicking away. 'It doesn't seem possible.'

'Well, it is possible,' says Ruth, though she has lain awake half the night wondering how she can possibly entrust her precious darling to the terrors of education.

This from a person with two degrees who works in a university.

'Come on, Kate,' says Ruth, holding out her hand. 'We don't want to keep Mrs Mannion waiting.'

'Is that your teacher?' asks Nelson.

No, she's the local axe-murderer, thinks Ruth. But she leaves it to Kate to tell Nelson that Mrs Mannion is very nice and that she gave her a sticker on the taster day and that she's got a teddy bear called Blue.

'We take it in turns to take Blue Bear home,' she informs him. 'But we've got to be good.' She says this doubtfully, as if it's an impossible condition.

'Of course you'll be good,' says Nelson. 'You'll be the best.'

'It's not a competition,' mutters Ruth as she opens the car door for Kate. But she has already had enough rows with Nelson about league tables and private schools and whether it's absolutely necessary for a four year old to learn Mandarin. In the end Ruth had her way and Kate is going to the local state primary school, a cheerful place whose mission statement, spelt out in multicoloured handprints above the main entrance, reads simply, 'We have fun.'

'You're exactly the sort of person who's against competition,' says Nelson, putting away his camera.

'What sort of person's that?'

'The sort of person who does well in competitions.'

Ruth can't really deny that this is true. She has always loved learning and positively enjoyed exams. This is why she wants Kate to have fun and play with potato prints for a few years. Plenty of time for formal learning later. Nelson, who hated school and left as soon as possible, is anxious that his children should waste no time in scaling the slippery academic slope. He and Michelle sent their daughters to private schools and both went to university. Job done, though Laura is currently a holiday rep in Ibiza and Rebecca has no idea what she wants to do with her Media Studies degree beyond a vague desire to 'work in TV'.

'Say goodbye to Daddy,' says Ruth.

'Bye, Daddy.'

'Bye, sweetheart.' Nelson takes a last picture of Kate waving through the car window. Then he puts away his camera and goes back to have breakfast with his wife.

Ruth takes the familiar road with the sea on one side and the marshland on the other. Bob Woonunga, her neighbour, comes out to wave them goodbye and then there are no more houses until they reach the turn-off. It's a beautiful autumn day, golden and blue, the long grass waving, the sandbanks a soft blur in the distance. Ruth wonders if she should say something momentous, tell Kate about her own first day at school or something, but Kate seems quite happy, singing a jingle from an advertisement for breakfast cereal. In the end Ruth joins in. Crunchy nuts, crunchy nuts and raisins too. Yoo hoo hoo. Raisins too.

It still sounds funny to refer to Nelson as 'Daddy'. When Kate was three and asking questions, Ruth decided to tell her the truth, or at least a sanitised version of it. Nelson is her father, he loves her but he lives with his other family. Does he love them too? Of course he does. They all love each other in a messy twenty-first-century way. Nelson had been appalled when Ruth had told him what she was going to say. But he realised that Kate – a bright, enquiring child – needed to know something and, after all, what else could they say? Nelson's wife, Michelle, also took the agreed line, which Ruth knows is more than she deserves. She's glad that Kate has Michelle in her life as Michelle is a proper homemaker, good at all the mother things. She would have done those plaits right, for a start (she's a hairdresser).

They drive past the field where the Bronze Age body was found in the summer. English Heritage have agreed to fund another dig and they will also include the project in their DNA study. There's even a chance that the dig might be filmed. Two years ago, Ruth appeared in a TV programme called *Women Who Kill* and, whilst the experience was traumatic in all sorts of ways, she didn't altogether dislike the feeling of being a TV archaeology expert. She's not a natural, like Frank Barker, the American historian who fronted the programme, but the *Guardian* did describe her as 'likeable', which is a start.

'Mummy might be on TV again,' she says to Kate.

'I hope Blue Bear does come to our house,' says Kate.

She's right too. Blue Bear is more important just now.

Ruth had been scared that Kate would cry, that she would cry, that they would have to be prised apart by disapproving teaching assistants. But, in the end, when Kate just waves happily and disappears into the sea of blue sweatshirts, that somehow feels worse than anything. Ruth turns away, blinking back foolish tears.

'Mrs Galloway?'

Ruth turns. This is an altogether new persona for her. She likes to be called Dr Galloway at work and she has never been Mrs anything. Mrs Galloway is her mother, a formidable Born Again Christian living in South London within sight of the promised land. Should she insist on Ms or would that blight Kate's prospects on the first day?

'Mrs Galloway?' The speaker is a woman. Teacher? Parent? Ruth doesn't know. Whoever she is, she looks scarily at home in the lower-case, primary-coloured environment of the infant classrooms.

'I'm Miss Coles, the classroom assistant. I just wondered if Kate was having school dinners or packed lunch.'

'Dinners,' says Ruth. She doesn't feel up to preparing sandwiches every day.

'Not a fussy eater, then? That's good.'

Ruth says nothing. The truth is that Kate is a rather fussy eater but Ruth always gives her food that she likes. She dreads to think of Kate's reaction when presented with cottage pie or semolina. But surely school dinners are different now? There's probably a salad bar and a wine list.

Miss Coles seems to take Ruth's silence for extreme emotion (which isn't that far from the truth). She pats the air above Ruth's arm.

'Don't worry. She'll settle in really quickly. Why don't you go home and have a nice cup of tea?'

Actually, I've got to give a lecture on Palaeolithic burial practices, thinks Ruth. But she doesn't say this aloud. She thanks Miss Coles and walks quickly away.

*

Nelson too finds it hard to stop thinking about Kate. He wishes that he had been able to take her to school but it was generous enough of Michelle to agree to the early morning visit. The late breakfast together was meant to be Nelson's attempt to say thank you but, when he reaches the house, Michelle is on her way out of the door. There's a crisis at the salon, she says, she needs to get to work straight away. She kisses Nelson lightly and climbs into her car. Nelson watches as she performs a neat three-point turn and drives away, her face set as if she's already thinking about work. Nelson sighs and gets back into his battered Mercedes.

But, when he gets to the station, there is some compensation. Amongst all the rubbish in his inbox, one email stands out. 'Dental records on skull found 17/7/13'. This is the American pilot, the one found in the summer behind the wheel of his buried plane. After Ruth had excavated the skeleton, an autopsy had found that death probably occurred as a result of the bullet wound in the temple. Here the investigation would probably have stalled without the generosity of the American Air Force, who had offered to fund DNA tests and extensive forensic investigations. Even so, the laboratories had taken their time. In August Nelson had rather reluctantly accompanied Michelle on holiday to Spain (far too hot) and had returned to find that no progress had been made. Well, it looks as if they have a result at last. Nelson clicks open the email, still standing up.

'Cloughie!' he calls, a moment later.

DS Clough appears in the doorway, a half-eaten bagel in his hand.

'Look at this. We've got a positive match for our American pilot.'

Clough peers over his boss's shoulder. 'Frederick J Blackstock. Who's he when he's at home?'

'Come on, Cloughie. You're from Hunstanton way. Don't you recognise the name?'

'Blackstock. Oh, those Blackstocks. Do you think he's related?'

'I don't know but I'm going to find out.'

'Why would a Yank pilot be related to a posh Norfolk family?'

'Your guess is as good as mine, Cloughie.'

'Bit of a coincidence, isn't it?' says Clough, scrolling down the email. 'American pilot found dead right near his old ancestral home.'

'Exactly,' says Nelson, gathering up his car keys. 'And I don't believe in coincidence.'

*

It's impossible to ignore the Blackstock name in the Hunstanton area. There's the Blackstock Arms, the Blackstock Art Gallery, even the Blackstock Fishing Museum. The smug ubiquity of the name reminds Nelson of the Smiths in King's Lynn, a comparison that isn't exactly reassuring, given that a previous investigation involving the Smiths ended up combining Class A drugs, an ancient curse and a poisonous snake. Unlike the Smiths though, the Blackstocks still live in their ancestral home, a bleak manor house built on the edge of the Saltmarsh.

They drive (along Blackstock Way) past flat fields crisscrossed with tiny streams, mournful-looking sheep marooned on grassy islands as geese fly overhead, honking sadly. The house is visible from miles away, a ship rising from a grey-green sea.

'I wouldn't like to live here,' says Clough. 'It's as bad as Ruth's place.'

'It's a bit grander than Ruth's place.'

Blackstock Hall is indeed grand, a stern, brick-built edifice with a tower at each corner, but there is no comforting stately home feeling about it: no National Trust sign pointing the way to the tea rooms, no manicured lawns or Italian gardens. Instead the grass comes right up to the front door and sheep peer into the downstairs rooms. If there was a path to the front door it vanished years, maybe centuries, ago. Nelson parks by the side of the road and he and Clough approach the house through the fields.

'Bloody hell,' says Clough, 'the grass is full of sheep shit.'

'What do you expect?' says Nelson, hurdling a stream. The sheep stare at him with their strange onyx eyes.

'I expect a proper driveway, since you ask,' says Clough. 'Bunch of gyppos would do it for a grand.'

Nelson ignores this, though he knows he should say something about the un-PC language. 'It's travellers, not gyppos, and we should respect different lifestyle choices etc. etc.' Instead he says, 'Hope there's someone at home after all this.'

'There's smoke coming out of the chimneys,' says Clough. 'Probably burning a virgin for the harvest.'

'I should never have let you watch *The Wicker Man*,' says Nelson.

Despite the smoke it seems at first that the house might be deserted after all. Finally, after almost five minutes, the heavy oak door opens slowly and a woman's face appears.

'Oh there is someone here,' she says. 'We only really use the back door.'

'I wasn't aware of that,' says Nelson stiffly. 'I'm DCI

Harry Nelson from the King's Lynn police. This is DS Clough. We'd like to speak to Mr or Mrs Blackstock.'

'You'd better come in then,' says the woman. 'I'm Sally Blackstock.'

The door opens with difficulty and Nelson sees that the hall is full of packing cases. Clearly Sally Blackstock was telling the truth about this entrance not being in use. She's an attractive woman in her mid-fifties, ash-blonde hair, blue eyes, no make-up. She reminds Nelson of an older version of Barbara in *The Good Life*.

'This is quite some house,' says Nelson.

Sally Blackstock laughs. 'It's a mish-mash really. Built in Tudor times, burned down during the Civil War, rebuilt in the Georgian era. The Blackstocks have lived on this site for over five hundred years and it feels we've still got all their rubbish.' She gives one of the packing cases a feeble shove.

'Are you moving out, then?' asks Clough.

Sally laughs. 'I should be so lucky! No, we're clearing up. George has got some mad idea about opening the house as a B&B. Lunacy, the whole thing'.

As they follow Mrs Blackstock down a seemingly end-less corridor, Nelson can't help but agree with her assessment. All the rooms in the house, though undoubt-edly large and well proportioned, are either empty or full of boxes. It's hard to imagine the place being transformed into a haven of breakfast tables and comfortable sofas. Eventually, though, Sally turns a corner and admits them to a large kitchen complete with Aga, armchairs and an open fire.

'We practically live in this room, I'm afraid,' she says when Nelson comments on the fire. 'The rest of the house is just too bloody cold. Now, what's all this about?'

The sudden switch from Barbara Good to Margaret Thatcher takes Nelson by surprise, as does the gear charge into an extremely patrician accent. He says, aware that he is sounding like a stage policeman, 'We've got some news regarding a gentleman whom we believe may be a family member. Frederick J Blackstock.'

Sally Blackstock's mouth forms a small, round o. 'Freddy?' she says. 'Freddy? But he died in the war. His plane went down over the sea.'

'Mrs Blackstock, do you remember reading in the local press about a Second World War plane being found near here? It would have been a couple of months back, in July.'

'Yes, I think I remember something.'

'Well, there was a body in the plane. Dental records have just identified the man as being Frederick Blackstock. I believe he would have been related to your husband?'

'Yes.' Sally Blackstock runs a hand through her hair, leaving it standing up in a crest. She waves a hand vaguely towards the armchairs. 'Do sit down, Detective er . . .'

'Nelson.'

'Yes. Nelson. Like the admiral. Frederick was my husband's uncle but he emigrated to America in the thirties. We knew he'd died in the war but we were told that his plane went down in the sea with no survivors. My husband will be amazed.'

'Where's your husband today?' asks Nelson, surreptitiously removing a dog's lead from the cushion of his chair.

'He's with Chaz. Our son. He's got a pig farm near here.' She pulls a face. 'I'll call him. Oh God, where's my phone?'

Clough finds it under a pile of *Horse and Hounds* and is rewarded by Sally putting the kettle on for tea. She goes into the pantry and they hear her leaving a message for her husband. 'Darling, something rather amazing's happened.' Nelson and Clough exchange glances.

Sally comes back into the room minus the phone. Nelson wonders where she's put it and whether she'll ever find it again. She is suddenly all charm. She leans on the Aga and beams at the two policemen. 'The thing is,' she says cosily, 'there were three brothers. Shall I tell you the story?'

'Yes please,' says Nelson, trying not to sound as if he's in nursery school. He wonders what Katie's doing now. Perhaps she too is listening to a story. He sees Clough trying not to laugh.

'Lewis was the oldest. He fought in the war and was a prisoner in Japan. Had a terrible time by all accounts. Anyway, he was never the same again and, in 1950 or thereabouts, he simply vanished.'

'Vanished?' repeats Clough.

'Yes. They all thought he'd killed himself, but no one ever said it aloud. George, my father-in-law, says it was an absolutely terrible time. His mother never could accept that Lewis was gone and she went a bit doolally herself. In the end, though, they had to admit that he wasn't coming back and Lewis was declared dead in the 1960s.'

'And Frederick had already died in the war?'

'Yes. He was the second brother. He hated this place, that's what Old George always says. He said that Black-stock land was cursed. He had a vivid imagination, like his mother. So Frederick emigrated to America and he fought in the US Air Force. He died in 1944, leaving George to inherit.'

'Your father-in-law?'

'Yes. He never expected to inherit, being the youngest son, but he tried to make a go of the place. My husband is his only child. He's called George too. Young George, even though he's pushing sixty.' She laughs and takes the hissing kettle from the Aga.

'So the family were told that Frederick's plane went down over the sea?' says Nelson, trying not to look as Sally sloshes hot water into the teapot. The police first aid course was a long time ago and he can't remember what you do about scalds.

'Yes.' Sally puts the tea in front of them and, after a few minutes' searching, adds a biscuit tin. 'That's why I don't understand how he could have been found in that plane in the field.'

'We don't understand it either,' says Nelson slowly. The buried plane had been fairly easy to trace. The single-seater Curtiss P-36 Mohawk 'D for Dog' had gone down in a thunderstorm in September 1944. The pilot had ejected and was found dead in an adjacent field. The plane had crashed into a disused quarry and was imme-diately buried by a landslide caused by the heavy rain. In the light of the fact that the pilot had been found, no attempt was made to recover the plane. Flying Officer Frederick Blackstock, on the other hand, was not meant to be anywhere near D for Dog. He was part of a five-man crew of a fighter cruiser which had been shot down over the English Channel four weeks earlier.

'That's partly why we're here,' says Nelson, watching as Clough selects two biscuits conveniently stuck together. 'If your husband would agree to a DNA test, we could establish beyond any doubt that this Frederick Blackstock was a family member.'

'I'm sure he'll agree,' says Sally. She rolls her eyes upwards. 'I wish I could tell George, Old George I mean.'

Her manner is now starting to seem slightly spooky. Why is she looking upwards? To indicate that Old George is watching them from heaven?

'When did George, Old George, die?'

She laughs again. The laugh, too, is starting to grate. 'Oh, he's not dead, Detective Nelson. He's upstairs having his mid-morning nap.'

RUTH GALLOWAY – BIOGRAPHY

Ruth Galloway was born in 1968, in Eltham, South London. Her father Arthur was an insurance clerk and her mother Jean was a dinner lady. She has an elder brother called Simon.

From the start, Ruth always felt something of an outsider in her family. She remembers devouring books as a child, sitting under the table reading *Alice in Wonderland* and Noel Streatfeild while her parents wondered aloud if this behaviour was normal. She was also fascinated by the past. Eltham is a South London borough but it has a very interesting history. Henry VIII was brought up in Eltham Palace, where an Art Deco mansion now occupies the castle's ruins. Nearby Shooter's Hill was a famous haunt of highwaymen and Well Hall House was once the home of Margaret Roper, Thomas More's daughter. Ruth loved stories about the past and remembers searching in the soil around Eltham Palace, hoping to find Tudor coins. She dates her interest in archaeology from that moment.

When Ruth was ten, her parents found God. Well, that's how they would describe it anyway. Arthur Galloway had actually been brought up in the Salvation Army but Jean was resolutely agnostic until she attended a Billy Graham rally. Eventually both Galloways were Born Again and from then on their lives were dedicated to the Almighty in the form of their local evangelical church. They took the children to services with them but, whilst Simon was silently compliant, Ruth was questioning. How do we know God exists? What's the evidence? If there is a God, why does he allow people to suffer? How do we know the Devil is evil anyway? At sixteen, Ruth declared herself an atheist and refused to attend church. Her parents' sorrow and resentment at this decision still linger. Incidentally, Simon is also no longer a Christian but, by keeping quiet about his views, he has managed to escape censure.

Ruth attended the local comprehensive where she excelled academically. In 1986 she won a place at University College London to study Archaeology. Her parents were bemused by her choice of subject. If Ruth was so clever, why couldn't she do something sensible like work in a bank or study accountancy? But the lure of the past was too strong. Ruth left Eltham to live in the university halls of residence and, apart from weekends and the odd holiday, never lived at home again. The long journey away from her parents had begun.

Ruth enjoyed university. She made some great friendships and revelled in the academic and personal freedom. However, she doesn't think she really became an archaeologist until she met Professor Erik Andersen. Graduating with a First, Ruth did a Masters at UCL and then embarked on a Ph.D. at Southampton, where Erik was her personal tutor. As Ruth once described it, 'Erik took my mind apart and put it back in a different shape.' Erik taught her how to look at the world, how to read a landscape, how to understand the language of stones and bones. Ruth worshipped Erik and his beautiful wife Magda. In 1996 she accompanied Erik to Bosnia, where they worked on excavating the war graves. Ruth still has nightmares about it. Returning from Bosnia, Ruth was offered a job at the new University of North Norfolk. She accepted, knowing that Erik was organising a dig in Norfolk that summer. The Henge Dig, as it became known, changed Ruth's life. It was on this dig that they discovered a Bronze Age henge on the Saltmarsh. It was on this dig that Ruth met Shona and Cathbad and Peter, the man who was to be her partner for ten years.

Although Ruth doesn't consider herself attractive (she thinks she's fat and ungainly), she has never been short of boyfriends. At school she went out with a boy called Daniel who adored her. As Jean never fails to remind Ruth, Daniel is now a very wealthy plumber. The relationship did not survive Ruth's move to university, where Ruth began an affair with a medical student called Tom. She lost her virginity to Tom and believed herself in love, but the couple broke up when Ruth moved to Southampton. There she had a few boyfriends but no one really serious until Peter. Ruth and Peter bought a house, adopted two cats and embarked on a settled life together. When Ruth finished the relationship because she felt that she no longer loved Peter, her mother was heartbroken. 'You've lost your last chance of happiness,' Jean told her daughter.

But Ruth lived alone quite contently. She loved her work and her cats and her cottage on the edge of the lonely Saltmarsh. Then, one morning in 2007, she walked into the university to find a strange man waiting for her. 'This is Detective Chief Inspector Harry Nelson,' said her boss Phil, in a tone of barely suppressed excitement. 'He wants to talk to you about a murder.'

And Ruth's life changed for ever.

ELLY GRIFFITHS – BIOGRAPHY

When people find out that I've published books under the name Domenica de Rosa, they assume that it's a pseudonym. In fact, Domenica de Rosa is my real name. It's Italian and means Sunday of the Rose. I don't know how I got such an exotic name. My dad was Italian but my parents hadn't gone mad with my sisters' names, Giulia and Sheila. I can only assume that they thought I was going to be a boy and didn't have a girl's name to hand. I was born at five minutes to Sunday, hence Domenica. If I had been a boy, it would have been Cesare.

Perhaps my romantic name influenced my decision to be an author. I don't know. I certainly know that I always wanted to write. I wrote my first full-length book aged eleven. It was called 'The Hair of the Dog' and was, perhaps significantly, a murder mystery. At secondary school

I used to write episodes of *Starsky and Hutch* (early fan fiction) and enjoyed making people cry as I ruthlessly killed off each character in turn. I read English at King's College, London and, after university, worked first in a library and then for the *Bookseller* magazine. After a couple of years checking proofs at the *Bookseller*, I got a job at Harper-Collins, first in publicity, then as an editor, eventually becoming Editorial Director for children's books. I had quite forgotten my dream of becoming a writer and only remembered it when I went on maternity leave before having my twins in 1998. Freed from the constraints of making money out of books, I wrote my first novel, *The Italian Quarter*, partly based on my dad's life.

Three other books followed, all about Italy, families and identity. By now, we had two children and my husband Andy had just given up his City job to become an archaeologist. We were on holiday in Norfolk, walking across Titchwell Marsh, when Andy mentioned that prehistoric man had thought that marshland was sacred. Because it's neither land nor sea, but something in-between, they saw it as a kind of bridge to the afterlife. Neither land nor sea, neither life nor death. As he said these words, the entire plot of *The Crossing Places* appeared, fully formed, in my head and, walking towards me out of the mist, I saw Dr Ruth Galloway.

I didn't think that this new book was significantly different from my 'Italy' books but, when she read it, my agent said, 'This is crime. You need a crime name.'

And that's how I became Elly Griffiths.

THE OUTCAST DEAD – BEGINNINGS

Sometimes I struggle to find titles for my books. Sometimes the title is there first and I have to find a story to fit it. I have had the title *The Outcast Dead* in my mind for a long time. There's a ceremony held every year at Cross Bones Graveyard in London. It's called the Service for the Outcast Dead and it remembers the people buried in unmarked graves: paupers, prostitutes, plague victims. I knew that I wanted to use this service in one of the Ruth Galloway books.

A couple of years ago, I was visiting Lincoln and, having some time to spare, decided to take the tour of the castle. The guide was brilliant – as they always are – and the tour ended up in the old prison chapel. In Victorian times, Lincoln Prison was run according to something called the 'separate system' whereby inmates were kept isolated at all times. Even in chapel they had to sit in separate little boxes, unable to see anyone except the preacher. I stood in this little room, divided into wooden cubicles, and thought that I'd never been in a spookier or a *sadder* place. I knew then that my next book would involve a prison.

I wanted *The Outcast Dead* to be set firmly back in Norfolk and, of course, Norwich Castle is a famous landmark. But the more I researched it, the more I knew that it was perfect for my story. Norwich Castle had been a prison and many criminals were executed there. It was briefly run on the separate system and Elizabeth Fry − one of Norfolk's most famous daughters − had campaigned against it.

In the book, whilst digging in the grounds of the castle, Ruth finds the body of one of Norfolk's most notorious murderers. I invented Mother Hook, the so-called 'baby farmer' who was accused of killing the children in her care, but her story is based on real cases of the time, including that of Amelia Dyer. I also wanted to bring in the 'resurrection men', grave robbers who sometimes went so far as to kill their victims to sell their bodies for experimentation. Against this rather gruesome Victorian background, I wanted to have a modern case of possible child murder and abduction. Ruth is a working mother, so I started to think about the feelings you have when you leave your child in someone else's care.

Put like this, the plot sounds rather bleak, but I wanted to have some light relief by introducing Ruth to the world of live TV as she finds herself becoming the face of a programme called *Women Who Kill*. This book also introduces Ruth to Frank Barker, a rather attractive American academic. Of course Nelson is here too, busy with the child abduction case, but aware of Frank and disliking him intensely. There is also a return for Cathbad's teenage daughter, Maddie, and a first appearance for Ruth's brother, Simon.

And Cathbad comes back. I could never keep him away for long.

Elly Griffiths

E LLY
G RIFFITHS

Read the whole Dr Ruth Galloway series now.

'Ruth Galloway . . . is an admirably gutsy heroine'
The Times

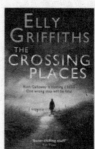

COMING SOON BY ELLY GRIFFITHS:

The Zig Zag Girl

Brighton 1950s. When a girl is murdered, Detective Inspector Edgar Stephens discovers the method was inspired by a magic trick linked to the shadowy WWII unit, the Magic Men, in which he served. Drawn back together, the men must solve the case before more innocent people die...

Sign up to the Elly Griffiths newsletter now:
quercusbooks.co.uk/elly-griffiths

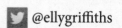 @ellygriffiths   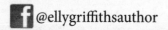 @ellygriffithsauthor